The First Key of Kalijor

Paul Lell

The First Key of Kalijor by: Paul Lell

© 2007 Paul Lell

Cover art by: Sooj

© 2007 Soojin .M.

All rights reserved.

ISBN: 978-0-6151-5955-3

For more information,

 See the author's website at

www.kalijor.com

For my family, I thank you all!

Riana stepped out of the gate from Talanor into the dark night and driving snow of the Southern Wastes. Briefly she nodded to the gate guards as she pulled her heavy hood up. Her body was alive with tactile sensations she had never imagined before. Every move, every turn, every breath caused her skin to scream out. The friction of the cloth across her now very sensitive skin sent spears of discomfort and pain to her aching head.

As she moved further from the city, the driving snow blocked out what light would normally be visible this time of year, which wasn't much really. The end result was that Riana was forced to shift her vision into its alternate state, allowing her to see the heat emanating from objects. In the total darkness and extreme cold, she still couldn't see much. She could see well enough to navigate and would know if anything warmer than a snowball was nearby. This brought a small degree of comfort because this frozen tundra was filled to overflowing with a nasty breed of Orc.

These particular Orcs were about human size, two-hundred to three-hundred pounds worth of solid muscle, and a pasty grey color with random black and dark grey/brown markings. They had sharp canine teeth that protruded from their mouths like wicked daggers, and evil eyes that glared red from beneath their boney brows.

"The snow is as thick as bread pudding," she whispered to herself, pulling her heavy cloak closer to try and shake the feeling of discomfort that always chased after her when she walked through the Wastes. The last thing she wanted was to attract the attention of an Orc scouting party, but hearing a voice, even her own, helped reassure her that she was still alive and well. Cautiously, she picked her way down the road, its edges barely visible to her keen thermal vision. Making every attempt to not shift or move too much, because it made the rough material of her heavy cloak rub against the sensitive, fresh tattoos covering most of her body. The dull ache in her head didn't help things much either now that she gave it some thought.

She hated that she had to go to Talanor to get it done, but no other artist in the realm was better than the master there. Master Dinendal had been surprised by what she had asked him to do, even more so when she had presented him with the vials of enchanted inks that she had spent months collecting rare ingredients to distil. It had taken some time to convince him to proceed, and a good deal of coin as well. But as he worked, his confidence grew. By the time he had finished, almost three days later, he was beaming with pride in what he had created. Of course, the process had left Riana's skin painfully sensitive. Master Dinendal had told her that normally such discomfort lasted for a week, but with the special inks and the nature of the work, he had no idea how long it would last. She hadn't really cared at the time, but now she was beginning to regret it as the thought of a three-day trudge through the

Southern Wastes settled in on her. The prospect of what it meant in the long run was more than enough to compensate her for a few days or even weeks of discomfort. But if her skin remained this sensitive for too terribly long, she would have to seriously reconsider her wardrobe. Thinking of her closet full of the heavy robes traditionally worn by wielders of the arcane arts, their weighty fabric covering almost every inch of the body made a small groan escape her lips.

"Mom's going to absolutely KILL me." She whispered to herself as she continued threading her way down the snow-packed road, headed for home.

"For what?" An echo of her own voice whispered next to her, causing her to nearly fall over in surprise. Turning sharply towards the voice, her cloak shifted and twirled around her, dragging itself painfully across her freshly tattooed body. Wincing in pain, she saw her sister standing in the middle of the road, looking at her innocently. It was like looking in a mirror, which made sense, since they were twins. Katrina had the high, thin cheek bones of a royal elf, her long, pointed ears concealed beneath her own cloak's hood. Her thin lips parted in a devilish grin, revealing slightly too sharp teeth that was a subtle indication of their mixed heritage. Her fine features were soft and attractive, even for the young twenty years old they were. There were some differences though. Katrina's eyes were an acidy yellow and she wore her fine, platinum hair down, in a manageable style, while Riana's eyes were a deep violet, and her hair was pulled back into a fancy array of 'pony tails' at the back of her skull, with a few strands hanging down around her face. At some point she had managed to turn her hair a vibrant, royal purple in an accident at the alchemy table. It had grown that way ever since and she had finally, after more than a year of trying, given up attempting to conceal it from their mother by dying it regularly. Their mother had sighed when she saw it coming in, in all its purple glory, then looked at Riana and said, "Just like your...father." She had then hugged her and walked away with a strange look on her face, the memory of the father they had never known clearly haunting her.

Looking deeply into her sister's eyes through the driving snow, Riana smiled weakly, "I'll tell you when we get home. I need to get out of these clothes and into something lighter. This is definitely not the weather for it."

Katrina admonished her with a parental look and then asked, "Why are you walking home? Didn't you buy a portal ring while you were in Talanor?"

Riana sighed the sigh of sisterly defeat. "No," she finally admitted, "I spent all my money on..." She took a deep breath before continuing, "well, you'll see when we get home." Her voice trailed off.

Katrina smiled, grinned rather, from ear to ear. "Then let's get home, and out of this weather, so I can see what you did! C'mere sis!" At that, a slender hand emerged from beneath her cloak, in its delicate fingers she held a portal ring. Its shiny gold band adorned with the vibrant, almost glowing ruby that was the symbol of their home city of Rathalon. She placed the ring on her finger and with a grin at Riana, turned it one-hundred eighty degrees, so the ruby was facing down.

The ring began to glow brightly for a moment, and an instant later, the light was gone. Between the girls appeared a series of red rings of magical energy floating in a column. They appeared to be composed of pure light, bobbing up and down lazily like a buoy might while floating in a calm harbor.

Riana looked at her sister and saw the ring on her finger crumble away into nothingness.

Katrina smiled and shrugged, "I still can't afford a rechargeable one, but these are pretty reasonable." Then she stepped into the column of glowing rings and disappeared in a dull flash of red light.

With a sigh of resignation and a brief wish that her head would stop its aching, Riana stepped into the column of rings and instantly found herself in a large, stone room, surrounded on all sides by armed guards. All of whom were looking at her expectantly.

"Ssstate your name and bussinesss." An imposing reptilian hissed at her from directly ahead. She looked at the guard. An impressive creature, standing some eight feet tall and heavy with strong, sinuous muscles, he towered over her lithe six foot frame. The deep emerald-green of his scales was accentuated by the golden plate armor of the Rathalon guard. In one hand he bore the signature weapon of the Rathalon Defenders, a short metal staff with a wickedly pointed blade jutting out of each end. The weapon was easily as tall as the creature holding it and was known throughout Kalijor as a vicious weapon that required a great deal of skill to use effectively. The weapon hung in his hand like a toy, despite its mass. His bright amber eyes stared at her unblinking from beneath the helmet that had been custom fit to his reptilian head. Although Riana had seen and talked with Captain Sselina on many occasions, she was still caught off guard every time she used the portal system and found him staring at her expectantly.

"Riana Thorindal, daughter of Ezrina Thorindal. My sister Katrina and I are on our way home." Indicating Katrina, who stood behind the captain, speaking in hushed tones to a merchant near the exit of the arrival area. Riana pushed her hood off her head revealing herself to the guards and causing a brief surge of pain. Her long ears perked up in the warmth and the presence of friends.

The Captain eyed her for a moment, before he nodded ever so slightly in her direction. "Welcome home Lady Thorindal." Then he made a barely perceptible gesture and the rest of the guards stood down and went about checking other arrivals.

"Good to see you again Captain," Riana said, feeling much more at ease now. She moved out of the inbound portal area where other people were arriving in brief red flashes. Rathalon was the center of Kalijor. As the mecca of commerce and travel, it was the largest city in the world. Everyone came through Rathalon at one point or another in their lives. A great many of those arrivals simply appeared here in the cavernous portal chamber. Looking around the room as she moved away from the arrival area, Riana felt the enormity of the chamber. It was a gigantic room designed with security in mind, with numerous large columns arranged in rows that would allow defenders to take cover from any invading force, firing arrows, bolts and spell missiles from positions of cover at the central area of the building where all arrivals appeared. Twenty steps led down into the arrival area, which was a giant octagon, some one-hundred feet across, giving the defenders a tactical advantage in the event of an attack through the portal system, by placing any would-be attackers well below the city defenders.

People flowed in and out of the building through the gigantic, intricately-carved main doors. Some headed toward the smaller, raised octagonal platforms that held glowing portals similar to the one that had brought Katrina and herself here to Rathalon, but these portals were a shimmering yellow, and always very busy. There were six such platforms in the portal chamber of Rathalon, but only five of them had portals atop them. One platform in the far back corner of the room, stood empty. There had not been a portal there for so long that no one remembered where it had gone when it had been active.

Making her way up the short stair way, she nodded to the Captain, and offered him a wry smile. He offered her the reptilian equivalent, baring rows of small, deadly sharp teeth. Then he moved further down the stairs to intervene in some dispute that had started up with one of the arrivals.

Riana wove her way through a few small groups of people that were milling about, causing her heavy cloak to drag across her skin. Gritting her teeth and forcing back the pain, she made her way to her sister's side.

"Hey Ree." Kat said at her sister's approach, "One sec and I'll be done here." Then she went back to haggling with the merchant about something or other.

Riana took a moment to pull off her heavy cloak, careful to cause as little friction with her body as possible. The silk skirt and blouse she wore underneath helped some, but she was still painfully aware of what she had done to her body. The garments she had picked for the trip had been chosen with two thoughts in mind, reducing friction against her sensitive skin and to cover her up as much as possible.

Carefully holding her cloak in her hands, out away from her body so as to keep it from bumping into her, she turned back to her sister just as Katrina concluded whatever negotiation she had been involved in.

Katrina grinned at her, stifling a laugh at the sight of her sister. "WHAT?!" Riana howled indignantly.

"Nothing." Katrina said, almost unable to hold back the laughter. "You just look like…"

"Like what?!" Riana asked, raising an eyebrow, her ears pointing straight back from her head in annoyance.

"Like…an old maid…" Katrina finished, and finally burst into laughter, unable to contain it any longer.

Riana's skin flushed red in embarrassment, her ears drooping down. "I guess I do." She said, sounding upset.

The blouse had long, billowing sleeves that came to a buttoned cuff at each wrist, and ended at the neck in a fancy collar that she didn't care for, but it served its purpose very effectively. Her skirt was long, ruffled, and of the same fine silk. Ending below her ankles, it almost completely covered her traveling boots, which were soft brown leather, and came up to her knees beneath the skirt. She knew it was not the best traveling attire, but she had other concerns to worry about on this particular trip. She wasn't even wearing her normal belt with her short sword, knife and pouches on it.

Suddenly Katrina grew very serious, the laughter gone, but still audible in her words, "C'mon Ree, let's go home so you can show me."

At that, the two of them were off. Weaving in and out of the throngs of travelers. Deftly avoiding traffic jams, as only two children could. The pain of moving nearly floored her, but Riana resolved to get home before giving up her secret. Her head hurt and her body ached, as she pushed herself to keep up with her sister. In an instant they were at the massive doors to the portal chamber. Then they were outside, in the full light of day. The momentary transition from night to day had taken place while they were inside the portal chamber, and now people were beginning to come out of their homes and add to the volume of travelers already thronging through the smooth, stone streets of the city. They wove their way through the crowds —down a back alley here, through someone's yard there, under a street merchant's awning, between two horse-drawn carts— making and taking every shortcut they could. As she strained the limits of her body to force it to keep up with her sister's pace, Riana began to realize just how far away home was. Every step she took caused her clothing, as well chosen as it was, to light up her nerve endings like a bonfire. Every time they dodged around someone or ducked under a clothesline, her body screamed out at her to stop. Slowly, she began to fall behind, even though she was pushing herself well past her pain threshold.

Rathalon was a gigantic city. The largest in Kalijor by far. Its population was in the millions, if you included all of the transients that were there at any time, although its actual residents numbered only five or six hundred thousand people. It had been carved from the head of the Uraval Mountains over the course of centuries. The spot was perfect as travelers had to round the head of the mountain range on their way from one side to the other. The mountains themselves were impassable. Not so much because of the treacherous terrain, which there was plenty of, but because something lived up there. Something less than friendly to travelers. And no one was known to have ever made it over the range. So all travelers had long ago taken to rounding the head of the range. And before too long, a great undertaking was begun. Some of the best stone cutters in the world had banded together and drawn up plans for something amazing. They decided to build a city at the head of the mountains in order to capitalize on the traffic that passed there, but their city would be nothing short of spectacular. So they began removing stone from the face of the mountain, and for generations they carried on removing stone from the mountain. Their children toiled away at it, and their children's children.

The city was still not completed to this day, but it was the most amazing thing Riana had ever laid eyes upon. A city capable of housing millions of people, carved from the head of the mountains. All of the buildings they ran past on their way home, the streets that they had learned so well in their youth, the walking paths where they used to play tag among the pedestrians of the city, the fountains Riana and Katrina had learned to swim in, all of it carved from the rock. Not a single piece had been brought in, or added to, any feature of the city. Even the massive stone gates of the thick outer wall, were hewn from the mountain's mass, hinges and all; Riana waved at the gate guards as they darted past the one-hundred foot tall gates, the action sending lines of fire up the nerves in her arm and chest, she staggered momentarily, but forced herself up and on after her sister.

The great wall that surrounded the city was one-hundred fifty feet high, and twenty five feet thick. Leaving the vertical face at the southern edge of the city, it extended northward and curved around to the west and back south to reconnect with the same vertical face. The girls ran along the base of the wall, towards their house. In her hyper-sensitive state, Riana was relieved by the realization that the glossy surface of the city's wall was actually as smooth as it looked. For years she had been amazed at how its near mirror surface would dimly reflect its surroundings, but now she was in heaven as she leaned against its cool surface and slid painlessly down the road.

There were fewer merchants on this road, but it was still a high traffic area and a great many people bought and sold, and just moved from place to place here. As they dodged through a crowd at the edge of the street, Riana brushed against a large man in heavy plate armor. He barely touched her svelte form, but the result was instant and startling to those in the area. Her skin sang its discomfort out to her nerves, sending her sprawling to the ground at the foot of one of the city's freestanding buildings. People stopped what they where doing and looked at the young elf, sprawled across the ground in a tangled mess. Tears of pain forming in her eyes at some unknown and unseen torture. Riana looked up at the man as he was staring down at her in confusion, trying to stammer an apology, "Miss, I'm sorry, I didn't..."

"She's fine! Just had a rough day!" Katrina was next to her, hoisting her off the ground, not realizing that her embrace was adding to her sister's pain.

Riana focused her thoughts on shutting out the pain and tried to get her body to obey her commands, wincing as her sister dragged her away from the crowd.

Once they rounded a corner, Katrina braced her sister against a wall to let her catch her breath. "Wow Ree. What was THAT all about?" Her face was distorted with worry for her sister, ears drooping low in concern.

"I'll be okay Kat. I just need a minute." Riana said, wiping tears from her eyes. Finally she willed her body back into her control and stood up. "Let's get home." She added weakly.

Almost home now, Riana gazed southward at the sheer rock face that stood thousands of feet high, towering over the rest of the city. In the face were carved balconies and windows, from top to bottom. Tens of thousands of people lived in the apartments carved into the cliff. In the center of the city, visible to the sisters as they crossed the last major intersection before reaching their building, was the palace where the governing party of Rathalon presided over the day-to-day activities of the city. It was a series of buildings in a square, interspersed with a few fountains, a few gardens and some grassy knolls. It was only called the palace because of its appearance however, as there was no actual royalty governing the city; rather, a group of elected citizens that served a term and then went back to their lives.

The streets teemed with life day and night. All civilized species were welcomed with open arms here, and most could be seen on any given day. As was evidenced by the mixed group the sisters wove through, their final destination in sight. Katrina sidestepped around a felinoid and then ducked between an Ogre's legs as Riana barely managed to get her complaining body out of the way of the wildly gesticulating arms of a Troll that was excitedly telling the crowd about some amazing point of interest or other in his last journey to the far reaches. Those of Riana and Katrina's race, the Elves, were in the minority by far with maybe a dozen families living within the city. Most of the elves tended to live closer to nature, in Pandoria, or even in one of the world's forests in unofficial cities that most sentients didn't even suspect existed.

The sisters approached their home, causing Riana to breathe a sigh of relief at the thought that she could soon shed the clothing that was causing her so much discomfort. Her relief was short lived however, as two things occurred to her. First, she was going to have to show her body to her mother soon. Secondly, they lived at the top of a three story building on the western edge of the city, which meant she still had three flights of stairs to get up. Living in the building with their own family were two other elven families, each fairly wealthy, either by heritage, or by enterprise. They burst through the front door and charged up the stairs to the door of their home. The spacious apartment consisted of four bed chambers, a living area, a study, a kitchen, two bath rooms, and had running water, both hot and cold, provided by the city's talented architects and designers.

The door to their apartment opened as soon as one of them touched it then closed again behind them. Katrina grabbed Riana by the hand and gently pulled her toward Riana's room.

Katrina moved Riana to the center of the elegantly appointed room, stripped her cloak out of her hands, and tossed it on the king size four-poster bed made of a dark, hard-wood with silk and chiffon hangings draped down at the corners as she spun around. Knocking the door closed and flopping down on a large pile of satin and velvet throw-pillows, she pulled her knees up to her chest and planted her feet in the plush rug that covered the stone floor. Katrina steepled her fingers together and set her chin on her finger tips, staring calmly at her sister.

"Ok," she said, "show me."

Riana looked at her, her eyes glazed over in something approaching abject terror. "I don't know Kat. I'm kind of scared." She would have wrapped her arms tightly about her body and rolled up into a ball, but she feared the pain it caused might be worse than her feelings about what her sister would think.

"It CAN'T be that bad Ree. Seriously. Show me." Katrina was sincere.

"Just you wait." Riana said as she began to unbutton her blouse, hands trembling, "You may yet change your tune."

Katrina bit her lower lip as she watched her sister slowly open her blouse. She was stunned, her mouth having fallen open as she stared at the slowly revealed intricate pattern of dark lines weaving around, serpent-like on her sister's alabaster skin. They covered most of her upper body. From her wrists up to her shoulders and down her torso. The markings were not so tightly packed as to cover all of her skin, in fact, most of her skin was untouched, but the spacing of the patterns was such that very little of her body was far from some type of mark.

Her back was covered as well, Katrina noticed as Riana slowly turned around, her ears drooping down in an obvious display of her uncertainty and concern for her sister's reaction.

Finally Katrina realized Riana was staring at her expectantly. "Ree… I had no idea…" Slowly she stood up and approached her sister, inspecting the complex patterns more closely.

"Are these Draconic?" She wondered aloud, reaching out to touch one of the marks on Riana's stomach. As she touched it, Riana flinched away, almost falling over. Katrina grabbed her sister's outstretched hand, stabilizing her before she completely lost her balance. "I'm sorry Ree, I imagine they are still sensitive huh?"

Riana nodded her agreement. "It's ok Kat. And yes, they are Draconic. It was the only language I could find in my research that would effectively do what I needed in single symbols."

Katrina nodded gravely, pretending to understand. She could recognize Draconic, but not actually read it. "Why did you do this?" was all she could think to ask as she reached out and stopped short of touching another of the vibrant marks.

Riana sighed, a full confession approaching her lips. "I was doing some research. Trying to find a way around the limitations of our mages. They, all of them, even you, can only cast so many spells at any given time. They require you to memorize them, and you can only memorize so many. They take concentration to cast, and time to speak the incantations. I was trying to find a way around all of that. And eventually I did." She sighed again, still unsure of herself.

"Go on." Katrina said reassuringly as she moved around her sister, inspecting each and every line with intense scrutiny.

"I found an ancient tome in the academy library. Back in the restricted section…"

Katrina stood bolt upright, almost knocking Riana over again. Her eyes as big as saucers, and ears standing straight up in amazement. The restricted section of the academy library was one of the most attentively guarded areas in all of Kalijor. Some of the books there were written before the great war, and contained spells and incantations so powerful that they could, and in fact had, leveled whole cities. Sneaking into the restricted area was not unheard of, Katrina had done it herself on more than one occasion just to see if she could; But to remain there undetected, for long enough to do real research, was something indeed!

"I know," Riana said narrowing her eyes. "That was almost the most difficult part of this whole ordeal. Next to having to tell mom."

Katrina giggled at that, and then crouched down again, resuming her inspection.

"So I found a book that detailed the research of a mage from before the war who sought very much the same thing." Riana paused before continuing, "he found that if he used the correct ingredients in his inks, and had them enchanted in just the right way, then he could have certain magical symbols permanently applied to his skin. It let him use the associated spells with little concentration, and no time memorizing them. The only problem he encountered was that he could only make it work with a single symbol for each spell, and he lacked the knowledge to divine appropriate symbols for all of his spells."

Katrina blurted out, "The Dragons have symbols for EVERYTHING! They invented most of our magics!!"

"Exactly," Riana replied. "So all I had to do was learn their written language. No small task, to be sure, but very possible. After that, it was merely about setting up my spell books, and convincing the Master in Talanor to do it."

"Do they…" Katrina gestured randomly about Riana's body, "…work?"

"Watch," Riana said with a touch of pride in her voice. She held out her hand and closed her eyes for an instant before a small ball of fire appeared in her outstretched hand. Katrina inspected the mark that had glowed as if in response to her sister's thoughts. The intricate pattern had glowed vividly for an instant in vibrant color before fading back to black. The flame hovered there in her hand, exactly as it would if she had conjured it through the normal, accepted means.

Katrina held her hand over the flame, as if to verify that it was real and not some kind of illusion or trick. Feeling the heat from it, she closed her hand around it as she recited a quelling incantation. Several seconds later the flame disappeared with a flicker.

Looking at her sister, eyes wide again, then to the rest of the intricate pattern spreading across her body. "Your legs as well?" She queried, amazement in her voice.

"Yes." Riana said flatly. "Both legs, from the lower calf up to the waist." At that, she lifted the hem of her skirt and showed one of her legs to her sister. The marks were there as well, standing out in stark contrast to her light skin.

Katrina was in awe. "I didn't know you could CAST this many spells!"

"I can't yet." Riana said. Now she was almost glowing with pride. "I included all of the arcane spells that I could find in the library. You see this?" She pointed to a symbol on her forearm.

"Yeah." Kat said with an eyebrow quirked.

"This is a spell I know how to cast. It's a sphere of light cantrip. But this one here…" Riana pointed to another, more elaborate image on the bicep of the same arm. "This is a fire ball spell that I have never cast before. Most mages can't for years. But as soon as I am able to channel the appropriate level of power, I will be able to use this one. I just need to keep practicing my focus and channeling abilities."

"Ree… This is…" Riana winced as she waited for her sister to finish her thought, to tell her she was insane, or stupid, anything but what came next. "This is AMAZING!"

Riana sighed heavily, relief flowing through her body. If Katrina could accept it that well, then their mother may just go mildly crazy, rather than kill her outright. Gently, she sat down on the edge of the bed and held her head.

"What's the matter Ree?" Katrina asked with a tone of concern, sitting down beside her sister on the edge of the bed.

"My head has been aching for a while. Nothing major. Just kind of a constant, dull pain." She said, as she massaged her temples with her finger tips.

"Since the tattoos?" Katrina said, obviously thinking there was some kind of connection.

"No," Riana came back quickly. "Since a week or so before that. Somewhere in the middle of studying up for the tattoos. I don't know what brought it on."

"Over a week?! Have you taken something?" Katrina was looking more worried by the moment.

"No, silly!" Now it was Riana's turn to admonish her sister, "I've been saying nice things to it in hopes it will get a confidence boost and move on to greener pastures!" Grinning wickedly at her sister, Riana punched her lightly on the shoulder. "Anyway, it isn't as bad as all that. Just kind of inconvenient. I need to find something to wear before mom gets home from Cohai. Help me pick something out Kat?"

"Of course!" Katrina said as she jumped off the edge of the bed. The headache temporarily forgotten in favor of a trip to the bazaar. "What did you have in mind?"

"Something… rather more daring than usual I think…" Riana said as a mischievous grin formed on her lips.

The Rathalon bazaar was something everyone should see at least once in their life. The two main roads through the city were lined on either side with merchant's awnings under which stood tables, racks, stands, buckets, bushels, and hangers filled with anything anyone could possibly want. The treasures of Kalijor were here for the taking, if only the price could be met. People of all creeds and colors, species and sizes wandered the streets, from tent to tent, corner to corner; haggling, bartering, trading, buying, and selling. The bazaar itself put all this to shame. Easily the largest building in the city, it was packed with ten times the merchants as all of the city streets combined.

"Welcome to my humble shop." The finely featured elf said as the girls tumbled through the door. "If there is anything I can help you with please let me know." He smiled happily.

Katrina nodded in his direction and smiled as Riana started digging through the racks of fine silk garments.

"I see you have an excellent eye m'lady. Those silks were imported from Avian just this morning. They were woven by some of the finest silk weavers in the land."

"Oh Kat! This is amazing! I can hardly feel this material it's so light and soft!" Riana cooed as she fondled a couple of the garments appreciatively.

Katrina moved over near her sister and picked up the sleeve of a hanging blouse. Sliding the material back and forth between her fingertips she nodded her approval then turned her head slightly so that she could see the store's proprietor in the corner of her eye. "It's nice. But I've felt better. Remember that nightworm silk merchant we ran into in Talanor the other day? That stuff was way softer than this." The man's smile faltered a bit but he returned quickly.

Riana was only briefly caught off guard by her sister's comment. Recovering her wits quickly she smiled slightly and began playing her part. "That's true. Such a nice little dwarf too! Hard to believe she was selling it so cheaply, it was just flying out her doors."

"Yeah. Maybe we should portal back over there and see if she has any more available. Remember that dark purple she had? It was amazing!" Now he was fidgeting a bit as he watched them.

"Oh! This one is nice." Riana said as she removed a sapphire colored silk tunic from the rack and gently held it up against her tattooed skin. "How much is it?" She looked at the uncomfortable man pointedly, turning slightly so that he could better see the garment.

"Eh… that one is fifty silver pieces m'lady." He smiled hopefully as she looked back at him with a skeptical glance.

Katrina turned around and leveled her gaze on the man, narrowing her golden eyes at him then turning back to her sister. "C'mon Ree, put it back, we'll go back to Talanor where the prices are more reasonable and the silk is better. It's worth the trip with as much as we're going to need in order to refill your wardrobe."

Riana put on her best pouting face as she reluctantly let her sister take the tunic from her hands and return it to the rack. "Alright. I suppose you're right," she acquiesced.

Dramatically they made their way to the street, lingering a bit too long with each step and fingering a garment or two as they paraded toward the door. Finally the owner had enough and almost shouted, "my ladies if you intend to purchase a quantity of items I am sure we could arrange for a volume price."

Katrina stopped half way to the door and turned slowly to look at him, her eyes narrowed again. "What sort of price?"

"Ah… well, I… How about thirty five silver…"

Katrina cut him off by turning back toward the door with a flourish and taking another step.

"Thirty! Thirty silver each…"

In an instant, Katrina whirled on the man and gave him her best stern look, her hands on her hips and ears parallel with the ground, pointing straight back from her head. "Twenty five silver each and not a copper more!"

The man looked like he had been slapped in the face. He hesitated for the briefest of moments, considering her words, during which time Katrina started turning toward the door again. Finally he came to a decision and called after them, "alright, twenty five silver each. But you have to buy a dozen or more."

Katrina turned back around and smiled sweetly. "Deal."

Numerous pair of soft suede boots, several bodices and tunics in different styles and materials, some skirts, belts, greaves, gloves, capes, cloaks, and various other odds and ends later they made their way home, laden with packages and parcels. All told they had spent nearly fifty gold pieces, but had returned victorious, with bundles of new things to wear. The only thing they had not purchased, mostly due to its high cost and their inability to talk the store keeper down, was a set of leathers that was a deep, glossy black color with purple trim. It was a complete set and had been magically enchanted to increase its strength and softness, and reduce its weight. Its cut would have worked perfectly around Riana's freshly tattooed skin, but the cost seemed simply too high.

They had immediately set about going through Riana's wardrobe, piling up all of her robes and other long, concealing things on her bed. Katrina was stowing the last of the new items when Riana stepped behind the changing screen to don one of the new outfits.

"Ok. Here goes." She said tentatively as she stepped from behind the screen. She wore a very light, elven silk scarf that covered her breasts and formed a cross over her heart then tied behind her neck. Her lower half was draped with a similar silk that hung low on her waist and covered her with a low hanging breechcloth in front and back. In all it was extremely revealing, and to her, felt as though she was wearing nothing at all because the fabric was so light. She breathed a sigh of relief at the feeling of no longer having coarse fabrics constantly lighting up her nerve endings. It felt so much better that she didn't much care what it looked like.

Katrina stared, mouth hanging open. "Ree, I… Oh wow," Was all she could manage to say.

Riana looked at herself in the full length mirror by her wardrobe, blushing from head to toe. "I see what you mean Kat, but it's the only way I'm going to get anything done. At least until these tattoos heal a bit more. Wearing normal clothing is almost debilitating." Looking in the mirror, she turned this way and that, inspecting her image from different angles and perspectives. It was very revealing, but nothing she couldn't get used to, she supposed. The dark lines covering her body in intricate patterns were all visible. Briefly she wondered if this was all just part of the price she would pay for her deed.

"Mom IS going to kill me." She muttered out loud.

"Maybe." Katrina chimed in from the other side of the room, "But you'll look darned good when you go."

Riana saw her sister's grin in the mirror and grinned back. Then put her fingers to her temples again and tried to massage away the dull ache once more.

"You should see a healer Ree." Katrina sounded worried again. "Maybe there are side effects… Something not in the notes. Or maybe something went wrong…"

Riana turned around and looked at her sister. "Nothing went wrong. Unless it went wrong enough for the wizard that recorded the procedure that they were unable to note it, there was no mention of it. Besides, like I said earlier, it started more than a week before I went to Talanor."

"Maybe so. But you should STILL see a healer!" Katrina was definitely worried, she never got this insistent unless she was deadly serious.

"Alright. I'll go see a healer tomorrow." Riana acquiesced.

"Why tomorrow?" Katrina pushed the issue still further.

"Because if mom kills me tonight, then I won't have to worry about a healer tomorrow!" Riana said mockingly. "That and it will be dark in a few minutes, and unless it is an emergency, most healers won't see people at night. I'll be fine until tomorrow." Riana busied herself with storing her robes and other displaced garments in a foot locker while she talked. Trying to keep her mind off her headache.

"Alright." Katrina finally gave in. "But you are going at first light, and I will go with you to make sure you get there!"

"Fair enough. Now help me get this mess cleaned up."

A moment later the brief transition into night occurred. The bright light of day quickly dimmed and faded away into night. It took less than two minutes to happen, and all at once it was night time. And with it came a knock at the front door.

The girls answered the door together, opening it to find a human male standing there. He wore dusty traveling gear, and looked as though he had just run a marathon. His light hair was matted to his forehead and he was winded, although his bright blue eyes shone with an inner energy. He was barely over the twin's six foot height, and looked as though he weighed in under two-hundred pounds, mostly lean muscle. He smiled broadly when he saw the sisters beyond the threshold, raising an eyebrow at the sight of Riana, wearing not much more that a couple of silk scarves.

"I am a courier. I was dispatched from the Burning Expanse this morning with a message for Ladies Katrina and Riana Thorindal. Might you be they?" His voice was a solid tenor and showed no signs of being winded, despite his outward appearance.

"The Burning Expanse?" Katrina wondered aloud.

"We don't know anyone in the Burning Expanse!" Riana chimed in.

"So you ARE Katrina and Riana Thorindal?" The man asked, obviously eager to deliver his dispatch.

"We are," the girls said in unison.

"Very well then," he said. He reached into a satchel slung over his shoulder and produced a sealed parchment. "My instructions say that I am to give this only to the two of you together, and that you must first show me the matching seal."

Katrina and Riana stared at him blankly for a moment. This was a very strange turn of events. Finally Riana shook herself and said, "Just a moment, let me get mine." Then she disappeared into her chamber for a moment and returned with her seal in hand.

She handed it to the messenger, who inspected it, and compared it against the wax seal on the parchment. Then nodded his approval and handed both items to Riana. "Here you are. Thank you." He then bowed to them and took a step back from the door, "Now if you ladies will excuse me, I have other deliveries to make."

"Of course! Thank you very much." Katrina said as she watched him head down the stairs, closing the door after he was out of sight.

Alone again, the girls inspected the parchment. It bore the family seal, which meant it had to be from their mother, as she had the only seal that was out of the house currently. Gently, Riana tried to slide her thumb nail under the wax seal, but it did not budge.

"He said together." Katrina said aloud. Then she placed her thumb on the other side of the seal and together they applied pressure. The seal popped loose, and the wax melted away into nothingness. Quickly, Riana unfolded the parchment to reveal the elegant, practiced script of their mother. It was a large letter, and it looked to have been written in something of a hurry, as the hand was not up to Ezrina's normal standards. Together they read.

Girls,

I know you were expecting me home this evening, and it pains me to write this letter to you rather than be there with you both. Unfortunately the pain my heart must endure does not stop there. It is time you both knew the truth. About your 'father'. Years ago, I was living in a keep with a number of companions that I adventured with regularly. We struck out often into the unknown wilderness in search of whatever there was to be found. Riches, knowledge, new sights, whatever took our fancy. One of these adventurers was an elven Wizardess named Kilishandra. Kilishandra Thorindal.

Katrina and Riana looked up at one another suddenly. "Thorindal. Dad?" Riana said.

"No." Katrina replied. "That can't be right. She said this Kilishandra was a wizardESS. Not a wizard!"

They stared at one another for a moment and then looked back to the letter.

Kilishandra and I shared many adventures together. As the best of friends. But there was something different in her soul. Something that I never would have expected until I watched her beat down the defenses of a castle single handedly, in order to profess her love, for another of the women that lived and adventured with us. I wasn't sure what to think or do about her after that day. I tried to stay close to her but I wasn't sure my heart could go where I thought she may eventually try and tread. Apparently our other friend felt the same as me, for she distanced herself from Kilishandra, and soon after, became engaged with a wonderful man, whom she eventually married and bore children with. Kilishandra was happy for them both, but I could see that she was crushed. So I spent more time with her, trying to keep her thoughts from the past. Eventually, years later, we encountered a Dark elf with a special

32

mission. He buried a cursed dagger in Kilishandra's ribs and disappeared, sobbing something about being sorry. I rushed her to our healer, who quickly dealt with the physical wound, but she did not get better. She lay in a fevered sleep for days, and whenever we tried to rouse her, she would scream obscenities and try to hurt us. So we had a healer keep her in a deep slumber while we tried to figure out what had happened.

Eventually, we discovered, through a series of events that leads me to believe the entire ordeal was very much orchestrated, that the dagger was a cursed weapon that would slowly open her mind to the powers of hate and discord. She would slowly become a being of evil and hatred unless we could do something. What's more, the Dark elf that stabbed her with the thing turned out to be the reincarnated first love of Kilishandra, whom had died hundreds of years prior, and now it seemed, had been called back and was being controlled by a powerful mage of unknown origins. The elf, Rhaeton, confessed that he was obliged to tell us his master's name, and said that it was Wyndel. While our friends fanned out in search of this Wyndel, I decided to see if the curse of the dagger could be broken if the dagger itself was broken. But in trying to destroy the thing, I pricked my finger with it, thus cursing myself to the same fate as Kilishandra.

After a time, our mages contrived a ritual that they said had a high probability of success in curing both Kilishandra and myself of the curse, but we had to act immediately, and it was a very dangerous thing to attempt. It involved the merging of our minds, along with a third person's. Their thinking was that, together we could chase out, or seal off the cursed parts of our minds, and then balance what was left, filling in gaps and holes from one another's minds. In effect, after the ritual, we would all be ourselves, but each of us would carry bits of the others within us. I agreed, as did the woman that had been the object of Kilishandra's affections years before, so we set up the ritual and performed it immediately.

I can not to this day describe the experience. But when it was over, it had worked. Almost perfectly. Kilishandra woke from a months long slumber, a changed person. But then so were the rest of us. I found that the pieces of her that had stayed with me, helped me understand her feelings, her confusion, her uncertainty in how she felt, and WHAT she felt. I knew in my mind that I could never have considered it possible before, but then, after the ritual, after the sharing, and baring of our souls to one another, I could not deny it. I HAD grown to love her in our time together, and although she had been trying hard to subdue her feelings, especially after what had happened to her the last time she shared them, I KNEW that she loved me. So, we went down that path, together.

I wish that I could say that we had years of happiness together after that day. But it was not to be. After a few brief days, she discovered who Wyndel was, and where he had secreted himself away. It seems that he was her estranged father, driven mad with power lust over centuries spent in its pursuit. He had struck a deal with a demon to provide it the perfect vessel with which to wreak havoc on the world in exchange for some ultimate power, and to that end he had brought back the soul of Rhaeton and had it strike down his own daughter. She snuck away from our bed in the dead of night and went to him to finish it. She left a note that I discovered when I roused at the realization that she was not with me that night. I could not have gotten to them in time if I had grown wings and flown. Although, gods know, I was close. I arrived just as the final blows were struck. Kilishandra and Wyndel destroyed each other before my eyes. My love lay dying in my arms and there was nothing I could do to stop it.

With her dying breath she professed her love to me, and pushed a parchment into my hands before closing her eyes for what should have been the last time. The parchment was a love letter of sorts, and directions to where she had hidden an amulet of her own creation. The amulet was enchanted with bits of her being in such a way that the first woman to don it about her neck would conceive a child, born of her and Kilishandra's bodies and souls.

I kept it secret. Hidden for years. I feared what my life would become. Not just in the having of children, but in the having of children with no father, but two mothers. I feared for what people would think of me. And of what they would think of my children. But after decades, my heart still ached for her. I longed for her touch. Her breath upon my flesh. I missed her so much that I decided that I would have a living piece of her in my life no matter what others thought of it. So I donned the amulet, and waited.

Not long after, the two of you came to me. I gave birth to you and it was the greatest miracle in my life. I raised you both as best I could, telling you all the while that your father had been killed in some great battle. I never had the courage to tell you the truth, for fear of what you, my children, would think of me. Know that I love you and that I have always loved you. You are both the products of pure love. A love between two people that could not be broken, not by curse, not by time, and certainly not by the prying eyes of other people.

I know that this must come as a shock to you both, but I had to tell you before I set you down the path that you must now follow. I am sorry that it is the two of you that must now complete the cycle of the curse that tried to destroy Kilishandra and myself all those years ago. If I could do it myself, I would, but it can not be me that does it. When I said that the ritual almost worked, I meant it. There was an unfortunate consequence. Some time after the ritual, the third woman, an elf by the name of Ambrai, began to follow a dark path. Long a Ranger of the wilds, she began to turn towards the dark magics, forsaking her roots in the forests and the wilds. She began to play with necromancy, and before long had exhumed the body of my Kilishandra and reanimated it to do her bidding. She caused much strife in the world before she was inexorably drawn to the dark side of the mountains, where the undead and demons of Kalijor roam free. I know she was hurt by Kilishandra, and I know she saw into her heart that day. I can forgive her, even for the desecration of Kilishandra's grave, but she is getting worse. I have long heard rumors of a dark ranger that roams the Plane of Sorrow and preys upon adventurers there. Recently I overheard someone that had seen her, talking about the amulet that this dark ranger wore about her neck, and I know it to be the very one that gave the two of you life. The one I buried with Kilishandra after you were born.

I did some research into some of Kilishandra's journals and spell books and it seems that one of the spells she used in creating that amulet was an ancient spell of life, from

35

before the great wars. I further researched the spell in the academy library and discovered that it has a dark potential when used as an enchantment. After it is expended, it can be recharged, through the infusion of soul energy. It takes hundreds of souls to replenish the power of the amulet, but the nature of the life created by it is directly proportional to the way in which the soul energy is harvested. Kilishandra filled it with all of her love for me, and blessed me with the two of you. And, I believe, because of the nature of your conception, your being born almost solely from magic, the two of you have come to surpass almost every mage in Kalijor, even at your young age. But I fear Ambrai, in her travels down the path of evil, now fills the amulet with a dark energy. If she were to conceive a child, born of that energy, and with your aptitude for wielding it, it would be a monster.

I am currently deep in the Burning Expanse, searching the catacombs here for some means to destroy the amulet. But it is to the two of you that I must entrust the task of collecting it. I have no idea how Ambrai will react to the two of you but I can imagine that it will not be pleasant, and I know that your experience will be difficult. You may have to fight her. Or even kill her. And it is very likely that she still commands the body of your mother, Kilishandra. Please understand that she is long since dead. If you must destroy her body, know that it is just that, her body. Her soul was freed decades ago, and all that remains is a husk.

Go first to Pandoria, and fetch a reliquary from the druid circle there. It should help you when dealing with Ambrai. I have sent a message there warning them of your coming and your needs. Then visit Gornin in Cohai, and ask him how best to proceed. He knows of your quest and will be ready to receive you.

Katrina. Riana. My loves. My life. I am very sorry for this thing that I have asked you to do. I would do it myself, but the part of my mind and soul that is Ambrai's would not allow it of me. So it is to the two of you that this task must fall. I am truly sorry girls. I love you both more than life itself.

Your loving mother,
Ezrina Thorindal

The girls looked at one another after finishing the letter. No words were said, but the exchange ran deep. Their whole world had just changed. In the blink of an eye, the reading of a letter, everything they knew was different.

"Get some rest." Riana said to her sister as she stood up and slowly padded down the short hall towards her bedchamber. "We'll leave in the morning."

Katrina stared after her sister as she moved down the hall, closing the door behind her.

-3-

They were both up before the daylight began, making preparations for their journey. Riana had gone out and visited the clothing shop where they had found the leather garments the previous day, waking the poor man well before he was used to getting up. When she told him she was related to Ezrina, whom he had known for a long time he had readily agreed to help her by discounting the articles slightly and further enchanting the materials to reduce the friction they would cause against her skin. He also cast a few enchantments upon a belt and pouches that she picked out that allowed them to reduce the weight of anything the belt supported.

Returning home just after light she began packing as lightly as she could, she stuffed a few of her new silk garments into a large pouch on her right hip. On top of those she put some carefully wrapped rations, and a medium sized water skin. Some other odds and ends went in as well, a compass, a set of utensils, some scraps of parchment, a small vial of ink and a couple of quills, and one-hundred feet of fine, magically-strengthened elven climbing cord; just in case they had to face a climb of some kind. On her other hip she sheathed her short sword and her dagger. Finally she rolled up her thin sleeping pad and blanket and set the roll across her back, securing it with a braided leather rope over her shoulder.

When she exited her chamber, she found Katrina ready and waiting in the main room of their apartment. She was similarly packed, although most of her things were in a back pack slung over her shoulder, and she wore her normal, conservative, mage robes. She smiled at Riana when she saw her, and gave an appreciative whistle, to which Riana blushed profusely.

Riana wore a tight fitting bodice above a breechcloth that hung to well below her knees in front and back and was settled over another leather garment that covered her private parts, but not much else. She had on a pair of sturdy but comfortable leather boots that came up to the middle of her calves, and a leather bracer on each forearm that covered from her wrists to her elbows. The coup de gras was a thick leather choker around her neck and the heavy belt that supported her short sword and dagger in new scabbards, as well as a couple pouches for coin and other odds and ends. All of the items were rich, black leather, soft and supple, with a royal purple beading and stitching that complimented her hair. To complete the ensemble she pulled on one of the more expensive items they had purchased. The fine black material of the elven cape rested nearly weightless on her shoulders, its rich purple interior wrapped around her comfortingly as she fixed the intricately detailed dragon's head clasp at her neck and let it rest against her leather choker.

"So," Riana said, trying to take the focus off of her exposed body. "We take the portal to Pandoria, and then speak with the Druids."

"Right." Katrina agreed crisply.

"Alright then. Do we have everything we need for a few days? I am sure we can resupply in Cohai before we set out for the Plain of Sorrow." She was trying not to sound scared as hell despite the fact that neither of them had ever been far from home for any length of time. While they had both been to Pandoria before, they were seeing life through new eyes now, and even their apartment seemed to have taken on a different feeling for them. As she headed for the door Riana looked around their home, her eyes landing on a painting by the dining table, the myriad of figures within its rich golden frame bent to the task of what she had always thought to be the construction of some great monument or structure. Now as she looked at it, she saw new details in the image, the forlorn faces of the workers, the stress lines on their faces, they were bent to no task of joy. Deeper in the background she saw the rows of stone markers for the first time. The figures were erecting a tomb, a grave site for some hero that had fallen.

As she reached for the door, Riana was taken with the sick feeling that she would never see this place again. It was not a feeling of doom, or some disaster, in fact she was quite confident in their success. Something was nagging at the back of her aching mind as if trying to tell her to let it all go. Pushing the door open, she dismissed it as being related to her headache and stepped out into the hallway. Together, Riana and Katrina took their first steps into their new lives. Riana wasn't sure if they were truly ready, but she knew they had no choice now in the finding out.

They appeared in the Pandoria portal chamber less than an hour later. This room was similar to the Rathalon portal chamber, but on a much smaller scale. There was a similar sunken arrival area, surrounded by columns. They were met by armed guards that wore leather and chain armor rather than the heavy plate ensembles of the Rathalon Defenders. Most of the guards here were elven, with some dwarves, and other fey folk mixed in. The room had only one raised platform, with but a single portal ring sitting atop it. Rathalon was the only city in Kalijor that had portals to multiple destinations. It was the only city that could handle the traffic.

This room differed from its counterpart in Rathalon in one other significant way, it was made of wood. In similar concept to Rathalon, Pandoria was built without adding additional material during the construction process, but Pandoria was built in and around massive, living trees. Many of the city's facilities were grown into the trunks of trees so large it could take a person the better part of a day to walk around the base of a single one. The portal chamber was a hollow in the trunk of such a tree. The floor was solid wood, worn smooth over centuries of pedestrian traffic, but the growth rings of the tree could still be clearly seen as Riana looked down. The columns in the room were wood as well, part of the living tree.

"State your name and business." An armor clad elf called to them from a few feet away. His armor was a finely woven chain mail that moved and rippled like water as he took a step toward them, a light, curved, wicked-looking sword in his hand.

"Riana and Katrina Thorindal. We are here on business. We must speak with the Druids at their temple." Riana said to the fair haired elf.

The guard looked at them for a long moment, paying particular attention to Riana. His gaze traveled over her form and she flushed a bit at the scrutiny. She could not tell if the intense look was because of her outfit or because of her tattoos. Finally he motioned them out of the arrival area and offered a curt, "Welcome to Pandoria ladies."

They moved up the steps and into the room proper. As they made their way toward the large double doors leading to the city, they passed one of the smooth wooden pillars growing from the floor to the ceiling. Riana gently touched the wood with her fingertips and felt the tree's life-blood flowing strongly through the pillar, supplying the vital nutrients to the still living, vibrant tree despite the massive hollow chamber held within its trunk. Rather than chopping and carving away at the trees, the druids that built Pandoria had used their magic to manipulate them. Forming open spaces within the trunks, weaving branches together into solid walk ways between trees and so on. They stepped out onto a tree branch that was wide enough for four two-horse carts to traverse side by side. The wood had been flattened out into a serviceable road, with gutters for water runoff, sidewalks and all the other features of a paved roadway.

There were people everywhere here as well. The merchants sold their wares from alcoves in the trunks of the trees rather than from street-side tents and awnings like the markets in Rathalon. Most of the people were on walkways around the trunks of the trees themselves, leaving the branches that spanned the space between trees fairly free of traffic.

The Druid temple was next to the lake, on the floor of the forest some eight-hundred feet below them. So Riana turned off on a branch that headed down a gentle slope. Katrina followed her sister towards another tree trunk that looked as though it had an inn or tavern of some kind housed within it. The air was warm, but not hot. The humidity was enough to keep skin well moisturized, but not so much so that people's clothes constantly stuck to their bodies. The light of day filtered down to them through the canopy of branches high over their heads, keeping things light, but not bright.

Riana noticed that the mood of the people here was much less rushed than those in Rathalon. Things moved at a slower, more leisurely pace here. The hustle and bustle of Rathalon became a relaxed stroll in Pandoria. The occasional warm conversation punctuated the gentle air of the city. Riana moved more easily here, keeping enough space around herself to prevent people brushing and bumping into her overly-sensitive skin. Even the most crowded areas of Pandoria moved at a slower pace, with much more room and no jostling or jockeying to get around.

The pair made their way down ramp after ramp, weaving their way back and forth between the hundreds of gargantuan trees that made up the city. After about an hour, they finally set foot on the floor of the forest. The ground was spongy and covered with a fine grass that was soft to the touch. It seemed to support the weight of a person without bending, but never caused any discomfort in even the most tender of bare feet. The blades were short, maybe a quarter of an inch high, but packed so closely together that one could barely see the soil beneath.

Children danced and played around them as they made their way across the forest floor towards the lake at the center of Pandoria. The children ran barefoot, playing tag and kickball with not a care in the world. Riana sighed, thinking about those days, not so long ago, when her only concern was whether or not they would find the time to go swimming.

"That seems like such a long time ago." She said aloud as she looked after the children, who by now had almost all dived into the lake and begun splashing one another.

"That was like, last week." Katrina said with a grin on her face. She turned her sparkling yellow eyes on her sister and resisted the urge to push her playfully.

"I know…" Riana mused. "But so much has happened since then." She paused briefly, thinking for a moment. "Kat? What do you think about all of this? About mom, and this Kilishandra person. Do you think it's really possible?"

Katrina's gaze dropped a bit, looking at some unknown spot on the nearest tree trunk. "I imagine it is true. I've never known mom to lie; but it seems so fantastic. It's hard to believe, I must admit."

"What does that make us?" Riana said suddenly, as she stopped in her tracks and looked at her sister pointedly.

"What do you mean?" Katrina looked her sister in the eyes. Riana's deep, violet eyes watering up in preparation to shed tears.

"I mean. What are we? Some kind of abominations? We have no father! We shouldn't even BE! It isn't natural." She was almost shouting, she was so upset.

Katrina thought for a moment before answering. "Honestly Ree, I don't know. I imagine that in the grand scheme of things, it really doesn't matter. We are. We have a loving mother, who conceived us with the help of someone she apparently loved very much. Why should anything else matter?"

"Yeah. Mom loved this Kilishandra person so much that she couldn't bring herself to tell us about her! US Kat! Their children! WE COULD NOT BE TOLD! What does that make us?!" She was almost screaming now; punctuating her words by throwing her arms about angrily. People near them quickly stopped and stared. Those further away quietly avoided them, moving on to some other spot on the forest floor.

"Ree. She had her reasons. I don't think she meant to hurt us." Katrina somehow still remained calm, even in the face of her sister's rising rage.

"NO!" Riana shouted back at her. "She didn't mean ANYTHING for us! She USED us to feel closer to this other woman!" Riana's violet eyes began to glow as she yelled.

Katrina saw it happening before she knew what it was. Her sister was angry, very angry, and her magically infused body was harnessing her anger. The markings were channeling it and they began to glow brightly as she screamed.

"Ree! Calm down! Something's happening! Look at yourself!" Katrina began to panic as her sister continued to rage, her body thrumming with palpable energy.

"Don't TELL me to calm down!" She shouted at her sister. "We aren't even real people! We aren't supposed to be! We were USED! Who the hell is this Kilishandra person anyway?!"

As the first fires erupted about them, Katrina sprung into action. Not knowing what else to do, she struck Riana hard across the face with her fist. The effect was instant. Riana spun around with the force of the blow, crumpling to the ground in a heap. The many small fires surrounding them fading away as she slipped into unconsciousness.

Leaping to her sister's side, Katrina picked up her limp body and cradled her head in her lap. "Oh Ree. I'm sorry. I'm so sorry. I didn't know what else to do. Oh Ree… Something isn't right. We'll fix it. You'll see. We'll make it all better soon. Just hang in there. We're almost ready." She sobbed the words, rocking her sister's unconscious body in her arms.

-5-

"There is nothing more we can do for her," the elf continued as Katrina sat on the edge of the bed, holding Riana's hand. "I am sorry, but there is nothing wrong with her physically."

"I know." She said through the tears streaming down her cheeks. "Thank you."

The elf bowed slightly, his dark hair falling over his brow before disappearing through a door in the small room. Katrina watched him go with a sigh. When she looked back at her sister, Riana's eyes were open, tracking her sister's movements.

Katrina hastily wiped the tears from her face and stifled her sobs. "Hey Ree. Welcome back."

Riana looked around the small circular room in surprise. It was fifteen feet in diameter with a door opposite the bed. A small round window next to the bed looked out onto the lake where the children were playing in the water, splashing one another. The small desk growing out of the wall midway between the door and the bed boasted a small serving tray with a steaming cup of tea and a small loaf of bread. The chair that Katrina sat on next to the bed finished out the furniture. She lay under a thin silk sheet, it's light pressure making her skin sing out in discomfort that bordered on real pain. Finishing her survey of the room, Riana's eyes fell back on her sister's tear streaked face. "What happened?"

"You went a little crazy for a bit, but its ok now." Katrina smiled weakly at her sister.

Riana was not so easily fooled. "What is it Kat? What's wrong?"

Katrina paused looking as though she was thinking about how to answer the question. Finally she spoke as another tear ran down her face. "Ree, there's something wrong. Something in your mind. The Druids can't fix it. They have no idea even what it is, or what could be causing it."

"In my… mind?" Riana looked confused. "They can't get a psychic surgeon to fix it?" She had never seen it done but it was well known that a psychic surgeon could fix basically any problem a person's head might have. Brain trauma. Swelling, bleeding, all of it.

"No Ree. Not your brain. Your mind. Something is not right in your mind. It isn't a physical problem." Katrina was crying again. With effort she continued, "They are fairly certain that is why you are having headaches, but there is nothing they can do about it."

Riana looked up at the wooden ceiling, counting the growth lines of the tree she rested inside. Trying to think of anything that might be helpful in some way, she knew it was deeper than the quick explanation she had been given. Katrina was pretty upset. Turning her head back towards her sister, Riana fixed her eyes on Katrina's and stared into them. "Kat. Tell me the rest. What else is wrong?"

Katrina wiped her tears away again, trying in vain to stem the flow. Shaking her head in disbelief she stammered. "They can't be sure of anything, but they think there is a good chance you could… die. If it keeps getting worse."

Katrina continued sobbing as Riana pondered this new information. She lay there for a while before finally coming to a decision. She sat up, causing the ache in her head to increase. Willing the pain away, she pulled the silk sheet about her and looked at her sister. Katrina was staring at her, with tears pooled in the corners of her eyes.

"We aren't getting anything done like that." Riana said to her simply. "Now, where are my clothes?"

Katrina pulled open a drawer under the lip of the bed with her free hand and pointed to the leather garments inside. Then looked back at Riana again, "What are you doing?" She asked as Riana stood up and started pulling her things from the drawer.

"I am going to finish what we started." She said as though it was the most obvious thing in the world. "I have a few questions for this Ambrai woman, and Ezrina as well."

Katrina blinked as she watched her sister gently pull her meager garments over her sensitive skin and fasten them in place. She had never heard Riana call their mother Ezrina before.

"Ree, you don't have to… we should go see…" Katrina began to protest, but Riana interrupted her.

"Go where Kat?! Huh? See whom?!" She sighed a heavy sigh. "The druids don't know what's wrong with me or how to fix it. Who knows more about healing then they do? Who is going to be of any more help? Besides, I am not even supposed to exist. What harm could there be in my passing?" As she finished speaking, she closed the clasp on her cape. Snapping up the belt with all of its pouches and scabbards attached, she stalked out of the room, kicking the door open as she pulled the belt snugly around her waist.

6

"Please take this reliquary, it will offer some protection against the dark forces on the other side of the mountains." The druid handed Riana a small, finely crafted wooden box. She took it and opened the lid with one hand. In the velvet lined box, lay a long leather necklace, with a small glass container on it. Inside the container was a bone of some kind. She touched it gently with her free hand, feeling the cold surface against her fingertips.

"I am sorry there is nothing else we can do to help you Lady Thorindal. Our hopes and prayers are with you on your journey." The elf spoke sincerely, and Katrina bowed her head to him and began to thank him, when Riana cut her off sharply.

"Don't call me that!" She snapped at the druid. Harshly she yanked the relic from the box, snapped its lid shut and thrust it back into the man's arms.

He looked dazed as he accepted the box and watched her settle the necklace around her neck. Turning around abruptly, she stormed out of the temple, not even looking over her shoulder to see if Katrina was following.

Running to catch up with her, Katrina shouted ahead to her sister. "Ree? What was that?"

"What was what?" Riana snapped back at her.

Kat finally caught up to her, drawing alongside, "THAT!" She said, stabbing a finger back towards the temple by the lake.

Riana sighed. How could she explain it any differently? "That…" She started to say something, but changed her mind, "was that."

Katrina stared at her for a moment as they walked quickley across the forest floor, then said, "What does that mean?! That was that? Those people helped us Ree. They deserve to be treated better!"

"They certainly didn't help ME any Kat. They handed me a death sentence! Am I supposed to thank them for that?"

Riana still had not looked at Katrina, who simply squared her shoulders and stared ahead, her voice shaking as she spoke, "Ree," She said simply. Riana kept stalking along the bottom of the city, moving deliberately toward the portal that would take them into the forest outside the city.

"REE!" Kat shouted at her sister's back.

Riana stopped abruptly. Her shoulders sagged and she turned around to look at her sister, with tears forming in her eyes. "What Kat?"

"They tried Ree! They did everything they could! I know you're upset but how is yelling at THEM going to make it any better?"

"It isn't," Riana acquiesced.

"They didn't say you were GOING to die Ree. They said you COULD die. If it continues to get worse." She tried to be optimistic.

Riana looked at her. Shaking her head as the tears rolled down her face. "You don't understand Kat. It IS getting worse. It has BEEN getting worse. Its gotten worse EVERY DAY for two months now."

Katrina looked as though she had been shot through with an arrow. "Two... months? But Ree you said it had been a couple of..."

"I lied!" Riana cut her off again. "I didn't want you to worry. So I lied to you. I'm sorry Kat. I know I shouldn't have."

Riana watched her sister stare at her. A distant look flashed across her face, as though she was concentrating very hard on something behind Riana. Then she opened her mouth in an expression of shock, and focused her eyes back on Riana.

"Oh Ree. This isn't good. We need to do something, we need to..."

Again, Riana cut her off, "We need to get going. Cohai isn't getting any closer with us standing here, and I sure as heck am not adding any sand to my hourglass."

"But Ree, there may be a way! Somebody may know!" Katrina was grasping at straws and she knew it.

"There isn't time Kat. We need to get this done. So let's just get it done. If there is time after, then we can go chasing whims. After we clean up Ezrina and Kilishandra's mess." Riana sighed again and made a gesture toward her bedroll that Katrina was hugging to her chest. Her sister approached her, offering the rolled up mat and sheets. Riana took it and gently settled it against her back beneath her cloak, tightening the rope against her body to prevent it bouncing around. The constant, dull pain of the pressure against her tattooed skin actually helped her keep her mind off the sharp, throbbing pain in her head.

She looked at her sister again, and seeing the fear and concern on Katrina's face, grabbed her by the shoulders and pulled her into a tight embrace. Riana squeezed her eyes closed against the pain she was inflicting upon herself.

"I love you Kat. I always will. Even into the next world. But you may have to go it alone for a while before we get to be together there. Just know that I always carry you in my heart, no matter what."

She held the embrace for another long, painful moment, Katrina squeezing her back. Then Riana broke the hug and held Katrina out at arm's length, still squeezing her shoulders. She looked her in the eyes and spoke, very calmly.

"Now. There are some things I need to ask this Ambrai person. And if I can make it that far, I need to speak to Ezrina as well. I need you with me Kat. I will need your strength to make it." Her tears were gone now. She was all business. Her long ears were pointed almost straight up, the small golden hoops in them hanging down against the edges.

Katrina stifled her own tears and looked squarely into her sister's eyes, "Aye, Ree, you can count on me. You sure as hell aren't going to be able to get rid of me. Not until it's all… over…" She tried her best to not cry again. Turning her head away from her sister's gaze and squeezing the tears back with her eyelids. Her ears drooped down in sadness, flushing red with her emotions.

Riana nodded at her sister gravely, then let go of her shoulders, wheeled around on her heels, and resumed her quick pace towards the portal to the forest.

Katrina watched her for a moment, wiping the tears from her eyes. "I don't know if we'll be ready in time." She said under her breath, before dashing to catch up with her sister.

7

The other interesting thing about Pandoria was that it didn't really exist. Not in a normal sense at any rate. The entire forest-city was constructed in a pocket dimension that had been created specifically for the purposes of its creators. As such, it was only accessible via portals. There were only two of those: The portal that was tied into the Kalijor portal network the girls had arrived through; and the portal that they had just stepped though, leaving them standing in the middle of the Forest of Brume.

The dark, dense forest of old hardwood trees was a stark contrast to the widely spaced, gigantic trees of Pandoria. The ground, where it wasn't covered in a thick blanket of mist, was instead blanketed in fallen leaves from the old trees. The air smelled of animals, decomposing leaves and wet soil; a very different feel from Pandoria's sweet, flower and fresh pine scents. Turning around to get her bearings, Riana looked back at the open portal to Pandoria.

Like a window into another world, it stood there. A pulsating, amorphous hole in reality. The forest of Brume stood all around it, but looking at the portal she could see the giant tree trunks and neatly groomed floor of Pandoria's forest. There was no frame or other delineation around the portal, creating a visual effect that could be quite disturbing to a first-time viewer as the scenery changed abruptly from one forest scene to another completely different setting, and then back again as one scanned the area.

"Ready?" Riana asked her sister, after completing her survey of their surroundings.

"As ever." Katrina said, as she set about cinching her pack tighter to her body. "Although I kind of wish we had gone to Cohai with mom once or twice before, then we could just take the portal."

"Yeah, well Ezrina said we would make it there when we were ready. I guess that is now." Riana said as she started to head up the path that would wind its way toward the Cohai pass in the mountains.

As they moved through the dark forest, they became acutely aware of that subtle phenomena one can only feel in an old, well established forest. They felt as though they were being watched. They felt like thousands of eyes were upon them, watching them move through the forest with great interest.

Changing her pace to keep her sister closer to her, Riana scanned around her in an attempt to see if she could locate any signs of life, any hint of what might be watching them. She knew it was probably just her nerves, but she still could not shake the feeling that their progress was being monitored.

The path they followed had been cut through the forest before anyone could really recall. The dirt track remained clear and serviceable beneath the thick mist due to regular, if not constant travelers and the occasional game animal. A sudden noise startled the girls as a small animal darted from a small gap in the underbrush and dashed across the trail, disappearing into another gap on the opposite side. Most of the animals in the forest had long ago stopped bothering with travelers, but occasionally there had been news of someone being attacked by a bear or a cougar. Any such stories were immediately investigated by hunting parties, which usually came back with some large animal they had tracked down and slaughtered, and travel continued unabated.

Uneasily, the girls made their way through the forest on their own for the first time. Occasionally they would cross paths with a merchant caravan that was to large to fit through the portals that would allow faster travel. After exchanging pleasantries and information about the road ahead they would part ways again and the caravans would head on to Pandoria or further south toward Avian or Loch Moore.

Three days later, they came to a rock wall indicating they had reached the western edge of the Uraval Mountains. Following the path along its base for a few hours they eventually came to a jagged cut in the stone. Barely wide enough for one person to pass though, the cut ran up out of sight above them. This claustrophobic pass was the only way to approach Cohai for anyone who had never been there before.

Peering into the crag, Riana saw a sprinkling of trees that clung to any arable soil in the tight chasm. Some were ancient trees, warped and twisted, reaching for the precious light at the top of the deep fissure. Some other, younger trees were scattered here and there in small clumps as if they desperately clung to one another, seeking some form of comfort in this dismal place. Occasionally there could be seen a single solitary giant shooting straight up from the ground and obscuring everything behind its massive bulk. The tiny path wound between the trees, disappearing from sight after the first few paces.

Slowly, Riana turned to look at Katrina, who was already looking at her. They both swallowed hard.

"Are we ready for this?" Riana asked, jerking her thumb toward the unfriendly looking pass.

"We don't really have a choice." Katrina replied, trying not to look worried.

"Not really." Riana gave in, "But that doesn't mean we have to like it." She stood up straight and handed her gear to Katrina before squeezing through the gap into Cohai Pass. Her sensitive skin scraped across the rough stone, making her wince. Once through, Riana took her pack from her sister's outstretched arms then reached back through the gap for Katrina's backpack. Watching as Katrina squeezed through the gap sent shivers of remembered pain dancing across her skin.

Once in the pass, the girls felt no better about it. The space was narrow, the path not much more than a game trail. Certainly not meant for people to travel, it wasn't even wide enough for them to walk shoulder to shoulder and the dense, twisted foliage made it nearly impassable. It was dark, oppressive, and cooler than the forest they had just left.

Riana thought she might die as her body was constantly assaulted by the branches and stone outcroppings. Her skin was screaming at her to stop the pummeling but she forced herself to forge ahead, tears constantly on the verge of flowing from the painful sensation. Katrina seemed to be having a difficult time as well, her robes catching and snagging on the wicked branches of the pass.

It took nearly ten hours for them to wade deep enough into the pass that it widened a bit. Now there was twenty or thirty feet between the stone walls, which allowed more vegetation to grow. The feeling of claustrophobia had diminished, but the path was no easier to traverse due to the ill-maintained trail. Eventually they decided to camp for the night.

Katrina cleared a spot against one of the rock walls for a camp fire while Riana collected some fallen branches from the area. After the fire pit was set up and stocked with wood, Riana summoned a flame in her hand with a brief moment of concentration and tossed the magical spark on the wood, causing it to immediately start burning. Then they rolled out their sleeping mats and broke out their meager provisions, sitting across the fire from one another, leaning against the wall and staring off towards the opposite side of the canyon as they ate.

Nothing but silence passed between them for a while, as they sat, eating their dried bread and meats, listening to the soft crackle of the fire. Finally Katrina broke the silence, a worried look on her face.

"Ree? Does…" She stopped suddenly, apparently thinking better of what she was going to ask.

Riana looked at her, her violet eyes glowing in the fire light. She sighed a heavy sigh and poked at the fire with a stick. "Does what Kat? Does it hurt?"

Katrina's eyes began to water up as she nodded.

"If I stop and think about it." Riana confessed. "Then it hurts. But if I keep my mind on other things, then I can stave off the pain." Gently she withdrew her stick from the fire and watched the end of it burn, turning it this way and that, playing with the flame, bending it with the force of her will as one of the marks on her body glowed brightly.

Katrina watched her sister, tears in her eyes, not knowing what to say or do. She was at a loss as to how to help her sister through this dilemma.

"Do you remember that time in the Plane of Serenity, when we ran into those goblins?" Riana asked, as she jabbed the stick back into the fire.

Katrina sniffled as she wiped some tears away from her face with the sleeve of her robes, "Yes." She said, visibly trying not to smile.

"Remember we both used up all our memorized spells? And we had to try and finish them off with our knives?" Riana continued, a grin forming on her lips.

Katrina pulled her knees up against her chest and ducked her face behind them, trying to hide her smile from her sister. "I remember." She said seriously.

Riana grinned openly at her sister now. "And that last one. Some kind of Goblin champion or something! Disarmed both of us!"

Finally, Katrina couldn't hold back any longer. She started laughing. "Yeah, so we both punched him and broke our fingers!"

"Yeah." Riana laughed openly, "The look on its face was priceless! It had no idea what to make of us!"

"That was the day we both agreed to learn how to fight, so it would never happen again." Katrina said, wiping tears of laughter from her face now.

"Aye." Riana agreed. "It was also the day I set myself to learning how to overcome the spell problem. The event that led me to this." She said, indicating the tattoos on her body.

Katrina sighed. "I just wish I knew what you are going through. I wish I could share it with you Ree. I don't want you going through it alone."

"That's my point Kat." Riana said in earnest. "I have never been alone, and I never will be. I will always have you with me. I have never feared being alone thanks to you."

Katrina nodded a bit and added," I know, neither have I. But now you are going down a road that I can't follow Ree, and I am scared. I am scared for you, and…" Katrina hid her face behind her knees again, her ears drooped down in shame and spoke in a barely audible voice, "for me. I am afraid of being alone if you leave."

Riana's face softened, and she looked at her sister with love in her eyes, her ears pointing straight out from the sides of her head in a show of affection, "Sis, you will never be alone. Even if I DO die after all of this. I will never leave you. You will never have to fear being alone Kat."

Katrina looked at her sister through her tear-filled yellow eyes, as though truly seeing her for the first time. "Ree. How are you doing this?"

"Doing what?" Riana said absently as she resumed poking the fire with her stick.

"Staying as calm and collected as you are. You know what may happen and yet you keep on as though it isn't even a possibility."

"Well," Riana said, "Let me put it this way. What choice do I have? I mean. I could spend time fretting about it, but what would that accomplish? It would make me a wreck and then this thing Ezrina has shoveled onto our shoulders would not get done."

Katrina nodded at Riana and then asked the question that she had dreaded asking since she noticed it. "Ree?"

"Yeah?"

"Why did you start calling mom 'Ezrina' all of a sudden?" She looked like a wounded animal as she asked it.

"Because she is not my mother." Riana said flatly.

Katrina reacted as though she had just been slapped in the face. "WHAT?!"

Riana just looked at her sister coolly, then went back to toying with the fire.

"Ree, you don't mean that!" Katrina almost yelled it.

"Why not? What makes her my mother?" Riana tossed back at her sister.

"Let me think a moment," Katrina said sarcastically, "the fact that she carried us in her womb and gave birth to us?" She stood up as she continued, her voice gaining volume. "Or maybe the fact that she raised us from birth with love and devotion?" Now she was tossing her arms about, pacing in front of the camp fire.

Riana watched her sister pace, her eyes cold. "Maybe. But what about the fact the she only conceived us so that she could be close to a piece of this Kilishandra woman? Kat the ONLY reason we are here is because of her own selfishness. And the fact is that if she had never put that amulet on, Ambrai would not have it now and Kalijor would not be in any danger from a love-sick Ranger-gone-bad."

Katrina stopped in her tracks and gawked at her sister, sitting there calmly, negating their existence. "Ree, if she had never put it on, WE would never have existed!"

"SO WHAT?!" Riana shot back at her. "What have WE done? What makes US so important to the world?! Eh? Think about it! You're upset because you are only thinking about yourself! Look past that Kat! Look beyond your own life! If we had never been born, the amulet would never have fallen into the wrong hands. It would have remained hidden safely away, maybe

64

forever! Kalijor would be safe, and Ezrina would still be lonely. Which she continues to be today, even WITH us around!"

"I can't believe you would say things like that Ree!" Katrina was yelling now. "You think a death sentence gives you the right to be cruel like that?!"

"NO!" Now Riana was standing, her stick forgotten. "But it has given me a new perspective on things. I'm sorry your feelings on the matter are too clouded to see it!"

Katrina was stunned into silence. She had no idea what to say. She stood there dumbly for a moment as she soaked in her sister's words. Then she broke down, and turned to make a run for the darker parts of the pass where she could cry and think by herself for a while. Turning on her heels, she began to dash away from the circle of light, and ran headlong into something large, and solid as stone. She fell backwards all at once, almost into the fire, looking up in confusion at a solid object that had not been there a moment before.

Riana watched the scene, not entirely sure what was going on, until the mass leaned forward into the fire light. It extended a thick grey arm, the color of the stone walls around them, with three clawed fingers and a thumb on the end of it. Slowly the thing bent down, reaching with its clawed hand for Katrina's exposed ankle. As it moved into the light, its head became discernable. Long, harsh shadows danced about its beak-like nose, its dark amber eyes glowed in the fire light.

"Gargoyle!" Riana shouted in realization of what they faced. Without a thought she yanked her short sword from its sheath and leapt over the fire, plunging the blade into the darkness where the beast's body was. She felt the tip of the blade find purchase in the creature's stone-like skin, and it let out a yelp of surprise as it staggered back a step. "Get away from her!!"

The beast stood up to its full height, towering over the girls and unfurled its giant, leathery wings in a display meant for intimidation. Riana responded by holding her left hand out and clenching it into a tight fist as she concentrated on a stun spell. Briefly her eyes glowed along with a tattoo on her back and the creature staggered back another step and stared at them, its eyes dull and confused.

"Get up!" Riana hissed at her sister as she grabbed Katrina by the shoulder, trying to hoist her off the ground bodily.

Katrina finally came to her senses and scrambled off the ground. Drawing her stiletto from inside her robes, she held it out in front of her and began to recite a spell incantation. There was a sudden flash of light as a bolt of lightning arced out of the sky and enveloped the stunned gargoyle in a flash of blazing blue-white light. Before the light faded, Riana had conjured a giant ball of fire in her left hand. Hurling it at the creature with all her strength, the gargoyle fell onto its back as the ball of flames exploded, showering the surrounding area with embers and sparks.

Shaking off the stun spell, the gargoyle rolled onto its haunches and climbed back to its feet with the assistance of a nearby tree trunk that was crushed into kindling as it applied pressure through its grip. Riana and Katrina stared at the thing, mouths hanging open. They had barely scratched it.

"Kat! Snare its feet!" Riana shouted at her sister over the din of the exploding tree trunk.

"I hope you have a plan." Katrina hollered back as she began an incantation. Shortly, the floor of the pass came to life. Vines and roots snaked out of the ground and wrapped themselves tightly around the monster's ankles, securing it in place. The gargoyle pulled at its legs, against the force of the living bonds at its ankles.

Katrina tossed a glance at her sister just in time to watch her violet eyes glow briefly. The ground began to rumble and shake. Riana raised her hands over her head and a fountain of boulders and debris from the rocky floor and walls launched itself into the air.

"MOVE!" Riana yelled at her sister, as the mass of rock and stone hung in the air.

Diving out of the way, Katrina rolled behind a tree as Riana brought her arms down in front of her. Pointing at the gargoyle still snared in the vegetation of the canyon floor. The blizzard of various sized projectiles followed her will and rained itself down on the monster, smashing it again and again with a hail of heavy, blunt stones. The whirling cloud of stone debris slammed into the gargoyle repeatedly, hammering the beast again and again before finally falling to the ground at its feet and piling up around it. Its amber eyes flashed as the stones struck. The beast flailed against the torrent, bashing away stones with its forearms, but its eyes grew dim and finally flashed out as it finally yielded to the crushing force of the assault.

The ground stopped shaking. Like a small rockslide in the wake of an avalanche the sound of the last few pebbles striking the pile before finding their final resting places could be heard echoing from the walls of the pass. Riana stood by the fire, panting from the effort of concentration.

Stepping cautiously out from behind the tree, Katrina surveyed the scene. In an instant, she was at Riana's side, checking her sister for injuries. "What the hell was THAT?" she spewed as she looked Riana over.

"What was what?" Riana panted, resting her hand against the cliff wall to support her exhausted body. She didn't think casting spells like this would be so physically taxing.

"That shower of boulders!" Kat said, pointing at the pile of rock towering over their heads next to the camp fire. "I've never seen anything like that before."

"I'm not sure." Riana said, finally starting to get her breathing under control again. "I just… Saw it in my mind and it happened. God Kat, I'm tired." She slumped down to the ground, her back against the wall of the canyon. The pain it caused her overly sensitive skin ignored as weariness washed over her. She was tired to her core, in a way that she had never felt before in her life.

Leaning down to look at her sister, Katrina's eyes fell on a small, rapidly drying trickle of blood running from her sister's nose. Barely discernable in the fire light, but there it was. "Ree! You're bleeding!" She said with concern as she wiped the trickle away with the sleeve of her robe.

Riana looked at her sister out of the tops of her eyes, her head slumped to her chest and her ears drooped down in exhaustion, barely conscious. "Huh?" she managed blearily.

"Oh Ree. I think these tattoos are really bad for your head. Look at you! You can hardly keep your eyes open and your nose is bleeding!" Katrina was almost in tears as she fussed over her sister.

A rumble of crashing and falling rocks made her turn suddenly however, before she could do more than straighten up the gargoyle's hand shot out from its presumed tomb of boulders to seize her by the ankle. Falling forward onto the ground at Riana's side as the beast's grip threw her balance off. Then it started dragging her toward the pile of stone.

Katrina let a wild yelp escape her lips as the monster dragged her toward it, the pile of rocks falling away from the beast, its beaked head visible again, amber eyes flashing maliciously in the flickering light of the fire. It was clear the gargoyle intended to finish what it started, and unable to focus her thoughts on an incantation, Katrina could not cast a spell while being dragged to her demise.

"LEAVE HER ALONE!!" Katrina caught the shrill of her sister's enraged voice as a flash of skin and leather streaked towards her captor. Riana clambered up the loose pile of rock that still buried more than half of the monster, her short sword still clenched in her right hand. Working her way around the pile as she ascended, she crested it behind the gargoyle's exposed head. With her left hand she reached around the beast and grabbed it by the underside of its beaked mouth. Holding her sword high over her head, the tattoos mirrored her eyes and began glowing all at once. Giving off a light as bright as midday in the open desert of the Burning Expanse, tiny points of light emanated from each of her tattoos, completely washing away any visage of the dark night in the canyon. Rolling like liquid light, the glow coursed up her right arm melding with her sword blade. The keen edge glowed brighter than molten steel in a blacksmith's furnace as she plunged it into the top of the gargoyle's head. An ear splitting screech escape the beast's maw as the glowing blade seared its brain and boiled its blood. Then all went silent, its life force expended.

Struggling to see what was going on behind her, Katrina caught a glimpse of Riana looking down at her from the top of the rock pile. A loving smile crossed her lips as she collapse around the beast's lifeless head, her hand still tightly gripping the handle of her short sword.

-8-

Riana opened her eyes and regretted it instantly. The diffused light in the canyon hurt her head. Her whole body was sore and the slightest movement caused her to wince in discomfort. Clenching her eyes closed again, she willed the pain in her head to subside. Not that she could stop it, but she was getting pretty good at ignoring it by now.

In a whoosh of fabric-in-motion, Katrina was suddenly at her side, grabbing her sister's hand. Riana opened her eyes again and looked around briefly. She found herself lying on her sleeping palette near the waning fire. The light of day gently filtered down through the trees. A short distance away she could see the pile of stones still packed around the gargoyle's lifeless body. At the summit of the mound was the beast's head. Her short sword still buried to the hilt in the thing's skull.

"What happened?" Riana said, surveying the scene groggily.

Katrina looked at her with concern, her eyes moist with tears. "That monster grabbed me and you screamed at it, and then all of a sudden you were up there," she pointed at the top of the rock heap absently as she rambled, "you grabbed its head and you were glowing and there was light everywhere. Then you stuck your sword in its head like that and passed out."

She took a momentary respite to breathe, and then continued as the tears began to flow. "I eventually freed myself but by then it was all over and you were out cold. I thought you were dead Ree!"

"Alright." Riana said as she forced her unwilling body to clamber to its feet. Climbing back up the pile of boulders she inspected the dead monster. Looking at the protruding sword, Riana noticed that there were indentations in the handle, running all the way around it. Tentatively, she wrapped her right hand around the handle and her fingers slid perfectly into the grooves. "So, what do you THINK happened here?" she said as she pulled on the handle, testing to see if it was as stuck as it looked. The sword didn't budge.

"I think," Katrina said with trepidation, "that you are not in complete control of your abilities." Katrina said half under her breath as she set about cleaning up their camp site.

"Why do you say that?" Riana quirked an eyebrow in her sister's direction and her ears perked up in curiosity. She removed her hand from the sword handle and made her way back down the shifting pile of loose rocks to help her sister break camp.

"Ree. You were glowing! And you can't even remember any of it! Can you?" Katrina accused, looking up at her sister.

Riana looked confused. "Not really, no."

"I mean that thing grabbed my ankle and started dragging me toward it and the next thing I know you are up there on top of the rocks, holding the gargoyle by its head, and your body was glowing so brightly that it hurt to look at you. Then you stabbed it and passed out. And you're bleeding from your nose again! I'm scared and I'm not sure what to do Ree…" Katrina let the words flow out of her mouth in a torrent, almost panting by the time she finished.

"Bleeding?" Riana said, as she put her hand to her lips and drew it back with a quantity of clotted, dried blood on her finger tips.

"I'm scared Ree." Katrina admitted as she lunged forward and threw her arms around her sister in a tight embrace. Riana winced in pain, but staved off the desire to recoil. Instead she returned her sister's hug.

"I know Kat. So am I."

Katrina sobbed into her sister's shoulder. "What do we do now?" she gasped between sobs.

"We need to move on." Riana said. "I have no idea whether or not these things have family. But I don't want to be here if its relatives DO come looking for it." She forced her sister to break the embrace and turned around to collect their things.

Katrina wiped her face and began helping clean up what was left of their camp. In a few moments all of their things were repacked, and they were moving away from the scene of the previous night's horror.

The rest of their journey through Cohai pass was uneventful. After a few hours, the pass widened yet more, climbing steeply uphill the whole time. The trees thinned out, eventually disappearing altogether, to be replaced with a few sparse bushes and shrubs. Then the grass and tall weeds gave way to lichen and slowly no vegetation at all, just rock. They were both breathing hard, chests heaving and bodies perspiring as they tried with little success to draw enough air to supply their burning lungs.

They could clearly make out the brightly lit mid-day sky above the still towering cliff walls on either side of them. Riana was checking behind them briefly when she heard Katrina gasp. Turning around in a flash and dodging around the sharp bend Katrina had disappeared around Riana had her hand on her dagger when the sight took her breath away.

They stood on a stone precipice. Looking down, the treetops appeared very much like the lichen covered stone they had just recently left behind. Green and yellow clumps and nodes of tree tops, all blending together into one undulating, amorphous pool. Even where there were breaks in the forest canopy, they could not make out the forest floor through the mist that always floated through the Forest of Brume.

What lay directly in front of them made them both gasp in fear and amazement. A rickety old rope bridge, looking more than a few centuries old, crossed a vast open expanse of empty air, and connected their precipice with a spire of rock some hundred feet away. There was a landing on the other side of the bridge, accounting for the only horizontal space on the spire that was outside an enormous protective wall.

Behind the wall, the Cohai Observatory rose up majestically, offering its occupants an unobstructed view of nearly all of western Kalijor. The observatory's many windows and balconies were all devoid of people, and the place was eerily silent.

The girls stared in awe. Neither of them had ever seen anything like it.

Finally, Katrina managed to pull herself together a bit and asked, "So now what?"

Coming back around, Riana blinked a couple of times before focusing her vision on her sister. "I guess we go knock."

"You first." Katrina said as she looked at the dilapidated wooden bridge, swaying gently in the wind.

Riana nodded, understanding her sister's trepidation. Gently, she grabbed the ropes on either side of the bridge and tugged on them a bit, throwing her weight into them to see what happened.

The bridge bounced and swayed, but she felt no sign that it was weak or on the verge of breaking, despite its appearance. After waiting for the swinging to calm down she placed her right foot on the first suspended plank. The board held as she applied more and more pressure to it, eventually even jumping on it once.

Turning slightly and smiling at her sister, Riana began to move across the bridge. Trying as hard as she could to focus on her feet or the planks under them, she looked at anything but the empty void of air between her and the forest floor far below her. Cold sweat poured from her as she moved across the bridge. A gust of wind sent it roiling and tossing, almost tossing her to the planks in sudden fear. When she reached the other side, her hands hurt from clenching the ropes and her legs were bundles of stiff muscles from being pushed constantly against the bridge. She turned around and waved Katrina across as she collapsed against the stone wall of the entryway.

Katrina had a different approach in mind. She grabbed the hand ropes on either side of the bridge, set her feet on the first plank, then closed her eyes and ran blindly across the bridge, making sure to keep her hands on the ropes. Barely stopping before she ran headlong into the door, she opened her eyes and smiled.

Katrina laughed at her sister's dumbfounded look and then turned to inspect the gates.

Shaking her head slightly from side to side, Riana's mouth hung open as she also turned her scrutiny to the gates.

There was no handle or knocker on the large gates, and they fit perfectly into the opening they had been made for, with not a gap on any edge that either of them could see. Made of a heavy, solid hardwood of unknown origin. Neither of them had ever seen any wood like it before. It hung on a set of simple metal hinges.

"Now, how do we get inside…" Riana wondered aloud as she took in the gate and surrounding wall.

"I say we ring the bell." Katrina pointed to an old bronze bell set within a small alcove in one of the walls. Next to it, a striker hung on a small length of rope, and on the bell, written in common were the words:

Only those that know the touch of tranquility are welcome within.

"What the hell does that mean?" Riana said as she read the inscription on the bell.

"I think," Katrina began as she lifted the striker and gave the bell a solid hit with it, causing it to ring out a single loud, clear note that sustained and reverberated through the stone entry way for long moments before finally, slowly fading away, "It means that we are supposed to wait here, without fussing or beating the bell to death, until someone comes for us." She took off her back pack, set it down on the stone floor of the entry way, and sat down beside it. Leaning against the wall, she smiled up at her sister.

"Well that's nice." Riana said as she pulled off her bed roll and set it on the ground for her to sit on. Slumping down on the roll, she eyed her sister suspiciously. "How do you know that?" She finally asked.

Katrina's grin widened a bit. "I asked mom about it a few years ago and she told me."

"And how long did Ezrina say it took?"

"For her?" Katrina replied pleasantly. "Three days."

Riana gaped at her sister, but knew she was right. Katrina was always right about such things; that was the problem with having a bookworm for a sister.

So they both settled in and began the long wait at the gates of Cohai.

-9-

A grating noise startled Riana out of a fitful sleep. The sky was light again, so she knew they had been waiting through the night, although she had no idea how far into the day it currently was. She looked up to see Katrina already standing up, facing the gates with her pack on her back and a radiant smile on her face. With some effort, Riana hauled herself off of her bed roll pulling it snugly into its place on her back. As she moved next to her sister, Riana realized the door was nearly three feet thick. As it slowly swung open the single person working the massive obstacle came into view.

That one person was a troll. Trolls were ugly creatures, with oversized, pointy ears that hung off the sides of their heads like those of wild dogs. Their faces were long, with pointy jaws and pointy noses. A maw full of randomly placed, randomly sized, but all very sharp teeth gave them a nightmarish visage. Their dark eyes were recessed back under their bony brows. Scarce amounts of hair shot out of their bodies from random locations in bunches and tufts with no apparent rhyme or reason. Tall, with long arms and legs, their skin ranged in color from tans and browns to greens and blacks, with spots and patterns not at all uncommon. Long spindly fingers and toes, all capped with jagged, ratty nails made their limbs seem even longer and their skin often looked diseased. They were rarely seen and most often regarded as unpleasant creatures that would sooner eat their own children than run out into the forest to catch a rabbit for meal time.

This particular troll, while far from attractive was nothing like his normal brethren. At seven feet tall, and two-hundred fifty pounds in weight he was smaller than most trolls by a good measure. His features were sharp, his eyes were a piercing shade of blue and looked deep and thoughtful. His skin was a deep yellow-brown and no hair could be seen on his body. His teeth were unnaturally straight and uniform. He wore a loose fitting, sleeveless gi and when the gate was open far enough for him to step though the gap, he stood up straight, stepped out and bowed low before the sisters.

"Welcome to Cohai, my name is Gornin." His voice was rough and low, like a heavy boulder being dragged across a field of gravel by a team of oxen. "How may I be of assistance to the ladies Thorindal?" He finished speaking and stood back up.

Riana's eyes flashed in anger at the mention of their family name. "Don't call me that!" she spat at Gornin acidly.

"Ree!" Katrina hissed leaning into her sister's shoulder with her body to try and keep her grounded.

Riana recoiled from the contact, stepping away from her sister to protect her sensitive skin, almost lashing out with a blow to her sister's body. "That isn't me anymore." She finally said.

"Then who are you? If not Riana Thorindal, daughter of Kilishandra and Ezrina?" Gornin asked calmly, seemingly unsurprised by Riana's outburst.

Looking at Riana, Katrina opened her mouth to speak but no sound came out so she closed it again and stared at her sister through glassy eyes.

Riana looked at her sister for a moment, then over to Gornin. "I..." she stammered, "I don't know." She said with a sigh. "I don't know who I am anymore."

Gornin looked at Riana and nodded, "Then perhaps I may be of some assistance. Knowing who you are is the only way to find balance. Only through balance can we overcome adversity."

Riana watched Gornin for a long moment. Tears welling up in her eyes, she heard Katrina stifle a sob.

"Do you have balance Riana Thorindal?" He looked at her unassumingly, tranquility emanating from his very core.

"No." she said after a long pause. "I feel so... lost. I don't know who I am any more. How could she do this to us?!"

"She has done nothing but share herself, her love, and her life with you." Not realizing that they had not even introduced themselves his answer reverberated through Riana's aching head. His calmness was aggravating, and his knowledge of them was as yet still unquestioned.

"She did it out of selfishness! She did it to be closer to this Kilishandra woman!" Riana's voice was shrill, her eyes flashing. A palpable energy surrounded her as emotions began to well up inside her and take control.

"Was it selfishness?" Gornin said thoughtfully, putting a hand to his chin and stroking its underside as though he were running his hands through a full beard. "Did you know she used to live in Pandoria? She moved the day she conceived the two of you. She knew you would never be accepted in Pandoria, so she moved here to give birth to her daughters. She was heir to the throne of Pandoria once, your mother."

The energy building up around Riana instantly dissipated, and Katrina let out a gasp. They both looked at Gornin with shock in their eyes.

"Please." Gornin said as he stepped away from the door and gestured to the opening behind him. "Come in, and we will talk further. I am sure you are hungry and tired."

In a daze, they slipped past Gornin and through the doorway. On the other side of the wall was a paradox that was unexpected to say the least. The courtyard surrounding the Cohai Observatory was a veritable oasis. Well groomed grass covered the ground from wall to wall. Immaculately manicured bushes, flowers, trees and shrubs decorated the courtyard. The air was sweet, scented by blossoms on the trees and flowers in the gardens. It was a study in vibrant colors and soft pastels as far as they could see.

Among the gardens and stands of trees all manner of people wandered. People from all walks of life appeared to be tending the living things in the courtyard, sitting and reading under trees, practicing katas or weapon techniques. There were people sparring and mages levitating fire balls. Everywhere people were practicing their skills or meditating.

Riana and Katrina looked around in amazement before they could ask. "What are all of these people doing here?"

Gornin said, "These people are all here on missions of self discovery. Each of them is here to broaden their understanding of themselves. To hone their skills."

"How does understanding yourself make your skills any better?" Riana asked with a note of disbelief.

"How could it not?" Gornin responded flatly. "Riana, everything we do in life is tied into our understanding of ourselves. Only through self understanding are we able to focus our energies to their maximum."

"No offense Gornin," Riana said, "But I don't see how 'knowing myself' will make my skills or abilities any stronger."

All at once Gornin stopped, Riana and Katrina nearly running headlong into his thickly muscled back side. Turning slowly to face them, Gornin had a strange look about him, as though he had been punched in the stomach.

"Riana Thorindal. Knowing who you are is the single most important goal anyone should have in this life. If you do not know who you are, then you are truly lost, adrift in a sea of doubt and uncertainty. Knowing yourself, truly knowing yourself, is the gateway to true power." At that Gornin turned to face a boulder larger than himself and with no hesitation or perceptible effort, stuck his index finger into the face of the rock, up to the third knuckle.

Katrina inhaled sharply, and Riana stared in wonder. Gornin pulled his finger out of the boulder, releasing a small spray of dust and debris. Riana walked over to Gornin and ran her hand over the face of the boulder. Trying to discover the trick in his display, to see how he had fooled them.

"There is no deceit," he said.

"You are trying to tell me that simply by knowing myself, I can punch through solid rock with my bare hands?" Riana asked him incredulously.

"No," Gornin said, "I am telling you that the gateway to your true power is through knowing who you are. Once you discover that, anything is possible."

Katrina nodded sagely, in complete agreement with the troll. Riana however, was more than skeptical and had no compunctions about showing it. Focusing her thoughts for a moment, her eyes flashed, and one of the tattoos on her back glowed brightly for an instant, then a bolt of lightning arced out of the clear, cloudless sky, and blasted the boulder into a shower of dust and pebbles that filled the area with a thick cloud of debris.

As the gentle wind of the high mountain pass cleared the area of dust and smoke, Gornin stood unmoved, watching Riana with his piercing blue eyes.

"And what have you proven?" He said in his maddeningly calm tone.

"That I don't need your mysticism to get the job done." Riana scoffed at him.

"I see," Gornin responded as he calmly bent down and picked up a pebble sized piece of the boulder debris. Then he held the small rock gently between his thumb and index finger and extended his arm out fully to his side with his hand turned so that Riana had a clear view of the stone. "Now do it again, but don't harm my hand."

Riana stared at the troll as though he had asked her to single handedly carve Rathalon from the mountainside in a fortnight. "Impossible!" she spat at him, "No mage has that level of control. It can't be done!"

"Indeed?" Gornin replied. Then he looked over her shoulder and called out to someone. "Exodus! Please, a moment of your time?"

The name struck a chord in Riana's mind, and a sharp intake of breath from Katrina said that she recognized it as well. Turning to see who Gornin was talking to, Riana saw a handsome human wearing the robes of a mage approaching them. He had a bald head and a well kept mustache that merged into an equally well managed beard of dark brown whiskers. His eyes were a clear, light-grey color and he had his hands tucked away inside his sleeves in front of his body. He smiled brightly as he approached and inclined his head ever so slightly to them as he came to a stop next to Riana.

"Exodus?!" Katrina gushed suddenly as she lunged forward and threw her arms around the man excitedly.

"Katrina!" He responded with equal enthusiasm as he returned her embrace. "How have you been? I haven't seen you in... years it seems."

Riana gaped at the interaction for a moment before she remembered the name from their time at the Magic Academy. He had been the instigator of many evenings spent in detention, cleaning floors and transcribing records. She had learned to dread his name despite the fact that he always led them on a merry adventure before the hammer fell.

"I see we know one another. Plenty of time to catch up later." Gornin said simply, with no hint of annoyance in his gravelly voice.

"Of course Master Gornin," Exodus said as he released Katrina and offered a short bow to the troll. "How may I be of service?" He asked in earnest.

"Do you know a lightning bolt spell?" Gornin inquired.

"I do." Exodus replied calmly.

"Would you please demonstrate?" Gornin asked moving his outstretched arm a bit to draw the mage's attention to the pebble he still held there.

"Of course Master Gornin." Exodus said, inclining his head again. Then recited a brief incantation and when he finished the spell he pointed his left index finger toward Gornin's outstretched hand, and an arc of lightning leapt off of his finger and pulverized the pebble into dust.

Riana's mouth fell open. She gaped at the spectacle she had just witnessed. No one had such fine control over the forces of magic. Such a thing was not possible.

"How… did you do that?" she stammered as her gaze slowly shifted to the man standing calmly next to her. She distinctly remembered him having a lack of control in their school days. In fact she was pretty sure she still had a case of writing cramps in her hands because of his lack of control.

"I pictured the objective in my head and cast the spell." He said simply.

"And how long have you practiced this?" She asked as she moved forward and seized Gornin's hand, inspecting it for signs of damage.

"That is the first time I have ever done anything like that." He replied.

Riana turned and stared at him, as Katrina let a giggle escape her lips. Turning to glare at her sister, Riana spoke to Gornin, "And you will teach me this power Gornin?"

Gornin sighed, an almost inaudible sigh, as though his patience had finally been pushed to its limit, but only for the briefest of instants. "No, Riana Thorindal, I will not teach you this."

"Then why show me?" She jerked her head around, violet eyes trying to pierce the troll's thick hide with their gaze alone.

"Ree, he's trying to say that once you learn who you really are, you will figure the rest out all on your own." Katrina offered from behind Riana.

At this, Gornin offered a smile to Katrina, his sharp, curved teeth making him look dangerous even in a display as benign as a smile. "Exactly, Katrina."

Riana released his hand and then jabbed her index finger into his chest, "Why do you keep calling me Riana Thorindal and then call her just Katrina? What are you playing at Gornin?"

Gornin stood there and absorbed her accusations, not even flinching as she jabbed her finger into his chest. "I am playing at nothing Riana Thorindal. Your sister is well on her way to figuring these basic truths out for herself. You, on the other hand, need somewhat more of a guiding hand. With as attuned as you are to the forces of magic, especially now," He then motioned to her tattooed body by way of explanation, "you should by all rights be the most powerful mage on Kalijor. Instead you are an emotional wreck with no more control over your abilities than a first year student at the academy. All of this stems from the fact that you are stuck on one thing. You feel that you have been wronged."

Riana gaped at him, unable to respond. "Riana Thorindal, the things that you cling to can not sustain you. You are angry with your mother for the things she has done in the past. But these things are long since gone, and none of us have any choice but to live with the results. Accept your mother, and your life, for what they truly are, gifts to be cherished for as long as they can be. Only then will you start down the road of enlightenment. Only then will you truly come to know yourself. Only then will this power, this focus, be yours."

Riana stared at him for a long moment before she finally slumped down on to a large rock left over from the demise of the boulder. She pulled her knees up against her chest tightly and wrapped her arms around her legs and started to weep. "I don't know if I can let it go." She sobbed. "The anger is all that is keeping me moving. My head hurts so badly I can hardly think half the time. The only thing I can do to block the pain and move on, is focus on the anger."

Katrina knelt beside Riana and gently wrapped her arms around her sister, squeezing her lovingly.

"The Druids told you that you may die." Gornin said. It was obviously not a question, but a statement of fact.

"Yes." Riana sobbed into her knees.

"This scares you." Gornin stated again.

"YES!" Riana screeched, her voice breaking up.

"Why does it scare you?" Gornin asked her as though her fear was the strangest thing in the world.

"Because I don't want to die!" Riana choked out.

"No one WANTS to die." Gornin retorted. "But we all know instinctively that eventually we will; even your kind who can live for scores of centuries. Everything living must eventually die. This is the most basic truth of the universe Riana Thorindal, and through this truth we will help you uncover your lost knowledge of who you are."

"How?" Riana lifted her head off of her knees to look blearily at Gornin through her tear-filled eyes.

"Like this." Gornin said as his hand flashed out at Riana in a blur.

The attack came so quickly that there was nothing Riana or Katrina could do about it. Gornin's hand moved with a speed that made it almost invisible. Katrina screamed as she tried to move herself into the path of the attack, and Riana closed her eyes and braced herself for the impact as she opened her arms in an attempt to keep her sister's body out of its path. She felt the impact on her neck just as her sister screamed out in mad fear, and then her world went dark.

-10-

Riana slowly became aware of a comfortable weight pressing down all over the front of her body. She was warm, and enveloped in silky soft smoothness. The air was pleasant and calm around her, and she could detect a soft, diffused light through her closed eyelids. Slowly she opened her eyes and saw the silken canopy of her own four-poster bed. Trying to make sense of what was going on she focused her thoughts on what had just happened, and realized that the pain in her head was gone. She remembered Gornin talking to her and then there was a flash as he moved. Katrina had screamed and then she was here, in her own bed.

Looking around her, she saw her room as it had been the day they left. Everything was in its place, exactly as it had been days ago. The soft light of day was drifting through her light silken drapes, bathing the room in a warm, indirect light from outside. She moved her limbs a bit under the heavy silken duvet that covered her over-sized feather bed and realized that the discomfort of her sensitive skin was gone as well.

Carefully she pulled the covers back and inspected her naked body. All of the tattoos were still there, in all their fine detail, but the discomfort was gone. Something was wrong here. She had been in constant pain for months now, since the headache had initially started building up. To suddenly be without that chronic pain, or any discomfort at all, was almost a pain in and of itself. She had no idea what to think or feel. She felt light and free. Unencumbered by all of the pain that had become her world over the past months.

Cautiously she climbed out of her bed, testing the floor to make sure it was solid. Gingerly she put her weight on her feet, afraid that they would be pulled out from under her at any moment. She wanted nothing more than for this to be real, knowing in the pit of her stomach that it could not be. All she had wanted for months now was for the pain to go away. And for the past few days she had wanted nothing more than to be at home again, with her sister and...

"And whom?" She heard a lilting voice come to her ears from across the room.

Riana jerked her head around toward the sound of the voice. She saw nothing but the other side of her room. Her full length mirror standing quietly against the stone wall next to the changing screen in the corner near the wardrobe.

"Who's there?" Riana called out, her ears perked up to detect any noise.

92

"Only me." The sing-song voice replied, again from the direction of her mirror.

Riana cautiously crept across her room, looking over her shoulder and into all of the nooks and crannies of her room as she closed the distance to her mirror. Drawing up on the object, she had no idea what to expect, but she was strangely calm, not at all concerned about harm or danger.

Looking into the mirror, she saw…herself. Almost. She stood looking at her reflection, except there were no tattoos and the hair was the metallic platinum color that her own hair used to be; the color of Katrina and Ezrina's hair. Otherwise, the image was her own, only it did not move with her movements as it should have. It just stood there, watching her.

"Hello?" Riana said tentatively to her near-reflection.

"Hello there." The image in the mirror responded in that lilting voice that seemed somehow familiar to Riana.

"Are you me?" Riana asked bluntly of the image.

"Not really." The elf in the mirror responded.

"Well, do I know you?" Riana asked.

"Not as well as you should." The image replied, smiling a matronly smile that at once calmed Riana and made her wonder what this person knew that she did not.

"Why doesn't my body hurt any more?" Riana asked, not sure if this phantom in the mirror would know the answer.

"Because none of that matters here." The platinum haired elf said, moving her arms around to indicate the room around them.

"Where is 'here'?" Riana queried, looking pointedly into the violet eyes of her near-doppelganger.

"I can't tell you that." The elf said flatly.

"Why not?" Riana looked confused.

"Because there are rules. Even here."

"Ok. So can you tell me who you are?" Riana said, changing the subject a bit.

"You know who I am." The elf said matter-of-factly.

Riana furrowed her brow at the mirror.

"Alright then." Riana acquiesced, "Then WHY am I here."

The image showed some excitement as she raised her arm up, index finger raised in exclamation, "Why ARE you here?"

Riana sighed heavily. "Let me guess. You can't tell me that either."

"Oh I can tell you THAT. Although I think you may know already, even if you can't admit it to yourself."

"I am here…" Riana began thinking out loud, "Because that troll, Gornin, attacked me!"

"No." Her mirror-bound tormentor replied. "That is how you GOT here. But it is not WHY you are here. The two have no connection. Except that he knew what would happen."

"That doesn't really help me much." Riana said with a tone of annoyance.

"Helping you is not really my job." The image shrugged noncommittally.

"What IS your job?!" She was getting upset now. Her violet eyes flashing in anger.

"My job is to help you understand what is truly important in your life."

"And you are planning on doing that by upsetting me with riddles and conundrums?" Riana shouted at the image.

"No." The elf in the mirror said flatly. "I am going to take you apart, bit by bit, and then together, we will rebuild you."

"Wha?" Riana took a step back from the mirror, concern growing inside her. Suddenly she felt her naked, exposed flesh. She felt the chill of the breeze through the room. She felt the tingle of fear in the back of her mind. Her ears drew back behind her as she prepared herself for an attack.

"You can't hide from me here." The lilting, soft voice came from behind her now.

Riana whirled around to see the other elf standing there behind her, in the middle of her room. Although their height and build were nearly identical, Riana felt somehow shadowed by the other woman. As though she were larger than she really was. Her demeanor was that of someone who was used to getting what they wanted. Not because they felt that was the way it should be but because they had grown accustomed to fighting for every inch. This elf was a woman of power. Power of her own making. And standing there before her, Riana wondered how she could have ever mistaken this woman for herself, even with them being nearly identical.

Suddenly, Riana knew the other had spoken the truth. She could not hide. Not here. Inside her own mind. Her own soul. Not from her mother. "Kilishandra."

As the realization sunk into her soul, Riana dropped her gaze to the floor. How could she look this woman in the eyes? This elf that Ezrina, no, that wasn't right. That her mother had loved with so much of her being that she had given up everything to share her life. How could she look at this elf whose appearance she mimicked so closely and yet she felt further from her than she did from her own life right now. She stared at the rug on the floor, tears welling up in her eyes.

Kilishandra smiled softly as she reached up, gently taking Riana's chin in the arch of her hand and lifting her daughter's face up. Their eyes met, four violet pools, like moonlight on the calm surface of a pond in the forest of Brume, locked together for the first time. "My sweet daughter. How I wish I could have been there for you. So many times I have wanted nothing more than to embrace you, to hold you to me and tell you how proud I am."

Riana let the tears roll down her cheeks unabated. Her mother's eyes were so calm, so clear, so full of love and compassion. She thought she hated this woman. Hated her and Ezrina for their selfishness, for what she thought had been acts committed solely for the feelings of the moment. But looking into her eyes, Riana understood that she had been there all along. She had never left them, even after her body had been broken.

Riana's body flushed, her ears drooping down in shame. She had no right to feel this woman's love. Not after the things she had thought. The things she had said.

Seeing the emotion on her daughter's face, Kilishandra smiled again, "Riana, you have done nothing wrong. Your feelings are natural. You cannot hide from them, nor should you be ashamed of them. Embrace them. Learn from them. Then move on with your life. You have much to do yet."

"But the things that I said. The things that I did!"

"They are in the past Riana. Let them go." Kilishandra took Riana by the shoulders then and pulled her into a tight embrace.

"I don't know how to do this." Riana wept into Kilishandra's shoulder.

"Yes, Riana, you DO." Kilishandra said as she hugged her daughter tightly. "The path is there before you. You have but to take the first step."

"I'm scared." Riana cried.

"I know. And it will not be easy. But you will have help. You will never be alone, you never HAVE been alone. Let Gornin teach you, he taught me, and he taught Ezrina. Listen to him Riana, he can help you free yourself of the pain, but you must know that it always gets worse before it gets better."

They stood there in a tight embrace for what seemed like hours. Riana crying into Kilishandra's shoulder the whole time. Kilishandra just stood there and held her daughter, letting her cry it all out, until finally she broke the embrace, and held Riana by the shoulders at arms length.

With a loving smile she said, "It is time, my daughter. You have to go now."

"I don't want to go. I want to stay here with you." Riana sobbed.

"I know. But you can't. You have work to do yet. Ambrai is a lost soul Riana, and she needs help. She has let the evil consume her because she feels that she destroyed me. She needs to know that she is free to live her own life. I can no longer convey that message to her. That is why Ezrina and I have asked you to do it. To be our messenger for us."

"I don't know if I can… My head hurts so badly when I am awake." Riana tried to stifle her tears, but could not. Every time she looked into Kilishandra's eyes, she started sobbing again.

"Listen to Gornin, Riana… You make me proud every single day…"

The voice began to fade away, and the room began to twist and turn around her, colors running together and swirling around until the room became a blur of grey. Riana tried focusing on something, but there were no solid objects around her. Her world spun and swam and she fell to the floor, a familiar pain growing in her head as she lay on the floor, and watched the sky spin around her. Her back began to ache, the familiar ache of coarse, solid objects against her sensitive skin.

Slowly she began to hear a voice. It sounded distressed, concerned. The sky slowed its spinning and resolved into the normal night time sky over Kalijor. The voice cut its way into her thoughts as she mentally forced the pain into the back of her mind where she had become accustomed to keeping it locked away.

"Ree!! Wake up Ree!!"

It was Katrina. She had Riana propped up on her knees and was sobbing into her ears, her arms cradled around her sister's prone form.

Reaching up, Riana put her hand on Katrina's shoulder. She squeezed it with all her strength, which wasn't much at the moment, and spoke, her voice barely audible, "I'm ok Kat. I'm back." She clenched her eyes shut and forced herself to concentrate on anything but the pounding in her head. Then she heard another familiar voice.

"Are you ready Riana Thorindal?" It was Gornin.

Opening her eyes, she focused them on the imposing form of the ever calm troll. She forced the words to come up from under the pain, "Yes Master Gornin. I am ready now."

"Very well." Gornin said as Katrina looked up at him, tears still pooled in her eyes. "We will begin at first light. Exodus will show you to your rooms, and see that you are fed and bathed. Rest well." Then he bowed low, turned and walked away into the garden courtyard of Cohai.

11

The inside of the Cohai Observatory was pure function. There were no frills, no ornamental features, nothing superfluous. The construction was immaculate, with every piece having been expertly carved by skilled hands. It was obvious that the structure was intended to fill a purpose, and that purpose was to put a roof over people's heads, not to be pretty.

The entire structure was hewn from the stone of the mountain spire it sat atop, with veins of color running through the walls and floors. The corners were smooth and rounded, but not decorative. No space was wasted anywhere, no area left unused. It was a study in utilitarian beauty. The doors were solid hard wood, the same type used for the main gate, albeit much thinner stock. The windows were simple holes in the thick stone walls, filled with single panes of plain glass.

Exodus led Katrina and Riana through the narrow passages of the observatory, up a few flights of stairs and around several blind corners, then finally stopped and turned to face the sisters.

"These will be your rooms," he intoned in his full tenor voice as he indicated a door on either side of himself with a widening arm movement. "There is a bath at the end of the hall behind me if you wish to clean up after your journey. The warm mineral water that comes up from beneath the observatory is quite refreshing. It is a community facility however, so be aware that you may be joined by others."

Riana gave her sister a strange look as she noticed her sighing at the sound of Exodus's voice. Disengaging herself from Katrina's shoulder she did her best to curtsey without falling over. "Thank you Exodus." She managed to say in a raspy voice.

"Yes, thank you sir." Katrina echoed her sister, and offered a polite curtsey and a mischievous grin.

"You are both most welcome. If you need anything, just ask anyone you see, they will either be able to assist you or locate myself or Master Gornin." Exodus then bowed low and finished with a grin of his own at Katrina, "Now I must return to my studies. Food will be brought to you within the hour. I would love to spend some time catching up on things with you tomorrow if that is alright Katrina?"

Katrina nodded with a grin and responded, "You had better!"

With that, he straightened, turned, and disappeared around a corner. The sisters watched him disappear, then looked at one another for a moment before they each grabbed a door handle and pushed open the doors into their rooms.

They were little more than stone cells. A narrow cot with some basic bedding materials on it rested against one wall and a small writing table with some stationary and a stool sat against the opposite wall. There was a single window in the middle of the wall facing the door. A candle perched on a small, simple sconce, ready to provide some meager light once the daylight had gone.

Riana sighed as she inspected the room. It was much smaller than what she was used to, but it was a far sight better than sleeping on the floor of the forest, or that terrible, rocky pass. Gratefully she undid the buckle on her belt and gently slid it, along with its various pouches and scabbards, off of her tender body. Tossing the whole affair onto the cot, she untied the bedroll from her back and deposited it on the floor next to the bed. As she was undoing the clasp on her cloak, Katrina popped into the room, having already stowed her traveling equipment in her own room. Sitting down on the stool as Riana removed her cloak and hung it on a hook by the door Katrina waited for her sister.

Riana dodged the inquisitive look as she sat down on the bed and worked at removing her boots.

"So… WHAT THE HELL HAPPENED OUT THERE?!" Katrina blurted out, aware that she was going to get nowhere with the subtle approach.

Riana's eyes lost focus for a moment as she thought about it. After a few minutes she finally said, "Kat. I'm not sure."

"It's ok Ree. You can tell me anything you know." Katrina moved over to the cot and sat next to her sister, gently putting her arm on her sister's shoulder.

"I think I just met Kilishandra." Riana stared at the wall blankly as she spoke, her voice on the verge of breaking up.

Katrina stared at her sister, her jaw slack in surprise. "Kili... Are you sure?"

Riana nodded, turning her head away from the wall to look her sister in the eyes. Katrina was looking into her own lap, mouthing something to herself with a strange look on her face. "Kat? Are you ok?"

Riana fidgeted a bit, jostling her sister to try and rouse her. Katrina's head shot up after a moment, eyes wide, looking at Riana.

"What? What's the matter?" She stammered.

"Are you ok? You looked pretty far away there for a second." Riana said with a note of concern.

"No! I mean. I'm fine." Katrina continued stumbling over her words. "So uh... Kilishandra?"

"I am pretty sure." Dismissing her sister's distracted behavior, Riana's eyes moved back to the blank wall across from the bed.

Katrina began pelting her sister with questions about the encounter, wanting all of the details as usual.

Riana tried to answer them all, pushing back tears as she relived the emotions of the experience, "She looked a lot like us. Her hair was the color of yours but otherwise she looks just like us. Her voice was a bit higher, and sounded like a lullaby." Riana sighed as she remembered the voice lilting through the room. "She was larger than life though. I mean, she LOOKED a lot like us, but it was obvious as soon as she strung a couple of words together that she was someone else entirely. She spoke like she had thousands of years of life to back up what she said. She was kind, and caring, and maddeningly cryptic."

"She sounds interesting." Kat said, her eyes still fixed on her sister.

Regaining some control, Riana sighed again as she thought about the experience. Replaying the event in her mind for the thousandth time since it happened. "She said that things were going to get worse before they got better."

"Well that isn't exactly encouraging." Katrina said as she scrunched up her nose at Riana.

"She also said she was proud. That she was happy every day for us, and that we would never be alone." Riana said with a contented smile.

Katrina smiled as well.

"Both Kilishandra and Ezrina studied for a while under Master Gornin." Riana added as she abruptly focused her attention back on the task of removing her boots. "We should learn what we can from him."

Nodding her ascent, Katrina released Riana's shoulder in time to see a dwarf knocking on the open door. He was a typical dwarf, around three feet tall with a full head of hair and long beard. The dark hair that was reasonably well kept hid most of his facial features, but his nose was easy to see as it was large and bulbous. His dark eyes smiled brightly as he looked into the small room at the two elves sitting on the cot.

"Master Gornin asked me t'bring up yer even'n meal. Would ye both be eat'n in'ere or should I be putten one'o these bowls in t'other room there?" His voice was low and gruff, thick with the dwarven accent and their typical good humor.

Katrina jumped up off the cot and swiftly moved to the door as she spoke, "Thank you master dwarf, what is your name?"

"Me name's be'n Dorin, an yours?"

"My name is Katrina and this is my sister Riana." Katrina said, indicating Riana. "Thank you very much for bringing this to us, I am sure it's not how things are normally done here."

"T'be sure. But I'm not mind'n much, Ah don' get too many opportunities t'be gett'n out o'da kitchen as it is. But t'do so, AND get t'meet a couple wee elven beauties such as yerselves is allright by these ole'bones." He winked as he finished speaking, and then offered the tray of dishes to Katrina. "Did ye want this Miss Katrina? R'should I be putting it on the table fer'ya?"

Katrina bent down to take the tray from the dwarf. "Oh, I'll take it. Thank you very much Dorin." She said as she lifted the tray from his arms and turned around to set it on the small table in the room.

106

"It's be'n me pleasure, Please don' esitate t'be callin on me in the kitchen if'n ye be need'n an'ting more." He said as he bowed to them and then disappeared down the corridor.

The sisters watched the dwarf disappear, then looked at each other and grinned.

"He was a jovial fellow." Katrina almost laughed.

Riana added with a chuckle, "And a little lecherous too."

"Yeah." Katrina agreed. "I wonder if his family knows he is slacking in that department. Most dwarves are more than just a little lecherous."

They laughed together for a few minutes before then turning their attention to the two wooden bowls of stew and fresh bread.

12

Riana flopped down on the cot, exhausted. Staring at the ceiling of her tiny stone room, her mind was blank. It had been a month since they had arrived at Cohai, and since that first night, Gornin had been relentless in his teachings.

"What did you do today?" Katrina's voice called over the short distance from the door.

Riana dropped her chin to her chest so that she could see her sister standing in the doorway. She was wearing her typical robes, although there seemed to be more ink stains around the sleeves lately. She had been studying with Exodus almost daily, trying to increase her control and general breadth of magic knowledge, and maybe just enjoying the company a little bit.

"The old goat had me meditating on top of a lodge pole, holding some kind of clay pot full of water in one hand and another full of bird seed in the other." Riana sighed.

"Wow." Katrina said as she thought for a moment about what her sister had described. "All day?"

"Since first daylight." Riana confirmed.

"Did you see any pretty birds?" Katrina said with a grin on her face.

Riana lifted her left arm and indicated her forearm with a look and a slight nod of her head. Katrina stepped into the room and looked at the proffered limb, gasping at the sight. Riana's forearm was covered with scratches and gouges, some of them thick with clotted blood. Katrina hissed through teeth clenched in sympathetic pain.

Riana shrugged returning her gaze to the ceiling. "It doesn't hurt any more. It's amazing how I am able to block pain now. I imagine it would have been agony a month ago."

Grabbing a small clay pot from the table across from the bed and a pile of light, gauzy cloth that lay next to it, Katrina pulled the stool closer to the cot. She sat down and began tending her sister's wounds, applying a thick salve from the pot to her wounded forearms and then wrapping them lightly with the gauzy material. After a few minutes of her ministrations Riana's forearms looked like freshly-wrapped mummy's arms.

Riana, laying there unflinching, took the time to marvel at the change. Only a month ago the gentle touch would have been agony. Her skin was still much more sensitive than it was before the tattoos, but it no longer hurt her to have cloth or other pressure against her skin. She wasn't sure if it was because the tattoos had healed or because her newfound ability to block pain had just dulled it along with her headache. She still preferred to wear her new clothing though, it was much lighter and more flexible than her old robes, allowing her to bend and contort her body more easily through Gornin's trainings. "Thank you Kat."

"You're welcome." Kat said as she inspected her sister's newly defined body. Her skin had darkened from a month of nearly constant exposure to the daylight. It wasn't nearly as dark as a human's skin could get, but definitely darker than most elven mages would ever get in a lifetime of studying books and scrolls. Her already lithe body had become toned and muscles could be clearly seen moving beneath her skin. Her dark purple hair was longer, and pulled back into a much more manageable single pony tail instead of her usual array of smaller ones. The tattoos on her body defining themselves and becoming more vibrant than they were before. It was apparent that Riana's progress was considerable.

"Ree…" She started to say something but stopped mid-thought.

"Yeah?" Riana prodded her, shifting her gaze to her sister. Sitting on the stool next to her, Katrina looked almost forlorn.

Sitting up and throwing her legs over the edge of the cot, Riana took her sister's hand in hers and squeezed it. Her ears spreading out in a display of sympathy for her sister. Concern filled her voice. "What's the matter Kat?"

"I'm worried about mom Ree. We've been here a month now and there has been no word about her. She should have found whatever it is she's looking for by now don't you think?"

Riana squeezed her sister's hand again, "I'm sure she's fine Kat. We don't even know what she is looking for. Master Gornin said it is some kind of artifact." She paused a moment, thinking about something, then continued, "Besides, we have to focus on our task. Mom will come through."

Katrina took a deep breath, trying to shrug off the feeling of dread. "How can we be sure?" She asked, locking eyes with Riana.

Her sister stared back at her, unblinking and unafraid. "We can't. But if we believe in her and what she fights for, then we lend strength to her fight. Just as she believes in us, and always has."

Katrina smiled and set the clay pot on the table next to her without looking. The jar sat precariously on the edge of the table for an instant and then fell off, rolling over in the air as it dropped the short distance toward the floor.

In a blinding flash, Riana's left hand shot out and snatched the small pot from mid-air, inches from the floor, rolling it over to keep the thick salve inside from sloshing out.

Startled by the quickness of her movement, Katrina gasped as she looked at her sister's face. Riana's eyes were still locked on her, she had never even blinked.

Riana's eyes were bright as she sat there, still looking at her sister. She smiled a bit as she gently placed the small pot securely back on the table. With her head still turned away from the door she said, "Good evening Master Gornin."

Katrina wondered for a moment if Riana was hearing things before turning her attention to the door of the small room, where she saw the troll standing serenely. He was still in the hallway, but he was turned so that he was facing into the room, watching quietly through the open door.

"Greetings." His low, gravelly voice rumbled through the room.

"How can we be of assistance?" Riana asked as she turned to face the troll, bowing her head.

"I have come to inform you that your time here is done." He said in his usual calm manner.

Riana's gaze snapped up to meet the troll's, a hint of panic showed for a moment then cleared away as she regained control of her emotions. "Master Gornin, I think there is still much I can learn. Why must we go now?"

"I have no doubt that you could learn much more Riana. But some lessons must be lived, they can not be taught. Time is catching up with us, and it is time for you to pursue the amulet, before it becomes a danger to the entire world."

"Very well. We will make ready immediately." Riana said, standing up from the cot.

"In the morning." Gornin said, motioning her to sit down again, which she did. "You need rest before you venture out again. I have asked Dorin to bring your evening meals. Please rest and meet me in the cellar after first light."

"Very well. Thank you Master Gornin." Riana said as he turned and disappeared down the narrow hallway.

"So, off we go again, eh?" Katrina said in a light hearted tone, trying hard to conceal her concern.

"So it would seem." Riana replied as she bent to the task of removing her boots. "I think I am going to get a warm bath before we head out. No telling how long it will be before we get another chance."

"Now that sounds like a plan to me." Katrina replied with genuine light-heartedness in her voice. "I think I will join you." Then her expression changed abruptly to one of sudden concern.

"What's the matter?" Riana raised an eyebrow at Katrina.

"I need to see Exodus before we go. You go ahead and get your bath. I'll see you in a little bit." Then she dashed out of the room without looking back.

-13-

By the time daylight made its way through the tiny window in Riana's room, she had all of her things packed in her pouches and was dressed and ready to travel. As she secured her belt around her waist she looked at the empty scabbard wistfully, wondering when she would have a chance to procure another sword. She had her bedroll cinched to her back and was just closing the clasp on her cloak when Katrina knocked lightly on her door and entered, her pack already secured to her back and Exodus on her heals with his hand in hers.

"Ready to go sis?" Katrina asked cheerfully as she examined her sister, then offered her an appreciative nod.

"Just now." Riana said as she swept her gaze over the small room one last time to make sure she hadn't forgotten anything. Satisfied, she indicated the doorway with a nod, looking past Exodus' shape in the portal and somewhat awkwardly they moved out of the room and into the hallway. Riana tossed Exodus a sideways glance, then looked at her sister a moment. Katrina rolled her eyes toward Exodus, signaling that she wanted a moment with him so Riana headed down the hallway to the stairs and leaned against the wall to wait. Looking back up the hallway she saw Katrina lean in to the human and kiss him deeply for what seemed like forever before breaking away and taking three steps backwards, reluctantly letting her hands slip from his and turning around to look where she was going.

When she caught up to Riana she was met by an accusatory look before the two moved down the stairs together. "What was that look about?" She asked after a moment.

"What look?" Riana said innocently.

"You KNOW what look." She playfully drove her elbow into Riana's mid-section, trying to keep the matter light-hearted.

"Nothing. I just didn't realize you and Exodus were…" She trailed off.

"Were what?"

"Were close. Like that…"

"Like what?" Katrina asked suspiciously, she knew where the conversation was headed but as a sister she felt obliged to make Riana work for her prize.

"You know… THAT. I mean… That was no friendly kiss goodbye. What have you two been doing in the library?!" Riana was talking almost under her breath and looking at the floor as she walked. She wasn't sure how to take this unexpected development. It was strange to suddenly realize that even though they had been together their entire lives, there were some things they just couldn't experience together. She couldn't help it but she felt a little bit betrayed by her sister's actions.

"Well," Katrina went on, seemingly unaware of Riana's deeper concerns in the matter, "we ARE old friends from the academy and… well it turns out we both sort of carried a torch and so one thing led to another and… Oh Ree you aren't upset are you?"

"No!" Riana lied. "I'm happy for you. I just… I guess I never thought about it before but we've never really done anything significant while apart from one another before. I guess I'm just kind of… I don't know really…" She gave up trying to express the strange emotion this had stirred up in her. "Let's just talk about it later ok?"

"Ok…" Katrina seemed worried now, not wanting to change the subject but at the same time not wanting to foul her sister's mood. "So, why do you think Gornin wants us to meet him in the cellar?" Katrina finally asked as they wound their way down the tight spirals of the staircase into the lower levels of the observatory.

"Not sure." Riana said, "Maybe there is something more he wants to share before we leave." She shrugged her shoulders unknowingly, still not wanting to talk much as they moved further down into the spire of rock.

At last they came to the cellar door, neither of them at all sure how far below the main level of the observatory they had traveled. The door was typical of the others in the observatory with two exceptions, its surface was reinforced

116

with several heavy metal bands and it bore a complicated locking mechanism. The lock itself had two key holes and a series of dials on its surface, all suggesting that whatever was within needed guarding, and a great deal at that. The door was slightly ajar as they approached it.

Placing her hands on the door, Riana noticed it was warm to the touch. Uncommon for wooden doors in a stone structure, she suspected that there may be more to this cellar than she had initially thought. Leaning into the door Riana and Katrina forced it open a little more on its heavy, reinforced hinges.

They stepped from the spiral stair-way into a small chamber where they were met by Gornin and Dorin. Riana bowed to the pair as Katrina curtsied. Gornin and Dorin both bowed to the sisters in return.

"Master Gornin." Riana said noting the door on the opposite wall that looked exactly like the one they had just come through.

"You have come far, Riana Thorindal, in a short time. However, you have further still to go. Do not forget what you have learned." Gornin's gravelly voice had a tone of earnest to it, he was concerned about something.

"I will endeavor to follow your guidance Master Gornin, I am already able to better stand the pain in my head, and my body is stronger than ever before." Riana spoke with energy.

"I know, but do not grow over-confident. All we have done is make you able to cope with the pain so that you can still function normally. We have not solved the problem." Gornin sighed a heavy sigh of resignation, "I truly wish we had more time, but things progress regardless and now we must take action. Take this, Riana Thorindal, and use it wisely."

Gornin punctuated his comment by raising his right hand, in which he held a large animal hide wrapped around an object. As his hand moved up, Riana could see the handle and hilt of a sword. Gently she took the weapon from Gornin and inspected the handle. It was a dark black material, soft and supple, but stiff, like metal. It was small, perfect for an elven hand and bore a series of elvish runes running in a sweeping curve from the black arc of the hilt down to the dark, mirror-polished pommel.

"Elkorine." She read the inscription out loud, "Light from Darkness." She translated the word into common. Rolling the weapon over in her hands, she twisted it out from under the animal hide to reveal the blade. It was about two feet long, plus the handle, and the blade was made of a material that was a dark, glossy grey color, almost black. It was impossibly light, and a series of elvish runes danced down the blade on both sides. Riana recognized them instantly as a series of power runes, not words. Although she had never seen them before she could guess at their potency, only master elven smiths were capable of successfully inscribing such runes on a blade.

Katrina stared at the weapon as her sister rolled it over a few times in her hands. "Gornin! That is amazing!" She said in awe.

"Yes it is Master Gornin. Are you sure you want me to take this? Its value must be…" Riana was suddenly cut off by Gornin.

"Beyond measure." He broke in. "Elkorine was forged before the great wars. It has played a part in every major event in the history of Kalijor. And now it is your companion."

118

Riana was taken aback by his words. "Master... I..."

"Treat it well Riana Thorindal, and it will do the same for you." He interrupted her again.

"An'fer ye Miss Katrina, I made this t'other day. Sure'n it'isn't as fantastic as Elkorine 'ere, but I think it'll be treat'n ye jus' as well." Dorin said as he tapped the end of a long metal staff on the floor several times in rapid succession and a sphere of intense white light appeared, floating above the tip of the high-end of the thing. The light was brighter than a torch, steady and pure white. Dorin grinned beneath his thick beard and then tapped the staff rapidly on the floor again and the sphere of light vanished. He then handed Katrina the stave.

Katrina accepted the rod with a quirky grin on her face and inspected it. It was just over six feet long, thin and light. Composed of some kind of metal, the thing was harder than any sword or staff she had ever laid hands on, but weighed less. It too was covered in runes, from top to bottom, although these were dwarvish, and seemed to make no sense to her as she looked them up and down. Although simple in design, the staff radiated strength and confidence.

Her eyes lit up with delight as she smiled at the dwarf. "Thank you Dorin! It is magnificent! Does it bear a name?"

"Aye, I calls it Chavan, Tha's dwarvish fer traveler's companion." Dorin said as he smiled with a touch of pride.

"And a fine companion it will be. Thank you Dorin." Katrina clutched the staff tightly and tested her weight against it on the stone floor.

"It is time." Gornin spoke up. "This door will lead you down into the depths of the tunnels that honeycomb the Uraval Mountains. There is a path marked through the caves that will lead you to a grove of trees that hide themselves from the Plain of Sorrow. You will be able to see the markings on the path only with your unique vision. Do your best not to stray from the marked path as the tunnels are filled with all manner of unpleasant creature. Once you are in the Plain of Sorrow you must locate Ambrai and then secure the amulet."

Katrina and Riana both nodded, trying with little success to conceal their fear and apprehension at delving into the unknown.

"This door can only be opened from this side." Gornin continued as he turned to work the complicated lock on the heavily reinforced door, "So once you are in the caves, there will be no return this way."

Riana slid Elkorine into the empty scabbard on her belt, stepping back as Gornin pulled the heavy door open.

A warm breeze rolled out of the darkness beyond. "At the bottom of the shaft you will find the enchanted spring that supplies Cohai's water. Follow the path from that chamber and do not stray from it." Gornin said. Placing a hand on Riana's shoulder he spoke again with sincerity in his voice, "Good journey to you Katrina and Riana Thorindal. I wish you both well."

"Thank you." The sisters said in unison as they moved between Gornin and Dorin into the darkness and watched the door close again behind them, sealing them into the caverns of the Uraval Mountains.

The darkness grew oppressive around them as they stood next to the closed door. The sliding home of the bolt mechanism, securing the solid panel, made them both aware of the reality of their situation; they were now locked in a dark, unknown cavern, days from home with nothing and no one to assist them if they came into trouble.

As they stood there listening to one another breathe, they became aware of another sound, that of surging water. Leaning close to the wall next to her, Katrina put her ear to the stone surface and gasped.

"What is it?" Riana said, forcing her eyes into their heat sensitive range of vision. Turning to look at the now bright, orange and white figure of her sister who was leaning against the equally bright orange and red wall, she stared. "Wow!" She added as she took in the scene. The wall on the opposite side of the tunnel was a cool blue, as most cave walls tended to be, but the reds and oranges of the wall near Katrina indicated that it was somehow heated.

"It's water!" Katrina said as she continued to listen to the wall with her acute elven hearing. "Surging through the wall of the cave!"

"Maybe it is Cohai's waste water." Riana surmised, "We should be careful down further, I don't think we will want to step in it, wherever it is going."

"No!" Katrina exclaimed excitedly.

Riana looked confused, not that anyone could tell in the darkness; even elven heat vision would not allow them to distinguish facial expressions with any accuracy.

"I don't think there is a cesspool below us!" Katrina said, still showing a good deal of excitement.

"Oh. Why not?" Riana put on her best curious demeanor, even though she didn't mean it at all.

"Because," Katrina paused dramatically for effect, "The water is going UP. INTO Cohai!"

"What?!" Riana couldn't help herself now, she really was curious. She leaned against the wall and put her long ear to the warm stone and listened intently for a moment. Telling which direction an aquifer was moving through solid stone of unknown thickness was not an easy task, but after a few moments she had to agree with her sister. There was a definite pulse to the flow and it seemed to start far below them and surge upwards against gravity, into the lower levels of Cohai.

"That is amazing!" Riana finally managed to say.

"Isn't it?" Katrina's grin could be heard as she turned around. "Let's see if we can find the source!"

"That appears to be in our direction of travel." Riana said as she pointed to the floor beneath their feet.

Katrina looked down and saw immediately what her sister was talking about. There on the floor was a series of triangular marks that stood out bright orange against the contrast of the cool blue of the stone floor. They were spaced a fair distance apart and all pointed the same direction, further into the cave.

"So it does." She said, standing up straight and cinching the straps of her pack tighter against her body. "Shall we be off then?"

Checking her own items and cinching her bedroll against her back Riana quickly ran a hand over the pommel of Elkorine. Nodding to Katrina she grabbed her hand and squeezed.

With a sense of trepidation, the sisters set off down the winding spiral of carved steps that carried them inexorably away from Cohai. As they descended deeper into the cavern the sound of the pulsing water grew louder in their sensitive ears. On the threshold of being painful it became a dull roar that pervaded their senses. After a while the tight hallway they were in opened up into a massive circular shaft. The stairs they traversed were carved into the outside of the shaft, still spiraling down into the depths below them. As they pressed on, a green glow began to suffuse their vision, eventually growing bright enough that they returned their vision to its normal state. The roar of moving water was deafening in their ears now, and it was instantly apparent as to why. In the center of the shaft was a column of water that rose up into the air from some source out of sight below them. The shaft of water lunged upwards into the ceiling of the shaft and disappeared on its journey into Cohai. The entire place was lit dimly by an eerie green glow that seemed to emanate from everywhere at once, even the surging column of gravity-defying water.

"Now THERE is something you don't see every day!" Katrina shouted over the din of the rushing water spout as they both stood and stared at the sight before them.

Riana just nodded dumbly, completely at a loss for words.

"You think maybe this is the source of those great hot mineral water baths we took every night?" Katrina continued speculating just loudly enough to be barely heard over the thunderous cacophony.

"Not sure." Riana finally started to recover her wits and shouted back, "Why don't you dive in and see where you end up?" She grinned as she challenged her sister.

"Maybe when we aren't on a schedule sometime..."Katrina paused for a second, thinking something through in her head, "...whenever the heck that happens." She finished up shaking her head a bit, her ears laying back as things settled down in her mind and the nature of their journey reared its head again.

A silence fell between them, almost as deafening as the noise that rolled up and down the shaft around them. Without further discussion, they turned back to the stairs and continued making their way down the inside of the spire that supported the Cohai Observatory.

They weren't sure how long the descent took them. All they knew was that they had camped and slept somewhere along the sheer wall, and taken several meals of their renewed provisions before finally reaching the bottom, and what they saw took their breath away. In the base of the open shaft was a lake, almost a sea, of glowing green water. It was enormous, extending far back and away from the vertical shaft. The opposite wall was only barely visible to them it was so far away. The surface of the great green lake was as calm and clear as a pane of glass, and numerous strange creatures could be seen swimming beneath the placid surface. Only where the immense geyser leapt away from the pool was there any disruption in the calm demeanor of the lake.

Their narrow stairway opened up into a wider path that followed along the edge of the lake. As they moved away from the shaft, the great cavern arched almost out of sight over the great body of water. The ceiling far above them was lit up with bright green motes of light that gave the illusion of a clear, starry night sky.

Following the marks on the floor led the sisters through the cavernous space, and after several hours, into a much smaller tunnel on the far side. The roar of the column of rising water was a distant rumble now, and faded quickly as they moved into the tunnel. The green glow of the subterranean lake faded as they moved down a gentle slope and around a soft corner, their world shifting into darkness once more.

With their vision returned to its heat-sensitive state, they could clearly see one another and the marks on the floor. As they moved forward, following the trail laid out before them, something began to nag at the girls. A constant scraping noise coming from somewhere up ahead, accompanied by occasional cracking and popping noises, as though someone was breaking up some long-desiccated tree branches, had replaced the drone of the column of water. As they moved further into the cave, the sounds grew louder and more numerous. It wasn't the noises so much as their unknown source that really began to set the twins on edge.

"Ya!" Katrina yelped and jumped into Riana's back suddenly.

"What?!" Riana hissed as she twisted around to look. Seeing nothing with her keen thermal vision she turned to look at her sister. She inhaled with a start as she saw the flash of something cold and blue disappear from in front of Katrina.

"I thought I felt something touching me." Katrina said sheepishly as she looked at her sister in the darkness. "We should have brought a torch or something."

"A torch gives off too much heat. It would have fouled our ability to see the marks." Riana whispered as she peered into the darkness behind her sister, waiting for whatever it was to move again.

"Why are you whispering?" Katrina whispered back with a twinge of fear in her voice.

"Because I don't think we are alone here." Riana said in a voice so low it was barely audible, even to Katrina's sensitive elven hearing.

"WHAT?!" Katrina flinched, moving closer still to her sister as she shouted the word.

As her sister closed the distance between them, Riana saw the flash of blue again, something dashing between them, something that had almost no heat. It was barely brighter than the walls and floor.

Quickly she grabbed Katrina's hand with her left hand and drew Elkorine with her right, holding the weapon at her side as she pulled her sister along the tunnel, following the markings on the floor.

"Definitely not alone." She hissed through her clenched jaw as they whisked down the passage as quickly as they could. The sounds were growing louder with every step they took. Popping and scraping noises issued forth from all around them, echoing off the stone walls and ceiling, ahead and behind.

Focusing on the marks that were their beacon in the darkness as they rushed through the cave, Riana finally stopped short, Katrina once again colliding with her backside with an exclamation.

"The hell?" She admonished as she looked ahead of them past Riana's shoulder. As she looked around them all she could see with her thermal vision was herself and her sister, everything else was a cool blue.

"The marks are gone." Riana said under her breath.

Katrina surveyed the area, but all she could see on all sides of them was the cool blue of empty space and cavern walls. "They are gone from behind us too." She whispered.

The scraping and popping noises were all around them now, and Riana felt something hard brush against her arm briefly. Flinching away from it, she bumped into something else that gave a bit and was followed by a series of more intense popping and scraping noises.

"Something's not right here." She hissed at Katrina, "We need a light or something."

In a flash of embarrassment, Katrina suddenly remembered the stave in her hand and what it was capable of. She rapped the end of the stave against the floor a few times rapidly and suddenly the cavern was washed in a pure-white, unwavering light.

The twins' eyes adjusted in time to see the mob of skeletons surrounding them take a collective step forward, grasping at anything their bony fingers could wrap themselves around. The skeleton's hollow eye sockets stared blankly at the sisters as they began pulling and tugging them in numerous directions at once.

Riana acted on instinct, lashing out with a fierce kick to the ribs of the closest of the things to her. The blow jarred the monster's bones apart, loosening its vise-like grasp on her arm. With effort she wrenched her arm free of the bony hands, their unyielding fingers tearing her flesh as it came free. Lashing out with Elkorine she removed the arms of half a dozen of the foul, fleshless things, but they didn't seem to notice as they continued to pull at her body and tear at her tender flesh. There was no pain the things could not endure, nothing seemed to stop them short of being dashed to pieces. Again, Elkorine's shiny grey flashed in the brilliant white light of Chavan's spell and more skeletal limbs clattered to the stone floor to be instantly replaced with more grasping hands, it was all Riana could do to keep her sword arm free of them. She was suddenly embroiled in a losing battle and she knew it.

Picking up on her sister's cue, Katrina was busy thrashing away at the tidal wave of bone with Chavan, her robes were torn and tattered, matted with blood from several wounds the monsters had inflicted upon her.

Relentlessly their weapons flashed in the bright light. Severed bone-limbs piled up on the floor at their feet, but the tide kept rising against them, the masses kept moving toward them. Their chests heaved and their lungs burned with the strain of the constant fight.

"This isn't going to go well if it keeps up like this." Riana grunted to her sister as she wrenched Elkorine free of a split skull, narrowly avoiding the grasp of yet another bony hand that darted through the mass in front of her.

"I think a less physical approach may be in order." Katrina's voice came back in raspy gasps, closing her eyes she began reciting an incantation even as the skeletons folded themselves around her now still form. She began to disappear beneath the engulfing horde as they pulled at her body, tearing her flesh and yanking tufts of hair from her scalp.

Barely finishing the spell Katrina spread her fingers as wide as she was able within her bony tomb and an arc of electricity issued forth from her fingertips. The lightning blast arced to the closest skeleton and then the next, and the next, jumping from skeleton to skeleton, arcing back and forth through the mass of animated bones, enveloping her in a brilliant white light for the briefest of instants. There was a sharp cracking sound as the air burned away, and then an explosion as the superheated bones exploded from within, showering the tunnel in dust and splinters of bone.

"Two can play that game." Riana remarked as she concentrated for a moment, one of her tattoos flashed and a similar burst of lighting issued forth from her free hand, followed by another explosion of bone and for a moment their immediate vicinity was devoid of the relentlessly advancing dead.

"We aren't out of this by a long shot." Katrina croaked through the dust-filled air as she looked down the tunnel through the settling cloud of debris, and saw that it was full of the things, all shambling toward them, arms outstretched.

Bent over with her arms on her knees, panting to recover her breath, Riana saw the advancing mass of bones and her eyes flashed. A wall of intense flames sprung up from the floor between them and the skeletons; the sounds of splintering and exploding bone could be heard from behind the flame-wall as the skeletons relentlessly pushed on, trying to shamble through the barrier. "That'll hold them for a moment." She said nervously then turned her head back to look ahead of them. Her ears drooped down in disappointment as she saw a similar mass of the things shambling toward them from that direction.

Riana's eyes flashed again as she issued forth another blast of electricity that annihilated a large group of them, but they kept coming.

"I can't keep this up." Katrina grunted as a gout of flames shot from her outstretched hand, burning some of the monsters to dark cinders. She was hunched over as well now, panting for breath, her arms felt like lead weights at her sides and her tattered robes were matted with her blood and clung to her body, further impairing her movement.

Riana was falling into desperation and was on the verge of losing control. Elkorine glowed a bright blue as she unknowingly charged the weapon with magical energy. Each time she swung it the weapon released explosions of electrical energy, bolts and arcs of lightning that would damage and splinter the skeletons nearby. Fatigue finally caught up with her as one of the monsters seized her arm, staying her flashing blade and bringing a look of terror to her face.

130

Riana's mind slipped away in that instant. Her concern for their safety drove it down, forced her body to keep fighting. But her concentration began to slip the further her mind got from her body, and as her concentration waned, the pain returned. The headache throbbed back to her in full force, snapping her mind back in an instant. With a scream of pain she tore her arm free of its bony imprisonment, tearing away more of her flesh in the process. Her weapon cleaved several of the skeletons in two as it arced through the air, glowing brightly with her channeled power before it was embedded into the solid stone wall of the tunnel and Riana collapsed to the floor under a tidal wave of skeletons.

Pressing her fingers to her temples and trying to drive the pain back she screamed again. Katrina gasped as the tunnel walls began to bend and twist. The stone contorted in strange ways that she had never seen even the most skilled geomancers cause. As she looked on, she saw the skeletons bending and twisting in nightmarish ways as well. Their attack completely forgotten, they writhed on the floor and slammed up against the deformed walls as what little was left of their bodies betrayed them in ways a sane mind could not even conceive.

Riana screamed again, the sound of a person in intense suffering and pain. Her eyes clenched tightly, her body doubled over, hands still pressing into her temples and a pool of blood forming on the floor beneath her as it poured from her nose.

Katrina dropped her stave as she dove across the distance between them wrestling her sister free from the few skeletons that still had a grasp on her. Cradling Riana in her arms and squeezing back the tears as she yelled over the din of her sister's screams. "Not yet Ree. We aren't ready yet! Pull it together!"

The last of the skeletons fell to the ground, their bodies twisted and contorted in ways that defied explanation. Some of them still twitched and moved, but none retained the ability to cause the sisters any harm.

As Katrina soothed her sister, whispering in her ear that everything was going to be alright, the cave slowly returned to normal along with Riana's breathing. Her screaming fell away into a muffled crying as she willed away the pain; driving it back into the recesses of her mind through sheer force of will.

"It's ok Ree. Come back to me. It's alright. C'mon sis." Katrina was repeating over and over again as she cradled her sister's body to her own and gently rocked her back and forth, unable to hold back her own tears any longer.

-14-

The pure-white light was painful to her as she forced them open, so she quickly snapped them shut again. Her head hurt. Keeping the pain at bay seemed impossible sometimes. It seemed to be getting worse by the minute despite her best efforts to stave it off. Keeping her eyes clenched tightly closed, she raised her arm to her head and used her hand to cover her eyes, blocking out more of the light. Moving her arm caused her an entirely different kind of pain, but under the circumstances, it was the preferred source of the feeling.

"Oh gods, you're awake!" Katrina exclaimed with a raspy voice as she was suddenly at her sister's side again, holding her other hand tightly.

Riana tested her voice by clearing her throat, confirming what she thought, her throat hurt and her voice was raspy from over-exertion. "What happened?" She croaked.

"Oh Ree! The walls started bending and twisting, and... and... well look!"

Riana heard her sister pick something up from the stone floor and turned her head in the direction of the noise, opening her eyes just enough to get a vague impression of what her sister was getting on about.

In her hand Katrina held the twisted mass of a pile of bones, all fused together and mangled. Some of them passed clean through others with no signs of breakage or stress and —had she cared to investigate— she would have found the entire skeleton there in that pile; every bone accounted for.

As she squinted at the gnarled mass, Riana spied the pool of drying blood on the floor and her eyes opened wide despite her better judgment. "Were you wounded?" She forced her voice to stay calm, but the urgency in her tone remained.

Looking down at the blood, Katrina sighed and shook her head. "Yes Ree, and so were you, but that blood isn't from either of our wounds. Your nose was bleeding again." A tear rolled down her cheek as she spoke, placing the remains of the skeleton on the ground next to the puddle of rapidly-drying blood.

Reflexively Riana pulled her hand from her sister's and raised it to her face, feeling for signs of damage or dried blood. When she raised her hand to look at it, it was clean. Only the numerous scratches and lacerations, all of which had been cleaned and salved, lingered as a reminder of the battle.

"I already cleaned you up a bit." Katrina said by way of explanation. "Do you think you can move? I don't think we will be safe here for much longer."

Riana nodded and took her sister's proffered hand. With Katrina's help she was on her feet after a moment, leaning against the wall and still holding on to her sister. She surveyed the area as her equilibrium restored itself. There were similar piles of bones all over the place, hundreds of them, all twisted into grim facsimiles of their former states. Then her eye spotted the handle of Elkorine protruding from the stone wall near her head.

"How did this happen?" She asked her sister, running her fingers over the handle of the weapon.

"You did that." Katrina said flatly as she stooped to snatch up Chavan from where it lay on the floor.

She recounted their battle with the skeletons, focusing on what had happened to Riana towards the end of the exchange. Frowning as she finished speaking, her eyes coming to rest on the handle of the sword protruding from the wall, "I tried to pull it out but it's stuck."

Riana nodded absently as she wrapped her painfully sore fingers around the handle, its cool metal surface instantly conforming to her grip. With almost no effort at all she slid the sword from its resting place and examined its perfect unblemished blade for a moment before looking at her sister.

Katrina had a look of awe on her face. "I tried for twenty minutes to pull it out." She protested against the reality of what she was looking at.

"At least I don't have to find another one this time." Riana said, regaining a little of her humor.

With a slight wince, Riana shrugged her shoulders and slid the weapon home in its scabbard on her belt then wrapped her arm around Katrina's shoulder and put some weight on her sister, bringing herself to a standing position.

"We certainly wouldn't want that…" Katrina replied with a touch of levity. Despite her being covered nearly from head to toe with scrapes, wounds, even deep fissures in her skin, and her robes being torn to tatters and matted in her own blood, she seemed as though a huge weight had been lifted from her shoulders as they moved on.

Even the constant twilight of the 'dark side' of Kalijor was welcome to their eyes as they emerged into the secluded glade from behind a rock outcropping. They had no idea how long they had been in the tunnels. Riana thought it had been about a week, while Katrina was leaning towards 3 days; but with no day-night cycle to judge by, neither of them could be sure.

The glade they found themselves in was pleasant, with tall leafy trees surrounding them on one side and the rock wall of the eastern slope of the Uraval mountains on the other, it felt like the Forest of Brume, but something was missing.

"There are no animals," Katrina said as she looked around for any signs of life.

"Doesn't look like it," Riana confirmed her fears.

"Think we should make camp here and then head out in the morning to look for her?" Katrina suggested, not really sure what to do at this stage.

"Sounds as good of a plan as any," Riana said off-handedly as she closed her eyes and took a deep breath, willing the pain back under her control. She wasn't sure how much longer she could keep it there. It was taking all of her willpower and concentration to keep from doubling over in agony. She had no idea how she was going to take on a Dark Ranger and her undead minion in this condition, especially when the minion was her mother, and the Ranger was as close as any family, with decades of experience on her side.

Riana sat down against the trunk of the nearest tree and slipped into meditation as her sister went about the task of setting up their simple camp, and collecting some fire wood for what would surely be a cold night.

You have work to do yet. Ambrai is a lost soul Riana, and she needs help. She has let the evil consume her because she feels that she destroyed me. She needs to know that she is free to live her own life.

The words of her mother echoed through her mind as she meditated. How were they going to finish this? How were they going to deal with Ambrai? What could they possibly do to defeat her? If the stories were true, she had been preying upon adventurers for years, constantly honing her skills to a keen edge. How could the two of them defeat her with their meager skills and lack of experience?

-16-

The Plain of Sorrow lived up to its name with astounding ease. Here was a barren, parched wasteland. The terrain was mostly flat with a few subtle dips and rises here and there, although not enough to actually obscure one's vision from reaching the horizon in every direction. It was covered in a ruddy-orange, clay-like dust that was just moist enough to cling to the boots and clothing of travelers and weigh them down, but not so thick as to gather in huge clumps. There was the occasional shrub or withered tree that could be seen but nothing else broke the monotony of the landscape. The perpetual twilight added to the gloomy feeling that permeated the area and kept hope from rising up in travelers in this cursed land.

The sisters' bodies were dry, unable to collect even a drop of useable water from their surroundings. They had been rationing their supplies, and those were beginning to run thin. Their skin was beginning to draw tight about their muscles causing their wounds to open up again under the stress; blood clotting instantly due to lack of moisture. Their joints were beginning to ache and grind as the fluid normally cushioning them was absorbed by their vital organs and blood. Their stomachs were empty, as their food rations were also running extremely low. They had barely enough energy between them to keep trudging across the barren waste that was their prison.

It had been days since they left the caves of the Uraval Mountains, and they longed now for the cool, wet environment of the dark caves there.

"We're lost Ree." Katrina's words barely escaped her parched lips, her voice was hoarse and rasped against their ears harshly.

Riana withdrew her compass from her belt pouch and opened its protective cover with her hand, its many tears and lacerations showing signs of slow healing. Examining the device through squinting, dehydrated eyes, she tapped on its side a few times and cocked her head as she examined it further. Then she snapped the lid closed and slid it back into her pouch. "We're still heading northeast." She croaked.

Riana had long ago heard of a great, dark city on the northern edge of the dark side of Kalijor, standing in the shadow of a looming, angry volcano. This city, a place where evil ran rampant through the streets and death stalked the unwitting around each corner, with markets rivaling those of Rathalon's Bazaar, but catering to a much baser clientele. The city of Bête Noire. Thinking that even a practiced ranger such as Ambrai would have to stop for provisions and simple creature comforts from time to time; the girls had agreed that Bête Noire was the likely choice. Where better to find such things than the one city in the entire world where no one cared who you were or what you were about? It was there that they would begin their search, if only they could survive this hellish wasteland long enough to find it. They knew the city lay near the northern barrier wall, but They did not know any more than that.

"Where are we going again?" Katrina asked for the thousandth time as she dragged her feet through the viscous orange dust, leaning heavily on Chavan for support. The end of the stave pushing deep into the earth with each labored step they took.

"Bête Noire." Riana replied for the thousandth time. She seemed to be having a better time of it, simply because the discomfort of her body allowed her to focus her mind on something other than the growing discomfort in her head. As she finished the thought, she felt a trickle of moisture run down from her nose and touch her upper lip. Gently she touched the spot with her finger and drew it back to examine it. The scarlet liquid of her life's blood covered her finger tip, thick and viscous from dehydration. Her mind reeled at the sight of it. Her time was growing short, and she knew it, she felt it. Quickly she wiped the trickle of blood from her face and licked the liquid from her parched finger; she could scarcely afford the loss of such a thing in this environment.

The sound of Katrina collapsing to the ground behind her came as no surprise to her half-conscious mind. Stopping in her tracks and slowly turning toward the sound of the noise, she saw her sister laying face down in the accursed orange dust, her stave resting on the ground beside her in a hollow depression created by its own fall.

Riana slowly dragged herself back to where her sister lay on the ground. Katrina was mumbling to herself about baths and goblets of wine in her delirious state. Dropping to her knees at her sister's side, Riana put her hands on Katrina's back and shook her as vigorously as she could. When Katrina failed to stir, Riana did the only thing she could under the circumstances; she fell over face first on her sister's back, nearly unconscious. But when her right hand splashed into a small pool of water and sprayed a few errant droplets of the cool liquid onto her face, Riana's eyes opened wide in an instant trying to focus on her hand, dangling in a small pool of water that was about six feet long, four or five inches wide and as many inches deep; at the bottom of which lay Chavan, sparkling in the reflected light of the mute twilight.

Bringing her fingers to her lips, Riana tasted a few drops of the liquid tentatively. It was cool, clear and pure tasting water, as though it had just been drawn from a crystal stream. Cupping her hand she drew up more of the liquid and drank it down greedily, then forced herself up off of her sister's still mumbling body. Cupping her hands together she brought a quantity of the sweet liquid to Katrina's lips and let it trickle down their parched line. Katrina started unconsciously lapping up the liquid, nursing on the vital fluid from Riana's hands.

A moment later Katrina was awake again and they were both bent over double on their knees, drinking from the pool, which seemed to never diminish, no matter how much they drank from it.

"Remind me to give Dorin a really big hug the next time I see him." Katrina finally said as she sat back on her haunches and examined the pool with the stave still resting at the bottom.

"I'll be right behind you." Riana replied as she removed her water skin from her belt pouch and dipped it into the pool. The mouth of the skin bubbled as the liquid displaced the warm air that had been the skin's former contents.

"Good idea" Katrina commented as she removed her own water skin from her pack and bent to the task of filling it as well. "I really thought we were done for."

"We're not saved yet…"Riana said, her voice trailing off as something caught her attention and she focused her vision on the horizon.

Seeing her sister's stare, Katrina turned around to look at what had Riana's attention, and there on the horizon she saw a thick, black cloud hanging low over a dark spot in the distance. "What is that?"

Riana rose to her feet, brushing off as much of the clingy orange dust as she could, cringing as the vile substance worked its way into her many wounds. Craning her neck, trying to focus her recovering vision on the spot in the distance, she slowly began to realize what it was, a volcano, belching forth a thick cloud of grey ash and black smoke.

"Bête Noire." She said, her voice trailing off again in thought.

They assumed it had been nearly two days since they had first spotted the cloud of Bête Noire on the horizon. Since then they had learned that Chavan had yet another interesting ability. By stabbing the stave into the ground and letting it stand upright, it would attract a small animal that would become so docile that they had no trouble catching it and cooking it. Approaching the outer gates of the city, they were no longer hungry or thirsty, but still felt unprepared for what lay before them as they took in the utterly different world of the dark city.

On the west side of the city stood an oppressive sight; the monstrous, smoke vomiting volcano that was Bête Noire. The mountain stood in the Plain of Sorrow like a giant festering sore on an otherwise unremarkable body. Its very presence was incongruous to the unbroken monotony of the ruddy orange plain. There were no other hills or mountains anywhere near the beast. It simply sprang up out of the ground, seemingly of its own volition.

In the shadow of the volcano lay its namesake, the dark city of Bête Noire. Surrounded by a low wall that was punctuated by large, open gates at regular intervals, the city was no fortress. The interior was filled with buildings of all shapes and sizes and representing a myriad of different architectural themes. Some rose five or six stories and stood next to single room cottages. There were mud dwellings, others metal, wood, stone or crystal. Some included all of the materials in a misshapen heap that was painful to look at, while others incorporated them all into a grand design that blended the materials superbly into a structure worthy of awe.

There was a very light, but consistent flow of beings heading in both directions through most of the city's gates. Most of the traffic seemed to come from the north side and head out to the south. Drawing nearer they could see that the people heading out the southern gates were typically in good health, their equipment in excellent condition. However, those people going in the southern gates were bedraggled, beaten, disheveled; their equipment typically in tatters.

"Fortune hunters." Riana stated knowingly under her breath as she and Katrina merged into a light stream of people heading in one of the southern gates.

"There must be some treasures in the southern areas still." Katrina offered insightfully as she examined the disparity between those heading south and those returning from the same direction.

"Must be some pretty valuable treasures" Riana said simply as they moved around a group that was dragging three dead comrades on a makeshift sled. "This will be the spot Kat. If we can't find her here, I can almost bet that someone here will have seen her, or even dealt with her before."

"You'll get no argument from me on that score." Katrina replied.

As they passed through the gate they were scrutinized by a rough-looking group of people in a hodge-podge of armor. All were carrying wicked-looking weapons and grinned toothily at the two elves, eyeing them hungrily.

"We don't exactly blend in here." Riana intoned quietly to her sister as they moved their damaged elven bodies into the crowd on the street. "We'd best stay on our toes... and out of dark corners."

"Ree, you'll have trouble getting me out of your sight. Let alone into a dark corner." Katrina said as she dodged around the grasping hands of a street merchant that was trying to convince them of their dire need for some kind of dead animal that smelled remarkably like skunk. "What's our first move?"

"We need an inn. Probably a larger one. With as many travelers as we can find." Riana went on to explain that a larger inn would probably be better for asking questions without drawing attention to themselves. She walked with one eye closed. Shutting the other tightly and rubbing the side of her head distractedly.

"Are you ok Ree?" Katrina asked tentatively when she saw what her sister was doing.

"No." Riana said flatly as she opened her eye and wiped a trickle of blood from under her nose. "But I am well enough. There, that one." She pointed to a large building across the street as she finished.

The building she indicated was three stories high and easily four-hundred feet on a side. It was constructed of an incongruous mixture of stones that looked almost haphazardly piled up into something resembling walls. The doors and windows were all framed in various materials ranging from burnt lumber to pristine hard-woods and even solid slabs of wrought stone. The front doors were double wide and large enough to admit two ogres standing shoulder to shoulder and there was a steady stream of people flowing in and out of the building. Its roof was a ramshackle mixture of tiles and thatching that looked as though a stout wind would send it wholly into the open maw of the volcano.

Crossing the rough cobbles of the street, the sisters squeezed their way into the building through all of the traffic. The interior was surprisingly warm and cozy feeling, in complete contrast to the outside. The main room was a high-ceilinged affair with beams of some dark hard-wood spanning the expanse from wall to wall, spaced at regular intervals. Between the beams hung numerous chandeliers, each bearing hundreds of candles. The floor was composed of a myriad of different wooden strips all laminated together and worn to a smooth, almost mirror-finish over decades of use. On two opposing walls there stood massive hearths, wrapped around equally impressive fire places in which roared great fires to both warm and light the room. On the far wall was a stone and hard wood counter with shelves of bottles behind it and several people bustling about fixing and serving drinks and food. The room was littered with tables and chairs of all shapes and sizes and in the center of the room was another large fire pit, this one with a set of metal rods and attachments anchored around it for the cooking of meals. Currently there was a large boar roasting, with numerous people taking turns rotating the large iron crank handle attached to the spit while they reminisced about some adventure or other.

The occupants of the room were easily as eclectic as its construction, if not more so. There were humans, dwarves, gnomes, ogres, trolls, orcs, felinoids, and lizardmen, but they appeared to be the only elves. Several more exotic species, some of which neither of them had ever laid eyes on before, finished out the mix. What was more interesting was the fact that all of these people were getting along, in the same room at the same time. Some of them were dire racial enemies, but here none of that seemed to matter to any of them as they enjoyed drinks, food, and stories in one another's company.

"And they say this is an EVIL city?" Katrina remarked to Riana as she saw the same thing.

"'Course they do lassies. 'Cause they c'na control it." A rough looking dwarf with several facial scars and an eye patch said as he limped past them on his way somewhere. A stein of ale jostled in his thick, scarred hand. "Tho I would'na advise goin' down any dark allies 'ere," he finished as he disappeared behind an ogre and was gone.

Slowly the girls made their way across the common room to the bar on the far side where they were met by a human with a balding pate of dark hair, dark happy eyes, and a warm smile on his face.

"Welcome to the Shadow of the Mountain! How can I be of service to two lovely elven ladies this day?" He practically sang. He was obviously ignoring their wounds and bloodied clothing as he spoke to them.

"We would like a room." Katrina said sweetly, ears perked up pleasantly.

148

"O'course!" The man said, "Would you be wanting a private room? Or a bunk in a community room?"

At that, Riana turned around and glared at the man icily, a trickle of blood making its way down her upper lip from her nose and her ears cocked back in annoyance.

"Ah... uh... private room it is then." He said, recovering his mood quickly. "I'll have a basin of hot water sent up with some clean linens so you ladies can get cleaned up." He added, nodding his head in Riana's direction.

Riana turned her attentions back to the common room, scanning the occupants for any sign of the elf they sought, or someone who might be in the know as to how to go about locating her.

"The price for a private room is fifty silver a night. That includes food in the common room and your first drink. If you want anything brought to your room or anything else to drink it will be extra." He said as he produced a brass key from beneath the counter and handed it to Katrina.

"That will be fine." She said, her tone still upbeat and happy. She produced two gold coins from her belt pouch and handed them back to the man. "I don't suppose you have a bottle of elven wine?"

The man accepted the coins coolly but was obviously excited to see the money. He smiled as he turned around and removed an elaborate blown glass decanter from the shelf and set it on a tray. Adding two wine goblets, a loaf of bread and a small block of cheese he then pushed the tray toward Katrina across the bar top. With a grin he said "Here you are m'lady. Shall I have someone bring it up to you?"

"No thank you." Katrina replied as she smiled at him and picked up the tray. Turning to leave, she bumped Riana with her shoulder to draw her attention. "C'mon Ree, let's go get settled and clean up some. We can look for her in a bit."

"Huh?" Riana snapped her head around to look at her sister, then seemed to soak in what she had said for a moment before reacting. "Oh. Yeah. Alright. Let's go."

As they moved away from the bar towards the wide staircase behind it the man called after them, "I'll have that water up to you in a few minutes."

The stairs were larger than they were used to, having been built to accommodate some of the larger species of the world. The sisters ascended them with some effort, rounded a sharp corner at the landing and headed up another flight to the third floor where they began inspecting the doors for the one that matched the number engraved on their brass key.

The room was small, the feeling intensified by the bed, troll sized by Katrina's estimate, it took up the bulk of the room. A foot locker sat near the end of the bed and a chair rested next to a small table in the corner. There was a fireplace in one corner near the only window in the place that looked down on the busy street they had just recently left.

Katrina set the tray of food on the table and removed her pack, setting it on the floor, she leaned Chavan up against the wall next to her pack and set about pouring two goblets of wine and cutting some cheese and bread for them.

Riana tossed some logs into the fireplace and ignited them with a flash of her eyes, then sat down in front of the blaze and slipped into meditation, trying to focus her mind so she could control the pain.

A solid knock at the door made Katrina jump a bit. Realizing what it meant, she flashed a look at Riana, who made no move to answer it. Pulling the door open an ogre stood there with a large basin of steaming hot water in his arms staring back from the hallway. She admitted the ogre, who set the basin on the floor in the center of their room and then disappeared again without a sound.

"Thank you!" Katrina called after him as he disappeared down the hallway.

Closing the door again she stripped off her tattered robes and underclothes, snatched up a clean wash cloth and began cleaning herself with the hot water. Sighing at the touch of the rough linen but happy at the prospect of being able to see her skin again, instead of the ruddy orange of the Plain of Sorrow mixed with her own dried blood.

After twenty minutes, Katrina had finished cleaning herself up, and had dressed a few of her deeper wounds with some salve and clean bandages. The water in the basin was now an ugly orange-brown color and there was a swirl of silt still playing on its surface. She had on a clean robe and was sitting down to some of the food when Riana came around, blinking at the change when she saw her sister.

"You look better." She said, smiling at Katrina.

"I feel much better." Katrina replied, and then pointed to the basin with a slice of bread she held in her hand. "I ordered you a new basin but this water is still warm if you want to get a head start on some cleaning up."

"That is an excellent idea." Riana said as she stood up and made her way to the basin, shedding her leathers as she walked.

-18-

The next couple of days were not terribly productive. The sisters spent most of their time in the inn's common room, watching and listening to people as they came and went, sharing their stories of adventure with anyone who would listen. Katrina and Riana had sat down with a few people who sounded like they may have run into a Dark Ranger, but when pressed it turned out none were able to provide a single detail and all were merely relating urban legends.

Riana's nose showed a constant trickle of blood now, and Katrina was in a perpetual state of worry. She constantly asked Riana if she was ok, or needed anything. Riana appreciated the fact that her sister was so concerned. Telling her to stay seated while she ran errands for them both made her sigh in exasperation. The headache was back in full force, and even with the meditation techniques Gornin had taught her, she could no longer block out the pain as it throbbed away behind her eyes.

Finally on the morning of the fourth day, something interesting happened. As Riana was speaking to a particularly belligerent ogre named Gromm, whom had just returned from the shores of the Dead Sea, she caught sight of a cloaked figure standing in one of the darker corners of the inn.

"So den I smash's dis zombie wit me club an as it falls over, dere she is... Dis dark ranger yer look'n fer. She's purty fer an elf, an starts call'n me to'er. But Gromm hear's 'bout dis ranger lady an he high tails it back to d'city. Gromm wants nothing to do with dark ranger lady." The ogre was going on about how he was not a coward for not facing the dark ranger, but Riana was not listening; instead she watched the cloaked figure in the corner who appeared to be watching her in return.

Katrina caught sight of the person her sister was eyeing and whispered to her, "You think that is someone important?"

"I don't know." Riana whispered back as Gromm continued to go on about his fine palette and high quality parentage. "But whomever it is, they moved into the common room, went straight to that corner and have been standing there ever since, looking this direction." Riana licked the blood from her upper lip as she finished speaking.

"Ok," Katrina offered, "but why is it odd that they are standing there? Lots of people come in here and just stand around."

"True." Riana acquiesced, "but look at them. They are STANDING in the corner. Not leaning against a wall or chair or anything. Just standing there, not moving..."

Even Katrina had to admit that was odd behavior for the patrons that seemed to frequent the Shadow of the Mountain. Most people rolled in the doors and folded themselves over a chair or stool as quickly as they could possibly get off their feet.

"I'm going to speak to them." Riana said suddenly as she pushed herself out of her chair. Tossing Gromm a smile, she licked the blood from her lip again as she addressed the ogre, "Gromm. It has been a pleasure speaking to you. I am afraid I must take my leave now. Please allow me to pay for your drink." With that she tossed a couple of silver pieces on the table and then strode away towards the figure in the corner, Katrina on her heels.

As they neared the figure, Riana could see that they were about her height and build. They were completely covered by a thick, black robe that hung loosely on their frame and kept their face concealed in shadow. The figure stood there completely motionless as the sisters approached.

"Hail." Riana said as they drew near.

The person's entire body turned to face them but they gave no other indication of hearing the greeting.

"We were wondering if we might buy you a drink and talk of your travels." Katrina offered with a wan smile on her lips.

Without a word, the figure moved between the sisters and almost glided across the common room towards the stairs behind the bar. The patrons in the inn seemed to instinctively move out of the figure's way as it approached them. In a moment it was at the base of the stairs and turned around to look at the sisters, still standing in the corner watching.

After the figure stood there, apparently waiting for them to follow, Riana and Katrina moved across the room, with much more difficulty. They dodged around and between people who made no attempt to ease their passage. When they arrived next to the cloaked figure, it whirled around and seemed to float up the stairs.

In a moment they were at the sister's door, the cloaked figure standing next to it looking at them expectantly from beneath its shadowed cowl. The girls were getting nervous now, not knowing what to expect. Was this person trying to get them alone so they could be dealt with in private? Killed? Raped? A thousand possibilities flowed through each of their minds as Riana slowly reached out and opened the door to their room. The door swung open under gentle pressure from Riana's hand, revealing the contents of their room in a gradually increasing panorama. Midway through its arc they could see a chair in the middle of their room with a female elf sitting in it, facing the door.

The elf had a mane of thick red tresses that framed her face and ended just below her shoulders. Piercing green eyes that looked like a poisonous tree frog's vivid skin unblinkingly watched the girls. Her face looked as though it was pleasant once, long ago, but had been wearing its piercing hateful gaze so long that it would have been hard pressed to let even the tiniest hint of genuine comfort or pleasure show. Her features were fine and attractive, but worn hard over the years of living in the wild. Her ears swept lazily back from her head, revealing her as being quite calm, but not restful. She wore a suit of chain mail that was nicked and worn, it was a dark emerald green color and covered her body from her shoulders to her knees and elbows. Her shins and forearms were covered with plates of some dark metal that seemed to absorb all light into their matte black surfaces. There was a thick leather belt around her waist and a scabbard on either hip, each bearing a sword with an ornately decorated handle and hilt, in the traditional elven style that made them look like they had been grown from winding vines and then dipped in metal.

The woman looked at the sisters appraisingly, taking in their appearance and nodding slightly to herself. She seemed to be sizing them up, judging whether or not they posed a threat, or even a challenge to her. Presently she spoke, her voice was like a brook in a peaceful grove of trees, but the undercurrents were there that made Riana think of a riptide in the Watery Expanse. "Come in girls, I hear you have been looking for me."

As Riana, Katrina and the cloaked figure stepped into the room, the door mysteriously closed itself behind them, corralling them into the space.

Katrina looked around the room appraisingly and decided that aside from the presence of the two strangers, everything was as they had left it. Turning to her sister, Katrina saw Riana looking at the flame-haired elf with a gaze that could bore through marble.

"Ambrai." Riana said flatly. There was no question or uncertainty in her statement. No one here was under any misconceptions as to who was present.

"Riana." Ambrai returned, a small, wicked smile turning up the corners of her thin lips.

Staring icily at Ambrai, Riana spoke again, "We have come to retrieve our mother's amulet."

Ambrai's smile was gone in an instant. She stood up from the chair and advanced on the sisters with frightening speed, crossing the room in an instant and stopping amid a small gust of wind, her face mere inches from Riana's. "I know why you are here, youngling. And you will not have it."

Riana balked at the sound of the word. Younglings were elves that were too young to be away from their families, too young to be out on their own, too young to take care of themselves. She narrowed her violet eyes and stared coolly at the acid-green orbs that looked back at her unflinchingly. Ambrai was a few inches shorter than her, but that did not seem to bother the woman any, if anything she seemed fiercer for it, looking slightly up at Riana, her seriousness was evident. "Your insults mean nothing to me. Give us the amulet and we will leave you be." Briefly Riana considered saying *please*, but then decided against it, if Ambrai immediately resorted to insults, she felt it unlikely that the elf would fall for a pleasantry.

Ambrai continued to stare into Riana's eyes for a moment, then suddenly straightened up and turned to look at Katrina. "So. The two of you have left the safety of your life of luxury on a whim. Headed into the great unknown on an impossible mission at the behest of a treacherous elf that can not even deign to set you to the task in person." Now she was wandering around the sisters slowly with her hands clasped behind her back as she spoke. "You have no idea what you face. But you bravely face it together. Come what may. It doesn't matter as long as the two sisters Thorindal face it together, eh?"

As she finished speaking she was standing very close to Katrina, looking accusingly into her golden eyes. Riana looked at them and thought for a moment that she saw her sister's eyes tear up. Ambrai walked around Katrina again. Looking up and down her robed form as she did so, never more than a few inches from her. Finally she stopped, standing in front of Katrina, looking up slightly to meet her gaze with her piercing, green eyes. "The TWO sisters Thorindal." She said accusingly, and for an instant, Katrina's eyes dropped to the floor in a look of near shame, before she seemed to gather her wits and look back into Ambrai's eyes.

Ambrai's look did not falter. She simply stared back into the pools of liquid gold for another moment. Then she screwed her face up a bit and grunted something resembling understanding at Katrina before she turned around and moved back toward Riana. For a moment she seemed lost in thought as she paced around the twins.

Riana was confused. Here was their mission, standing before them, and yet she could not bring herself to take action. She had thought about this moment thousands of times during their trip. Thought about what she would do when she came face to face with the woman that had been the focus of her being for so many weeks now. Ambrai simply wasn't what she had expected, and something in the back of her mind was keeping her from attacking the flame-haired elf outright. She had no idea what it was, or why it was holding her back and as she tried to concentrate on it, she was suddenly overcome by an excruciating pain in her skull.

Riana screamed in pain as she fell to her knees, clutching her head with her hands and curling up into a ball on the floor. As she screamed, the room warped around her. The furniture twisting and bending in impossible ways. The effect did not seem to directly affect the others in the room, but they were all bowled over by the effect of the distortion. All except Katrina, who was instantly at her sister's side, wrapping her arms around Riana squeezing her tightly.

Riana howled again as her head throbbed like a mad dwarven drummer. The room twisted around her as though it was trying to give physical form to her pain. Ambrai stood up from where she had fallen and staggered across the twisted, deformed floor to the girls. Standing over them with one armor clad leg on either side of the puddle of blood that was forming under Riana's painfully balled up body, she bent down and wrapped her arms around Riana's back, moving her lips close to the girl's ears. With a wicked grin, she spoke.

"I am going to leave you to your pain and suffering, as I would never wish to distract anyone from something as exquisite as your pain seems to be. But I am going to leave you with one nugget of information to think on." Her wicked grin twisted a bit and took on a much more malicious look as she spoke her next words. "Ezrina Reyals only ever bore one single child. One child. Not two. There is but one daughter of Kilishandra and Ezrina."

Katrina looked up at Ambrai with a visage of pure hatred and malice as the shorter elf smiled back at her, her mane of fiery red hair moving like a lava flow as she gracefully stood up and continued grinning menacingly down at the prone forms on the deformed floor of the room. "I am bound for the Dead Sea. There are some adventurers heading that way and I think they will work nicely for my collection. If you still think you can take the amulet from me, you can find me there, on the northern shore."

Riana howled in pain again, squeezing her hands against the sides of her head, trying to stave off the assault. Ambrai's words were drilling into her mind, even as it revolted against her. She was unable to process the information, but every word found purchase in her inflamed mind.

With less effort than one might have thought possible, Ambrai made her way across the nightmarish twists and turns of the floor toward the now oddly-shaped door of the room and pulled it open on its somehow still functional hinges. The cloaked figure fell in behind her as she moved.

160

Standing up in a flash of defiance, Katrina whirled on the pair and pointed accusingly at Ambrai. "You bitch!" was all she could think to say as tears ran freely down her pained face.

Ambrai looked over her shoulder at Katrina's tear-stained face and her evil grin returned. "Me? That's a laugh. I'm not the one that has been lying to her for her entire life. There is no deception in what I am about, whoever you are."

Then she was gone, the door closed behind her and Riana's screams of agony turned slowly into sobs of pain and confusion. Eventually she passed out on the twisted floor of the inn room while Katrina held her, rocking her gently and repeating over and over again, "Everything will be alright soon."

Riana's eyes opened in a flash. The room was brightly lit by flickering flames from the hearth of the fire, as well as numerous candles and torches that were strewn about the room. She lay naked in the bed, covered with the coarse fabric of the inn's sheets and the heavy weight of the feather-filled duvet on top of her. Her headache returned in full force as she stared up at the ceiling, listening intently to the sounds in the room, in an attempt to discern whether she was alone or not. Finally deciding that she was indeed by herself, she sat up on the stiff, uneven mattress, pulling the covers up around her body, and surveyed her surroundings as she fought to push back the throbbing in her brain.

The room looked as though it had been torn apart and rebuilt by someone with a fancy for unusual geometry, and an impossibly masochistic eye for detail. The floor was rippled and twisted, looking similar to the face of a cliff attacked by a gang of dwarves that had gotten it in their minds to deface something, but all of the wooden planks and boards fit perfectly into the nooks and crannies that had been formed from the previously comprehensible construction. The grain of the wood flowed perfectly from one face of a board to the next, even though they might be at severe angles to one another. None of it was damaged or broken, just warped to the point that it was barely discernable as being what it was originally.

The nightmare did not stop with the floor either. The walls bowed and bulged. The door and windows were warped, no longer square, but showing curving arcs and sharp angles. The ceiling, the furniture, indeed the entire room and everything in it had been twisted in a similar fashion.

That explains why the bed is so uncomfortable.' She thought to herself as she realized that it had been contorted into something barely resembling the inviting sleeping surface that it had been yesterday.

Gingerly she put her feet to the floor, discovering that the parts that still remained flat, which were admittedly few and far between, were still smooth and comfortable to walk on. Dragging the bed-sheets with her, she wandered around the room, examining and touching the newly disfigured surfaces, while she mentally wrestled with the memories of what had happened before she had lost consciousness.

There had been the four of them in the room. Ambrai, Katrina, the strange cloaked figure, and herself. There was some posturing and threatening, before Ambrai had insulted them, called them something… Riana's brain screamed out at her to stop whenever she tried thinking too hard these days… *'Younglings!'* it screamed at her with a pulse of pain that shot down her spine like a crossbow quarrel. Then the pain had started, she had fallen to her knees as Ambrai circled them one at a time, gloating proudly about how they would never, COULD never take the amulet back.

She remembered the pain vividly. It had filled her consciousness to overflowing. Forcing out all other thoughts in her mind, the pain had become the only thing in her world. There was something else, something Ambrai had said as she was standing over her own prostrate form, something she had almost whispered into her ear. Riana forced her mind to relive the experience, and at once she felt the familiar trickle of blood running down her upper lip. She didn't care any more though. All that mattered was getting that damn amulet back! All that she cared about in the world right now concerned that single artifact and the safety of her sister!

'Wait,' she thought suddenly. *'My sister…'*

That was it. Something about Katrina sparked a memory. A dim recollection of what Ambrai had said to them before she had strolled out of the room. Then it hit her and she staggered as the words came back to her.

"Ezrina Reyals only ever bore one single child. One child. Not two. There is but one daughter of Kilishandra and Ezrina."

As she stumbled backwards, Riana's heel caught in one of the pits in the newly deformed floor and she went reeling back, out of control. Unable to stop herself and not near enough to any piece of furniture to make any attempts at catching herself, she tried to spin her body around in an attempt to break her fall with her arms. Turning in mid-air, the world moved in slow motion around her. She saw Katrina appear in the room, seemingly from nowhere; looking around the room as though she had just entered it and was checking to see if everything was the way she had left it.

164

Much too late to do anything about it, Katrina saw Riana falling and shouted out, "REE!!" She dashed across the room in time to watch the side of Riana's head collide with the mangled floorboards.

Riana barely felt the impact through the throbbing headache and the single driving thought that was bouncing around in her addled brain, *'Where the heck did she just come from, and how did she appear in the middle of the room like that?'* Then her world went dark again as she lay on the floor and felt the warm puddle forming beneath her head.

-20-

When she opened her eyes again Riana instantly recognized the deformed ceiling of their inn room. She was in the bed again, its odd twists and turns contorting her body into a strange, but not wholly uncomfortable position. Immediately, her head began to throb again, but there was a new pain added to the usual pressure there. There was a sharp throbbing near her right ear and she gently touched her hands to the area in question. Finding that it was bandaged thickly with clean wrappings. She must have hit her head pretty hard when she had fallen.

"Ree!!!" She heard Katrina's voice from across the room in a panic, and following a series of thumps and yelp of pain, her other hand was scooped up in Katrina's. Riana looked up into her sister's golden eyes and was at once very grateful, yet scared of the person behind them. She had known her all of her life. She had never had cause to doubt her sister in any way. Still there was uncertainty twisting around in her gut, making her wonder if it had all been a colossal lie. Realizing belatedly that Katrina was staring into her eyes questioningly, she forced herself to smile.

"Hey." Riana said finally. "How long was I out this time?"

"Only a couple of hours. You hit your head pretty hard!" Katrina looked down at her sister, concern evident on her face.

"So I noticed." Riana said as she gingerly touched the bandage on her head again. Looking up into her sister's eyes, Riana felt the question bubble up out of her before she could stop herself, "Kat, what did Ambrai mean about only one daughter?"

Katrina stiffened when she heard the words and her eyes opened wider in mild surprise. She was quiet for a moment as she looked into Riana's eyes, seemingly searching for something, then she finally offered a weak smile and said, "I am sure she was just trying to mess with our minds. Make us try and second guess one another."

She had looked away as she spoke, her hands idly smoothing the duvet over the surface of the twisted bed. Riana had no idea what was going on. She could not conceive of a reason for Katrina to lie to her, but she knew her sister better than that. Katrina was not telling her something. Ambrai had struck very deeply with those words, and Katrina's reaction spoke volumes about the accusation. Something was definitely not right.

"I feel a little light-headed." Riana finally said as she formed a strange thought in her head.

Instantly Katrina's gaze snapped back to her, golden eyes bright again. "You've lost a lot of blood recently, between the nose bleeds and cracking your skull. I'll run down stairs and get some soup or something for you. It should help a bit." Katrina was standing up again now, moving towards the door as she spoke. "Now stay in bed so you don't hurt yourself again." She finished as she opened the door with ease despite its looking like it had half-melted into the floor.

The instant the deformed door clicked closed behind Katrina, Riana jumped out of bed. Her head spun, causing her to stagger and latch a hand on to the frame of the bed for a moment as the room stopped spinning around her. When the world had righted itself again, Riana moved to the foot of the bed as swiftly as her spinning head would allow and yanked open the footlocker.

She pulled her leathers out and dressed herself quickly; with practiced movements that let her mind stay blissfully unfocused. After a moment she was dressed and buckling her belt around her waist. Reflexively she checked Elkorine to make sure it was snug in its scabbard, then rifled through the room and collected any of her things that were laying around. She picked up the last bit of bread from the tray and filled her water skin from the basin by the door, settling the supplies in her belt pouch.

Opening her coin purse she took quick stock of her money. Concentrating briefly, her eyes glowed before her form shimmered and faded as the invisibility spell cloaked her from sight just as the door opened again. Katrina entered the room carrying a tray heavy with dishes and crocks of food, concentrating on not spilling the tray. Riana slipped out of the room behind her an instant before Katrina kicked the door closed again.

Now alone in the hallway she was struck by the extent of the damage to the inn. The walls and doors in the hall were as twisted and warped as their room had been, the floorboards warped and writhed down the hall like some great serpent twisting around its own body as it slithered along the ground. As quietly as possible, Riana made her way to the end of the hall, down the stairs, and after a few minutes of effort to keep clear of others, through the common room. The sight of the large room gave her pause as she entered it. While there was less warping than the upstairs, some of the windows were oddly shaped, and the massive beams that arched across the high ceiling were bent into strange shapes, but still managed to span the gap from wall to wall. Riana stared in awe for a moment, trying to figure out how the twisted beams still managed to support the building above them.

Under her invisibility enchantment, she made her way up the street and around a few corners without bumping into anyone, which was a real challenge in a city this crowded, even for a visible person. Finally she canceled the spell and appeared in front of a massive stable. It was three stories high and disappeared out of sight behind its humble street-facing front door, over which hung a simple sign that touted:

Animal boarding and sales
Common, exotic, magical,
tack, feed, supplies

She licked the blood from her upper lip as she headed through the over-sized doors and wandered into the huge building, in search of its proprietor.

As she wandered through the cavernous space looking for someone to speak to, she passed rows of stalls containing all manner of animal. She saw horses of all shapes, sizes and colors and camels of several types that watched her lazily as she wandered by. There were bulls bearing wide, wicked horns and glowering red eyes that bored into her as they glared unblinkingly. She passed stalls containing buffalo that stood calmly with an air of majesty about themselves. Rounding a corner, still searching for someone that worked there, she passed an antelope tied to a hitching post, long legged and thin with its antlers sweeping back from the top of its head in a graceful arc and ending in needle-sharp points. The animal was wearing a bridle and custom saddle, and stared back at her as though it would gore her if she got too close. She moved on past a few stalls containing stags, standing huge and proud, looking regal with their arrays of antlers filling the stables. As she rounded another corner she realized that the huge building went on down the block. A giant, cavernous space lit by the flickering light of torches and a few windows set high up in the walls.

Moving into this portion of the building she came upon stalls filled with much more exotic creatures. A Pegasus stood calmly near by, eyeing her curiously and ruffling the feathers of its carefully folded wings as she passed. Giant hulking lizards with broad shoulders and long, snake-like tails glowered at her as she slinked past, trying not to get too close. Nightmares, inky black stallions with featherless bat-like wings and glowing red eyes watched her pass by with palpable disdain for her very presence. A giant stag beetle, easily fifteen feet long with cruel horns twisting away from its head and shining like metal in the torch light, clicked and chattered at her loudly, causing a slicing pain in her head. Further down the long row Riana thought she could see the form of a dragon-like creature. Although small by dragon standards, the creature was something entirely different for an elf her size.

Gazing toward the creature as it lazily unfurled its wings, Riana rounded yet another corner in the place and nearly bowled over a small person that looked mostly human. Long twisted horns sprouted from his forehead and curved back sharply, ending in slightly up-turned, blunted points at the back of his head, sweeping over his shock of dark, matted hair. He was five feet tall, with pale yellow eyes set in a gaunt face. He had the look of a man that had spent several lifetimes toiling away at hard labor. He wore a cloth shirt that fit loosely around his well-muscled upper torso and was thick with dirt and grime from a long day's work. His pants were leather, and bore several patches of various sizes and colors.

The man smiled faintly at her as she stammered an apology, revealing a set of teeth that were slightly too sharp to be human, but not unsettling. "Hello little one. Been expectin' you." He growled in a basso voice that rumbled through Riana's chest like an earthquake as he looked up at her. "What'll it be then?"

"I need a fast, hearty steed." Riana said looking around the room at the menagerie. "I need to get to the Dead Sea as soon as possible, and I need to leave in haste." As she spoke she pulled her coin purse from her belt and opened it, peering inside. There was a small fortune there, more than eighty pieces of gold and several of silver and copper. As she licked the blood from her lip again, she noticed that the trickle was becoming a flow, and thought, *'at this rate there will be no return trip for me to worry about anyway.'*

"Wait. Did you say you were expecting me?" She raised an eyebrow at the man as she pulled the pouch closed.

"Aye." The man said, looking her directly in the eyes, "Bu'then that's not exactly say'n somth'n as I am also expectin' pardon from Rathalon any day now."

Riana sighed and tossed the coin purse to the man. "I want the fastest, heartiest, and most easily manageable creature here. Along with a quantity of appropriate provisions and riding gear for the animal." She said as the man stuck his nose into the pouch. His eyes suddenly became as large and round as saucers.

"M'lady." He said as he pulled the pouch closed and buried it in the bottom of his own belt pouch. "Let me show you an animal that I think you will enjoy very much."

At that, he turned and strode off down the aisle toward the back of the building. Turning an abrupt corner to another row of large stables stretched out in front of them he walked half way down that aisle before stopping suddenly.

"This," he said as he bowed and indicated the stall to his left with a theatrical flourish, "is Xanthe."

Riana looked into the stall that he indicated and her breath came up short. In the stall was a large reptile of some kind. It was easily fifteen feet long and stood about four feet off the ground. Four powerful looking legs ended in three deadly, clawed toes. A slim serpent-like body led seamlessly into a long neck that tapered elegantly into the animal's head. Thick pointy horns arced back from the top of its skull and two bright blue eyes were set on the front of its head. There were no discernable ears, and a set of large nostrils flared curiously on the tip of its pointed snout. As the creature looked over the top of the stall at her, it peeled back its thin lips to reveal its needle sharp, gleaming white teeth and much larger canine fangs. Its tail accounted for more than half of the animal's length, and the entire thing was only as thick as Riana's forearm. It ended in a large knot of bone that had a blade-like protrusion jutting out from it, looking like a short sword or large dagger on the end of the animal's tail. The animal's skin looked as smooth and as shiny as liquid silver but was in fact covered in scales that were so fine that they were barely discernable. Deep blues and a darker silver rippled and shined as the torch light played across its body.

"Xanthe." She sucked in a breath as she realized that the animal was looking at her in much the same way that she was marveling at it. Their eyes locked for a long moment and she felt a prickle at the back of her skull. Then Riana felt a wave of trust wash over her as her consciousness touched Xanthe's. Instantly she knew that they would be leaving together. She could feel the animal's feelings, sense its thoughts and for an instant she could have sworn she was seeing herself through its eyes.

"Ah… I see you've bonded. Well then, that there pretty much settles it." The horned man's rumbling voice broke Riana out of her reverie. Blinking in astonishment about the connection she had just experienced, she noticed that the man was strapping a saddle to Xanthe. It was a minimalist affair, not much more than a few sturdy leather straps with a small seat and some stirrups to it. As he moved about the animal tightening the buckles he spoke out loud, "How's tha? Not too tight is it fella?"

Riana was somewhat shocked to see Xanthe twist his head around and nuzzle the man affectionately. He then reached up and scratched behind Xanthe's eye ridges for a moment before putting a bridle on the animal's head. There was no bit in the bridle, just a couple of straps that secured a set of reins that lay along Xanthe's neck ending near the saddle on his back. Xanthe nuzzled the man again and received an affectionate pat on the shoulder. As he moved around the stall making sure everything was in order the man continued speaking pleasantly to Xanthe telling him to be good to his new friend. After a moment the man made his way out of the stall, leaving the door open behind him, and stood next to Riana.

"He's a good'n that Xanthe. I'm gonna miss him bein' about. But I have a feeling that you two will do just fine together." Riana could swear there was a tear welling up in the man's eye as he spoke, looking back at Xanthe with affection.

"What is he?" Riana finally managed to get some words out of her mouth, "What does he eat?"

"Ah. He is a rare breed Xanthe. That there's an Equus-Draco. Rare breed that is, an every one of'em is as loyal and loving as can be... quite unlike their larger full blooded kin, who tend to be a little grumpy and territorial, 'specially after a few centuries'o bein hunted by adventurers and such."

"Larger kin?" Riana mulled the statement over in her bitterly protesting mind for a moment as her tongue snaked out of her mouth and lapped up the blood on her upper lip. "You mean dragons?" She let out with an air of revelation.

"Aye little one." The man said as he looked up at her and smiled. "Now, he'll eat jus'about anything that has meat in it, so this here's loaded with some smoked meats and such, good for the both of ya, and there's a couple skins'o water in t'other side." He spoke as he handed her a sturdy leather saddle-bag. "He ken go days without eatin, but you're better off givin'em a bit'o something every day, jes a few bites while you're eatin should be fine. An a handful o'water each day as well."

Riana was amazed at the animal. Xanthe just stood there calmly and looked at her as the man spoke. When he stopped, Riana nodded at him absently and then stepped cautiously into the stall with Xanthe, who continued to look at her curiously as she gently placed an outstretched hand upon his smooth, scaled neck. He was warm to the touch, not cold as she would have expected, and smooth as the magically hewn stone wall that surrounded Rathalon. Xanthe leaned in to her touch, seemingly finding pleasure in the contact as she ran her hand down his side.

"...ye said ye was being in a hurry little one?" The man broke Riana out of her trance again.

"Wha?!" was all she could manage as she looked at him vaguely, blinking her eyes as if trying to wake up from a dream.

"I said, didn'ye say ye were in a hurry?" He was smiling at her. Obviously aware of what was going on between her and Xanthe, the connection that was forming.

"Oh. Yes. I am." She forced her screaming mind to focus. Settling the saddle bag on Xanthe's back, just behind the saddle, she then looked at his great blue, cat-like eyes and asked, "Is that alright there?"

To her surprise, Xanthe nodded his large head, then lowered his body closer to the floor and lifted his front leg so that she could use it as a step.

Tentatively, Riana put her weight on the proffered leg and with very little grace, she managed to hoist herself into the small saddle and slid her toes into the stirrups. Gently Xanthe nuzzled her as she took hold of the reins, then he turned to the horned man and nuzzled him one last time.

"The Dead Sea be straight south o'here. Jus follow the trail o'fools out the gate and head straight on. Xanthe knows the way, he's been down there more than once. And don'be lettin tha'red headed pain get the best'o ya once ya get there."

Riana mulled over what he had said, sorting through the directions in her addled brain. When she finally realized what he had said, she looked around wildly to ask him how he knew what she was about, but she couldn't find any sign of the man anywhere, and Xanthe was moving towards the stable door of his own accord, apparently eager to get started.

When they made it out the large stable doors and onto the open street, Xanthe picked up his pace a bit, loping though town as quickly as traffic would permit, and most people moved out of the way if they saw them coming down the road. In moments they were at the south gate and after a short wait in line with the stream of adventurers leaving the city, they were out in the open Plain of Sorrow again, rapidly putting distance between them and Bête Noire.

Riana forced her mind to focus as Xanthe seemed to keep picking up speed in the miserable clay-like terrain of the Plain of Sorrow. The soft, pliable surface didn't seem to bother him at all, but the constant motion of his stride began to worsen the pounding in Riana's head. Just as she thought her head might actually burst open from the pressure however, he changed his gait to a smoother stride that lessened her pain slightly. Gently she laid a hand on his neck and silently thanked him as the ruddy orange ground continued to fly by underneath them.

She wondered what Katrina was doing now. She hadn't really wanted to leave her behind, but she couldn't keep her mind off what Ambrai had said about them not being sisters. As absurd as it sounded, she actually believed what the Dark Ranger had said, and her statement had only been reinforced when she had seen Katrina appear from nowhere in their room. She knew Katrina had not mastered any teleportation spells, and only the most powerful of mages were able to teleport at will into any location they wanted. Most of the less powerful mages that learned those spells had to teleport themselves to predetermined locations, or powerful magical objects such as obelisks or magical circles.

Still, it was difficult to discount all the years that she and Katrina had spent together. As many years as she could remember, as far back as she could recall. Katrina had always been there. Ezrina had always treated them both as her daughters, and she was fairly sure her mother would have mentioned it if Katrina had been a stranger, or even adopted. No, she had always called them both her daughters and treated them as such. They had been through so many adventures and misadventures together. Exploring and learning, getting into and out of trouble as a team. Always together.

But Ambrai's words still rang true in her ears. Only one daughter.

She focused her mind on these thoughts as Xanthe bounded across the Plain of Sorrow, every smooth stride bringing them inexorably closer to the answers that she was no longer sure she wanted to hear. Closer to the confrontation that neither of her mothers had been able to face. Closer to the Dark Ranger that was spoken of in whispers by the stoutest of adventurers, both good and evil. Closer to Ambrai.

She had no idea how long they had been on the move. The constant dusk of the dark side of Kalijor made it impossible to determine night from day. There was merely a perpetual state of neutral light and overcast skies. They had stopped periodically to eat, drink, and rest, but most of their time was spent on the move. Xanthe seemed to require almost no sleep at all and after what seemed like forever, Riana had finally grown accustomed to the way he loped along, finding a way to catch small naps here and there in the saddle without falling off.

Her back ached from the repetitive motion, and the rest of her body was sore to the bone with the constant strain of trying to stay in the saddle. Her head, pounding harder than ever, seemed to do so in rhythm with Xanthe's gait now. The trickle of blood from her nose had been steadily increasing and was now nearly a river. For a while she had tried plugging her nose with one of her silk garments in order to stem the flow, but eventually she had given up after trying for what felt like an eternity to keep the silk wedged in her nostril. It had fallen out again and again, soaked with blood to the point that it could absorb no more, or on some occasions it plugged her nose up so completely that the blood had backed up through her head and begun flowing straight down her throat. For a while she had thought about leaving that arrangement in place as it seemed a more efficient way to get the vital fluid back into her body, but in the end she just couldn't handle the constant flow of liquid and had given up entirely on the prospect of stopping the river, and taken to drinking water on a more regular basis.

Knowing her supplies were limited she was coming to understand that there was little if any chance of a return trip, so conservation of food and water had moved down a few rungs on her list of things to worry about. With the long hours of travel Riana had begun to prioritize the things she needed to get done before she lost the ability to keep herself moving. Getting to the Dead Sea and dealing with Ambrai was at the top of her list. Getting the amulet back to her mother, or at the very least secreting it away somewhere that it would be nigh impossible for someone to locate it was a close second, although she honestly didn't think her head would cooperate for that long. She wanted desperately to find out what the story was with her sister, or whoever she really was. Honestly, making sure there was enough food and water to get back to familiar territory was now the furthest thing from her mind since she was convinced that she would likely be dead in a day or two at the most.

The nearly debilitating pain in her head combined with this jumble of thoughts managed to keep her distracted enough that the large creature that had been stalking them for the better part of a day continued to go unnoticed. Its four eyes—two vivid green orbs set into the front of its head, and two much smaller glossy black ones positioned one on either side of the thing's head just in front of its huge ears—went unnoticed by her as they followed her progress across the monotonous landscape. Its long, whip-like tail stuck straight out behind it and twitched in anticipation as it prowled along behind them, waiting for an opportunity to acquire its next meal.

It happened all at once. Riana winced as a wave of pain washed through her head, and as she leaned forward in the saddle to cradle her forehead, the beast pounced knocking her out of the saddle and bowling Xanthe over in the process.

Riana hit the ground with a thud, rolling over a few times and flinging a wall of the sticky orange soil into the air as she tumbled head over heals, finally coming to a stop on her back, looking up dimly into the great green eyes of the monstrous feline creature that was looking down on her with its many rows of wicked teeth bared. The thing's mouth was more like a great shark's than any land based predator, with multiple rows of short, serrated teeth that all pointed back toward the animal's throat. As she tried to shake her vision clear and make sense of what she was seeing, it took her a moment to realize that the animal had her pinned to the ground.

Desperately, Riana tried to get a hand on Elkorine, but the beast had her arms pinned to the ground with its six powerful legs in such a way that even if she could get a hold of the blade, she probably could not get it out of the scabbard, and definitely could not make effective use of the weapon. With a cry of pain she closed her eyes and concentrated her will on casting a spell. A wave of agony washed over her as her mind fought back against her desire to focus, but she won out in the end and one of the marks on her body glowed brightly for a second.

Instantly the surface of the plain was broken up as hundreds of plants sprouted up from beneath Riana and the creature that had her pinned. The plants grew thicker and stronger as they reached up out of the ground and began lacing around and through the multiple limbs of the animal which howled fiercely at the sudden restraint. Within moments the tangle of plants was so thick that Riana couldn't see the animal above her any longer, but she felt its weight come off her body, and instantly rolled over onto her stomach and started dragging herself out from under the mass of plant and animal that was now thrashing about wildly above her.

As she moved a few feet away from the viciously wailing mass she thought for an instant that she might have succeeded in containing the beast, but no sooner had she thought it than she heard a horrible ripping sound and rolled over again in time to see the creature shredding the mass of vines to bits with a set of foot-long razor sharp claws extending from each of its six feet. Without thinking she gripped Elkorine and unsheathed it, holding the weapon aloft, point towards the ferocious beast as it leapt from the mass of quickly dying plants, back onto Riana, again pinning her limbs to the moist soil.

"Damn you!!" She shouted as she tried in vain to cause some serious damage to the thing's leg with her sword.

The monster seemed to sneer at her in response to her exclamation, peeling back its lips and baring its frightening teeth again in some horrid parody of a grin. Drool as thick as river-bottom mud slid off of the thing's teeth and hung down in several long dangling ropes over her body as the creature reared its head back and opened its jaw impossibly wide in preparation to deliver the killing blow.

Refusing to close her eyes to her fate, Riana looked up at the thing, expecting the blow to come any second. She held her breath as she saw the animal's head start to jab foreword toward her. When the animal's gaping maw was mere inches from her head, a streak of metallic silver-blue flashed across her diminishing field of vision and the animal was gone, its weight removed from her body.

Blinking dumbly for a moment, she heard a commotion to her left and quickly rolled over to her knees and looked in the direction of the noise. There was Xanthe, locked in melee combat with the feline predator. They stalked around one another in a tight circle, lashing out with their wicked sharp jaws repeatedly as they moved. The predator's blood was pouring from several large bite wounds now, and it had a slight limp in its middle set of legs but it seemed even more ferocious than before as a result of the damage.

Riana looked on as Xanthe lashed out with his white, dagger-like teeth. The other animal reacted so quickly that Riana almost didn't see it move. It side stepped the lunge and caught hold of Xanthe's neck in its own powerful maw. Xanthe let loose a panicked warble as he tried to jerk his neck free of his enemy's grasp. To her surprise Riana felt a shooting pain in her own neck as

181

the creature bit down on Xanthe's neck. Unable to break free, Xanthe changed tactics on the other animal, bringing his thick, powerful tail around and pointing the chisel-pointed knot of bone at the animal. There was a snapping sound and Riana saw the chisel of bone separate into three wicked blades that then lashed at the creature, cutting a great gash in its side.

The predator bellowed in pain, releasing Xanthe's neck in the process and staggering away from the bladed tail that was now swishing around wildly in an attempt to keep the thing at bay. Xanthe staggered sideways and stumbled to his knees howling in pain. Riana could see blood seeping from between the fine scales on his neck and feel the pain coursing through his nerves. Without a second thought, she dashed forward and was at his side, her hand on his neck as she glared at the cat and pointed Elkorine at it menacingly.

The cat hissed at the pair of them and stalked back and forth just outside the reach of Xanthe's tail for a moment as it considered what it was up against. All at once it seemed to make up its mind and act out its decision as it leapt sideways toward them. Xanthe lashed out at it with his bladed tail, but the creature twisted around in mid-air to face them, and Xanthe's attack missed its mark by several feet leaving them vulnerable to the creature's attack. Riana acted without hesitation, leaping at the creature, sword in hand, she lashed out at it, slicing through flesh, muscle and tendon along the inside of three of its legs. The wounds were up high on the legs, where they met the body, and they ran deep, all the way to the bone. The animal cried out in pain and twisted again mid air, snapping its other three limbs out as it fell.

Riana screamed out in pain as she felt her flesh sliced open. The great cat cut her across the stomach, chest and face with two of its paws, slamming her to the ground and knocking the wind out of her. Blind with pain and gasping for breath she struck out blindly with her sword in the direction she thought the monster was headed. When she felt the blade stick into something, she simply pushed on the pommel with all of her remaining strength, driving it deeper into the flesh in which it had found purchase. There was a great, pained, wailing sound, accompanied by a violent shaking of her sword in her hand, and then the world went silent and still around her.

It took her several long minutes to regain her breath and force the pain in her head back enough to get her bearings again. Slowly she opened her eyes and forced them to focus through the pain that lit up her nerves like a continuous lightning strike. On the ground at her head lay the corpse of the predator, it was a large cat-like thing with sparse, bristly hair that was a sickly grey color, its six legs were folded under it awkwardly and bent in funny angles. Elkorine was buried up to its hilt in the thing's chest, dwarfed by the animal's bulk. At her feet, Xanthe was standing up shakily, and seemed to be taking an interest in her as he found his balance, a look of deep concern filling his gaze.

Looking down at herself Riana saw a long gash across her stomach and another across her chest, just under her collar bones, she chuckled a bit at the realization that her magically enhanced leathers had protected her from the bulk of the creature's assault. The garment seemed totally unharmed, although she immediately regretted the laughter as another spike of pain drove through her skull. Both of the wounds were bleeding steadily, although not profusely. Almost on instinct, she forced herself to act, removing some of the silk scarves from her belt pouch, she wrapped them around herself, binding the wounds inexpertly but enough to staunch the flow of blood.

"Just a little longer." She mumbled, wincing in pain as the silk worked its way into the open wounds. "Not much further now. Hold on."

Xanthe was next to her now, sniffing at her curiously, he licked her face with his rough, forked tongue and she screamed out again when the contact caused a jolt of pain across her face. Worried by what she might find she put a finger to her cheek and her fears were realized, there was an open wound on her left cheek running vertically from her jaw bone up past her mouth and along her nose to where it stopped a hair's breadth from her eye. She knew she was lucky to still have the use of the eye.

She looked at Xanthe seriously for a moment and then reached out to him with her bloody hand. He let her grab hold of his neck and helped her stand up. Leaning heavily against her companion, she reached down and extricated Elkorine from the body of the feline creature, and wiped off its dark grey blade on the animal's coarse-haired pelt as she examined the fallen creature with clinical disinterest.

With great effort from the pair of them, she managed to perch herself in his saddle once more, leaning fully forward and wrapping her arms around the base of Xanthe's neck instead of holding the reins. She set her face against his smooth, scaled body and spoke weakly.

"On to the Dead Sea friend… Not much longer now…" Her words slid out of her mouth as her body went numb and her mind shut down. Blackness closed in on her again as she felt Xanthe fall back into his familiar stride.

-21-

The gush of freezing cold water on her face had Riana awake and on her feet in an instant. Her hand found the handle of Elkorine as she spun around once to take in her surroundings. She was on the shore of a large lake that was nearly obscured by a thick, soupy, green fog. She was next to a well-stoked camp fire, standing on her bed roll. Behind her lay Xanthe, watching her intently with his curious blue eyes. Standing in front of her, an empty cup at her side and a jovial grin on her face, was Ambrai.

"Welcome back." She said, her grin widening. Then she turned around, tossed the cup onto a pile of her things and bent down to minister something cooking over the fire.

Behind where the Ranger had just been, Riana saw the cloaked figure standing stiffly, hood still drawn up around its head and face, not so much as breathing.

Riana's mind roiled in confusion as she tried to make sense of what was going on here, but the throbbing made it difficult to even focus her thoughts. This was the elf that she had been sent to confront. The elf that had told her, in no uncertain terms, that she would not capitulate to the demands of her mothers. What was she doing taking care of her, and smiling at her?

"Wha…" Riana began to speak, but a sudden stab of pain shot through her body as soon as she made a sound, forcing her to her knees, she pressed her fingers to her temples and massaged them roughly to try and calm the pain.

"Probably best if you don't speak." Ambrai said conversationally as she finished rotating the meat that was cooking over the fire, and turned to face her. The smile was gone now, but her face still held no malice. Shortly she moved to Riana's side and knelt down beside her, wrapping a chain mail clad arm around the taller elf as she winced from the pain in her head.

"You were going to ask what you were doing here? Why I am taking care of you?" Ambrai almost whispered in Riana's ear. Even at that volume level, the throbbing pounded in time with Ambrai's words.

Riana managed to nod her head in agreement, but even that action sent knives of searing hot pain through her mind. Clenching her jaw and wincing against the pain, she thought she saw the ground beneath her warp and twist briefly before returning to normal when the pain subsided a bit.

"Try not to make any sudden moves or sounds." Ambrai said as she helped Riana roll back into a sitting position on her bed roll. "There that should be alright. Just stay calm and try not to focus too much. I'll explain in a moment."

At that, Ambrai set about pouring a cup of steaming liquid from a small kettle near the fire, drawing a large Kukuri knife from a sheath on the back of her belt she used it to slice off a sizeable chunk of meat from the animal that was roasting over the fire. Setting the meat on a small plate, she resheathed the knife and brought the meat and cup of steaming liquid over to Riana, setting them on the ground in front of her.

Riana looked at the Dark Ranger suspiciously, her violet eyes narrowed at the other elf, who smiled briefly and then set about making herself a copy of the meal, then she sat down in front of Riana and took a sip from her own cup.

"It isn't poisoned. If I'd wanted you dead, don't you think I would have dispatched you while you were unconscious?" Then she smiled her wicked grin again, the one from the inn room in Bête Noire and finished by saying "I am a Dark Ranger after all. No compunctions about slaying innocent adventurers and all of that." When she finished speaking, her face returned to its normal, pleasant visage and she took a small bite of the meat on her own plate.

Riana just stared at her in wonder, her fingers still roughly pressing into her temples and her jaw slack in confusion. The blood from her nose running into her mouth of its own accord now.

"Eat up. You're going to need your strength very soon." Ambrai said as she swallowed another bite. "I'll try and explain as you eat."

Giving up on understanding for the moment, Riana turned her attention to the food at her feet, and suddenly was overtaken by the desire to have a cooked meal. She had no idea how long she had been eating dried meats and water, but it felt like years as she chewed tentatively on the small bite of succulent meat and washed it down with a sip of the hot, pungent tea from the cup.

Seeing that Riana was well into eating her food, Ambrai began to speak. "Its been a long time. I was beginning to wonder if you would come. My task is almost complete and I must be stopped before it is." Her voice was weak, a little distant, as though she were talking from a trance. Looking up briefly, Riana saw what looked like tears welling up in Ambrai's green eyes, now slightly clouded with emotion.

"I know it must sound strange, me asking you to stop me from completing my task. But you need to understand that this task is not my own. Something happened, during that ritual. Kilishandra and Ezrina's minds were cleared of the curse, but a piece of it burrowed into my mind before it was eradicated. Slowly, very slowly, over the years, it grew into something different, something malevolent in a way I have never experienced before. It makes me do things, terrible things. Hurt people. Kill people. Steal. I have become that which your mothers and I fought so hard against all those years ago."

Riana had stopped eating now. Her mouth hung open as she looked deeper into the green pools across from her, and she saw the truth of Ambrai's words. She had never expected this. Never expected to find sympathy for this elf that had wreaked so much havoc in the world, and on her mother's soul.

"It gets worse than that though. The worst part is that when it takes over, when I slip into darkness and begin following its commands, I like it." Ambrai now wore a look of pure hatred and disgust on her face, her ears cocked straight back in anger. "I don't know if it is some part of me that has been long buried and dug up by the thing in my mind, or if it is something put there by the creature. But when it is awake inside me, I follow its orders willingly, happily, reveling in the pain and destruction that it demands me to wreak."

Without looking up into Riana's eyes, Ambrai continued, almost as if she was trying to confess something on her deathbed and had to say it before she lost her strength and took her words with her to her grave.

"When the monster sleeps, my mind returns, and I am left to deal with the consequences of my actions. I have done so much that can never be atoned for. Caused so much pain." Her eyes were leaking tears now. "It wants a body. A powerful body. Originally it made me dig up Kilishandra's body, intent upon reanimating it and possessing it, fully aware of how powerful a mage she had been in life. But when I found her body, I also found the amulet, and then the plan changed. The monster in my mind knew instantly what it was, and it immediately set me to work on recharging the magic of the amulet."

Ambrai's eyes were reflecting the deep pain she felt, her voice held steady through force of will alone as she recounted her story, "It knew that if we charged the amulet with souls that were freed of their bodies through violence, that the child created from it would be extremely powerful, and wickedly evil, and so it set me to the task of recharging the thing with the souls of adventurers that it made me cut down."

Finally she broke down, burying her face in her hands to hide her weakness from Riana. "So many. I've killed so many people. And I have savored every death. Tasted their suffering, tortured them before they died. There is no fate cruel enough for me Riana." The Ranger sobbed into her hands, shaking her head as the tears rolled down her forearms, her hair waving about her head as it shook.

"I only retained my own consciousness because of your mothers. There are pieces of both of them in my mind as well. They help me guard my mind against being totally destroyed by the monster. They help me even now, holding it at bay so that I can talk to you as me, instead of that creature I have become. It has become more difficult over the years though. I can feel myself slipping away, and I know that it is only a matter of time before I become that person forever."

She lifted her head from her hands and looked into Riana's stunned eyes. "That is why I have waited for you. Why I told you where I was going. Why I arranged for Xanthe to come into your company. I need you to end it for me Riana. I need you to stop the monster in my mind." She made no attempt to wipe away her tears as she spoke, wearing them proudly as she asked for the thing that time would never bring her as an elf.

"What?" Riana asked, immediately regretting it as another lance of pain stabbed through her body and the flow of blood from her nose increased.

"I need you to destroy me. Take this body from the creature so it can't complete its plan. I asked Ezrina to do it once before, but she couldn't do it. Something in her mind stayed her hand. She said she would find a way. That she would send an emissary to do the thing that neither of us was allowed to do. I hoped it would be you. I can die well by your hand."

Riana's eyes were pouring tears now, despite her best efforts to stop herself. This elf was begging her to end her life. This elf that had been friend to both of her mothers, years ago when their lives were much less complicated by circumstances beyond any of their control. Then a thought occurred to her, what had Ambrai meant about her sister?

"Sister?" Riana asked as quickly as she could through her clenched teeth, ready for the pain that arced across her head like a lightning bolt. As she winced, she was sure she saw the ground flex and twist in time with the throbbing in her head, even the water in the still sea behind them seemed to be affected as small waves rolled about the surface.

"Katrina." Ambrai confirmed, her tears now drying up. "I don't know who she is Riana. I know for a fact that Ezrina only bore you. I watched it happen through a window near the top of the Cohai Observatory. There was only one child. But to this day Ezrina swears that you are both hers. Katrina came from nowhere it seems, just appeared one day, and everyone else acted as though she had always been there. I think Gornin knows the truth, but aside from him and me, everyone else seems to think that you and Katrina are sisters. It doesn't make sense to me, but I know that she is not of the same blood as you Riana."

Riana's eyes were wide as she listened to Ambrai, her mind reeled as she tried to grasp the idea that Katrina was really not her sister.

Through tear-filled eyes she looked at Ambrai. The Ranger's vivid green eyes looked back pleadingly, her ears drooped down out of sight into her thick scarlet curtain of hair. Riana's resolve strengthened as she saw in Ambrai's eyes, the true desire for this, her need to stop the thing that had control of her. She had traveled across Kalijor for this task, and now that she was here, she found herself wanting to do anything but complete it, even though she knew in her heart that it must be done, that it was the right thing to do.

Riana closed her eyes and clenched them tightly against the throbbing pain in her head for a moment, then slowly moved her hand to the handle of her sword as she opened her eyes again and looked at Ambrai.

"Wait." Ambrai said, reaching out and touching Riana's forearm. "It won't be that easy." She added as she inclined her head towards something behind her.

Focusing her vision over Ambrai's shoulder she saw the cloaked figure standing there as motionless as ever, noticed that it was facing them now, its shrouded face looking directly at them both. Looking back at Ambrai, Riana raised an eyebrow at her questioningly.

"She will defend me against any aggressor." Ambrai said. "It was one of the conditions of the spell used to reanimate the body."

At these words, Riana's eyes opened wide in surprise as she looked over Ambrai's shoulder to the cloaked figure.

'It couldn't be.' She thought, not wanting to believe what Ambrai was asking her to.

"You will need to immobilize me, then destroy her. She is too strong of a mage to be immobilized for any length of time."

Riana shook her head violently, causing pain to race across her nerves like fire. She refused to move, or act against what she knew was beneath the cloak. She couldn't do it. Her mind railed against it. Her head throbbed again, forcing her to close her eyes against the wash of pain, this time she felt the ground move beneath her. She knew her own time was drawing near. Almost any action was causing her nearly unbearable pain, and when she felt that level of pain, it seemed to affect the world around her physically. She was also becoming a menace to those around her, even if it wasn't a malicious curse taking over her mind. Slowly she opened her eyes again and looked at Ambrai, who was looking back pleadingly.

"Please Riana." Ambrai was almost in tears again as she pleaded for her end, her vivid green eyes locking with Riana's violet orbs.

With a sigh Riana closed her eyes and dropped her chin to her chest, nodding faintly. She heard Ambrai moving around then, and took a moment to focus her thoughts and energies on what was about to happen, what she was about to see. Slowly she sat up onto her knees and wrapped her right hand around the comfortingly cool surface of Elkorine's handle and opened her eyes in time to see Ambrai toss her sword belt across the camp, where it landed near Xanthe, who gave the object an unconcerned look and went back to watching the three figures.

Without a word Riana sprung into action. Her eyes glowed as a forest of vines broke though the ground around Ambrai's legs and quickly grew up around and entangled her limbs, holding her tightly in place. Then in one fluid motion Riana rolled to her feet and unsheathed Elkorine facing the cloaked figure.

As Riana came to her feet, her sword aloft and ready for action, the cloaked figure let loose a banshee wail that split the air like a lightning bolt and drove into Riana's pained body like a white-hot spike, driving her to her knees. The figure leapt across the distance between them in a flash, the rush of wind blowing the cloak free of its shadowed form.

Riana looked up as the figure was suddenly revealed for what it truly was, an elf that looked to be nearly a mirror image of herself. Kilishandra's skin was pale, almost white, and drawn tightly across her delicate frame, but it was still very much intact. Her facial features were sunken a bit, but discernable, and her vivid violet eyes looked sharp and observant. Her platinum hair was pulled back into a pony tail at the top of her head and the length of it fell down her back to her waist. She wore a tattered, black silk robe that looked as though it was being held together, and to her body by numerous leather straps. The billowing silk garment hung in the wind, blotting out the sky as she came down on Riana, screaming with a voice that cut through her like a knife.

Riana forced her body to roll to the side as Kilishandra landed where she had been only a moment before. Rolling to a crouching position facing her assailant, Riana hefted the sword in her hand and readied herself for another attack. She focused her groggy mind on Kilishandra's form an instant too late, realizing the undead elf was making shimmering glyphs in the air with her hands and chanting in elvish.

Riana closed her eyes and concentrated, manifesting a shimmering shield just as the lightning bolt struck her. She screamed out as the electricity coursed through her body, clenching all of her muscles as it went to ground beneath her.

'And that was partially deflected.' She thought as she pulled herself back together. Opening her eyes she saw Kilishandra working another spell, but summoned a gust of wind to knock her off her feet before the spell could be finished.

Kilishandra was bowled over by the wind, falling on her back and losing her concentration. She rolled to the side as a fire ball scorched the damp ground where she had been.

Cursing to herself, Riana tried to focus her thoughts through the pain in her head. If she couldn't focus, this was going to be a very one-sided battle. As a spark of blue-white energy arced toward her, she stuck Elkorine into the path of the missile, the sword absorbed most of the energy, but Riana's arm went numb from the overflow. Her eyes flashed as she fixed them on Kilishandra and the other elf's feet began to sink into the soil-turned-quicksand by Riana's spell. Without hesitation, Riana cast another spell, and an arc of lightning dropped out of the sky, only to be deflected by Kilishandra's counter spell in a blinding flash of light.

"REE LOOK OUT!" Katrina's voice shouted seemingly from nowhere.

Riana felt her ribs crack as she was kicked hard from the side. The added pain caused her to vomit where she landed. Her head was pounding away and the soft, moist ground felt like a sponge beneath her. Looking down she saw a pool of blood where she had thrown up. It was almost over now. Just one more thing to do before she was through.

"You little bitch! What were you thinking?! That I couldn't break free of a simple ensnarement like that?" Ambrai was on top of her again kicking her in the ribs and stomach as she spoke. Riana felt more of her bones give way under the assault and nearly blacked out from the pain.

"Get off of her!" Katrina screamed as she hit Ambrai in the back of the head with Chavan.

Ambrai recoiled from the attack, wheeling around on Katrina and lashing out with a swift punch to her face. Katrina's nose exploded, blood pouring freely from the damaged flesh. She leaned on Chavan heavily just to stay standing as her eyes watered and her knees wavered from the force of the blow.

"You can't stop me!" Ambrai shouted at Katrina. "Nobody can stop me!" She reached out and grabbed Katrina by the front of her robes and spun around, launching her across the short distance to where Riana lay coughing and sputtering on the ground.

Katrina, stumbling as she covered the distance, landed bodily atop Riana with a thud. Flattening them both out on the ground under the force of the impact. Riana howled in pain as the ground rippled out away from her like the surface of a still pond after someone dropped a stone in.

"Damn it!" Riana cursed, willing away the pain the words drove through her mind. She winced as she pulled herself out from underneath Katrina's crumpled form. She felt her hairs rising up on her head and knew only too late that she was in the path of another lightning bolt. Trying to focus her thoughts on a counter spell, she knew it was too late as she smelled the ozone around her.

Clenching her jaw against the inevitable pain, she waited for it, an instant, then two, then three, but the blast didn't come. Opening her eyes she looked around and saw Kilishandra staggering away from Xanthe who was slashing at her with his bladed tail.

Riana smiled grimly at her friend then turned to Katrina who looked up at her weakly and said, "Hey sis."

"Hey." Riana replied and then fell to her knee as the pain shot through her body.

"Don't talk Ree. Just go get her. On three." Katrina panted as she struggled to her feet and began casting a spell to help Xanthe against Kilishandra.

Riana focused her will on Ambrai and prepared to try something she had never done before.

"One." Katrina said as she started mumbling a spell under her breath.

Riana's mind hurt so badly that she could barely remain conscious, but she forced herself to concentrate on the spell, one of her tattoos began to come into focus and glow dimly.

"Two." Katrina said, continuing to mumble her spell. Kilishandra continued to struggle against Xanthe, but she was clearly not used to fighting a physical battle. Every time she began casting a spell Xanthe would bite her or check her, knocking her around and disrupting her concentration.

Riana opened her eyes and focused her clouding vision on Ambrai, who was dashing across the camp to retrieve her weapons from where they had landed earlier.

"Three!" Katrina finished casting her spell at the same time Riana's tattoo began glowing brightly, her violet eyes flashing in the perpetual twilight. Instantly, Kilishandra and Ambrai stopped moving, as did everything around them as Riana's spell sped the trio up in time.

Katrina's spell completed and a spell bolt arced from her hands towards Kilishandra's frozen body. Katrina's missile slowed down as the temporal displacement began to affect it as well, and Riana's eyes flashed once more as she disappeared from sight.

All at once, time returned to normal around them. Katrina erected a barrier around Xanthe to prevent him being hit by her attack just as

Kilishandra was blind-sided by the appearance of Katrina's spell bolt that was already on top of her. With fluid grace, Kilishandra spun into a pirouette to try and dodge the missile but it was too late. The energy bolt caught her fully in the body and exploded in a torrent of magical destruction.

Kilishandra screamed her banshee wail as she fell to her knees, clutching her side. As Katrina began chanting another incantation the shield around Xanthe disappeared and he dove at Kilishandra, jaws spread wide for the final attack, but the elf called out a power word in time to disappear from sight just as Xanthe's powerful jaws clamped down on the air where she had just been. She reappeared a few feet away and began chanting another spell as Katrina and Xanthe adjusted themselves to her knew position.

Riana appeared out of thin air just to the side of Ambrai as she dashed toward her weapons. The Ranger was caught by surprise as Riana brought her sword around in a wide arc. Elkorine sliced through chain mail as though it were mere fabric and opened a wide gash in Ambrai's side eliciting a yelp of surprise from the woman. She spun around and glared at her attacker with dulled green eyes. Riana stared back at her, looking her in the eyes and realizing that Ambrai was gone. The life in her eyes was no longer that of a smoldering passion, rather it was hatred. Hatred of all things living. A shiver ran through her and she staggered as she tried to hold her sword at the ready. Her head felt like it was split open and her vision fogged from the pain.

Ambrai touched her fingers to the wound in her side briefly before bringing them up to her face to inspect the bloody digits. She smiled cruelly as she sucked the fingers into her mouth and cleaned the blood from them. "You're hopeless." She sneered as she slid the fingers slowly from her lips. "And your friends are both going to die because of it."

Riana's gaze flitted briefly toward Katrina and she instantly knew it was a mistake as she saw a blur of green motion in front of her. An armored knee drove forcefully into her stomach causing her brain to explode with pain and forcing her to her knees again as she wretched violently.

"You! Help Ree!" Katrina shouted at Xanthe as she finished another incantation and the sky opened up and poured pebble-sized hail down on Kilishandra in a virtually solid stream. The undead elf was obscured from view under the torrent as Xanthe's head snapped around to see Riana crumpled up on the ground beneath Ambrai who had her arms over her head, poised to bring them down on Riana and knock her out of the fight, or worse. Coiling his powerful legs beneath him, Xanthe sprung across the distance opening up his tail blade in mid-air and slashing it toward Ambrai who twisted around suddenly and managed to catch only a glancing blow from the wicked blade. Xanthe landed with one of his front legs on either side of Riana's form, facing Ambrai and growling loudly with teeth bared.

Katrina, absorbed by the efficiency of Xanthe's movements turned to notice that Kilishandra had vanished again. Spinning around as soon as she heard Kilishandra's voice she caught sight of the glowing sphere just before it slammed into her body and knocked her across the camp-turned-battleground. Sprawling to the ground at Ambrai's feet coughing and sputtering, Katrina was followed by Kilishandra. The look of malice on the elf's sunken features as she joined Ambrai in looking down at Katrina and Riana mirrored the vile hatred bubbling in the Dark Ranger's gaze. Her eerie undead voice rose above them as Kilishandra began chanting another spell, one certainly intended to finish them off.

"NO!" Riana screamed, not even feeling the lance of pain stabbing through her head as she dove from beneath Xanthe with Elkorine held tightly in her hand. She threw herself toward Kilishandra with nothing on her mind aside form the desire to save Katrina.

Xanthe followed suit, stabbing his long tail through the air at the undead mage who was forced to leap back away from the crumpled form of Katrina to avoid the double attack.

Ambrai laughed cruelly at the scene as she nonchalantly strolled out of harm's way and walked toward her swords again.

"SHUT UP!" Riana screamed as she recovered her balance and leapt at the ranger's back with her sword at the ready. All at once her vision was filled with black silk as Kilishandra threw herself between Riana and Ambrai. Elkorine pierced her back between the shoulder blades and drove straight through her chest. The tip of the sword protruded out between the undead elf's breasts and she clutched it spasmodically with her hands as she dropped to her knees and howled her eerie wail.

Riana dropped to her knees behind her, as she was still clutching Elkorine's handle tightly. Her eyes were as large as dinner plates as she realized what she had done. Kilishandra's wails came to a halt and her body slumped over forewords, dragging Riana down to the ground on top of her.

Like a log on a roaring fire, Kilishandra's body began to turn to ash, starting at her extremities, her hands and feet falling to the ground and burning away into near nothingness. As her legs and arms followed, Riana began crying.

"I'm sorry mom…" Her voice broke up through the pain as her mother's body turned to ash beneath her.

"Look at you! You can't even stand up! How could you possibly hope to stop me?!" Ambrai gloated as she moved over Katrina's prone form and began kicking her repeatedly.

"Sssssstop…" Riana's voice was barely audible, but it got Ambrai to stop kicking Katrina for a moment.

"What did you say youngling?" She hissed down at her, laying on top of the pile of ash that had been Kilishandra.

"I… ssssaid…ssstop…" Riana repeated with more volume as she forced herself to her hands and knees and began dragging herself out from under Katrina.

Ambrai laughed at her menacingly and kicked Katrina a few more times. Katrina coughed up some blood and rolled over trying in vain to get away from the assault. "Stop what?" she laughed cruelly.

Riana dragged herself to a standing position, her knees bent severely and her back hunched over, trying to keep her stance wide and her center of gravity low so that she could stay on her feet. She held Elkorine loosely at her side, and her eyes were a vivid, clear violet that made Ambrai inhale sharply. As Riana glared at her threateningly, a river of blood poured from her nose. She looked as though she should be incapable of breathing, let alone standing.

"Stop… hurting… my… SISTER!!"

Ambrai took a half step backwards but stopped when she heard a low, deep growling sound. Looking over her shoulder she saw Xanthe standing behind her, barring his teeth at her and narrowing his eyes menacingly, on the ground beneath him lay her sword belt. Turning to face Riana again she smiled cruelly at her. "You couldn't hope to defeat me if you were healthy. Now you are a mess and look at you, thinking you stand a chance."

"You hit her again and I'll cut your heart out." Riana spat. Her head and body hurt so badly that she had gone numb to the pain. She could barely feel anything at all, so she took advantage of her situation and tried to look as menacing as she could. Standing up straight she strengthened her grip on Elkorine and took a steady step toward Ambrai. "Now give me my mother's amulet."

Ambrai looked surprised by Riana's sudden surge of strength, but at the mention of the amulet she sneered at her, twisting her face up into a nasty grimace. "NEVER!"

"Fine." Riana said as she focused her thoughts on the pain in her head, forcing herself to feel it again, forcing her body to accept the excruciating fire running back and forth across her mind.

She screamed in pain as she dropped to one knee, but she kept her eyes on Ambrai the whole time, focusing on her, thinking of nothing but her. The ground around them warped and bent, and Ambrai stumbled as her footing changed underneath her without warning, and then screamed out in pain as the reliquary hanging from Riana's neck began to glow brightly.

Ambrai dropped to her knees as her body refused to obey her commands. She screamed in pain and cursed at Riana with all of her strength, her acid-green eyes projecting pure hatred at the other elf. But suddenly they changed, softened, and looked at Riana pleadingly.

Riana looked into those green eyes and felt a connection; she knew it was Ambrai now, not the monster that lived in her head. She was lucid and clear now. Carelessly she wiped at the torrent of blood streaming from her nose as she looked at Ambrai.

"Please..." Ambrai's voice issued forth from the tortured figure. "Please do it now... I can't hold it back any longer..."

Without hesitation Riana lunged forward. Elkorine drove home, right between Ambrai's breasts. The blade effortlessly plunged through the magical chain mail, piercing her flesh, bone, and heart. A small gasp issued forth from Ambrai's lips as Riana's world went dark and the two of them bowled over onto the ground.

Ambrai smiled faintly as the world returned to normal around the pair, and her life's blood poured out onto the Plain of Sorrow. "Thank you." She said weakly as her eyes faded.

"NO!! REE!!!!" Katrina gasped as she crawled toward the two elves. Every muscle in her body hurt, she had several broken bones and her lungs burned with every breath, but she didn't care. She dragged herself to her sister and rolled her over onto her lap. Cradling Riana to her she ran her fingers through her sister's purple hair and cried.

"Hang in there Ree. We're fixing it now... Hang in there... Don't die on me Ree. I'll never forgive you if you die on me. C'mon Ree... Stay with me..."

Katrina was sobbing now, rocking back and forth as she clutched Riana's dying body to her chest. She looked up into the sky and screamed with all of her might, "Now damn you!!! Do it now!! She can't hold out any more! Start the transfer!! What the hell are you waiting for?!"

-23-

Riana came around slowly. Keeping her eyes closed against a soft light that seemed to surround her completely, she simply lay where she was and concentrated on the most exquisite feeling that she thought she had ever experienced in her entire life. Her head no longer hurt. She didn't know why, or even care. She was simply overjoyed that there was no more pain throbbing away behind her eyes. As she lay there thinking about what had happened between Ambrai, Katrina and herself, she came to the conclusion that she didn't give a damn if Katrina was her sister or not, she had shown up when she was needed most. That was all that Riana needed to know, or cared to know for the moment. She would have to tell her as much as soon as she finished enjoying the pleasant feeling of being totally free of pain.

As she concentrated on the feeling, she came to a startling realization; she could not feel her extremities, not her hands, her feet, her legs, arms, none of them. While panic threatened to overwhelm her she forced herself to be calm, to take stock of her situation. Tentatively she tried to open her eyes, but the lids would not obey her silent command. Panic reared up in her mind again until she realized she could hear something… A faint voice… no… several voices… and something else, something completely alien to her ears. Something that sounded almost like a musical instrument, playing a single note over and over again in a steady rhythm

………beep…………beep……………beep……………beep………

Focusing on the voices, she forced herself to listen to them in order to keep her mind from the panic state it was trying so hard to reach.

"Her brain waves are moving from delta to alpha. She almost went straight into beta, crested the needle a couple times and then brought herself under control. She has a strong will, that much is for sure," a tenor male voice said from somewhere across the room.

"Her cardiovascular system is now operating fully autonomously, BP is a steady one-twenty over eighty. Right on target." A confident female voice said from the other side of where Riana lay.

"Neural activity is nominal, nerve tissues appear to be taking well to the new spinal cord." This very nasal voice came from near the female's, and was almost certainly male. It sounded to Riana like a goblin talking through its nose, although what he actually said sounded like something a gnome might say.

"Cerebrospinal fluidic pressure is nominal, and fluids are circulating within predicted parameters." The female voice spoke again.

"She is listening to us," the tenor voice said with a note of surprise. "Look at these readings, hovering between Alpha and Beta states, and the computer says the audio receptors are fully functional and receiving our conversation."

"Her pulmonary system is running autonomously. Pressure is stable and air flow is well within specified parameters," the goblin-voice said.

"All of her systems seem to be functioning within parameters. Close her up and get ready to start booting up motor control sub-systems. Bart, please check the circuits in the inhibitor one more time, before we start with gross motor control." It was the female voice again.

"You've got it Gayle." Then a series of footsteps on a hard surface could be heard. "Oh! Hello sir!" The tenor, Bart, responded. He sounded surprised by the person entering the room.

Riana could hear a measured step approaching her, the foot falls sounded like those of a metal shod horse walking on a smooth stone lane. Click, click, click. The sound stopped and she could almost feel the presence of someone very close by, leaning over her, inspecting her. Her mind raced as she tried to imagine the scene around her. She was fighting with every fiber of her being to stay calm, but she was quickly loosing it, sliding into panic.

"What is her status?" The voice sounded like it was in her head the speaker was so close. It was a male voice, a deep baritone with a timbre to it that made Riana think of a dwarven melody sung around a camp fire on a warm summer night in the Forest of Brume. The voice simply dripped with confidence, and something else...

"She is awake sir." The female voice, Gayle, responded almost immediately. "We were just getting ready to start booting up her motor control sub-systems. Did you want to stay and watch?"

"Of course." The man's voice responded. This time it was slightly further away, as though he was still bent close to Riana's ear, but looking another direction.

A few more sharp footsteps as he moved away from her preceded him speaking again. "And send for Willhelmina. She should help things along a bit."

"She's all closed up Gayle." Came the Goblin's voice again. "Nanites are sealing the incision, aaaaannnnnnnddddd done!" There was a rustling of cloth for a moment before he spoke again. "All covered up."

"Thank you Wayne." Gayle said

"I still would rather have used less dramatic ears." The baritone man's voice said, "She looks... Like an elf."

"Technically sir, she IS an elf. We decided on that structure for her ears to help her with the transition. Our psychology team went rounds about them for weeks." Gayle responded. "We can still change them if we want to later; we have complete cont..."

"Ahem." Bart's interruption stopped the conversation abruptly. "She IS awake and listening to us, if I may remind you all. These concepts are completely foreign to her, and we should take care not to cause her undue stress. Inhibitor circuits all pass muster Gayle."

"Ah yes. Bartholomew, the consummate psychologist. Very well then. Get Willhelmina. I would like to say hello to our elf here," the as yet unnamed man said.

His voice rolled over Riana like a waterfall, soothing, crisp, full of purpose, and power. Her mind was racing, thinking about what was going on around her. Why couldn't she move? What was going on here? Who were all of these people around her and what were they talking about? They used words and language she had never heard before and had no idea what they meant. The missing pain in her head was being slowly replaced by panic, dread, and confusion.

"She's already been notified sir. She should be here momentarily." Gayle responded.

"Excellent. Thank you." The man said coolly.

Then came another new sound. The sound of bare feet padding very quickly along a stone floor. Someone lithe and strong taking large strides, almost leaps down a tunnel and into the room. Another person came to a halt near Riana, panting heavily.

"Did I miss it? Is she awake?" The new person's voice lilted through the air like a zephyr.

Riana would have cried out at the sound of that voice if she could have. She would have known it anywhere, in her sleep, or from the other side of a tavern common room filled to overflowing with inebriated dwarves. Katrina! It was Katrina's voice! The realization calmed her some. If Katrina was here then she was likely in good hands.

"Of course not Willhelmina. We would never begin without you. Whom else can we trust to keep our lovely Riana here calm in the face of so much?" It was the baritone voice again. His voice was silky smooth, but carried the sort of edge that was used to keep soldiers in line.

"Xavier, please don't talk like that. She'll be fine. She's smart. She can handle it." Willhelmina responded, her breathing coming under control after her apparent exertion in getting there.

"But of course." Xavier's amazing baritone voice responded. "But all the same, we would not do this without you present."

"Thank you Xavier." Willhelmina replied. Her voice was louder now, as though she were facing Riana while she spoke to the man across the room.

"Are we ready Gayle?" Xavier asked the other woman in the room.

"Just finished up the final diagnostics sequence now sir. Everything checks out, the inhibitor is online. We can go on your order sir." Gayle responded.

"Very well then." Xavier said smoothly, "Let our elf open her new eyes."

"Starting up motor control sub-systems now sir. System is responding to input." Gayle seemed excited about something as she spoke.

"Neural links are all green across the board. Inhibitor is functioning as anticipated." Wayne said.

"System registers continuity. Muscle control and tactile response should be coming on-line now." Bart said happily.

And suddenly, Riana's eyes snapped open.

-24-

The first thing she saw was the ceiling. The ceiling was white. A stark unblemished white that she had never seen before in her life. The finest silks in all of Kalijor could never be that bright, shining, white. Light seemed to emanate from everywhere and nowhere as she was unable to see any shadows but neither could she see any discernable source for the pure white light radiating throughout the space.

The next thing she saw was the face of a woman who looked slightly familiar. She had high cheeck bones and a small nose with full lips and sharp, green eyes that looked both loving and worried at once. Concentrating on where she had seen it before, it began to dawn on her. The ears were shorter, more like a human's, and her hair was black instead of platinum. The eyes were a different color, green rather than yellow, but her facial features were the same in almost every detail, and the look she was giving Riana spoke volumes.

"Kat?" Riana said tentatively, unsure how well her voice would work. It rang out crisp and true, as good as she had ever heard it sound.

The woman smiled down at her, tears forming at the corners of her eyes.

Riana felt a gentle pressure on her left hand and briefly looked down to see the woman squeezing it tightly. Her own strong, thin arms were almost shaking with nervous energy. Riana swept her eyes around the room quickly. There were four other people there.

Gayle, the only other woman there, stood behind some sort of counter with many colored lights playing off its surface and dancing in the air above it. Gayle looked to be of medium height, with sandy blond hair that was pulled back severely into a bun at the back of her head. She wore a white garment that fell to the floor, covering her arms and body completely except for a hint of something green beneath it at the collar. Her face was gaunt and serious and her dim grey eyes were partially concealed behind a pair of small round glasses.

Next to Gayle was what could only be described as a tall goblin. The man stood maybe four feet tall and had thin, wispy strands of hair floating around his head like a living halo. His face was unpleasant, with a distinct upturn to his nose, a large collection of wrinkles and pock marks and a flat, featureless expression that did nothing to add life to his cold, hazel eyes. He was also wearing a floor length, white garment that was closed up tightly around his neck, revealing nothing underneath. She was sure that was Wayne.

Bart, or Bartholomew, was a taller man with fair hair and skin, and a clear complexion. He was grinning from ear to ear from behind another

214

counter on the opposite side of the room from the others. He had icy blue eyes that warmed when you encountered his jovial, pleasant smile. He too was wearing the white frock that covered his arms and fell to the floor, but the front of his was fully open, revealing a pair of dark pants that shimmered like metal in the light of the room, and form fitting tunic of blazing red. She watched the strange fabric move over his skin for a moment before her eyes moved on to the last occupant of the room.

Standing at the foot of the bed was a tall man with dark hair and dark eyes that stood unmoving. His hands rested on top of a knurled wooden cane that looked like the branch from one of the great trees in Pandoria. The cane was planted on the floor in front of him and stood out in stark contrast to his over all appearance of cool, simple efficiency. His eyes were sharp, as were his facial features, although they were toned down a bit by the mustache and goatee that merged together on either side of his thin lips. He had a very intense look about him as he appeared to be appraising her in much the same way she was him. He was dressed in a dark colored jacket over pants of the same color. Both garments looked to be made of a heavy silk and had very neatly pressed lines that Riana had never seen the likes of before. Beneath his dark silk jacket was a much brighter white silk shirt threaded with what looked like strands of liquid gold. His look was intelligent, appraising, serious, and seemed to lack humor, even though his lips were beginning to curl up into something resembling a smile.

Riana's eyes fell back on the woman at her side, and scanned her briefly before returning to her face. Willhelmina was wearing some kind of tight black outfit that seemed to be made of the same material as Bart's shirt. Her exposed skin was shining with a layer of perspiration, as though she had just run a marathon, but the material of her clothing remained dry and did not cling to her body as a sweat-soaked garment would.

Looking back into her eyes, Riana forced herself to speak again. "Kat. Is it really you?"

The woman smiled warmly. It was an inviting and caring smile that Riana would have expected to see if she had just returned from a years-long journey, or perhaps a near-death experience?

"Yes Ree. It's me." She replied as a couple of stray tears made their way down her cheeks.

"What's going on Kat? Where are we? Who are all of these people? What happened to you? You look so different, so…human…" Riana's thoughts flooded out of her mouth all at once.

"One thing at a time Ree. How do you feel?" The woman asked, still grinning uncontrollably. She almost looked as though she was seeing Riana for the first time.

"How do I…?" Riana thought about the question for a moment as she squeezed the woman's hand in her own. Then she raised her other hand from the bed to put it to her head. She felt as though she was swimming in a vat of tree sap. "I feel alright I suppose. My arms feel a little heavy though. How long was I out Kat?"

As she spoke, the three people wearing white frocks sprung into action all at once. Gayle started moving the lights on her counter top around with her fingers and making thoughtful noises to herself as Wayne moved over to another, smaller structure near her and began doing the same. Bart began looking at an object he held in his hand and Riana realized that whatever it was was casting a show of lights onto his face as he looked at it intently.

"Does your head hurt at all Ree? Is the pain gone?" The woman next to her kept pushing for details.

"To be honest I don't think it has ever felt better." Riana said with a touch of excitement that belied her concerns about what was going on with all of these people.

"Neuro-kinetics look good, well within parameters." Gayle announced to no one in particular as she continued manipulating the lights floating above her counter.

"Muscle response is on target across the board. All motor control sub-systems are operating within specs." Wayne announced from his smaller counter as he looked up towards Bart on the opposite side of the room.

"I think it's the inhibitor." Bart said almost under his breath, but loudly enough for everyone to make it out in the small room. "I am going to dial it down five percent and see if that does anything."

Bart then touched the object in his hand and dragged his finger across it a bit and Riana instantly felt her muscles begin to work better. Staring at her arm, she moved it around in a circle, stretching it out and back again and clenching and unclenching her fist a few times. Then she looked up at Bart, her eyes wide with concern and interest. Finally she turned her attention back to the woman at her side and locked eyes with her.

"You aren't really Kat are you? Who are you? What is going on here? Why are these people talking about me like I am some kind of specimen being dissected?" Her voice began to sound panicked as the fear was edging back into her mind. Confusion about what was going on and how that man could have such an effect on her body started to cloud her rational mind.

"We'll tell you everything Ree. Just stay calm. My name is Kat. But that is short for Willhelmina, not Katrina. I am the same person you have known for your entire life, please trust me on this. These people are here to help you recover from your break-down." The woman said in her lilting, smooth voice.

"Kat... Willhelmina... Break-down? What break-down? The last thing I remember is stabbing Ambrai through the chest with Elkorine and then passing out. I thought I was dying. What are you talking about?"

Willhelmina looked at her with compassion as she spoke again. "Ree. Do you remember what the Druids said about your mind?"

"Yes." Riana said immediately. "They said something was wrong, and they didn't know what it was, but that it could possibly kill me if it continued to get worse. And it WAS getting worse. A LOT worse. I thought it was all over when I passed out." Reflexively her free hand went to her face and wiped at the spot on her lip where she was so used to finding a river of blood from her nose. She looked at it for a moment when it came away clean before locking eyes with Willhelmina again. "What happened?"

"Ree this isn't going to be easy for me to explain, or for you to understand. But I feel that I owe you the truth. You deserve to know what Kalijor is really about." Willhelmina went on, a strange look playing across her face as she spoke, "Kalijor isn't real Ree. It's a fake, simulated world that exists only inside a powerful, thinking machine called a computer."

Riana looked at Willhelmina blankly for a long moment, blinking deep violet eyes. "Not real? Kat what are you talking about? We have lived there our whole lives! How could it not be real?"

Willhelmina's expression became hard to read then, as though she was wracking her mind, trying to think of a better way to explain something to a child. "Yes Ree, you did grow up there. You have in fact spent your entire life in Kalijor up to this point."

"Are you saying I am not real? That I am some phantom from a dream world?" Riana's voice was uncertain, her mind was heading in several directions at once and a mixture of emotions was playing across her face as she spoke. "I'm dead aren't I? This is all some bizarre hallucination."

"No Ree. You are very real, and very much alive. But yes, you are from a dream world of sorts." Willhelmina looked as though she wasn't sure if she was helping things or making them worse.

"So I am a phantom from a dream world? Kat what are you talking about?" Riana sighed the words with exasperation.

"Miss Thorindal. If I may?" The silky, baritone voice interrupted the two women and Riana looked up to see the dark haired man in the dark silk outfit smiling faintly as he spoke. She blinked at him a couple times and then nodded.

"Thank you," he said and then pointed to Gayle who manipulated more of the colored lights on her counter. A rectangle of light appeared in the air next to the man's head and he inclined his head toward it slightly.

Within the rectangle of light Riana could see the city of Rathalon from a bird's-eye perspective. Her violet eyes lit up at the sight of it. "A scrying device!" She exclaimed as she turned her gaze back and forth between Gayle and the shimmering image of Rathalon floating in mid-air.

"Not exactly Miss Thorindal." The man continued. "That is a computer. A machine that allows us to perform complicated tasks very quickly and efficiently. Right now it is showing us an image from within the world you know as Kalijor." He nodded toward Gayle slightly then and as she manipulated another mote of light, the image of Rathalon shifted and blurred, eventually resolving into an image of the interior of Riana and Katrina's home, but it looked slightly different. It looked more like Riana remembered it being when they were little girls. Suddenly she saw herself as a youngling chasing Katrina through the house with a wooden sword.

"These are events that were recorded so that we could replay them and examine what we saw in order to better understand you." The man said calmly.

"Understand me?" Riana repeated. "What about me? How much of my life have you recorded like that?"

"All of it Miss Thorindal. We have recorded every moment of your life. From the very moment that we realized your uniqueness until the very moment that you left that world and entered ours." As he spoke the image moved into a blurred fast forward display of her life. She watched as it showed recognizable snippets and pieces. Memories long since dormant in her mind came flooding back to her. Within a few minutes the image had sped through her entire thirty years and finally froze on an image of her body slumped over on top of Ambrai's lifeless form, their blood mingling in a pool beneath them on the shores of the Dead Sea.

"As to why we would do this…" The man spoke as though she should already have accepted everything he was telling her. "That answer is something we still seek. You see Miss Thorindal, in all of Kalijor you were unique. In a world created by us for our own purposes, you came to be in an impossible set of circumstances. Thus far we have been unable to replicate, or even understand what happened."

"What do you mean?" She asked in a confused tone.

"Let me frame it for you this way Miss Thorindal. Nearly everyone in Kalijor is a puppet. They are very lifelike puppets to be sure. But never the less, they are all puppets that we have designed and breathed pseudo-life into through the computer that houses Kalijor. We tell these puppets how to behave. How to react. We tell them what they do for a living, where they live and what their dreams, aspirations, and problems are. There is nothing any of them are capable of doing, that we have not taught them, and told them to do."

"Puppets? But how? Why would you do something like that?" Her eyes were clouding as she tried to absorb the information. Why would someone say something like this? Why would they make up a story like this?

"The answer to that question is at once quite simple, and extremely complex Miss Thorindal. As to how we have done it, that is the simple part, we have done it through these thinking machines, these computers. We tell them our desires and they create them for us. As to why we have done this, as I said earlier, we created Kalijor and everyone in it simply for our entertainment. It is an interactive simulation that allows us to enter it and interact with it. In these simulated worlds we can do whatever we want. We can live wherever we want and in a lifestyle that may not otherwise be possible. We, Miss Thorindal, are in the business of creating people's fantasies for them, and letting them experience them in such a way that their minds and bodies think them as real as the real world."

Riana gaped at the man. She had no idea what to make of this. After that statement she was leaning toward the entire situation being a hallucination she was having while she lay dying on the shores of the Dead Sea. After a moment she decided to play out the fantasy and see where it led. With a note of sarcasm in her voice she asked, "so my whole purpose for existing was to amuse someone else? Someone who wasn't even a part of my world?"

"That is more or less the case, yes. You see Miss Thorindal, we have a myriad of these virtual worlds, each of which is a different setting. A different environment with different rules and themes. Your world in particular is one that has been evolving for more than one-hundred years." He sounded proud of himself with that last statement.

"But Kalijor has a history. It is millennia old. There are stories, fables, history scrolls. My MOTHER is more than one-hundred years old!" Her voice still carried her sarcastic tone and inability to accept what she was hearing as the truth. Briefly she looked at Willhelmina who was still at her side, squeezing her hand firmly and nodding at her in agreement with the man.

"As I said Miss Thorindal, we built your world. As part of that somewhat monumental task we also designed its history, its past, its fables, and lore. We wove them all together with the skill of a conductor leading a talented orchestra. Every inhabitant of Kalijor is a part of the tapestry. As the world continues to thrive, its inhabitants mature, marry, have children, grow old, and die, just like in the real world. This process makes everything easier to accept for those within it, as well as keeping the history of the world in motion. Simply put, it makes the world more believable for those of us that visit it."

"So none of it is real? Not the great war? The fall of the elven empire? MY MOTHERS?!" Her voice was somewhere between hysterical and angry.

"That really depends upon your perception of 'real' Miss Thorindal. From your perspective it was and is very real. You grew up in that world and have a lifetime of memories and experiences, all from that world. It is as real as you need it to be. But the fact remains that it is an artificial world created by us for our own amusement.

"Then why am I here? HOW am I here if I never really existed in your world? If I am nothing more than a phantom puppet for your 'kompooter' to manipulate, how am I here now having this conversation with you?" Her face contorted as though she were trying to cry, but no tears came as she fought against the thought that her entire world, indeed her entire life, had been someone else's dream.

"That is the magic question Miss Thorindal. Approximately seven years ago, you were born to Ezrina Reyals-Thorindal in the Cohai Observatory, very much outside our designs for the world of Kalijor."

"You mean I wasn't part of your tapestry? Your grand scheme?" She seemed somehow slightly relieved by this thought.

"Indeed not." He said as he raised an eyebrow at her curiously. "In point of fact, your birth into the world caused a ripple of chain reactions that began tearing the world apart. It took us months to smooth it all out and get things back on track. By the time we had things working smoothly again, something even stranger had happened with you." He paused for a moment, looking deeply into Riana's eyes before continuing.

"By the time we got back around to you, there had been another anomalous event in the system. Somehow the programs that governed your behavior had been altered from the system's normally prescribed patterns. Your mind had somehow become more complex than it should have been able to and as we monitored you over time, your mind became increasingly more and more complex. Eventually you became a fully sentient, feeling, thinking consciousness. In simplest terms, you came alive and began thinking for yourself."

"This happened two and a half years after you were born, and as soon as we realized what was going on we decided to let you grow up in the system and see what happened. But in order to monitor your progress more closely, we inserted an agent into the system to stay as close to you as possible." He inclined his head almost imperceptibly in Willhelmina's direction then.

Riana turned her eyes on Willhelmina's green liquid pools, and Willhelmina simply offered her a comforting smile and a nod.

"We inserted Willhelmina into the system and changed a lot of things in order to have the world accept her as your twin sister. That way she could constantly stay close to you and report back to us on anything unusual."

"So what happened? How did I get out here? If I was never real, how do I have a body in your world?"

"As you became more and more self aware, and expanded your consciousness and knowledge, the system became less and less able to cope with you. You were simply growing too quickly and becoming much too complex for it to handle. So as you began to stress the system it began to break down around you. You perceived this breakdown as pain, localized almost entirely in your head, the most complicated part of your program. Soon we realized that eventually the system would break down entirely if we allowed you to stay in Kalijor." He paused briefly, allowing her to think on what he had said for a moment before continuing.

"We conceived a plan to create a new computer that was significantly more complex, and transfer your consciousness to that computer so that we could continue to monitor your development. But before we began, Willhelmina came to me with an interesting proposal. She suggested that we build you a body, rather than just a shell. So that you could move around in our world, experience things, and continue to develop."

Riana's eyes locked on Willhelmina's again as she started to realize that this was probably not some kind of dieing hallucination. An unspoken understanding formed between them. These people were going to lock her mind in a box, and Willhelmina had convinced them to give her a body instead. "So you can just conjure up new bodies for people at will?" She asked tentatively, a touch of fear edging into her voice now.

"On the contrary Miss Thorindal. We painstakingly crafted your body using some of the most advanced technology available. It is one of a kind, unique in the entire universe, just as you yourself are. The perfect vessel for the most unique mind ever born."

"You built this body? Built it from what? Am I not flesh and blood? What am I?" She looked at her arms and except for the lack of tattoos, she appeared totally normal.

"All in good time Miss Thorindal. For now, you have had a busy first day with us and I am sure you would like some time to rest and think on things. I will take my leave and see to it that you get some time alone." At that he swept his eyes across the room and jerked his head slightly towards the corner.

Almost instantly the other people in the room seemed to spring into action. Gayle and Wayne manipulated some of the lights over their counters causing them to go dark. Then they and Bart moved to the corner of the room where a door that was blended seamlessly into the wall silently slid out of the way and they filed out.

Willhelmina began to get up but Riana squeezed her hand more tightly around Willhelmina's and said, "Please stay for a while."

Willhelmina looked briefly toward the man who nodded at her, smiled briefly, and then said, "Very well. I'll leave you two ladies alone. Willhelmina if you could please make yourself available to help out with getting Miss Thorindal acclimated over the next few weeks?"

Willhelmina looked at him and smiled. "Of course, Xavier!"

"Then I will leave you to it. Good evening ladies." Inclining his head slightly towards them, he then turned around and walked out of the room the same way the others had gone; his cane making a click, click, click noise on the floor as he disappeared from the room leaving Riana and Willhelmina alone.

-25-

After the room was empty Riana stared at Willhelmina for a long moment. Their eyes were locked as unspoken words passed between them. Finally Riana broke the silence with a question.

"So this is all true then? I haven't just died and dreamt this all up?" She asked, still trying to make sense of what was happening.

"It is Ree. Every word of it." Then she started crying.

"What's the matter?" Riana was bewildered by Willhelmina's sudden outburst.

"I'm just happy you're ok. They said you may not survive the transfer. Oh Ree… I was so worried. And I have to apologize…" She was almost unintelligible she was speaking so quickly.

"Apologize for what?" Riana asked, squeezing Willhelmina's hand.

"For lying to you all these years. I wanted to tell you all of this so long ago, but they said you wouldn't be able to accept it." She was sobbing now, almost doubled over in the chair, her hand squeezing Riana's like a vice.

"Kat, it's ok. I'm not certain I do accept it." Riana looked around the stark white room, "This is all pretty strange."

Willhelmina stopped short, tears rolling down her cheeks as she looked into Riana's eyes for a moment, then leapt out of the chair and threw her arms around Riana, squeezing her tightly. Riana returned the embrace with equal vigor.

"Oh Ree. I am so happy you made it." She sniffled and wiped away her tears with the back of her hand.

"Me too. Considering the alternative." Riana replied. Then she pulled away, holding Willhelmina by the shoulders and looking into her eyes again. "Is it ok if we talk about all of this later? I think I need some time to think."

"Of course. I have a room just down the hall and if you need me you can just press this here." She pointed to a large red rectangle on the wall at the head of the bed. "Do you need any food or anything?"

"No I think I'm alright. Thank you."

"Ok, get some rest then and we'll talk more tomorrow." Willhelmina hugged her again and then backed out the door in the corner as if she was scared Riana would disappear if she lost sight of her.

As the door slid silently closed and sealed her alone into the room Riana took a moment to look around in more detail. The room was white from floor to ceiling and all of its surfaces seemed to be as smooth as glass, with the same glossy shine. The edges of the floor curved seamlessly into the walls with soft arcs. The curve was mirrored where the crown molding would have been in their house in Rathalon. There were no harsh angles anywhere in the room that she could see. She still couldn't tell where the light was coming from either, it just seemed to be everywhere at once. As she looked down she saw that the bed she was on was small but seemed well made and fit the room nicely. To one side was the large counter where Gayle had been standing and manipulating her lights and on the other side of the bed was the smaller pedestal that had also been covered with a series of dancing lights but was now blank.

Her mind was reeling from everything she had seen and heard in the last hour. She had no idea what to make of her situation and was still not convinced that any of it was actually happening. As she thought about the ramifications, she felt a familiar pressure building up inside her bladder and suddenly realized she had no idea where the facilities were in here.

"All this tinkering and super-magic; building bodies and glowing rooms and I still have to pee. I guess they can't fix everything after all." Somehow the thought comforted her as she spoke it aloud to the room, but it still didn't get her anywhere closer to where she could take care of the problem.

"Nobody bothered to tell me where the damn toilet is," she said as she swung her feet over the edge of the bed. When she looked up from the bed she saw a door in the corner sliding soundlessly open. A light came on in the small room to reveal a sink, mirror, toilet, and a small booth with some pipes sticking out of one of its walls that looked a lot like the magically fed shower they had had in Rathalon. It was all so familiar to her, yet at the same time so very alien. Everything she knew was suddenly set on its edge by this new reality that had been foisted upon her.

She only hesitated for an instant before pushing herself off the bed with a heavy sigh to go take care of her business.

The floor felt exactly the way it looked, perfectly smooth, although the fact that it was warm to the touch came as a pleasant surprise to her bare feet. Tentatively she put some weight on her legs, testing them out. When they held up she put her full weight on them and stood there for a short time, testing her balance. After a moment or two of shifting her weight back and forth, she made her way across the room to the open door. After relieving herself in what appeared to be the appropriate receptacle she performed a quick check of her body parts, reassuring herself that they all appeared to be accounted for and at least looked normal. Standing up and looking at herself in the mirror, seeing her reflection for the first time since she couldn't remember when, she began an appraisal of herself and her situation.

Her dark purple hair was something of a mess, falling down around her shoulders to the middle of her back, it looked as though it hadn't been brushed in ages. Her violet eyes were bright and vivid, and her long tapered ears, pointed upwards in general interest. Around her neck was a thin metal band that did not appear to have any seams or clasps on it. She moved closer to the mirror and turned sideways. Running her fingers through her hair and along her scalp, searching for any signs that she was anything other than what she appeared to be. She could find nothing, save the absence of her tattoos, which would make her think anything was different about her body. Her skin was still soft and supple and if anything her muscle tone seemed much better than she remembered it being.

As she poked and prodded herself in front of the mirror a strange feeling of anger began to roil around in her. Everything seemed to be in place. Every single hair accounted for. Her ears, her eyes, the color of her skin and hair, every little detail. In a desperate gambit she closed her eyes and concentrated on the simplest of her fire incantations. Her arm raised in front of her, hand open and palm up to the ceiling. She pushed her mind with all the willpower she could muster. Envisioning the flame, willing it into existence, trying to force it to appear there where she wanted it, no not wanted, needed it to be. Opening her eyes after what she was sure was several long minutes of intense concentration she was greeted by the sight of her own empty palm.

"Dammit!" She cursed as she drove her empty hand down into the sink basin. The result was a loud thud and nothing more. She looked down at her hand and rolled it over to look at the back of it. Not a mark showed on its surface. Nor was there any hint of pain that she could feel from the impact. Eyeing her hand suspiciously she curled her slender fingers into a tight fist and smashed them down into the basin again with all of her strength. This time the sound of the impact reverberated throughout the small room, sounding like a metal tub being severely beaten with a heavy stick. Again, she felt no pain from the impact. She could feel it. She knew she was hitting it hard and could feel that as well, but there was no pain from it at all and still no sign of damage to her hand as she inspected it once more.

Finally she smashed her fists into the mirror, shattering it into thousands of tiny glass shards that showered down around her like crystallized rain drops. She was covered with the tiny, dagger-like fragments in an instant. Driving her fists into the mirror frame repeatedly she made sure there was no amount of the reflective surface still in its frame then looked down into the sink where the majority of the shards had fallen. Her vision clouded suddenly with fear and renewed anger as she saw herself reflected in the hundreds upon hundreds of tiny mirrors. The emotions welled up inside of her as she raised her hands again and brought them down on the captive fragments repeatedly, pounding them to a fine dust with blow after blow as she sobbed uncontrollably.

When her vision cleared she was on her knees with her arms draped over the counter and dangling in the sink basin which was now slightly deformed and bore a thin coating of shiny silver dust. Raising her hands out of the sink she looked at them hopefully but again found they were unscathed by the outburst. Sobs escaped her throat as the thought of what was going on began to finally sink into her clouded mind. When she raised her hand to wipe away her tears she was horrified when she felt no moisture there at all. Instantly both hands flew to her face and she felt frantically for the rivers she knew should be there but again they came back dry, sparkling slightly from the remains of silver mirror dusting them.

As the realization of what she had become began to sink into her she slumped over backwards against the wall and curled up into a tight ball with her arms wrapped around her knees. "They turned me into a golem... I'm nothing more than a monster now..."

"Wake up sleepy!" Willhelmina beamed as she slid past the still-opening door into Riana's room. She was now dressed in a rather unflattering one piece jump suit in a neutral grey color and carried a small container of some kind. Her raven hair was pulled back in a simple ponytail behind her head and her green eyes were bright and alert as she smiled broadly at her friend who was still sitting on the floor in the bathroom, staring blearily at the overly cheerful woman.

Riana looked at Willhelmina with no small amount of contempt and ran her fingers through her shock of matted purple hair as she considered whether choking the life out of her would help things at all. "Hello." She finally managed to get out.

Willhelmina stopped suddenly when she saw the mess that Riana was sitting in. Still covered with the fine, glistening dust. She looked as though she hadn't slept at all and was still very upset about whatever had kept her up. "Oh my god! What happened in here?!"

"I…" Riana looked around herself at the few shiny pieces of glass that had survived her fit by falling to the floor and lay reflecting the room's light up from the floor into her tired, violet eyes. "I'm not even human… At least you get to be human. I'm just some unfeeling golem…"

"Oh Ree!" Willhelmina hastily set the container on the bed and moved toward her friend. Kneeling down beside Riana, she set her hands on the other woman's shoulders. "Ree you aren't a golem. You are more human than you might actually think."

"Really?!" Riana screeched suddenly as she shrugged off Willhelmina's hands, knocking the other woman onto her haunches. Riana quickly snatched up a knife-sized shard of glass from the floor and jammed it into her other hand with enough force that it should have passed clean through. But instead, the glass merely cut a shallow gouge across her palm before shattering into more tiny pieces. Jamming her palm into Willhelmina's face it showed a shallow, inch-long scratch that was barely even red. As she looked on the scratch quickly turned white then faded away entirely and a moment later there was no sign of there ever having been any form of damage at all. "So what do you call that?" Riana finished loudly.

"Ree your body is made out of some materials that are different from normal flash and blood." Willhelmina stammered out defensively, her mind reeled as she tried to find some way to defuse the situation.

"Oh really? You think?" Riana shouted back as she stood up and ground her bare foot into the glass shards littering the floor of the room. Again there was no sign of any damage to her foot.

"Ree it's all they could do. They said they had to make your body that way so it could properly interface with your mind."

"Yeah, just like using a crystal in the heart of a golem! The proper vessel for the magic. So what is it now? Am I supposed to sally forth and destroy your enemies? Or just do your heavy lifting ad infinium?!"

"Riana please! I'm trying to help you. I would never do anything like that to you. And it hurts me to know that you would think I would." Willhelmina deftly sprung to her feet and wheeled around as she spoke, headed for the door. "There's food in that tray, help yourself and I'll come back after you've had a chance to calm down a bit."

Just before she reached the door Riana panicked. Willhelmina was the only person here she even remotely recognized and she suddenly couldn't face the thought of being alone any more. "Wait! Please. I'm…"

Willhelmina stopped short of the door and waited, her hands poised on her hips and her back still to her friend. "You're…"

"I'm… scared… I'm really scared…" Riana wrapped her arms around her chest tightly, wanting desperately for something to make sense to her.

"Is that all? You're just scared?" Willhelmina prompted without moving.

Riana looked suddenly embarrassed, her ears drooping down low in shame. She knew this routine well, Katrina had done this to her more times than she could count when they were growing up and a twinge of recognition ran through her with a shiver, making her feel slightly more comfortable. "Alright... I'm sorry Kat. It's just..."

Willhelmina's whole demeanor changed in an instant. Suddenly she whirled around again and was at Riana's side, guiding her deftly to the bed where she sat her down on the edge and hugged her tightly. "It's ok Ree. I'm here for you. I'm not going anywhere. We'll get through this together. Now come on. Let's get you ready for the day, they have a lot planned for you."

"Planned? Like what?" Riana asked, still more than a little upset.

"Tests and so forth. To see how you are adjusting to your new body. I'm not sure what all is planned but I will be there with you throughout so don't worry." Willhelmina reached for the small tray she had carried in and pried off the semi-transparent lid to reveal a plate of scrambled eggs, bacon, and toast, all steaming hot.

Riana's mouth began watering almost uncontrollably at the smell of the food and she looked up at Willhelmina hopefully.

"Go ahead, it's for you." She grinned even wider.

"Thanks!" Riana beamed, feeling much more at ease suddenly as she snapped up the fork and dove into the food. "So can I ask you some questions?"

"Sure." Willhelmina said, smiling. "I'll answer whatever I can but some stuff you may need to ask the techs as I'm not really familiar with a lot of the technical details."

"What is your part in all of this?" Riana asked around a mouthful of bacon.

Willhelmina sighed heavily and her eyes lost focus for a moment as though she was reliving some painful memory, then she focused back on Riana and spoke, "They brought me here to be as close to you as possible. To watch you and try and guide you."

Riana stared at her with an unsure look on her face. "Guide me toward what?"

"I'm not exactly sure how it works, but they kept saying you needed to make certain decisions in order to really achieve true sentience, and then in order to prove that you really were sentient." Willhelmina's eyes glazed over a bit as she talked about it, as though she were simply regurgitating something someone else had said to her.

"So they were manipulating me? Through you?" Riana looked more than a little disgusted at the prospect, some of her familiar fire crept back into her voice and she started working her hand around the fork, squeezing it roughly.

"Not so much manipulating really, at least not the way they described it. They said that you would just need a nudge every once in a while." She was obviously trying to defuse the situation and wasn't very clear on what their intentions had been to begin with.

238

"So. You have been... Somehow inside Kalijor... This dream world... For what? Twenty years? Please don't be offended but you're human right?" Riana swallowed some eggs and seemed to consciously reign in her temper. She wasn't sure she trusted this person yet but of all of them, Willhelmina would be the most likely for her to trust, she seemed so much like her sister despite the fact that she looked so different.

"Of course I'm human silly!" Willhelmina's eyes brightened up then, happy to be on a new subject. "We all are!"

"Even that little Wayne person? He looks like just about every goblin I have ever seen." Riana's eyes were wide with a bit of surprise, thinking of Wayne as human.

"Oh my GOD!" Willhelmina exploded into laughter. "I never really thought about it before, but you're right. He DOES look like a goblin!" She continued laughing for a moment before, trying to put on a straight face again. "Really though. He is human too. Everyone is!"

"Everyone? There are no elves? Or dwarves?" Riana knitted her brow in thought as she said it.

"No. All human. Most of the creatures and races in Kalijor are fictional. Some of them are described in our ancient mythology. Some are just made up by artists."

"I see." Riana's face turned a bit sad.

"What's the matter Ree?" Willhelmina looked upset at Riana's reaction.

"Well. If everyone is human, and the elves and the dwarves and everything else that I know is all made up, what is there for me here? Who am I?" Her violet eyes were clouded with confusion and her long, pointed ears drooped down in sadness.

"Oh Ree. You are who you always were. All any of us can do is try and make our way using what we have." She smiled a caring smile.

"I suppose you're right. So uh... how did they do this?" Riana said looking back into Willhelmina's eyes again.

"Which part? It was a pretty involved process. Nothing like it has ever been done before."

"Well let's start with this body. How did they build a body? What am I made of?" Riana held up her bare arms again, bending and flexing her joints, making fists with her hands and then opening them up again and fanning out her fingers a few times. "I don't feel any different." She paused for a moment as she wiped some of the fine silver dust off of her hand, "Until I hit something that is..."

"I'm not sure what materials they used to create your body really. I know you have a metal skeleton and some kind of new material that they won't tell me about was used in your muscles." Willhelmina was clearly not fully aware of what had been done to create Riana's new body. But she was trying to remember the things she had heard about it.

240

"So my body is mechanical? Like some sort of gnomish contraption?" Riana balked at the prospect, screwing up her face as she looked at her arms more closely. "I still have flesh, and there is blood in my veins. I can feel it."

"Yeah, that's the point Ree. You still have all of the normal things a person has. Real skin, a real mind. You still need to eat and sleep and…" She nodded toward the bathroom in the corner, "You know…" A sheepish grin formed on her face and again Riana was reminded of her time growing up with Kat in Rathalon.

"Metal bones…" Riana said to herself as she inspected her knuckles, stretching and distending the skin on her hand in different ways as though she was trying to see though it.

"Technically you are a cybernetic organism. It's like a…" She seemed to be searching for some example that she could use in order to make sense. "Well when you take a person and they get hurt… Or… they want to…" Again she seemed to be having trouble until finally she looked up and said, "A fusion of living and artificial components, all controlled by a living mind." Willhelmina said the words as though she was repeating them verbatim from an encyclopedia.

Again Riana recognized her sister in Willhelmina. Her mannerisms and quirks all seemed to be whole and in tact in this person sitting before her. "Are there many 'syboorneetik' organisms in this world?" Riana asked, looking up from her hand at Willhelmina.

"Lots! Most are people who for one reason or another have had parts of their body replaced by artificial pieces."

Riana looked confused at that statement. "Why would they do that?"

Willhelmina smiled. "Well some do it because they are replacing parts that were lost in accidents. Others do it because they want or need to be stronger, or faster. Soldiers often get enhancements in order to be better soldiers. Still other people do it just because they think it's cool."

"Cybernetics make people cold?" Riana raised an eyebrow. "I don't feel cold."

Willhelmina laughed out loud at the comment. "Not cold Ree. Cool. It means... Neat. Trendy. Interesting."

"I see." Riana nodded then looked down at her body. Covered in a thin white shirt that clung to her body flatteringly. Putting her hands to her stomach she squeezed and kneaded her body in different places, her hands roving around, testing every spot they encountered. "Cool." She repeated absently as she continued her inspection.

"What do you think?" Willhelmina asked her after a few minutes of silence.

"It looks and feels just like my body always has." Riana shrugged absently. "Except my tattoos are gone."

"They didn't have time to have them done, and we weren't sure if you would want them or not. There were a lot of technical problems toward the end there, and they were focused on those. We can have them done later if you want." Willhelmina said as Riana shifted her inspection from her body to the room around her.

"What kind of problems?" She asked as her eyes roved around the room.

"You would have to ask the technicians for details. They said something about your brain tissue not interfacing with your nervous system or something." Willhelmina shrugged nonchalantly as she finished.

"My brain?" Riana repeated, massaging her temples slightly as though she could feel the grey matter on the other side.

"Yeah, although technically it's MY brain."

"What do you mean YOUR brain?" Riana looked more confused than ever.

"They cloned it from my own brain tissues. Made an exact copy of my brain so that you could have one of your own. Of course they didn't fill it with anything until they removed you from Kalijor and put you into it. If you think about it though, we really are related. Twins even, in all the aspects that count. Anyway it's my gift to you. Besides, I have one of my own to use." Willhelmina grinned widely, not even sure if Riana understood half of what she was saying.

"So, what do you think?"

"It's just like I remember it. Except for this thing." Riana replied as she held her hair back with one hand and touched the metal band gingerly. "You said my brain was real living tissue?"

"Yes." Willhelmina replied. "I'm not sure what that metal band is. You'll have to ask one of the techs."

"I understand that final surgery to install your brain in your body is what was holding things up. We had planned on transferring you into it much sooner, but things weren't ready until the very last possible moment." Willhelmina's face was serious now as she looked at Riana. "We nearly lost you forever there. You were fading fast."

Riana looked confused. "Fading? What do you mean?"

"You really were dying Ree. The computer that runs Kalijor couldn't contain your mind any longer. The whole thing was breaking down. The system was designed to correct any problems that disrupted its normal operation, and your consciousness was a pretty big disruption. So basically it was trying to delete you from the program. That is where your headaches were coming from. It was trying to root you out like your body would a cold or flu virus."

Riana had a blank expression on her face as she looked at Willhelmina. "Uh huh." She finally managed. "So. Now I am here. What do we do? And where is 'here' anyway?"

Willhelmina's face brightened up a bit. "Well. The techs will all want to spend some time with you. Probably ask you a lot of questions and do a lot of physical examinations to see how you're doing. But around all of that I am sure we can find something for you to do." Then she smiled a devilish smile. "And as to WHERE you are. Check this out." She then moved back across the larger room to the head of the bed. When she got there she touched a rectangle on the wall behind the bed. The panel lit up brightly and Willhelmina touched a few of the different colored lights.

Riana gasped as a portion of the wall slid away, revealing a window that looked out on a black void that was speckled with multi colored motes of light twinkling away in the distance. In the center of the window was a beautiful blue-green orb with white swirls and patches around its surface. The orb hung there in the black emptiness, the white wisps slowly changing and drifting across its surface.

Without realizing it, Riana had moved across the room and was standing mere inches from the window, staring in awe at the sight before her. The vastness of the empty, black space was inconceivable, broken only by the tiny sparks of light, and the exquisite beauty of the blue-green orb.

"Wha…" Riana stammered. "What is that?"

"That." Willhelmina said, drawing up next to Riana and looking out the window alongside her. "Is Earth. The cradle of the human race. Our home-world."

-27-

The next few months passed in a blur. She saw the four people from that first day in her room often. Wayne and Gayle usually ran her through her paces in the gym. She was asked to lift weights in increasing amounts, and run around a circular track for hours on end. She swam innumerable miles in a small pool with a current in it that kept her in the same place no matter how hard she pushed herself. She learned that the collar around her neck was an inhibitor used to keep her body under control while she grew used to its strength. At one point, she lifted two stacks of thick metal weights joined together by a metal bar with such ease that a whole group of onlookers was shocked into silence. Later they told her that the weights had totaled more that five-thousand pounds.

Bart on the other hand, would sit her down in a comfortable chair and talk to her for hours on end about her feelings, desires, wants, needs, and expectations for the future. He would ask her thousands of questions about how she felt, what her plans were, what she wanted out of life, how her mother had treated her when she was young (as if they hadn't recorded every moment of her childhood), and a myriad of other, broad, philosophical, and infinitely more personal questions.

She spent countless hours with Willhelmina as well. Those hours always seemed to fly by in an instant, before it was back to being poked, prodded, and quizzed by people in white 'lab coats'. Thanks to her time with Willhelmina, Riana had learned some of the basic functions of the computers in the facility and was quickly catching on to some of the peculiarities of the people's speech.

Using the computers she also saw some of humanities less glorious achievements. Wars. Weapons. Killings. It was all so very familiar to her in a strange way. They had patterned their fantasy worlds after their real one and they all seemed predisposed to hurting one another.

She had begun learning about the history of the human race in this new world, about their rise from the animal kingdom thousands of years ago and their crossing of the Earth's great, blue oceans for the first time. Learning the power of flight! Leaving their planet for the first time. Building homes on some of the other planets in their 'solar system' and their subsequent expansion out into other near-by regions of space. She learned that the facility she now called home was a 'space station' positioned in something called a Lagrange point, which was a point in space where two bodies' gravitational forces cancelled one another out. This particular Lagrange point was located between the Earth and its solitary moon, which Willhelmina had taken her to a large view port in the station to see. A great grey mass; smaller than the Earth and pockmarked with craters. It had numerous great domed structures that twinkled brightly with lights in the darkness of space.

Willhelmina explained that when the population of the Earth had grown to the point that it was no longer capable of supporting more people, they had struck out and built cities on the moon. Before too long they had similarly colonized the next closest planet, a beautiful red orb called Mars. Over a few hundred years they had pushed further and further out into their solar system, colonizing some of the other planet's moons and building space stations to collect and process raw materials from wherever they could find them. Eventually the inevitable happened and they started pushing even further beyond the Earth and sending ships out of their solar system, into other regions of space.

Trillions of human beings now populated thousands of planets, moons and space stations in and around their solar system. Technology had quickly been developed to allow them to communicate instantly across the vast distances between worlds. As was typical, they quickly began using the communications medium for more than just speaking to one another, adapting it into a form of relaxation that had been common since the early twenty-first century, video games. Over the course of a few decades the games had become a source of interest to the corporations and several branches were now focused entirely on their design, production, and maintenance. The most successful of these organizations was one calling itself Solidarity Online; which owned and operated this facility, the computers that ran Kalijor along with hundreds of other, similar game worlds, and had built Riana's body.

Xavier was another story however, as he would stop by from time to time and watch her going through her paces with a faint smile on his lips. One evening he stopped by her room unexpectedly. "Ms. Thorindal." His baritone voice slid over her like a fine silk robe from the other side of the door to her room.

"Xavier. Nice to see you. What can I do for you?" She said cheerfully as she stepped aside and waved him into her apartment. It was a nice arrangement with a bed room, a bathroom, a small kitchenette and living room space. It wasn't fancy but it was private and allowed her to spend her evenings and nights reading about her new world.

Xavier stepped over the threshold, his gnarly wooden cane tapping the metal deck-plates of the floor with a crisp clacking sound. He inclined his head to her slightly in thanks for her invitation to enter then cast a critical eye about her sparsely furnished space. She had little in the way of possessions and the computer terminal was tied into the station's mainframe so she had no need of actual books as she could access the entirety of documented history and literature from the terminal. Still she liked having a book in her hands and had managed to procure a few tomes which she had set on shelves around the room. Finally he looked toward her to finish his inspection of her space. Her dark purple hair rolled unrestrained down to the middle of her back and her violet eyes were shining, her long, tapered ears perked up as she looked back at him. She was wearing comfortable clothes and no shoes and bore a thick tome in her right hand, her index finger marking her spot in the book.

"Are you finding your accommodations to your liking?" He inquired with little feeling as though he didn't really care but felt compelled to ask.

"Oh, yes. I'm fine. I could use some rugs or something to cover the floor but there's more than enough space and everything is 'cool'." She smiled as she used the word, sure she had gotten it correct.

Xavier cast her a disparaging look that caused her ears to droop low. Seeing her reaction he forced his face into a slight smile before speaking again. "I see you are learning a great deal about the subtleties of the language." Then he nodded slightly toward her right hand and his forced smile turned into a genuine one, "And an interest in literature as well. What are you reading?"

She looked down at the thick volume in her hand briefly before looking back up at him. "It's a book written by a man named Sun Tzu."

"Ah!" He seemed overly excited all of a sudden, his eyes livening up and showing a genuine surge of emotion. "The Art of War."

"Yes." Riana responded. Her ears perked back up a bit at his change of emotion and she moved across the room to retrieve a book mark which she placed in the tome and set it on the glass table in front of her couch. Then turned back to Xavier, "Please, come in."

Xavier moved further into the apartment and inspected the book more closely. His mouth went slightly slack when he realized the book was an untranslated copy, the title written in embossed golden Chinese characters. "Ms. Thorindal, this book is written in Chinese."

She glanced down at the book for a moment and then back up at him, her ears drooping again. "Is that bad?"

He looked up at her and raised an eyebrow as he searched her expression. "That depends. Can you understand it?"

She smiled sheepishly. "Yes. It took me a couple of days but I figured it out. Bart said it was best read in Mr. Tzu's native tongue."

He grinned widely at her now, openly excited. "You taught yourself to read the Chinese language in a few days?"

"Yes…" She replied tentatively.

Abruptly he changed the subject. "Ms. Thorindal, I have been monitoring your progress thus far and I must say that I am very pleased. I was wondering if you and Willhelmina would be willing to join me for dinner on the promenade this evening?"

Riana looked at him questioningly, unsure of what had just happened or where she stood with this man. "Ok." She said simply.

"Excellent. I will see you there at seven sharp." At that he nodded slightly and was gone from the room, his wooden cane clicking down the hallway as the door closed behind him.

They had arrived at seven exactly, resplendent in their evening wear. Riana felt like a fairytale princess in the silky garment. Unlike their daily wear, the dress was tailored to hang loosely about her frame. After trying for an hour to walk in the high-heeled shoes she had finally given up and was instead sporting a pair of fancy flats. Her hair was pulled up in a stylish, timely do that Willhelmina had arranged. She had even been talked into wearing some color on her lips and eyes. Willhelmina was similarly decked out, although she had long ago mastered walking in the torturous heels and now stood a couple of inches taller than Riana.

As they entered the promenade, Riana was struck speechless. The room was an enormous round space sitting beneath a dome of transparent material. Outside the dome was the full grandeur of space with half of the Earth visible on her left and the top of the moon on her right. The stars were shining brightly as a backdrop to the few craft floating gracefully to and fro above the dome. Riana had no idea how long she had been standing there before she realized that Willhelmina was talking to her, prodding her to move into the room and sit down with Xavier. He stood next to his chair at their table waiting for them. Even he looked more dressed up than usual, if such a thing was possible.

The meal was served almost the instant they had seated themselves. It came in courses almost too numerous to count, each seemingly more exotic than the last. Several items looked terrible to Riana but in an effort to not be rude she tried them all, and found most of them to be quite tasty.

Conversation was kept casual throughout and it seemed that all in all everyone seemed happy and excited that she was adjusting well, but at the same time there was an air of confusion about what to do with her. Their testing had slowed down a bit recently and Xavier explained that they were moving into a long term monitoring phase. Which meant that for the most part they would be watching her go about her daily life to see how she handled things in the long run. She still had daily check-ups and tests, both mental and physical, but nowhere near the barrage she had experienced in the beginning. As they were starting on their dessert Xavier had taken a call on his communicator and shortly excused himself saying, "Ladies, I am afraid that business never rests, please enjoy your desserts and the rest of your evening." Then he had excused himself and disappeared.

After dinner Riana had walked Willhelmina back to her room and then set about wandering the station since her new body required almost no sleep. The station had a day/night cycle similar to that of Kalijor so as the other people in the station would sleep she would wander the halls aimlessly looking for ways to pass the time. It was during one of these late night wandering sessions that she happened across Master Jonin in the gym.

She wandered into the gym on a whim. It wasn't as though she could make her body stronger or faster through exercise, but for some reason she had just felt the desire to wander through the place. She almost didn't enter the cavernous space when she saw the man in the boxing ring on the far side of the room. Not through any fear or concern for anything other than not wanting to disturb him. She imagined that any normal person that was up at this hour would likely be wanting some form of solitude in order to get themselves back into a sleeping state as quickly as possible.

She was ready to pass the windowed door by and wander off somewhere else when she saw the figure begin a series of almost hypnotic movements that made her pause and watch for a long moment. Here was a tiny man that looked to be old even by elven standards, frail in appearance yet imposing all the same. He stood in the middle of the boxing ring practicing an elaborate series of movements that was as graceful as a ballet, yet evoked a sense of awe and power as she watched him. Before she could think to question why, she was through the door and heading across the room.

As she approached the man she saw that he had his eyes closed and still executed his movements with flawless precision. Drawing nearer to him, her jaw slack in appreciation of his focus she was surprised when he suddenly smiled at her.

"I'm sorry, I didn't mean to…" she stammered as she began to back away from him again.

"It is alright. Please stay and watch if it pleases you." His voice was steady and strong, like a bird singing a confident tune to the wind.

"Are you sure? I don't want to intrude."

"I would not have invited you to stay if I was unsure. Please make yourself comfortable." Throughout the entire conversation he kept moving, each action precise, delicate, and yet full of power and discipline.

Riana moved closer to the ring and sat down on a bench where she watched him finish his dance-like movements. When at last he came to a halt he opened his eyes and looked at her, a slow smile spreading across his lips as he inspected her.

"And what is it that I can do for you at this hour?" He asked sincerely.

"I was just wandering around, I didn't mean to intrude on your… um… whatever that was." She blushed at her own ignorance.

"That was a kata. A series of movements designed to help one focus their mind, spirit and chi."

"It was beautiful."

"Thank you. One could spend a lifetime practicing katas and never master them, for to master katas is to master aspects of oneself. You cannot have one without the other."

254

"So, it is a spiritual… dance?" Riana raised her purple eyebrows at him, her ears perked up in curiosity.

"Very much so. Although it also has more practical applications. So tell me Miss Thorindal, what is it that keeps you wandering the halls at night?"

Riana blushed again, looking away from the man as he stood there unassumingly in front of her. "I… I just don't seem to need as much sleep as anyone else. It seems like a couple of hours is more than enough and I get lonely so…"

"So you wander the halls of a never-changing space station in search of answers that you know you will not find here."

She looked up at him suddenly, her violet eyes wide with amazement. "How did you…"

"It is plain enough in your movements, your speech patterns, the way you hold yourself. I myself am no stranger to being lost in this world. A long time ago I was in much the same situation, emotionally of course. It is a difficult thing at best."

"So what did you do?"

"I met a man. Quite by accident, although as it turns out it may have been more by design than I had at first suspected."

"What did this man do for you?" She asked, her embarrassment forgotten.

"He taught me that all things in the universe are connected, and that through certain refinements of being we can begin to see those connections, to appreciate the grander pattern of things and how we fit into them."

Riana almost laughed at that statement. "Well I don't think that will help me much. I'm not even supposed to exist."

"And yet, here you are. Curious is it not?" He smiled a knowing smile at her.

She looked at him for a long moment. Her ears flattened out, pointing straight back behind her. "What are you saying? That there is some purpose for my being here? That I am not just some anomaly in a computer program?"

"I am saying nothing of the sort. I merely suggest that you try to see things from a broader perspective before discounting yourself wholly. We all have a place in the universe Miss Thorindal, whether we realize it or not. But those of us who come to realize our places tend to live richer, more fulfilling lives. Those that make every effort to see the larger picture and themselves within it spend less time adrift in uncertainty and self-doubt."

Riana sighed heavily, her ears drooping lower as she inspected the man standing there placidly. "And you are willing to help me? See the bigger picture?"

"If such is your will." His bright eyes shone as he bowed low to her.

Riana thought about the past few months as she walked down the corridor toward Xavier's office. One wall of the hall was filled with slanted windows, looking out into space, and presenting an awe inspiring view of the station itself. Riana looked out the windows as small cargo vessels and skiffs floated about elegantly in the station's local space, hauling chunks of machinery, supplies, and various other items around between several docked ships and the station itself. The ships themselves were mostly of what had been described to her as the 'short range' variety, used mainly to ferry supplies and personnel between the station and the orbital ring that encircled the Earth, or the moon bases. The ships had stubby, thick wings that swept away from the fronts of the vessels at severe angles, and curved up slightly at the tips. They reminded her of arrowheads she had used to hunt small fowl, with blunt tips and wide bodies, designed to strike a killing blow and then come to rest point down so the arrow shaft would stick up in the air, making the bird easier to locate.

"What're you looking at?" Willhelmina's voice startled Riana out of her daydream.

Snapping her head around, she saw Willhelmina standing next to her, wearing her normal station uniform. She had her raven hair tied back in a tight bun at the back of her head and her brilliant green eyes were smiling mischievously.

Riana smiled briefly at Willhelmina before turning her gaze back to the space ballet. "Just... everything really. It's like watching a ballet in slow motion."

"I suppose it is. I never really look anymore. I guess you just sort of get used to it after a while." Willhelmina had turned to look out the broad windows as she spoke, her eyes focusing on one of the small skiffs that seemed to be hauling a large crate into the station.

"I can't imagine ever getting used to this." Riana said as she watched the same skiff spiral around a larger cargo hauler and zip silently into an open cargo hold on the ship's gleaming silver skin.

"I can't imagine what you are going through sis. This must all be so amazing to you." Willhelmina had turned to look at Riana's wide, violet eyes. Her lips formed into a smile as Riana turned to look at her.

"Did you call me sis?" Riana asked, a little bewildered.

Willhelmina thought about it for a moment, replaying her comment in her mind. "I guess I did. Do you mind? I mean, I know we aren't related really, but neither of us really have any family to speak of, and we HAVE spent most of our lives together, whether virtually or in reality."

Riana stared at her for another long moment before she lunged forward, embracing Willhelmina tightly. "Oh Kat. Thank you." She squealed into Willhelmina's shoulder as she squeezed her tightly.

"I wouldn't have it any other way." Willhelmina pulled Riana off her and grinned at her slyly. "So, what're you doing down here anyway?"

"Xavier asked me to come and see him. He said it was time to talk about my future here?"

"Ah. Well that sounds just like him to me. Don't worry about it sis. He probably just wants you to start doing some stuff around the station." Willhelmina started walking toward the double doors at the end of the hall, grabbing Riana's hand and dragging her along.

"I welcome the opportunity. All of this testing and wandering around is beginning to drive me crazy." Riana said as she allowed herself to be pulled down the hall.

"Still," Willhelmina added "it's kind of odd for him to invite me along for this. I wonder if something is up?"

Riana was about to ask what could possibly be up, but they had reached the doors, which were sliding noiselessly into their recesses in the walls, revealing Xavier Quinn's office for the first time.

For what must have been the millionth time in just a couple of months, Riana's breath caught short in her chest. As the double doors slid apart to reveal a tube, maybe a dozen feet in diameter, that was completely transparent with the exception of a two foot wide section of the floor. It felt almost as though she was standing in an open door, looking straight out into space.

Gently, Willhelmina tugged at her hand, leading her into the tube which curved sharply underneath them. Riana had a sudden realization that they were about to walk off the edge of a sharp drop off, all she could see if she looked straight ahead, or up was the starry vastness of space, and if she looked down, the floor curved out from under them into that void. As Willhelmina pulled her gently forward, their feet never left the surface of the floor.

As the floor leveled out again it opened up into a large, transparent dome. The floor of the dome was criss-crossed with six-inch wide solid strips that radiated out from a two-foot diameter circle in the center of the room like a spider's web. The top was a fully encircling dome that looked out on the void of space, on one side of the room was the Earth, and on the other was the moon. As Riana looked around she could hardly contain her amazement at the room and the spectacle of the view.

At the opposite side of the domed room was a large transparent desk with several holographic panels and readouts floating over its surface. Behind the desk sat Xavier, tapping away idly at some piece of information and watching the two women enter his domain. He motioned to one side where a set of comfortable looking chairs and a large black, leather couch waited around a transparent coffee table on which rested a delicate glass tea pot and cups. The table also bore a large bowl of fruit, some assorted candies and a

260

plate full of pastries. Dominating the opposite side of the room, a large conference table was circled with high-backed leather chairs similar to the one Xavier sat in.

"Every time I think I am getting used to things here…" Riana mumbled half to herself, sinking down into one of the chairs and looking between her feet at the station stretching away beneath them.

"Amazing isn't it?" Willhelmina said as she moved toward the couch.

"Tea? Willhelmina? Miss Thorindal?" Xavier said as he approached them.

"No thank you." Willhelmina smiled as she tried to find a comfortable spot on the sofa without falling into its seemingly bottomless cushion.

"Oh, sure. Thank you." Riana replied distractedly, her eyes still roving around the office.

Xavier poured a cup of the steaming liquid, handing it to her before pouring himself one and then sitting down fluidly in the other chair. He inhaled the aroma of the fluid as he held the cup under his nose for a moment then took a small sip and smiled over the cup at them.

Riana followed suit, taking a deep breath, inhaling the tea's strong scent. Not like the bitter teas she could remember from her other life in Kalijor. Tentatively, she put the cup to her lips and tasted the steaming fluid. Its bitter-sweet flavor filled her mouth, tingling at the edge of her senses.

"I love a good tea." Xavier was saying as he looked at the girls thoughtfully. "So, Miss Thorindal. Have you given any thought to what you would like to do with your new life?"

Riana looked at him over her tea cup, his face slightly distorted by the steam emanating from its surface. She mulled the thought over in her mind for a moment. She finally said, "I don't even know what there is to do."

"Understandable." Xavier replied after taking another sip of his tea. "Especially since we have had you cooped up here on the station, and constantly in testing to make sure you are adjusting well to your new body."

"That has slowed down a bit." Riana said with a note of happiness to her voice.

"Yes." Xavier said thoughtfully as he watched a small tug moving a larger ship past the dome. Then his eyes returned to Riana, "Jonin tells me you have been spending quite a bit of time in the gym lately."

Riana glanced at Willhelmina, who was still struggling slightly with the sofa. "I suppose I have." Riana finally replied, "I find that spending time in the gym is relaxing after a day of being poked, prodded, and questioned." She had begun splitting her precious free time between the computer's data banks, and the gym with Master Jonin. Studying under him, especially the mental practices of meditation he followed, seemed to help alleviate the 'strange feeling' she had ever since she woke up in this new body. She suspected the feeling was related to her lack of magical powers. Even the engineers were unsure what to make of it but she had grown up connected to magical forces, even if they were virtual, and their sudden absence seemed to have a definite, even if only perceived impact.

262

Xavier watched her intently. A genuine smile crept across his face when he spoke again. "That isn't a bad thing Miss Thorindal. Simply an observation. In fact, Jonin tells me that you have taken very readily to his teachings."

Riana blushed slightly at the compliment. "Well, he is usually up in the middle of the night, so I can take a break from the computer and go get some exercise." It was kind of a misnomer she knew, as her body didn't need exercise. Her muscles would never atrophy through lack of use, or strengthen through constant training, but it gave her a single point on which to focus for a while and that was a much welcomed change from her normal scattered musings about this new world and her place in it.

"Well Miss Thorindal. I spoke with Jonin this morning and he says you are doing exceptionally well. When I asked him to classify your level of skill he responded in no uncertain terms that you are at a class two ranking. To put that in perspective for you, most of our extremely well trained soldiers have a class three rating, and Jonin is a class one, meaning he is legally registered as a deadly weapon, bare handed." Xavier spoke with a note of pride, but whether that pride was for her, or Master Jonin, Riana wasn't sure.

Willhelmina was staring at the back of Riana's head with an intensity that made Riana's skull itch. Slowly she turned to face the raven haired woman and raised her eyebrow questioningly.

"Class two?! Ree I'm a class three and I beat you all the time!" Willhelmina exclaimed. "No WAY are you a class three unless…" Her voice trailed off and her eyes narrowed. Riana simply offered her a sheepish grin in return. How did you tell someone you had been letting them win for weeks straight?

"Anyway," Xavier said with a grin of his own spreading across his face. "I thought I might suggest something you could do. At least for a while. You are of course welcome to stay here on the station for as long as you like, as our guest. However, if you would like to see the solar system, and do something to fill your time, I happen to need a couple of new couriers for the company. We normally try to hire from within whenever possible and I can't think of two more capable insiders who would work quite well as a team. If, of course, you are interested."

Riana felt more than a little confused by what Xavier had said, but when she looked to Willhelmina for some insight the other woman was positively glowing with excitement.

"You will of course be paid the usual courier salaries, plus room and board here at the station and allowances for layovers in remote locations, a small vessel with a pilot, unless one or both of you wish to qualify in that regard as well." Xavier continued, looking Riana in the eyes the entire time.

"But…" Riana stammered briefly as she began to assemble the picture in her head. "Why are combat skills important for this work?"

At that, Xavier smiled broadly, genuinely impressed, before he replied. "You are pretty sharp Miss Thorindal. I can see that you will indeed be an asset to the organization. The reason is simple enough really. Solidarity Online is constantly pushing the boundaries of both hardware and software development in order to keep the quality of our games at the top of the market. Our competitors have agents in the field that will stop at next to nothing in order to acquire advanced copies of any of our materials. Make no mistake, this is a dangerous undertaking, but the rewards are extreme. Our couriers are among the most highly compensated people in the solar system."

Riana looked back at Willhelmina when she felt a tug at her arm. Willhelmina had leaned forward and was grinning at her. "I know a restaurant on the moon you would LOVE to see. It will be good to get out of the station and see the solar system don't you think?"

Looking from Willhelmina's glowing face to Xavier's more serious one, Riana paused, unsure. "So there is really a chance of... what? Dying?"

"There is. Although it is uncommon for a courier to be killed outright. Several have simply gone missing, a few are recovered in the field and retired on disability for loss of limbs or senses. We at SO try to play the corporate espionage game fairly straight Miss. Thorindal, but some of our competitors will go to great lengths to get ahead." Xavier said directly while sipping thoughtfully at his cooling tea.

"All of this over games? Virtual worlds?" Riana said, aghast, her ears drooping down.

Xavier raised an eye at the physical sign of her emotion, clearly unimpressed. "Yes Miss Thorindal. All of this over games. The entertainment industry is big money. Huge money in fact. Last fiscal year SO grossed over thirty five trillion credits solar system wide. That is not counting our long distance holdings in near-by Barnard's Star and Alpha-Centauri. We make more money in a year than the entire planet Mars. Believe me when I say Miss Thorindal, this is a cut-throat business."

Riana's eyes were wide in amazement, her ears perked back up. She had no idea what to make of any of this, but she knew she wanted to get out and do something, anything really. Although the idea of being in harm's way was not a new concept to her, she was not certain if she was ready to accept it again as a way of life.

After a moment she looked back at Xavier and asked, "Can I have a while to think it over?" Willhelmina let out a small sigh of disappointment next to her.

Xavier smiled again, setting his tea cup on the table   between them. "Of course you may, Miss Thorindal. I need an answer within twenty-four hours however, or I will have to make the positions available to others."

Riana nodded her understanding. "Ok." She replied, then added as an afterthought, "Can you call me Riana? Miss Thorindal sounds so… strange."

"That wouldn't be appropriate Miss Thorindal. You are my guest and potentially an employee of my company. It wouldn't do to speak to you as informally as that." He stood up easily and inclined his head to them before he began moving back toward his desk.

"But you call Kat by her first name." Riana protested as she worked to free herself from the chair's embrace.

"You are not my daughter," he replied simply as he rounded his desk and seated himself in the leather chair. "Good day ladies. I look forward to your reply."

-29-

As they moved back along the corridor Riana and Willhelmina looked at one another.

"You never told me you were his daughter." Riana said.

"You've been letting me beat you?!" Willhelmina said at the same instant.

They stopped for a moment at the corner that led to the lift staring at one another with a playful ferocity.

"You first." Willhelmina said. "How long have you been holding back on me in the gym?"

Riana crossed her arms defensively and started moving toward the lifts, forcing Willhelmina to keep pace with her. "I don't know… two weeks… maybe three. I just didn't want to hurt your feelings." Her ears drooped again as she spoke.

"You're more likely to hurt my feelings by holding back and then not telling me." Willhelmina replied.

Willhelmina was the only family she had and she didn't want bad blood between them. "I'm really sorry Kat."

"You will be forgiven just as soon as we get to the gym and you show me what you're really capable of," Willhelmina said briskly as she jabbed the call button on the lift.

"I don't know Kat," Riana hedged, "I don't want to hurt you or anything. I still don't know what I am capable of in this body." Riana was genuinely concerned for her friend's safety.

"Then don't hurt me Ree. Master Jonin'll be the first to tell you that martial arts are all about control. Besides, if he has given you a class two rating, then I'm sure I have nothing to worry about. He obviously feels pretty strongly about your skills." Willhelmina said simply as the lift door slid open silently. Stepping into the car she said clearly, "Rec Center."

The lift doors slid closed and they began moving with an almost imperceptible start. "Alright. One fight." Riana acquiesced, looking at the floor as she kicked the back of her left foot with the toe of her right absently. She looked up at Willhelmina and changed the subject, "Ok. Your turn."

Willhelmina sighed heavily, as though she was preparing for a war, before she turned and looked at the control panel on the wall of the lift. "I'm an orphan. My parents were killed in a compartment fire when I was seventeen. I spent a lot of time in Kalijor before the fire. When the community found out what happened, there was an out-pouring of support from a lot of people, including Xavier." She paused, drawing in a deep breath before continuing. "He took me in, brought me here to the Tyconderoga and raised me as his own child."

Willhelmina looked back over at Riana as she finished speaking, only to be enveloped in a nearly crushing embrace.

"Oh Kat! I had no idea. I'm so sorry, I didn't mean to drum up bad memories." Her ears were cocked back as she gushed her apology.

"It's ok." Willhelmina responded, returning the embrace for a moment before gently pushing Riana off of her and looking her in the eyes. "There was a malfunctioning control circuit that sparked against an oxygen line in the ventilation system. I only survived because I was in my game pod at the time, and it protected me from the blaze."

"He even put me to work on your project in Kalijor shortly afterwards. He said it was to help keep me going. To get me to move on with my life. Xavier remained my father figure as I've grown up. And Ezrina was kind of my mother."

Willhelmina quirked her mouth into a grin as the lift stopped and the doors slid silently open, admitting them to the cavernous space that was the station's gym level. "We can talk about it later if you want. But right now, you owe me a fight."

Riana's burst of laughter echoed as they exited the lift and moved into the gym. The room was huge, with a high, vaulted ceiling. Stacks of weights, lifting machines, running and biking machines, stationary swimming tanks, mats, poles, ropes with rings and bars dangling from them stood between the girls and their goal.

Stopping at the edge of a large mat with a square painted on it, Riana pulled off her boots and vest and set them neatly at the edge of the mat. Willhelmina also removed her boots, then unzipped her jumper down to her waist, shrugged her arms out of the suit and then tied the sleeves around her waist like a belt, leaving her wearing what looked like a baggy pair of pants and a thin tank top.

Together they moved out onto the mat, standing in opposite corners and looking at one another as they both secured their hair in pony tails behind their heads.

"Ready?" Willhelmina asked from across the mat.

"Yes." Riana said sheepishly as she moved into a passive stance, raising her arms to shoulder height and setting her feet shoulder-width apart.

"You're not going to hold back this time right?" Willhelmina asked as she set herself in an offensive stance, her feet closer together and arms set closer to her waist.

"Yes." Riana replied.

"Good. Then here we go." Willhelmina said as she moved swiftly across the mat and threw a lightning fast jab at Riana.

Riana reacted instantly, shifting her weight to the side, grabbing hold of Willhelmina's wrist and setting her shoulder against the other woman's chest. With a loud thud Willhelmina was sprawled out on the mat, looking up into Riana's violet eyes.

"Wow." She said with a tone of amazement.

"I know." Riana replied.

"Let's try again." Willhelmina huffed as she kipped up to her feet and spun around to face Riana again, slipping into a new stance with practiced fluidity.

"Ok." Riana answered as she moved back into her neutral stance.

Willhelmina smiled for a moment and then cut loose with a flurry of kicks as she advanced on Riana who was ducking, weaving, and deflecting them all with what appeared to be no effort at all. Switching to a series of combinations, Willhelmina moved in closer, bringing her elbows, hands and knees to bear. But Riana simply moved and dodged, contorting her body around Willhelmina's attacks in a parody of some complicated dance as they moved around the mat.

"You aren't attacking." Willhelmina panted as she broke off her assault and took a step back. Her hair was trying to work its way out of the pony tail tie and she flicked a stray strand out of her face.

"I don't want to hurt you." Riana said calmly. Her cybernetic body kept her breathing calm and regular.

"Then DON'T!" Willhelmina shouted as she leapt across the mat with a powerful flying kick that Riana rolled forward underneath her to avoid. Spinning around as she stood up, Riana lashed out with a quick open-handed jab that landed squarely on Willhelmina's shoulder, combining with her forward momentum and driving her face first into the mat. Riana calmly brushed a wayward bit of purple hair back into place, much as Willhelmina had done.

Not to be dissuaded, Willhelmina pushed herself up to her knees then hopped lightly to her feet with her back to Riana. Swinging her leg around in a sweeping reverse round-house kick, she gasped as Riana intercepted it, grabbing her ankle and hefting it higher into the air. Willhelmina rolled into a ball and used the momentum to flip over, then throw out her legs as she fell to the ground face first again. This time she landed the blow, both of her feet landing squarely on Riana's chest, knocking her off balance and they both hit the ground at the same time.

In an instant they were both on their feet again and Willhelmina grinned at her friend briefly before advancing again with another flurry of punches. Riana knocked Willhelmina's hands away from her body, opening her chest and stomach up to an attack, then raised her knee up quickly toward her groin. Instinctively Willhelmina reacted by curling up into a ball to absorb some of the blow, but it never came. Instead Riana smiled down at her as she dropped both of her hands down on her friend's shoulders, knocking her to her knees.

Willhelmina rolled backward away from Riana and back to her feet grinning broadly as she considered her next moves.

After twenty minutes, most of the other people using the gym had congregated around the mat. There was 'ooo'ing and 'ah'ing, and people pointed and talked as the girls continued to dance back and forth. Some of them mimed moves to themselves as though trying to learn from the experience while others just stood and stared.

Finally, Willhelmina stopped Riana with a raised hand as she crouched down, panting and pouring sweat. Looking up at her friend and then scanning the people that had gathered to watch them. Riana stood there calmly, her breath slow and even, no sweat evident on her body. Her expression was calm and passive as she watched Willhelmina gather her breath.

"Good fight sis. Master Jonin knows what he is talking about after all." Willhelmina grinned up at Riana. She raised herself up to a standing position as her ragged breathing began to slow down. "C'mon, let's go get a shower and some dinner. We need to talk about Xavier's offer."

Willhelmina put her arm around Riana's shoulders and together they headed toward the showers.

-30-

"You really think this is a good idea?" Riana asked as they sat down at the desk in her room and prepared to call Xavier. She was having serious misgivings about this courier business.

"Ree. SO couriers make over a million creds a year, plus perks. We'll have access to some of the best equipment, ships, and training. It'll give us a chance to see the solar system. We can do it for a few months, or a year, and if you don't like it then we can find something else to do." Willhelmina had been seriously trying to wear down Riana's defenses throughout dinner and all the way back to her quarters and she was finally starting to see some success.

"I'm just not sure if I like the idea of being attacked by random people just for being there you know?" Riana looked into Willhelmina's eyes trying to see some hint of the motivation for her strong desire to do this.

"How is that any different from walking through the forest of Brume?" Willhelmina retorted.

"It… well…" Riana stammered. She knew Willhelmina was right. "I guess it isn't any different. But that was a fact of life there. Here I have a chance for something different. I don't HAVE to live like that."

"Like what?" the raven-haired woman shot back expectantly.

"You know what! Sneaking around every corner for fear of what might be waiting there. Constantly honing my fighting skills, fighting for my life, RUNNING for my life. It doesn't have to be that way anymore." In truth, Riana admitted to herself, she had no idea what else she would do.

"A constant adrenaline rush, huh? Sounds alright to me. C'mon Ree! Just do it with me for a while? It'll give you a chance to get around and see what else there is you might be interested in." She was finally starting to see a response to her badgering.

"I have no idea what an adrenaline rush is, but I'm not sure I like the sound of it much. I guess you're right about the rest. It would give me a chance to see some things. Just tell me why you are so excited about this would you?" She pointed her finger at Willhelmina playfully as she finished.

"I've just never been off the station since my parents… well, since Xavier took me in. It's been almost ten years! I want to get out and do SOMETHING and this seems like a good start." Willhelmina raised her hands as if to indicate she had no idea what to do with her life either.

"You've never been off this station? In ten years?" Riana's eyes grew large in amazement and her ears flattened out from her head as she looked at her friend.

"Well... No. I had you to look after in Kalijor which was just about a twenty four-seven deal so I never really had a chance to. But now that you are here, we can go experience things together!" Willhelmina spoke without a hint of remorse for her time spent plugged in to Kalijor, she seemed to hold nothing but vibrant energy for the future. Riana found it slightly annoying, but also infectious.

Smiling at her friend, 'No.' She thought, 'Not friend. Sister.' Smiling at her sister, she finally gave in. "Alright. We'll give it a go."

Grinning from ear to ear, Willhelmina turned to the computer on the desk and keyed in a call request for Xavier. A moment later a glowing, three-dimensional image of his head appeared over the desk and he smiled as he looked at them. "Ladies." His silky voice issued forth from somewhere in the room. "How can I be of assistance?"

"Ree's decided to become a courier Xavier, and so have I." Willhelmina burst out, unable to contain her excitement.

"Are you sure Miss Thorindal?" His image raised an eyebrow at Riana as it looked at her intently.

"Yes." Riana said, trying to sound as though she meant it seriously. "For a while at least," she added hastily.

"The minimum commitment is twelve months, not counting any training time we provide for you. Do you find that to be acceptable?" His tone was all business now, no longer the fatherly figure.

Riana glanced at Willhelmina questioningly, her ears splaying out as she considered her future. Willhelmina was grinning and nudging her with her shoulder. "Yes." She finally said to the image. "Twelve months is fine."

"Very well." Xavier replied. "Please stop by my office in the morning and we can finalize the paper work. Then we can get you two into training and get you ready for some field work." His image nodded curtly to them and then winked out of existence, leaving the two women alone in the room.

-31-

The next day they walked down to Xavier's office where he offered them more tea before getting to business. He set two sheaves of paper thicker than Riana's forearm in front of them. They reviewed the terms of the contracts, then Willhelmina signed hers gleefully. Riana paused for a moment, pursing her lips somewhat nervously, then signed hers as well. Seeing the documents signed, Xavier pressed a button on his desk and a tall man, who Xavier introduced as their flight instructor, entered the room and whisked them away to a small room somewhere off the deck of the main hangar bay with not even a modicum of ceremony. After extensive training he had certified them alongside a few others to fly almost any small spacecraft. Next they worked in depth with another instructor who taught them everything regarding fire arms. Time seemed endless as they were constantly cleaning, maintaining, adjusting, firing and reloading weapons of all kinds. In between these hands-on sessions, they learned more about the principals behind each weapon than they ever thought possible.

Finally they were asked to combine their skills by flying a small ship through an obstacle course constructed in the Tyconderoga's local space. They had to land the ship under fire, and charge into a secured bunker. Once in the bunker they retrieved a case or data disk and then had to return to their ship and lift off again. Each time they ran the course obstacles would have shifted, guns would fire from different locations, doors would be moved or locked. They had to improvise constantly, never lapsing into habit.

Throughout it all Riana still spent her evenings in the gym studying with Master Jonin. He had stepped up his training retinue to a furious pace. Despite her trepidation, Riana admitted to herself that she was having a great time. Learning new skills and the constant rush of having her skills tested day and night made her feel more at home than ever before. She had never thought about how much adventure was a part of her former life, but now she could not think of a day without some unexpected, potentially life-threatening turn of events cropping up.

Having been thrown together in front of blazing enemy guns Riana and Willhelmina learned very quickly how to trust one another implicitly. Knowing full well that one day either of their lives could very easily be in the hands of the other. They had grown closer than ever outside the training as well. Willhelmina tried as hard as she could to keep up with Riana, and she had a great deal of success. There were still times when Riana ended up carrying her newly found sister to her waiting bed after she had worked herself to the point of passing out from exhaustion.

ICE breaking was described to Riana as using a computer to break down the firewalls and other defenses around another, secure computer, in order to access information or otherwise make the computers do what they wanted. The instructor was a skinny man with a mousy face and a neatly styled head of hair. His skills with the computers were obviously considerable as he guided them deftly through the motions of defeating countermeasures and surmounting virtual barriers. It was in the middle of one such class when Xavier entered the room and informed them that they were needed immediately and dismissed them from the session.

The excitement and tension was palpable as Xavier led them through the labyrinthine halls of the Tyconderoga. Near the hanger bay they stopped at a small, sterile briefing room. Its stark white walls, reminded Riana of the room she had woken up in months ago. There was a podium at the front of the room, facing three rows of chairs with small computer interfaces on the arm rests. Xavier motioned for them to take seats in the room and then moved up behind the podium and cleared his throat meaningfully as he tapped a series of controls and the lights dimmed.

"I am sorry to pull you away from your training ladies, but a need for your services has arisen. You are the only two couriers we have on-board currently and so the job falls to you. It is simple enough though. We simply need this data disk delivered to one Hakiro Yamato in Tranquility." His baritone voice slid silkily across the room as he keyed in another sequence and a holographic image appeared displaying a three-dimensional image of a high capacity data disk. It was matte black and very unimpressive, in stark contrast to the image of Mr. Hakiro Yamato that appeared a moment later. He was a skinny man with slightly upturned, dark eyes, and his shockingly orange hair set into a short mohawk.

Riana stared in a mixture of amusement and awe at the man's image. She had never seen anything like it before. His hair looked as though it would stand a full foot off the top of his head.

280

"Mr. Yamato is one of our top programmers from the security division. He needs to receive the disk within forty-eight hours. The contents of the disk are a closely guarded secret and its destruction should be your number one priority should it somehow fall into the wrong hands." Xavier looked at each of the girls in turn as he finished the last sentence, making sure they both understood how serious he was.

"Mr. Yamato's residence is in the alpha sector of Tranquility. The Indra Towers, apartment two-seven-one-seven. He is of course expecting your arrival and anticipated resistance is minimal. You are authorized to draw Class B weapons and equipment from station stores and your shuttle is being prepared for departure as we speak." He then looked at them pointedly again, as though he was sizing them up, watching for hints of fear, anxiety, insecurity, anything. Finally he finished, "Any questions ladies?"

Riana and Willhelmina exchanged looks, then looked back at Xavier and said in unison, "No sir."

"Very well then." He replied. "You have two hours to prepare for departure. Good luck ladies." He then tapped a few more controls on the podium, returning the room lighting to normal and causing the holographic images to wink out of existence. Bowing slightly to them, he snatched his cane from the podium and excused himself from the room.

As soon as the door closed behind him, Willhelmina jumped up and exclaimed, "Our first mission Ree!!"

Riana looked at her friend with uncertainty. "I guess so." She conceded. Her ears drooped down, betraying her feelings. She still wasn't certain she wanted this, even in light of her feelings about the training sessions they had been running through for nearly two months now.

"It'll be fine Ree. You'll see! Now let's go get ready." Willhelmina grabbed Riana's hand hauling her out of her seat and towards the door.

-32-

Ninety minutes later the pair was making their way to the hangar bay. Willhelmina was wearing a form fitting black body suit, with a cropped grey jacket. She had a belt on with various items clipped to it, and a pair of sturdy, knee high boots that sported a series of buckles up the fronts. She was wearing a handgun strapped into a tactical holster on her thigh, with a few clips on her belt along with the myriad of electronic gadgets. "Just in case" she had said as she had carefully placed each item in a pouch or clipped it to her belt. Her raven hair was hanging down to her shoulders freely and she wore a pair of sleek sunglasses over her emerald eyes.

Riana had decided to stick with the more conservative appearance that she had grown accustomed to on the station. She still wore her black and grey jumpsuit over a grey shirt that was exposed by the partially undone zipper. She wore a shoulder harness under her jumpsuit that supported a handgun under one arm and several clips of ammunition under the other. The new addition seemed to be making her slightly uncomfortable as she walked down the corridor, shifting her shoulders around and constantly tugging on the open edges of the zipper. She wore a pair of rugged, buckled boots nearly to her knees and her hair was pulled back into a lengthening, thick tail at the back of her head. She had even finally let Willhelmina talk her into wearing a pair of dark glasses over her violet eyes.

Willhelmina hadn't stopped grinning since the briefing and as the door to the small hangar slid aside, her smile only widened. On the pad was a small, sleek, two-person shuttle. It looked like a huge bird of prey with its outstretched wings sweeping forward and hanging on top of the body of the vessel. The tip of the shuttle curved into an almost knife-edge point that looked exactly like the beak of a griffon, the slightly opaque cockpit view port sat right where the animal's eyes would be, and it's four landing struts bore large three fingered pads that did nothing to detract from the griffon-like appearance of the ship.

Standing calmly next to the open hatch on the starboard side of the vessel was Xavier. He looked like a statue standing there, his hands both planted atop the cane in front of him. He examined the girls as they drew near. Seeming satisfied by their appearance, he offered a small nod in their direction as they stopped in front of him.

"Ladies." He said simply to them in greeting. "Do you have any questions before you leave?"

"No sir." They replied in unison.

"Very well. Here is the data disk." Xavier produced a small metal case from his suit pocket and held it towards them in his open hand.

284

Riana and Willhelmina looked at it, then at one another. For a moment their eyes locked and both sets seemed to scream, 'you take it!' to one another. Finally Riana reached out and snatched up the proffered item. Carefully she put it in a pouch on her belt and sealed the flap over it.

"The data on the disk is proprietary, and a closely guarded secret, however, it is not known to exist by anyone who may want it, so this should be a fairly simple run. Your ship is prepared and ready to go." Xavier motioned to the open hatch as he finished speaking, "Have a good trip and I look forward to your report upon your return."

The girls thanked him and then stepped through the hatch of the sleek, silver ship. Riana moved into the cockpit and started a preflight system check as Willhelmina cycled the hatch closed and checked all of the aft compartments to make sure everything was secured. A few moments later they were both strapped into their seats and moving away from the Tyconderoga's space. As soon as they were clear of the stations harbor buoys Riana kicked the ship's engines into after burn and spiraled into a tight barrel roll, bearing for the moon.

"Stop that!" Willhelmina admonished her, looking a little sick.

"Just getting a feel for it." Riana said with a grin. Even though they couldn't really feel the movement of the ship, the fact that the moon was visible meant that they could see the rotation against a fixed object and Willhelmina had a bit of a weak stomach when it came to spinning.

With a smile still on her lips Riana straightened the vessel out and backed off the engines a bit, settling into a nice straight flight path towards the lunar city of Tranquility. It was easily visible to them already, even thirty-two thousand miles away. The ship's ion drive closed the distance very quickly, bringing the bright silver domes of the lunar cities into greater detail with every passing moment.

Tranquility was a mega city built into the craters forming the Sea of Tranquility. A five-hundred mile diameter geodesic dome, made of some of the strongest materials the human race had ever conceived covered the massive metropolis. Two of the most important functions the dome served were keeping harmful radiation and space debris from harming the city's inhabitants, and of course keeping the breathable atmosphere contained. The entire structure glowed from within, a pale artificial light that was broken up by the spider web of supports that held the whole thing together.

Willhelmina's smile had still not lessened, and Riana still had knots in her stomach. They chatted idly as the moon loomed larger and larger in the front view port. After an hour they were contacted by Tranquility's flight control system and were given clearance to land. Riana guided the ship down to a small hangar on the outer rim of the gigantic dome. The girls unstrapped themselves from their seats and set about making sure they were ready to go as the hangar door closed and atmosphere was cycled into the room.

"I thought I read that the moon has less gravity than the Earth-normal we use on the station." Riana commented as she gently hopped a couple of times to test the gravity.

"It does." Willhelmina commented with a grin as she watched Riana. "The city includes gravity leveling technology that increases the field strength in and around the habitable area. It insures people can move from planet to planet and station to station with no ill effects since everything is kept at one-G."

"That makes sense. Ok, let's go."

A moment later they were closing the door of their shuttle behind them and heading out of the hangar into the space port of the lunar city of Tranquility.

At first the spaceport looked very much like the Tyconderoga with long, winding hallways of gleaming white materials, spotlessly clean floors and pure white illumination seemingly emanating from nowhere. But, after a brief conversation with a customs officer, who ushered them through in a hurry once they had presented him with their credentials, they walked through a door into the public portion of the facility.

As had happened on so many occasions in the past few months, Riana was awe struck. They had stepped into a cavernous room, easily as large as the underground lake chamber they had passed through under the Cohai Observatory. The floor of the chamber looked as though it had once been the same gleaming white of the customs area but long since they had given up trying to keep it that way. There were people everywhere. Coming and going, saying hello and good bye. Long separated lovers reuniting again with passionate kisses and squeezing embraces and dearest friends separating with tear-filled exchanges. The ceiling of the room was made of some transparent material and through it Riana could see a bright, sun-lit sky with puffy white clouds drifting lazily about the open blue expanse. The light from above washed over everything and everyone in the space port, leaving only soft shadows here and there as the light reflected back and forth off of the dingy white surfaces of the space.

The people were dressed in a rainbow of different colors and fashions, and while most of them were unmistakably human, Riana spied the occasional person with long pointed ears, or cat-like slitted pupils. She thought she saw a man with small horns on his forehead, but he moved off into the crowd before she could get a clear look at him. The place was a hive of activity but the acoustics of the structure dampened the sound and made it easy to have a private conversation.

"Isn't it beautiful?" Willhelmina's voice snapped Riana out of her gawking.

"It is." Riana replied simply and resumed soaking in the sights and sounds of the space port. "How can there be a sky and clouds in here? Aren't we in space?" She finally asked.

Willhelmina looked up through the transparent roof of the space port and smiled. "It's because the interior of the dome is so large. There are a lot of parks and open space areas with growing things in here, all of that combined with the people and animals creates a lot of water vapor and over time it just developed its own atmosphere and weather patterns."

"Weather?" Riana looked at Willhelmina with wide eyes. "In here?"

"Yeah. We get rain from time to time in here. Not much in the way of wind though. It's usually pretty tame." Willhelmina said as they made their way through the throngs of people toward the nearest exit.

"You say 'we' as though you live here."

Willhelmina looked sad for a moment, staring off into the depths of the cavernous facility before she responded, "Well, I used to live here. Before... well, before my parents died."

"I'm sorry Kat." Riana screwed up her face, realizing what she had said only too late.

"It's ok Ree. It was a long time ago." Willhelmina sighed as she seemed to collect herself again and they resumed their winding path to the door.

Stepping out the door into the full light of Tranquility's day Riana was overcome by a wave of emotions and memories. It felt like it had been years since she had stood in the open air with the day light shining down on her. For a long moment, she just stood there looking up and thinking about her life in Kalijor. So many things had happened since she had been harshly thrust into this new, vast world of science and technology. Even her body was a product of that science. A complex machine created by the hands of human beings. Standing there beneath the filtered sun and sky of a city built on the surface of an airless planetoid hurtling through the void of space, she was overcome.

"C'mon Ree. Let's finish this. Then we can go sight-seeing if you want." Willhelmina's soft touch on her arm and her lilting voice in her ear brought Riana back to the here and now. Her violet eyes fluttered open again; she hadn't even realized she had closed them.

Looking at Willhelmina's smiling face, she blinked a few times. "Ok." And after a moment, "Let's do it."

Together they made their way down the ramp from the space port to the street below. They joined a throng of people waiting at the transit station as the sleek train moved toward them. The thing slid up to the curb almost soundlessly and the door slid open permitting their entry.

Willhelmina was in the vehicle and sitting down before she realized Riana was still standing on the curb staring at the train. Leaning half way out of the passenger compartment she snagged Riana's arm and dragged her through the open door and into a seat.

-33-

The Indra Towers were two of the tallest structures Riana had ever laid eyes on. She remembered the day she had first seen the Magic Academy and thought that she would never see a taller structure. Little did she know at the time what the world was really about. The buildings stretched upwards toward the captured sky that obscured the dome covering the city. The tips of the buildings were just within sight, tiny pin points that looked as if they might be in danger of puncturing the protective dome. The area between the two towers of glass and steel was overflowing with lush greenery, trees, grass, and flower beds filled with a myriad of colors and fragrances. People were wandering around the park area, going about their business. Some were sitting and eating beneath trees, children played, couples took advantage of their semi-seclusion and stole a kiss.

Willhelmina hooked her arm around Riana's elbow and pulled the other woman toward the building on the left of the park. "C'mon sis. Odd numbered apartments will be in this one."

They stepped together into the grand lobby of the building. The floor was a solid sheet of white stone, streaked through with veins of black. The stone floor reflected the light streaming into the lobby through the glass roof that soared hundreds of feet over their heads. There were benches and chairs scattered around, all of them made of polished metal, and separated by large trees that sprouted up from the soft earth of their small planters and soared into the air at least twenty feet before the single solid trunk fanned out into an array of wide, green leaves.

Riana stopped and stared at the trees for a moment, trying to figure out what it was about them that was bugging her. Finally Willhelmina supplied her with the answer to her unasked question. "The trees are fed by a hydroponics system. That's how you get such a large tree in a small planter. The soil is there mostly to make it look more natural for people. We have to be efficient with every resource, despite our affinity for open spaces and greenery."

"Cool." Riana said simply as they set off again.

Willhelmina led her companion through the huge lobby to the back of the room where a series of doors lined the wall. She pressed a button between two doors and they stood there a moment waiting, as Riana continued to examine everything around them discreetly.

Just watching the diverse crowds coming and going could fill weeks on end. They were all so different and new to her. Not that she had never seen crowds of people before, but the way they dressed and acted startled her. On the Tyconderoga most of the crew and personnel wore the grey or white jump suits, or lab coats. She had obviously become too accustomed to seeing because being here was like being thrust into the bright colors of the Rathalon Bazaar.

Finally the lift doors slid noiselessly open and a small throng of people moved out of the tiny compartment. A young woman with dark, earthy green hair falling down her back, pointy ears and slitted green eyes brushed by them and looked at Riana for a moment, her eyes drifting around Riana's face and body for a second before she smiled and said, "Oh! I love your ears! Where did you have them done?"

Riana's ears splayed out widely in consternation at which the other woman's face lit up. Riana finally managed a confused, "Done? What do you…"

But then Willhelmina cut in, leaning between the pair, she grabbed Riana's arm and hauled her into the lift with a curt, "It was a gene-doc on Earth-station a few years ago." Then she smiled at the green haired woman as the doors closed smoothly, breaking off the conversation.

"Who was she?" Riana asked, her ears perking back up again as she looked at Willhelmina. "I thought you said everyone here was human?"

Willhelmina grinned. "I did say that yes. I also said that some people had had their bodies and features altered to look differently. She was just as human as I am; she just had her features changed around a bit is all."

"To look like a nymph?" Riana asked in amazement.

"I guess." Willhelmina shrugged. "I don't know why you are so surprised though. I mean, we must have seen droves of altered people at the space port."

Riana thought about it for a moment, replaying the scene of the space port in her mind. "I guess you're right. I just didn't think about it until now. So, is it... permanent?"

"Some of them are. Most can be removed without too much trouble though. Some doctors are doing the alterations at the genetic level now." Willhelmina was leaning against the back wall of the lift as it accelerated smoothly up the tower.

"What does that mean?" Riana asked, not at all sure what the implications behind the word genetic were.

Willhelmina's smile deepened as she explained. "Genetics are what make people up. Tiny instructions inside every cell of our bodies that tell us how we look, what our strengths and weaknesses are, whether we are male or female, stuff like that. So if they are making these changes at that level, not only would they be permanent, but they would also pass the changes on to their offspring."

"So..." Riana thought out loud. "If two parents had their ears done like that woman's, then their children..."

"Would have a good chance of being born with pointed ears, yes." Willhelmina finished as she pushed herself off the back wall into a standing position just as the doors of the lift slid open again.

The two women stepped out into the sterile, white hallway and made their way down the corridor, looking at number plaques on the walls next to each door as they moved. Riana was clearly preoccupied though, still thinking about people permanently altering their bodies to look like elves and nymphs.

"Here we are." Willhelmina called out from a few paces down the hall. "Twenty-Seven Seventeen."

Riana moved up the hall, closing the distance between them in a few strides and stopping next to her friend, looking at the door. It was a flat, white, featureless panel, set into the wall just enough to make it visible. On the right side was a metal plaque with the numbers '2717' on it with a blue light leaking around their edges. Below the plaque was a touch screen with an announcement button glowing on it. Riana reached out and gently touched the button and instantly the hallway melted away around her.

Suddenly she was hot. Extremely hot. Looking up she saw the full light of day blazing away above her, and looking down she saw that she was no longer standing on the antiseptic white floor of the hallway. Rather, she was now standing on an endless sea of blazing hot sand. Tentatively she took a step in the direction she was facing. The sand gave way beneath her foot exactly as she would expect. Her bare skin began to feel dehydrated as she took a few more steps. Looking down she saw that she was wearing her black leathers, and her tattoos were back, glowing vividly in the full day light.

After a moment she crested a low dune and saw a rocky fissure in the desert on the other side. There was a small camp set up at the edge of the fissure and a small group of some kind of creatures seemed to be tearing the place apart. Placing a hand to her forehead over her eyes she strained to see what was going on below her. The creatures looked like giant bugs of some kind with long, whip-like tails curling upwards from their backsides and eight chittenous legs. They could easily be five hundred pound scorpions, except for the human torsos, arms and heads that sprouted from where the bug's heads might have otherwise been. Their human features were ugly. Tough, leathery, and dark from constant exposure to the sun, and all along their backs and the outsides of their arms, their skin looked lumpy and chittenous, just like their scorpion-like lower bodies.

The creatures seemed to be ransacking the camp. Over-turning boxes and chests, tearing into the four small tents and dragging out bedding and other personal belongings into the desert heat. There were half a dozen of the creatures and they seemed to be so engrossed in what they were doing that they did not notice Riana atop the dune watching them.

Carefully, she took a few measured steps toward the scene, trying to get a better look at what was going on. But as one of the creatures dragged a large object from one of the tents, Riana stopped short. Her breath caught up in her throat and her heart began to beat furiously in her chest. The object looked like a body, clad in mage's robes, and trailing a long mane of platinum hair behind its obviously feminine form. She couldn't tell from this distance but she thought she recognized the body. She broke into a run, barreling down the face of the sand dune toward the scene.

Finally the creatures appeared to take notice of her and they formed up into a defensive line, brandishing an array of spears, tridents, whips and nets in her direction. But as she drew closer she could clearly see the long pointed ears on the body and the fine features of the dead elf's face, including her golden eyes, staring lifelessly at her as she approached in a panic.

"MOM!" She shouted as she bore down on the scorpion creatures. One of them made to stab her with its spear but with a wave of her hand, all of the tattoos on her body flared up at once and the creatures howled in pain as their bodies melted away into the desert sand, leaving only their weapons and trappings laying on the sand where they had once been.

Riana didn't stop until she was on the ground cradling her mother's lifeless body in her lap. "MOM!" She cried again as streams of tears washed down her face. The body felt so cold and lifeless in her arms. As though she had been dead for days before the creatures had discovered her body. Hugging her mother's body tightly to her own, Riana rocked back and forth on her knees and sobbed uncontrollably.

"I'm sorry mom. I'm sorry I wasn't here for you. What happened to you? Who did this to you? I should have been here. I should have found a way to be here with you." As she cried and rocked her mother's lifeless body, Ezrina's hand fell to the desert sand and her dead fingers opened slightly allowing the day light to glint off something shiny that caught Riana's eye.

Stifling another bout of sobs, she mopped the tears away from her eyes with the back of her forearm and then reached for her mother's hand. Prying it open the rest of the way she saw a large, pale blue crystal. As she looked at the crystal she saw an image floating deep within its center. Focusing her eyes on the glyph through the lingering tears she thought she knew it from somewhere. Then it hit her. It was an ancient elven symbol for 'a closely guarded secret'.

Blinking at the object and trying to understand what was going on, the entire world began to turn white around her. The desert sand melted away into a flow of white water that solidified into a hard, smooth surface and the next instant she was back in the hallway outside apartment Twenty-Seven Seventeen.

Riana blinked a few times and then looked down to see her finger still poised on the call button. Looking at it doubtfully she turned to look at Willhelmina who was still standing next to her, but now cast her a sour look.

"Were you going to press the button? Or just stand there and gawk at it a while?" She said with a touch of annoyance.

For a moment Riana considered telling Willhelmina about what had happened, but she wasn't sure if it HAD happened. She definitely didn't want Willhelmina to think she was crazy, and she didn't want to mess up their first assignment. So with more than a little concern for what might happen this time, she pushed her finger down on the call button, almost cringing as it pressed into the panel slightly and then sprang back normally. They could hear a faint tone from behind the door panel, then some movement and a moment later the panel slid open.

-34-

A man that could only be Hakiro Yamato stood in the open doorway looking at them. He was very skinny. Almost skeletal. His skin was pale and his dark eyes had a slight up turn to them. His head was shaved bald except for the flaming orange mohawk bisecting his skull from front to back. The man looked at them for a second, then without saying a word stepped sideways allowing them to enter the room.

Willhelmina and Riana moved past the man soundlessly, and he closed the door behind them. The room was dark, the only light in the place seemed to be emanating from one corner of in the room. Once their eyes adjusted they could see what looked to be pieces of various electronics and computer components were scattered everywhere.

Looking toward the source of the light, Riana saw a very large computer console dominating the far corner and most of the two attached walls. There were multiple displays, both flat and holographic, and every surface of the console seemed to be completely free of any kind of dirt, debris, or trash.

"Do you have it?" The man's voice startled the girls. It was rough and painful to the ears. Like the sound of a cat being scrubbed with a blanket of sandpaper.

Riana winced at him as she said, "Yes we have it." Opening the pouch on her belt, she removed the silver metal case and offered it to the man who snapped it up from her hand. Making his way through the sea of parts to a console, he sat down and placed the disk into a receptacle somewhere on the apparatus. Bent toward a display and typing away furiously on a keyboard, he was completely absorbed.

"I guess we're done here." Willhelmina said sarcastically, not trying to keep her voice down at all.

"I guess so." Riana replied absently, her eyes had fixed upon one of the displays above Mr. Yamato's head. Floating lazily above the holographic projector was the ancient elven glyph that stood for 'a closely guarded secret'.

"So we should just go then?" She raised her voice as she directed her question to the hunched form on the other side of the room.

The man waved them away with one arm, not even sparing them a glance when Willhelmina keyed open the door and turned to leave. When Riana didn't move, she turned around, grabbed Riana by the elbow and yanked her back into the sterile white hallway, the door cycling closed behind them.

As they walked back into the court yard between the two buildings, Willhelmina tossed Riana a sideways glance. "What's up?"

"Huh?" Riana snapped her head around to look into Willhelmina's eyes.

"I said, what's up?" Willhelmina repeated, looking more concerned now.

"Oh." Riana's expression changed into one of deep thought and she shifted her eyes back to the bright blue sky of the domed city. "I'm not sure."

"You're not sure what's up?" Willhelmina asked with a doubtful look on her face. "Or you just aren't talking about it?"

"I... saw something." Riana replied sheepishly, completely ignoring her friend's sarcasm.

Willhelmina turned her eyes to the sky, scanning around the area to see if she could confirm whatever it was.

"Not out here." Riana said hastily. "It was inside."

Willhelmina stopped and turned around to look at the building they had just left, as if she could see through the steel and glass structure and detect whatever it was that was bothering her friend. "What was it?"

"I'm... I'm not sure... I don't... Is there any way to get back into Kalijor?" She finally blurted out.

"Uh." Willhelmina said, looking more than a little confused.

"I need to see mom. Can I plug in? Or jack in? Or whatever it's called?" Riana was looking earnestly at her friend now, her eyes pleading.

Willhelmina saw at once how Riana was feeling, and changed mental gears to be more accommodating and less cynical. "I'm not sure. We'll have to ask the techs I think. We can find out when we get back to the Tyconderoga."

Riana nodded then looked around helplessly for a moment before settling her gaze back on her friend. Willhelmina was positively glowing in the day light and open air of the city, thick raven hair framing her face and making her green eyes shine brightly.

35

"I just don't understand WHY you would want to go back in." Gayle was saying, her voice now rough from the hours of debate.

"Because I need to see my mother!" Riana half shouted across the meeting room.

They had asked Xavier immediately upon their return if it would be possible for Riana to reenter Kalijor. After admitting he wasn't sure, he had set up a meeting with the three technicians most familiar with Riana's internal workings and systems. For multiple hours now they had been debating about whether it was technically possible, but in the end it came back down to the psychology of it. They all wanted to know why she wanted to go back.

"But it isn't REALLY your mother." Wayne said with exasperation in his voice. "It is merely a computer simulation of a person."

"Yes, I understand that Wayne." Riana said icily, glaring at the diminutive, goblin-like features of the man across the table. "But that does not change the fact that she raised me. And I want to see her! Now is it possible or not?!" She swept her violet eyes across the panel of scientists, her ears swept back in anger and frustration.

"Yes. Of COURSE it can be done. You must understand that it would never be permanent. You would be entering as a player and the system is designed to treat players differently. She may not even recognize you, let alone realize that you are of any relation." Bart intoned, his voice still sounding fresh and unperturbed after the hours of debate. "Not that you are even remotely similar to her any longer."

Riana leveled her eyes on the blond man who seemed to sink into his chair slightly under the weight of her gaze. "Look," she spat out at them, her temper rising up again, "I don't give a damn about what you think is going on here. I only want to know if I can get back in there and see her. If she doesn't know me then fine, so be it. But I need to know for myself. Who the hell are you people to tell me who she is anyway?!"

Suddenly Xavier cleared his throat, silencing the room instantly.

Riana swung her head around toward the door. He and Willhelmina were standing in the open doorway, apparently having just entered the room. Willhelmina made a move to catch Riana's eye, and gave her a great grin from behind Xavier. Riana stared at the pair, her eyes narrowed slightly but an iota of hope was winding its way through her mind.

"Can it be done?" Xavier asked simply of the entire room.

"Yes sir, but…" Gayle began but Xavier cut her off abruptly.

"Excellent. Make it happen. I need them both in-game in ninety minutes." He turned around and moved to step out of the conference room then hesitated a moment to speak to Willhelmina. "Willhelmina, if you and Riana could please meet me in my office for a moment?"

"Of course!" She responded brightly.

Xavier inclined his head slightly. Snapping up his cane, he disappeared into the hallway.

Instantly, Riana came up out of her seat, cast a chilling glare around the room at the techs and then moved across to Willhelmina and dragged her bodily out of the room.

"What was that about?" Willhelmina stammered as she caught her balance and moved to match Riana's faster than usual pace down the corridor.

"Fools." Riana said under her breath, still glaring ahead at some unseen spot on the wall at the end of the corridor.

"What?" Willhelmina asked, not at all sure what was happening.

"Idiots!" Riana raged, stopping in mid-stride and turning around suddenly to make a rude gesture at the closed conference room door. "Sanctimonious, self righteous, conceited… FOOLS!!" She gestured at the door again as Willhelmina turned around to see what she was doing. Riana then whirled around again and started off down the corridor, leaving Willhelmina standing there staring at the conference room door.

"REE! What happened in there?!" She hollered at her friend's back as she ran to catch up again.

"They told me Ezrina isn't my mother!! They said she was just a computer program!" Riana stormed, waving her hands around frantically by way of explanation.

"Well, technically she IS just a com…" Willhelmina was in the middle of saying when she realized Riana was staring at her with an intensity that could have bored a hole through the deck plates. "I mean she IS your mother. There's no doubt about that at all. But she IS a computer program too."

Riana glared at her for a moment longer before sweeping off down the hall again toward Xavier's office. "That doesn't change the fact that she is my mother, and I need to be there for her if she needs me. I'm JUST a computer program as well, remember?!"

The rest of the trip to Xavier's office was made in total silence. Each of the women rolling thoughts around in their heads until before either of them expected it, they were there.

"Ladies." Xavier called to them from his giant glass desk. "Have a seat please. Help yourselves to some refreshments and I will be right with you."

"It seems like we were just here doing the same thing." Riana whispered to Willhelmina, trying to bridge the silence built up in the hallway as they sank into the overly soft leather couch.

"Yes. It does." Willhelmina said as she shifted uneasily in the couch just as she had done before. "I have always despised this couch," she mumbled under her breath.

"I'm sorry Kat. I didn't mean to jump down your throat earlier." Riana said as she looked at the space station below them through the transparent floor.

"I know." Willhelmina replied, stopping her fruitless struggle with the sofa and looking at her friend with a warm smile. "I lost someone once. I know what it feels like to want to do whatever you can for them."

Riana looked up at her friend with a weak smile. "Thank you." She said simply. Willhelmina smiled affectionately.

"All made up and ready for work?" Xavier's silky voice slid between them, making them turn to look at him. Somehow he had managed to slip into one of the leather chairs and pour himself a cup of tea without either of them noticing. He sat there with an inscrutable expression on his face, holding a saucer in one hand and the tea cup in the other. Watching them through the steam rising from the cup, he took a small sip and returned the cup to its saucer.

"What do you mean work?" Riana asked with a tone of concern. "I thought you said I could go into Kalijor and see my mom."

Xavier smiled then and set his tea cup on the table, exchanging it for a small black box with some buttons on it. "Quite right. So I did." He replied in his carefully controlled voice. "As it happens I have something that needs dropped off with someone in Rathalon, and you two being couriers for me, I thought you would be willing to run the errand for me while en route to see your mother."

Riana stared for a long moment, trying to figure out if he was joking or testing them. He smiled simply, watching her trying to figure things out.

"Drop something off in Rathalon…" Riana repeated. "With someone?"

"Indeed." Xavier replied, the knowing smile still at the corners of his mouth.

"Wait." Riana said, holding her index finger up in the air and screwing her face up as though she were trying to force a series of thoughts together with brute force. Then she looked at Willhelmina, eyes open wide and ears perking up in sudden comprehension. "I get it! Kalijor is more than just a game world! People use it to conduct business! Have meetings and make exchanges!"

"This is amazing!" Riana was talking quickly now. Trying to get the thoughts out before she managed to convince herself that they were false. "Almost everything in this world is driven by data! The vehicles, the computers, life support systems, even the currency is all virtual. In a world like this nearly everything passes through a digital medium at some point or other, and in some fashion. So it stands to reason that in a virtual environment real meetings and real exchanges could take place. It would allow parties to meet in near anonymity and exchange information freely, but in difficult to detect and capture forms. Items, scrolls, gems, even swords and such could all be virtual representations of information."

308

Willhelmina looked at her calmly. Xavier on the other hand, was looking at Riana with a strange look she had never seen on his face before. It was a look of… appreciation? She wasn't sure, but he seemed to be impressed with her. Finally he spoke again when it was apparent that Riana was done.

"You are very astute Miss Thorindal. Especially for one so new to this world of ours. Kalijor has long been used as a middle ground for parties wishing to have meetings, negotiations, exchanges, and even the occasional war to settle disputes. Kalijor has always been much more than a simple game world to amuse bored teenagers." The lights dimmed in the domed room and a hologram of a scruffy looking human male with dark hair, brown eyes and a scar running down the left side of his face, just barely missing the eye appeared. He was wearing finely-woven chain mail over his upper body, arms and legs, with simple metal plates over his elbows and knees. Sturdy leather boots, gauntlets with metal plates attached to them and a scabbard on his back with an ornately decorated long-sword strapped across his back finished off the image of a burly warrior.

"This is Malice." Xavier said after they had a moment to take in his appearance. "He is a shady individual who happens to have something I want. I have worked a deal out with him via correspondence and all that remains is the actual exchange." He pressed another button on his remote and the image of Malice faded, replaced by a scroll of parchment with an ornate wax seal on it.

"This is what he wants, and what you two will deliver to him. In exchange, he will give you this." Again the image faded and when the new one appeared, Riana gasped quietly. Willhelmina didn't seem to take any notice of her reaction, but Xavier raised an eyebrow slightly, clearly curious.

The new image was of a large gem. It was ornately cut and was adorned with an elven glyph floating in its heart. Riana instantly recognized the bauble. She was taken aback by the image, her mind reeling.

"Something troubling you Miss Thorindal?" Xavier said with a tone that may have passed as concern.

"Wha?" Riana snapped her eyes away from the image and looked at Willhelmina and Xavier in turn. They were both looking at her curiously now. "No. I um…" She didn't want to tell them about the vision. She would do nothing to endanger her chances of going to see if her mother was alright. "I recognize that symbol. I saw it this morning in Mr. Yamato's apartment."

"Indeed." Xavier said coolly. "This is interesting news."

Willhelmina was now looking back and forth between the other two, the conversation having changed directions and left her behind.

"Do you recognize the symbol? Can you translate it?" He asked her with a raised eyebrow.

"Yes. It looks like ancient elvish. It stands for 'a closely guarded secret'." She kept her eyes on Xavier's while she spoke, looking for some sign of what the object was, but as usual his face remained unreadable.

"Very good." He said simply. "And as couriers of Solidarity Online, I would expect you both to keep it that way."

"Of course sir." Riana said automatically. She wanted to know what it was and she knew that she would do whatever she had to in order to find out;

but there was no way she would tell him that. Although her mother would still take precedence. "How do we…"

"Get it to me?" He finished for her, the smile returning to his face. "Just make sure it is on one of your persons before you log out and I will get it." He pressed another button on his remote and the image changed yet again. This time it displayed the exterior of a tavern Riana had seen before.

"The Crossed Swords." She said aloud as she looked at the image of two long swords forming an X through the middle of the sign. She had seen it many times in Rathalon throughout her youth. It had always been the sort of place even curious, rule-breaking young elves would avoid. She looked at Willhelmina who was also staring at the sign with an air of recognition.

"This is where Malice will be. The meeting is set for tomorrow afternoon at one PM our time. That will give you just under two days Kalijor-time to take care of business. I want you out of the system the moment you take possession of the item."

Riana looked at him again, searching his eyes. Would two days be enough time to find her mother and have a talk with her, assuming she was still alive? If she was dead in the Burning Expanse, it would take more than two days to get there and back again from Rathalon. She needed more time.

Xavier seemed to pick up on her line of thought and responded before she could open her mouth. "I am sorry about the time frame, this came up suddenly and it is urgent. You may, of course, log back in and take care of your business Miss Thorindal. AFTER I have the item."

Riana smiled slightly then. She felt better now. "Thank you sir." She said.

"Of course Miss Thorindal. I do understand the importance of family, even if circumstances make it a bit odd." He gave Willhelmina a faint smile and nod. "Are there any questions before you head down to the game deck?"

"No sir." The girls replied in unison.

"Very well then, best of luck to the both of you. I will see you tomorrow afternoon." He inclined his head to them, stood up from the chair, snapped up his cane and made his way deftly across the office to his desk, leaving Riana and Willhelmina to make their own way out of the office.

36

Fifteen minutes later, they entered the 'gaming' level of the station. Riana stared at the rows of computer terminals stretching off in every direction. A few technicians were bustling about here and there making minor adjustments to the various systems in the room as Riana followed Willhelmina through the rows and rows of computers. At the back of the room, Gayle and Wayne were bustling around a pair of what looked like giant eggs.

"What are those things?" Riana asked Willhelmina as they continued to move toward the strange objects. They were easily seven feet tall and four of five feet around. The stark white matched the walls of the room and a thick bundle of cables snaked away into a near-by computer terminal.

"Those are game pods." Willhelmina said with a smile. "You can play without them but they really add to the experience. Keep out outside stimulus, let you focus on the game world. One of those saved my life when my parent's apartment was burned," she said appreciatively.

"You were in one of these things? In the game when it happened?" Riana asked, her eyes large and round, looking at Willhelmina with a new sense of appreciation for what she had gone through.

"Yeah. The whole place burned down around me. In fact they had to cut me out of it. The fire was so hot that it fused the hatch." Willhelmina replied as they drew next to the pods and techs.

Gayle glared at Riana as she approached, apparently still upset about the meeting. Riana returned her look with a hard stare, her violet eyes flaring and ears sweeping back daring her to make a challenge.

"We're all set here." She said sharply, her eyes lingering on Riana for a moment before sweeping across Willhelmina and then returning to her computer console.

"What do we do now?" Riana asked the techs, but looked at Willhelmina.

"This pod is Willhelmina's." Wayne said, his troll-like features contorted in concentration as he indicated one of the pods with an absent gesture.

At that, Willhelmina moved to the pod and pressed a recessed button on its surface. The side split open, twisting upwards out of the way. Inside the pod an extremely comfortable-looking, ergonomic seat faced a computer terminal with several displays. A thick cable hanging down from the top of the pod ended in what looked like a mechanical centipede on the end of a string.

Willhelmina slid into the seat and made herself comfortable. Tapping a few buttons on the terminal caused the displays to light up. Reaching above her head, she grabbed the strange, dangling apparatus and pulled it down toward her head, cable paying out from a hidden supply in the top of the pod. She rested the device on her head fiddling with it a bit before all of the displays in the pod lit up brighter, registering a connection.

"This harness picks up electrical activity in the brain and translates it into instructions for the system." She said as a panel lit up and displayed some information. "It also translates computer output into carrier waves that your brain can interpret as sensory input."

"You mean the computer can make you see and feel things?" Riana said curiously.

"Exactly." Willhelmina replied with a smile as she settled back into the seat. "These systems can feed all of the computer output directly into your brain, or you can use the other displays for secondary information, system status and so forth. It all depends on your personal preferences and ability to process all of the information."

A humming noise behind her made Riana turn around to see the other pod opening up. The interior was identical to Willhelmina's with the exception of the conspicuous absence of the dangling headpiece.

"Where's my harness?" Riana asked Wayne and Gayle.

"You don't need one." Wayne replied, looking at her. "Your interface is more direct and efficient than encephalographic induction."

"What do you mean?" Riana looked skeptically back at Willhelmina who offered her little help in the form of an unknowing shrug.

"You are a cyborg." Gayle said coolly. "As much machine as living tissue. More machine in fact, in your case."

"So?"

"So." Wayne moved over to the pod and pulled a single black cable out of the right arm rest of the chair and brandished it as though it was an amazing technological breakthrough. "You will use this, connected to your onboard computers, rather than a less efficient EI harness."

"I have onboard computers?" Riana looked down at her trim body wondering where such things would be kept and why she hadn't realized they were there.

"Of course you do. There would be no other way to make your brain interface with all of the mechanical parts. What are you looking for?" Wayne stopped suddenly as Riana began looking inside her sleeves and cuffs and down the inside of her top at her chest.

"The plug." She said flatly. "Where does that thing go?"

Wayne looked at her like she was completely out of her mind. "Please sit down Miss Thorindal. I'll show you."

She made to move toward the pod Wayne was standing next to, then stopped and cast him a doubtful look. "It isn't somewhere... indecent... Is it?"

Wayne's mouth dropped open and he let go of the cable in his hand, which recoiled back into the pod with a loud snapping noise. His jaw worked up and down as he tried to formulate an answer. Finally, he gave up and looked helplessly to Gayle and Willhelmina. Willhelmina burst into laughter and even Gayle sniggered a bit from behind her console.

With a huge grin plastered on her face Riana closed the distance to the pod and seated herself on the ergonomic chair. Wayne turned and looked at her, shaking his head in consternation but managed to get back to business. He reached back into the pod and paid out the cable again.

"This may feel a little strange at first, but it should be over quickly." He said as he lifted her right arm and bent down to get a better look at the inside of her wrist. Slowly he moved the end of the cable nearer to the base of her palm until the cable lit up and a small opening formed in her skin, revealing a small plug just beneath.

"Here we go." He said, as he pushed the cable home.

Riana's body convulsed briefly as her mind interfaced with the computer. Her vision stretched and warped, the colors reversing and melting together before the room faded and her world was enveloped in darkness.

37

The darkness lasted mere heartbeats, although it felt like a lifetime. It was long enough for the panic to seep into Riana's veins and make an icy course through her heart. She could feel nothing at all, as though her mind had been completely disconnected from her body. She had no sense of time or where she was and for the briefest of moments she considered the possibility that they had shut off her body and this was 'death'.

Then there was light. Daylight. Bright, streaming, warming, comforting daylight. Slowly she opened her eyes and looked around. She was standing in a green grassy field that stretched out as far as she could see. Turning, she saw what was unmistakably the outer wall of the great city of Rathalon.

"The Plain of Serenity!" She exclaimed out loud. Her mind was flooded with a stream of emotions. She was at once happy, apprehensive, confused, and scared. She was ecstatic about returning to her home, but now it was cast in an entirely different light. Now she knew the truth of things.

As she pondered her feelings on the matter, she became aware of a smooth warm object pressing into the bare skin of her back and wheeling around, her hand dropping reflexively to the hilt of Elkorine, she was met by the gaze of Xanthe's deep blue eyes. The animal nuzzled her again and she wrapped her arms around its neck with a sense of joy.

Xanthe seemed a bit confused by her behavior but responded affectionately, seemingly enjoying the attention.

Stepping back from Xanthe, Riana examined him carefully, looking for any signs of damage or wounds, but he looked just as amazing as the day she had first seen him. Then she took a moment to look herself over and was elated to find all of her tattoos were back. She was wearing her black leathers, and Elkorine was slung low on her left hip while Ezrina's dagger was snug on her right. Her clothes were clean and looked brand new. Her body was also clean and undamaged, surprising when she thought back to the state she had been in as Ambrai had fallen.

"One of the perks of having admin privileges." A silky, lilting voice trickled over her shoulder.

Riana snapped around yet again, this time to find Katrina standing there in her robes, looking immaculate and clutching Chavan in her right hand. She had a huge grin plastered across her face, driving home the fact that Katrina and Willhelmina were in fact one and the same as Riana took her in, eyes wide.

"KAT!" Riana exclaimed as she pounced on her sister and wrapped herself around the other elf in an embrace that would have stifled a barbarian.

Katrina staggered under the assault, but recovered gracefully, prying Riana off of her and stepping back with the grin still on her face. "It's good to see you happy again Ree."

"Oh I'm so excited to be back again!" Riana bubbled brightly as she turned a few circles in the grassy plain and then embraced Xanthe in another bear hug.

"It is nice, isn't it?" Katrina remarked, turning around slowly, taking in the scene. "The scenery is much nicer than on the station at any rate."

Riana chuckled as she disengaged herself from Xanthe and turned to look at her companion. Katrina had crouched down and was rummaging through her pack for something, finally producing the scroll that Xavier had shown them in his office.

"So, we have a couple days to burn, then we need to get this to this Malice person." She said as she put it back into her pack and secured the top.

"Right." Agreed Riana, drifting away in thought for a moment.

"So, where do we start? What's the plan?" Katrina looked at her sister questioningly.

"Well." Riana thought out loud. "We should check our house and see if mom is there. Beyond that I'm not sure really. Maybe Gornin would know something if she isn't in Rathalon?"

"Seems as good a line of thought as any." Katrina agreed, then gave Xanthe a questioning look. "You think he'll be ok outside while we are in town? He won't eat the cattle or anything?"

Riana looked around at Xanthe, who was standing there calmly looking at them as they spoke. She stepped in closer to him and ran her hand down his smooth, finely scaled neck. He made a deep 'cooing' noise in response. "Will you be alright out here for a little while friend?"

Xanthe nuzzled her approvingly, pushing her in the direction of the city's west gate. After another long moment looking at him the girls started moving that way while Xanthe moved off into the open field poking around the occasional bush and small tree curiously.

"It seems he will be fine." Riana said with a grin, her ears perked up with happiness as they neared the gate with its formidable looking guards. They were just as Riana recalled. Decked out in the glimmering plate mail of Rathalon's standing army and holding double-ended sword-staves in their hands, the guards watched the girls approach suspiciously. As soon as they were within conversation range one of the guards, a burly human with dark eyes and a face covered in bushy bristles beneath his helmet, hailed them.

"Good morrow travelers. What is your business in the fair city of Rathalon this day?" His voice was gruff as he stared at them each in turn.

The sisters sighed and looked at one another knowingly. For as long as either of them could remember, they had had to answer that question every time they came through the gate. What's more, Corporal Edmonds had been the officer on duty at the gate for more than ten years now, and he still questioned them every time they passed his post.

Riana feigned a serious expression and stood at a rigid attention, then saluted the man and barked off a reply. "Sir! We are just returning from a six month sojourn into outer space where I found out that I was just a computer program in a vast virtual world that had been created for the entertainment of the masses, sir! But I wanted to see how our mother is getting on sir, so we logged back in to see if we could track her down!"

When she finished shouting her response, Katrina punched her playfully in the shoulder and gave her a cross-eyed look. Meanwhile Corporal Edmonds was staring at them both, his eyes blinking slowly as he tried to figure out if they were in need of a healer for some sort of head trauma.

"Ladies Thorindal. You make less sense every time I see you. Although admittedly it has been more than a year since you have passed through the west gate of the city, so I am sure…" He stopped mid-sentence and his expression changed. He stared off between the girls. Finally he raised his free hand to point at something behind the elves. "What on Kalijor is THAT?"

They both turned around curiously. A set of clawed feet wiggled in the air above the grass and a tail lashed about wildly. Briefly, Xanthe's serpentine head poked up out of the grass and looked back at them all as they watched him. His great blue eyes blinked a few times curiously then his head retreated back out of sight into the grass and he resumed rubbing his back on the ground with his wild, writhing motions.

"Oh." Riana said, as she turned back around to face the Corporal. "That would be Xanthe. He's alright. He's a friend of ours." She smiled sweetly at the man who was still looking suspiciously at the creature.

"Is it safe?" He asked point blank.

"Oh, he's just a big kitten really." She responded, eliciting a giggle from Katrina, "Although I wouldn't recommend sticking your arm down his throat or anything."

"And it's just going to wander around out here is it? While you are away in the city?" He shifted his eyes to Riana as he finished the question, clearly not wanting to be left with the creature while it's master was out of sight.

"He's fine. Really." Riana said, patting him on his armored shoulder as she slipped past the man towards the gates that two of the other guards were holding open for them.

Just then Xanthe rolled over suddenly and hopped to his feet, his brilliant blue eyes watching Riana and Katrina disappear around the corner into the city. Then he shifted his gaze to the guards and cocked his head to one side as if trying to work out what to do about them. Finally he turned around with an abrupt twist, the blade-like bone tip of his tail slashing around behind him with the sudden movement sent a rooster tail of cut grass shooting up into the air in a great green wave and then he galloped off into the fields.

"I think I should speak to the General about a raise in pay." The Corporal said under his breath as he watched Xanthe moving further out into the plane.

38

Everything in their home was covered in a thick grey layer of dust. It appeared that no one had been there in a very long time. As they moved through it, Katrina pointed out that they were leaving a trail of footprints in the dust that had settled on the floor. Clearly, their mother was not there, but Riana proceeded to check every room in the house regardless. She swept up and down the hallway, diving into each room, rummaging around for a few moments and then returning to the hallway again to dive into the next.

She checked every room in the house at least three times before finally giving up. A large cloud of dust billowed up around her as she plopped down into a chair in the dinning room. Her deep sigh of disappointment was abruptly cut off by coughing and wheezing from the inhaled dust.

"How long were we gone?" She asked Katrina, who had chosen a seat more than half an hour ago and was looking through her spell book.

"Uh." Katrina looked up at her, screwing her face up in thought. "We did a couple months of getting you used to your body, then around three and a half or four of training so that's around six months, multiply by… I would guess around three and a half years. Maybe a couple months more or less." She finally decided.

"Nearly four years?!" Riana looked as though she had just been slapped hard in the face. "But it was only six months!"

"Earth time." Katrina said off handedly as she stuck her nose back into her spell book. "There is a differential of seven to one. So every day you spend in the real world, seven days pass here."

Riana was flabbergasted. She had no concept how much the passage of time in Kalijor would have changed things. "Why?" She finally managed weakly.

Katrina, looking up from her book again, forced her eyes to focus on Riana across the table. "Oh. It's done that way for a few reasons. One is so that the players can actually see the world evolving and changing, with a one to one time factor that would not really be possible. Another reason is because some things only happen at certain times in Kalijor, like night, or in September. So Time is sped up here to give people more chances and less waiting around in order to get things done."

"What kinds of things?" Riana asked. Still looking blown away by the whole idea.

"What? Oh." Katrina lifted her face from her book again, then set it down on the table, apparently coming to the conclusion that she wasn't going to finish her spells until Riana had been fully briefed on the inner workings of Kalijor. "Ok. Remember when we would deliver those strange plants and stuff for that nice Neville man down at the end of Main Street?"

"Yes!" Riana said enthusiastically. "He used to give us half a silver apiece for it too!"

"Exactly." Katrina replied in the tone of a teacher. "That is what is called a quest by the game developers. An NPC asks you to do something, and offers you some reward for the task once it is complete. However, some quests can only be done at certain times. So remember if you will that Neville never was around to have us run errands for him on Saturday or Sunday. That is a very simple time limited quest. He will also only pay you to run his errand once per day remember? No matter how much stuff he had laying around, he would never ask you or let you deliver more than one plant or vegetable in a day."

"Wow." Said Riana, looking thoughtful. "I had no idea it was so complicated.

"Apparently very few people do." Katrina said, as she pulled her spell book off the table, letting a little cloud of dust up into the air as she did so. "Or so the developers tell me anyway." She shrugged noncommittally as she stuck her nose back into the book again.

"Almost four years." Riana murmured to herself. "What could have happened in four years? Where could she have gone?"

Katrina shrugged again from behind her book.

"We should go ask Gornin. He seemed to know quite a lot about what was going on before. Maybe he has heard from her recently." Riana had flashes of Ezrina laying on the ground as she spoke. It wasn't like Ezrina to be away from home for so long and she obviously had not returned home in the years her daughters had been gone from the world. Her search in the Burning Expanse seemed important, as it had to do with Kilishandra and her legacy. Riana could easily imagine her mother fighting to the death over it. The real question in her mind was, whom would pursue Ezrina out into the middle of that scorched wasteland and then kill her over something like that bauble Xavier had shown them?

"We should go and ask him, now." Riana said resolutely, standing up.

Katrina looked up at her for a moment then sighed slightly as she packed away her spell book. "Alright. Let's go and ask him."

39

"Your mother is safe Riana Thorindal." Gornin's gravelly voice rolled across them with a measured patience.

Riana was livid. They had arrived in Cohai via the Rathalon portal yesterday. An entire night had passed before Gornin had come to meet them. Time was running short and Gornin was insisting that Ezrina was fine but refused to tell them where she was or what she was doing.

"Gornin, I need to see her, I NEED to know that she is alright!" Riana hissed at him, her ears cocked back threateningly.

"Riana. You did a very good job of dealing with Ambrai. You have come a long way since I met you. But you still have a long way to go yet, and forgive me for not making your path more difficult." Gornin's voice was as calm and collected as ever.

"What are you talking about Gornin? Where is my mom?" The anger was rising up in her and she was fast losing the desire to even try and stem it off.

"If you can not see the path laid out before you, it is not my place to illuminate it. You must discover this for yourself Riana Thorindal. Your mother is safe and continues in her efforts to locate some means to destroy the amulet."

"Yes. But WHERE?!" She shouted at the troll.

Gornin gave her a reproachful look. She didn't care much about what he thought at the moment anyway and pressed the attack.

"She's my mother! I have the amulet that she sent me after. Isn't she going to need the amulet in order to destroy it? Shouldn't somebody give it to her? How is she going to follow through on her end of the deal if she doesn't have it?!" She was stabbing Gornin in the chest with her index finger as she shouted at him, but he simply stood there and allowed her to vent.

"You will understand one day. But for now all I can tell you is that she is safe." Gornin's eyes looked sad, as though he wanted desperately to tell her what she wanted to know.

"ONE DAY?! What the hell does that mean? One day I will know? Gornin, we chased half way across Kalijor for this damn amulet. I killed my mothers' best friend for it! I even destroyed my mother's body to retrieve it. I think I deserve a little more than 'one day you will know.' This is intolerable!"

Riana paced around the portal chamber, tossing her arms about wildly as she ranted.

Katrina had long ago slunk away behind one of the defensive columns in the room, trying to stay out of the fray. Riana tossed her an icy glare as she stalked past her on her angry circuit around the room.

"I know it is frustrating Riana. And yes, you have done much. But you need to understand that this is larger than you and your mother. All of Kalijor is at stake, and much beyond as well." At that he eyed her with a knowing look that made Riana start.

'What is he talking about?' She thought as she raised an eyebrow at him. His eyes returned to a passive look.

"What are you talking about?" She finally gave up and asked him point blank.

"I am talking about the future Riana Thorindal. The future of your world, and mine." He said simply.

Riana's retort came up short as she realized what he had said. She focused her violet eyes on him in earnest and twitched her ears up in sudden curiosity.

At the same time, Katrina moved up to Riana's side. Both girls examined Gornin. The troll stood there unimpressively, watching them.

"What do you…" Riana began to ask, but he cut her off with a pleasant wave of his knobby, thin fingers.

"I know a great many things about this world Riana Thorindal. And about your new world as well. Now is not the time to discuss these things. Suffice to say that your mother is safe, but if too many people know where she is, or what she is doing, her life could be put in great peril. Now, if I am not too much mistaken, I believe you have an appointment in Rathalon. Do take care to keep yourselves out of trouble ladies."

Riana and Katrina gaped. He nodded, bowed low to them, then turned around and left the portal chamber, pulling the heavy door closed behind him.

"What was that all about?" Riana asked Katrina, not taking her eyes off the closed door.

"I have no idea." Katrina replied, her eyes similarly glued to the door.

"I thought he was an N…P…P…?" Riana said, unsure of the term.

"NPC." Katrina corrected her. "And yeah. I thought so too. But he can't be if he knows about the real world can he?"

"I suppose not. But how can he be a real person? Hasn't he been here for hundreds of years?"

Katrina mulled this over for a while, pacing the room now as she contemplated what they had just learned. "Well," she began, thinking out loud, "I was here for most of your life. SO set me to the task when I was twenty years old and I was more or less in-game constantly for better than four years real time which makes us around thirty years old in game. The last time I heard Gornin was over three-hundred years old, so either there is a person jacked in somewhere that has been plugged in for more than forty years, or something fishy is going on here."

As she listened to Katrina working things through, Riana glanced out one of the high, slit-like windows of the Cohai portal chamber to the clear blue sky. "We have to go Kat. Malice will be at the Crossed Swords soon."

"Alright." Katrina said absently, her mind still working furiously on the newly arisen issue of Gornin's strange confession. Together they walked into the shimmering, glowing rings and vanished from Cohai with a faint popping noise.

40

The Crossed Swords stood by itself on the northeastern edge of the city, across from the huge public coliseum. Nothing was constructed within a dozen paces of the building in which they both now stood, and although she had lived in Rathalon up until a few months ago, she had never entered the establishment before today. Now she knew why her mother had always warned them away from it with such vehemence.

The large building was built around a small pit that was sunk into the floor and surrounded by bleachers. Tables placed on tiered platforms allowed everyone in the place to get a good view of the action in the pit no matter where they sat. Even at mid-day, the place was full of people that seemed to be overly interested in what was going on in the arena below them. Riana realized as they moved deeper into the building's dark interior that a bloody battle between two were-creatures was the center of attention. The creatures slashed each other to ribbons with their razor claws, drawing whooping and howling from the spectators who seemed to be enjoying themselves a little too much for Riana's taste.

The room was barely lit by torches and candles, as there were no windows in the building at all, which added a flickering, orange pallor to the people as they yelled, pumping their arms in the air in support of their chosen fighter.

As they continued onward in search of Malice, Riana realized that the fight was no longer the center of attention for many of the people in the place. For the first time since the day she had put them on, Riana felt nearly naked in her leathers. Her skin turned crimson as she felt dozens of eyes rove over her tattooed body. Closing the short distance between herself and Katrina, she grabbed her sister's arm and pressed her body up against Katrina's to try and shield herself from the lecherous gazes.

"This must be where every creep within a thousand miles comes to hang out in their off time." She whispered in Katrina's ear, as she flung icy glares that bounced off of the watching crowd like a hail of blunt arrows.

"You could be right about that." Katrina offered in solace, "Although you aren't exactly wearing what most would consider to be conservative clothing." She grinned.

"Yeah? Well it never bothered me before. I guess I can handle the occasional roving eye, but a whole room full! And they are all armed and scarred to boot!" Her voice was a hiss in her sister's ear as she tried to keep it quiet.

"Very true I suppose… Oh, there he is." Katrina pointed to a table in a dark corner on the far side of the room where the bearded human was sitting with a pint of ale in his hand and his giant sword close at hand.

The girls made a direct line for him, moving with purpose across the room. Riana noticed that as soon as people figured out where they were headed, the looks ceased almost immediately. Attention returned to the fight in the pit, although it seemed to be done out of fear rather than out of any interest in the fight.

Malice inclined his head as they approached his table. Taking a hearty swig off his ale, he wiped his mouth with the back of his hand and pointed toward the two other chairs at the table. Obligingly, the girls sat down, facing the gruff man who eyed them each in turn, with appraising looks that made them feel like they were sitting before a jury. His eyes lingered on Riana for much longer than they did on Katrina. He leaned forward in his chair with his eyes on Riana, looking her up and down as though he were inspecting a prize mare.

"Interesting." He said in a gruff voice that had a tinge of a growl to it. "So, he sends his new cyborg mongrel and her handler to do his work eh?"

"Excuse me?!" Riana exclaimed, standing up so quickly that her chair went clattering to the floor behind her.

Katrina turned a look of pure hatred on him, but remained sitting, with one hand on Chavan and the other clearly visible on the surface of the table. "Malice." She said with a tone of dislike that she did not bother hiding. "I believe you have something for us."

"Oh. I've got something for ya, sure enough." He sneered at them. "But first I want ya to answer a question for me."

"We aren't here to play question and answer with you." Riana said coldly, leaning over a bit and planting her knuckles on the surface of the table with enough force that Malice's tankard threatened to tip over.

Looking entirely nonplussed, he snatched his ale before it had a chance to spill. Taking another swig, he stared at Katrina, his eyes full of mirth. "Your mongrel is out of control. You should reign in the leash a bit."

Riana was half way over the table with her arms outstretched toward the man's neck before Katrina managed to stop her. Wrapping her arms around Riana's waist, she heaved her off the table and planted her bodily into the chair she had just vacated with a small thump. "Ree. We're here on business. He's just trying to rile you."

"Well he's doing a damn good job." Riana replied, not trying to keep her voice down at all and pushing upward out of the chair. Malice smiled at her in return.

"Yes. He certainly is." Katrina responded, putting a hand on Riana's shoulder and pushing her back down into the chair once more. "Please Ree. Just a couple more minutes. I promise you can maim him after we get what we came for." She smiled a knowing smile, her golden eyes glittering in the flickering torch light.

Riana relaxed noticeably, slumping into the chair with her arms folded over her chest and violet eyes glaring at the man across the table with pure, murderous intent.

"Ask your question." Katrina said calmly as she stooped to pick up Riana's toppled chair, planting herself firmly on it before returning her gaze to Malice.

The man sneered a bit in Riana's direction, but didn't actually make eye contact with her before looking back at Katrina and smiling. "Very well." He paused long enough to take a pull from his tankard, draining it dry and slamming it forcefully back onto the table. "My question is this. Why, do you suppose, that a company like Solidarity Online, and more to the point, a man like Xavier Quinn would go to the trouble of adopting a poor orphan after her parents were killed in a mysterious fire? And more to the point why do you think they would take said orphan back to their most closely guarded stronghold instead of putting her up at the facility closest to where they found the orphan?"

Katrina's mouth had fallen open in shock. Even Riana was stumped by his question, her arms had fallen into her lap and all desire to throttle him had temporarily left her, although the look in her eyes said the desire was fast rekindling.

"I ask only because it has never happened before, or since your, *'unfortunate accident'*. After which of course they put you to work straight-away on their top secret research project. I was just wondering what extraordinary attribute it was that you possess that would make them do something so out of character." He laughed cruelly. "Anyway, I can see by the stunned, vacant look on your face that you don't know any better than I do. So I guess we'll just do our deal and be off."

He stood up from the table and removed a small leather pouch from his belt, tossing it carelessly onto the table. "I believe you have something for me as well?"

Katrina removed the scroll from her pack and handed it to him absently. Her eyes were on him but could not focus through the cloud of emotions. Malice snapped up the scroll, hefted his large sword and swept out of the room before either of them could even think to question him.

-41-

"Come in Ree!" Willhelmina's voice lilted through the intercom unit next to her door with a bit more vigor than Riana was used to hearing lately.

Riana keyed the door open and slipped into the spacious apartment. The walls were the same glistening white as all the walls in the Tyconderoga, where they could be seen, but they had been covered from floor to ceiling with pictures, artwork, movie posters, and a myriad of other objects. Her shelves were cluttered with various trinkets, little figurines and long-saved toys. Books of all kinds were stacked up in corners, on shelves, and under furniture. Video and computer disks piled up in untidy stacks and heaps in the spaces between all of the other items. It wasn't terribly messy, but it was certainly a bit disorderly. It felt much more lived-in than Riana's own apartment. This felt much more like home to her and she wasn't sure if it was due to the clutter and lived-in feel, or just because it was Willhelmina's place and Willhelmina was her most solid link to this new life of hers.

As she moved across the main room towards the bedroom she heard the fervent tapping of Willhelmina's fingers on her computer console and sighed heavily as she realized what her friend was doing. It had been more than two weeks since they had met Malice in Rathalon. Ever since, Willhelmina had spent every waking moment she could spare in her room, searching through old data records. She wasn't sure what Willhelmina was looking for, but she knew that this new obsession was not healthy and tried to get her out, to the gym or the hydroponic botanical garden or anywhere really, whenever she could.

Stepping over the threshold into Willhelmina's bedroom, Riana saw her friend frantically tapping away at her computer console as usual, but now she wore a happy expression on her face and her emerald eyes were bright with excitement. Clearly she had encountered some measure of success.

"You found something?" She echoed her thoughts out loud.

Willhelmina turned to look at her and her face lit up with a wide grin. "I did. Com'ere and look at this a sec."

Riana slid into another chair near Willhelmina's desk and looked at the holographic display hovering in the air above the console. Two jagged lines ran horizontally across the display with a series of peaks and valleys breaking up the otherwise monotonous, fuzzy lengths. There was a series of numbers running horizontally under each of the lines, and more vertically on either end of each. Riana recognized them as graphs of some kind, she had been taught about them in one of her recent math courses with the station computer.

"What are we looking at here?" She asked patiently raising an eyebrow at her raven haired friend who was still beaming with pride and excitement at what she had found.

"Power consumption for two separate locations during the same time frame." She said matter-of-factly as though that should explain everything.

"Ok. What locations and what time frames are we talking about?" She had no idea where Willhelmina was going with this.

"Alright, here's the deal." Willhelmina began with exuberance. "After Malice asked me why SO adopted me and put me to work after my parent's death I started racking my brain trying to figure out why they had done it. I never really thought about it before, but he's right. They've never taken on a legal ward. I mean they do plenty of charity stuff, donating money to orphanages and so on, but never before or after me have they taken a child on."

"So I started thinking about the accident and what was going on around that time in my life that may have been significant and I finally found something. I remembered that just days before my parents were killed I was taken to the hospital for an electrical shock that originated from a faulty power regulator in the sub-station near our home in Tranquility. Loads of people were hit by it, nothing major came of it though. We were all just fine after some minor treatment."

Riana looked at Willhelmina and nodded her head slightly smiling a bit to encourage her to get to the point.

"Well, when I checked the records of all the injuries, I found out that mine was different than everybody else. Maybe even unique in the entire solar system to date." She paused for dramatic effect here, causing Riana to roll her eyes in mock suffering. "I…" She continued dramatically, "took the bulk of the shock through my head because I was in Kalijor at the time, which means I was wearing my EI rig on my head, a perfect path for the current to travel down."

"Ok, so you were wearing your harness, and in Kalijor at the time it happened. So you got shocked in the brain by the power surge, that really does explain a lot about you." Riana recapped playfully, netting a punch in the shoulder from Willhelmina as she feigned hurt feelings.

"Actually it explains more about you than it does me." She carried on with a grin. "You see. This first line represents the power consumption at the sub-station in question on that day, this spike here represents the power surge. Now, this second line represents the power consumption by the Kalijor main server here on the Tyconderoga during the same time frame. Notice the same spike at the exact same time."

Riana's eyes widened at that. Suddenly she was much more interested in what was being said. "Wait a minute. How is that possible? I mean, the two locations are separated by, what? Thirty-thousand miles? There is no physical connection between them at all. How could a power surge possibly translate from the moon to this station through the void of space?"

"I don't know." Willhelmina admitted with a shrug. "All I know is that there was an identical power surge here on this station at the exact same time and it can't be a coincidence. Look, here's one more thing I found just as you were coming in."

Willhelmina tapped a few more keys on her console and a third line appeared between the other two. This line was perfectly straight except for a single spiked peak that lined up perfectly with the power spikes in the other two graphs.

"What's that?" Riana asked with a raised eyebrow, her ears perked up in curiosity.

"This line comes from the husbandry database on the Kalijor server. They track every NPC birth on the system so that they can establish family history and inter-family relationships and so forth. The entire ecology of the world is basically automated but the designers like to know who came from where so they can write quests and plots and so on. Anyway this particular bit of the database shows all the births that occurred within the time frame, when the power surge happened. There was a single child born during that time frame, and that child was born at exactly the same time as the surge. Also, curiously enough, if you expand the frame of reference to twenty four hours, there was only one single birth in all of Kalijor that day. And there it sits, at the exact moment of the power surge."

Riana had no idea what to make of the information by this point. She could not deny the voracity of what Willhelmina was telling her, but she had no idea what it all meant. "I don't understand how this all ties together Kat."

"Alright. I know you don't know our calendar system very well yet so let me pull up the name registry for the birth in question." She tapped a few more keys and the display changed again to a pair of dates, one in Kalijor reckoning and one in the real calendar date.

Riana's eyes opened wide as she read the date. It was her birthday. The display then changed again, back to the three lines, this time with the dates superimposed over the spike on the birth line and under the spike was her name, Riana Thorindal. For the life of her she could not think of a single thing to say. "Are you sure? Of all of this?" She finally managed to get out in a barely perceptible whisper.

Willhelmina smiled and shrugged. "As sure as I can be. I mean the power information for Tranquility is public domain, and I have access into the appropriate systems on the Tyconderoga here. I don't know why anyone would fake this stuff, or more to the point I can't imagine your average Joe putting these three pieces together without a lot of inside information, so I don't think any of this has been altered or doctored in any way. "

"So…"Riana's head was spinning. She felt a nagging sensation at the back of her head that told her she should be prepared for another shock to the system. "What does it all mean? I mean if it isn't just coincidence. What is the end result?"

Willhelmina's smile widened and her eyes twinkled as she spoke again. "Think about it Ree. I was in Kalijor. There was a power spike that surged electricity through my brain while it was linked to the system. Somehow the spike was translated through the subspace network into the Kalijor servers and at that exact moment, you are born. You then go on to become the first fully sentient artificial intelligence mankind has ever seen. To top it off, when it was decided to go ahead and construct a body for you, they refused to try and make a computer system, or to grow a generic wetware nervous system for you. Instead they insisted, INSISTED that they use T-Cell samples from my nervous system to grow your nervous system." Willhelmina was nearly bursting with excitement as she continued. "It can't be coincidence that I was connected to the system when you were born, and I was chosen to be there with you as you grew up, and in the end it was my nervous system that was cloned in order to give you a body!"

Riana almost slid off her chair, her mind was racing with the possibilities of what this could mean and yet it still hadn't clicked home for her. Until Willhelmina finished her dissertation with a simple statement.

"We really ARE sisters! Or as close as we could possibly be under the circumstances anyway."

That was it. Riana was obviously not prepared for the final blow. As Willhelmina turned around from the computer display with a smile on her face, Riana's mind shut down. The room spun and shuddered around her and then her vision went dark as she vaguely felt her body slip out of the chair and onto the floor.

-42-

Riana woke up on the soft duvet in her room, looking up at the delicate silk and chiffon canopy above her. Blinking away the sleep in her eyes, she stretched lazily in the early morning light streaming in the windows. After a few moments of contemplation she finally sat up cross-legged and inspected the stone walls of her room, the dark hand carved wooden furniture and colorful rug. The pile of cushions and pillows on the floor in the corner was exactly where it belonged.

She stretched again, arching her back with her arms over her head, fingers brushing against the smooth, cool fabric of the bed's canopy sending a rivulet of small shivers down her spine at the sensation. She giggled a bit before relaxing again and giving some thought to what she had to do today. She had the vague impression that something important had recently happened concerning her sister, but she couldn't quite remember what it was.

Finally, after nearly an hour of lounging around in bed she forced herself to get up and dressed, pulling on a couple of silk wraps to cover herself and deftly tying them behind her neck and at her hips. Her tattoos almost glowed in the morning light as she dragged a fine, silver comb through her violet hair, inspecting her image in the mirror with interest as she did so. Something was odd about her reflection but she couldn't quite place it. She looked more intently for a moment before it came to her that her reflection's hair was a metallic platinum color rather than purple, and the image bore none of her still-glowing tattoos. Realization came with a sudden pang that brought recent events crushing down on her like a load of ore.

"Kilishandra?!"

The image smiled back at her sweetly and then placed its own silver comb on the vanity. "Pity, I was enjoying the feeling of running my fingers through your hair." Kilishandra's voice lilted through the room like a cascade of tiny crystal raindrops.

"Where are we?" Riana's mind was finally starting to put things together again, she had just been in Willhelmina's room on the Tyconderoga. She was nowhere near a Kalijor terminal let alone her bedroom in Rathalon.

"We are exactly where you know us to be dear. I am sorry for the suddenness of things, but I needed to speak with you about something of the utmost importance." Her smile was gone now, replaced by a look of determination.

Riana looked at her mother for a moment, her jaw working furiously as she thought about what to say. Did she tell her mother that she was just a computer controlled simulacrum of a person? How would that affect her? Or could she really have something important to say? She wasn't sure but just being here seemed tantamount to a miracle. So she supposed there may actually be something to what Kilishandra might have to say.

"I realize your skepticism Riana. But you must hear me out." Her mother's reflection said from the mirror as though she had been reading the younger elf's mind. Riana stilled herself and looked directly into the violet eyes of her mother's reflection.

"Thank you my daughter." The reflection said before carrying on. "Ezrina is working on this from a secret location here in Kalijor with the help of the Obscuri."

"The Obscuri?! Master Gornin refused to tell me where she is." Riana interrupted with a snort.

"And he is right to do so." Kilishandra replied soothingly. "If you knew her location, they could tear it from your mind and track her down in no time at all."

"What is going on? How is it that you and Gornin and mom are all aware of what Kalijor really is and moving back and forth between there and here? And if you all knew this why didn't you tell me?!" Riana raised her voice at the reflection in the mirror.

"Because your mind was not ready Riana. If you were to just stop a moment and really think about it, you would realize this. But I haven't the time to talk about it now. My time is short, they are looking for me even as we speak."

"Looking for you? Who is looking for you?" Riana's expression shifted from anger to concern. Looking over her shoulder, she expected someone to climb in through the window with a crossbow.

"Don't worry about that just yet. The important thing is that you know…"

"Know what? I thought we just established that you weren't going to tell me anything!" Riana blurted out.

Kilishandra's eyes turned hard for a moment, quelling Riana's temper instantly. Softness crept back into them and she smiled sympathetically. "I know this is difficult my daughter, but in time all will become clear. For now you must know that you have control. YOU! I have unlocked your subconscious, and now you need but take control."

Riana was confused now, more than ever before. "Take control of what?"

"You will see. Give it some time and it will all become clear. Meanwhile, Xavier is going to send you on another mission, a recovery assignment. Beware Riana. They know about it and they are laying in wait."

"Who is waiting? How do you know Xavier? Mom what is going on here?" Her mind was fogging with emotions, clouding her responses and thoughts.

"I can't keep up this link, they've found me again. I have to go Riana. Please be careful. Look behind the dumpster when they spri…"

There was a powerful jolt to her body, like a bolt of lightning coursing through her mind. The room swam around her for an instant and the next thing she knew she was sitting bolt upright in Willhelmina's bed. Willhelmina was kneeling next to her, holding her hand tightly, with an expression of concern on her face.

"What happened? Where did she go?" Riana stammered, blinking her eyes repeatedly as though she might open them and find herself in her bedroom in Rathalon again.

"Where did who go Ree? What happened where?" Willhelmina's voice was cracked, it sounded like she had been crying.

"I was…" Riana looked around again in confusion, trying to make sure she was where she was. "I was just in my room… in Rathalon. Talking to Kilishandra. She was in the mirror."

Willhelmina looked at her with her green eyes. The whites were pink with veins from crying. "Ree, you never left here. I told you what I had found out and you collapsed on the floor. I dragged you to the bed and you lay there completely still for fifteen minutes. I was just about to call the techs."

"No." Riana said simply as she rubbed absently at a mild pain that had appeared suddenly on her left wrist. Looking at Willhelmina's face she tried to offer her a warm smile, unsure how it came off she finally followed it up with some reassuring words, "I'm fine Kat. It's not the first vision I've had."

"What? This has happened before?" Willhelmina's eyes were wide with concern. She also looked a bit hurt by the fact that she was only just now hearing this news. "When? What happened?"

350

Riana sighed. She was resigned to it now, she had to tell her. Slowly she recounted the tale of how she had suddenly found herself in the Burning Expanse and charged down the hill to save her mother from the monster scorpion people only to find Ezrina was long dead and clutching on to the very item they had themselves delivered to Xavier mere weeks ago.

Willhelmina listened attentively, with an ever growing look of horror on her face as Riana finished telling her the story. Finally, when she had stopped talking, Willhelmina thought for a moment, then half screamed, "AND WE JUST LET XAVIER TAKE IT?!"

Riana looked shocked, scooting back on the bed a bit in an attempt to reduce the volume of her sister's bellowing. "Well, yeah. I mean. He's our boss, and he's done so much for me already. I thought maybe he was doing something with it that would, you know... help mom out." Now that she vocalized it, she knew it sounded naive. She had considered stealing away with the object but she had no idea where she would go in the virtual world or what she could do to keep them from simply unplugging her and taking what they wanted. She scratched the irritated spot on her wrist again without thinking as she continued, "And I... well, I didn't want to scare you or cause you any trouble."

"Thanks for that." Willhelmina said, her tone somewhere between thankful and sarcastic. "So. What did Kili say? You know... in this vision."

"She said there was some sort of trouble brewing, in this world and in Kalijor. But she wouldn't say what it was. She said something about me taking control, but there again, she didn't say what of. Really it was all more cryptic nonsense. Except that she said that mom was with the Obscuri somewhere, and that she was fine unless 'they' found out where she is." Now she was scratching at her wrist forcefully as she looked at her sister, searching for any sign of…anything.

Willhelmina glanced briefly at Riana's wrist. Clad in her usual jump-suit nothing looked out of the ordinary, except that she kept clawing at it. Swinging her eyes back to the violet pools across from her she asked, "So, she didn't say anything specific? Just a bunch of *'them's'* and *they's*?"

"Yeah, pretty much. Although, now that I think about it, as she was sending me off she did mention that Xavier was going to send us on some kind of recovery mission, and that somebody knew about it." She paused for a moment to dig her fingernails forcefully into her sleeve, this time quite conscious of what she was doing. "And there was something about a dumpster?" She added as she looked back up at Willhelmina.

"A dumpster?" Willhelmina grimaced. Then she sprung across the bed and snatched Riana's arm. "What the hell is going on with your arm?!"

"I don't know, just all of a sudden it itches really bad. I've never felt anything like it before." Riana confessed with a look of concern, her ears drooped down low.

In a flash, Willhelmina yanked Riana's sleeve up to her elbow and gasped at what she saw beneath it. "What the heck is that?!"

Both of their eyes went wide as they inspected Riana's wrist. Just behind the heel of her left hand was a red patch of skin that looked like a burn or other severe irritation, but the shape of it was not that of a random bump, or scrape. The red spot was very noticeably in the shape of an ancient Elven rune that they both immediately recognized.

"Is that...?" Willhelmina stammered, unable to believe what she was seeing.

"I think so." Riana replied with a tone of amazement. There on her inner wrist was a patch of deep red skin. "The ancient elven glyph..." She said out loud.

"For a closely guarded secret." Willhelmina finished.

Both of them stared at it for a long time as the gravity of the situation slowly made itself plain to them.

43

The orange-red ball of dust loomed in the view port as the Kestrel raced towards it. They had named the shuttle after a small bird that Riana had found images of in the station's computer banks; she thought it fitting considering the ship's small size and nimble flight characteristics and Willhelmina loved the name instantly.

The trip had taken the better part of the day, having left the Tyconderoga in the early hours, and it was now early evening. Their trip promised to last another hour at least. Immediately after discussing Riana's visions, Xavier summoned them to a briefing room and told them he was sending them to the Martian city of Achilles. Their job was to pick up a case containing a new processor prototype for use in Solidarity Online's up-and-coming game servers. He warned them that several other companies had become aware of the prototype's existence and he wanted it relocated to the station as soon as conceivably possible. As he authorized them for Class C weapons and reactive body armor, he told Riana that the technicians would relax her inhibitor collar a bit. This statement, more than anything else, struck her like a lightning bolt and continued to haunt her even now, hours later.

Her mind swam through a mire of possibilities as she considered the ramifications. She had been wearing the device around her neck for nearly a year now without a second thought. Until Xavier mentioned it, she had almost forgotten it was there. She had been treating it like a piece of jewelry that she never took off rather than an electrical appliance that was… What? Keeping her docile? Making sure she was under control? What other reason could there possibly be?

"Hey Ree! You in there?" Willhelmina's voice sliced through Riana's musings like a monofilament blade.

"Huh?" Riana swiveled her head to see her sister looking at her expectantly from the co-pilot's chair.

"I said, can you confirm our flight path and landing instructions?" Willhelmina raised an eyebrow as she spoke, very aware that something serious had been going through Riana's mind.

"Oh." Riana scanned her displays, called up the navigation logs and nodded an affirmative. "Yes, we are cleared to approach Achilles on a south-bound vector at plus nine-hundred feet. Docking bay twelve is prepped and awaiting our arrival."

"Confirmed Achilles flight control. Thank you for your assistance, and we will see you in thirty. Kestrel out." Willhelmina spoke into the comm.

Switching it off, she looked back at Riana seriously. "Alright. What's going on?"

"Nothing." Riana lied. "Just thinking about the future."

Willhelmina looked at her skeptically before nodding. "Fine. Tell me when you're ready, but for now we need our minds on the game."

"Yes Ma'am!" Riana snapped a crisp salute and grinned widely. She changed the subject smoothly. "So. Is the name Achilles significant some how? It doesn't sound much like the names of other places we have been."

"No. It wouldn't." Willhelmina smiled knowingly as she tapped a few controls, pulling up a topographic map of the planet. The globe revolved slowly between them until Willhelmina reached out and touched a long, dark scar running east-west on the equator. It wrapped almost a quarter of the way around the planet's circumference. "This is the Valles Marineris, the longest and deepest canyon on the planet. During our early history there was an author named Homer who wrote of two rivals, Hector and Achilles. They fought a great war over a woman. The war destroyed an entire city and both of their lives."

"So. These cities are named after two fictional people who killed themselves over a woman?" Riana looked at Willhelmina pointedly.

"Yeah. I guess you could say that." Willhelmina looked a little concerned at Riana's shift in attention.

"So, does anyone ever do anything for real? I mean you live in fantasy worlds, write fantasy books. Create fantasy films and video programs. Do your lives constantly revolve around things that exist only in your minds?" She was becoming upset as she spoke. She couldn't even explain why the idea frustrated her so much.

Willhelmina looked taken aback "I... well... I don't know Ree... I guess... we..."

"Don't worry about it. We need to get ready to land; I am picking up the beacon now." Riana turned back to the Kestrel's controls, happy to be off the subject, and ran through a systems check as the navigational beacon transmitted final approach instructions to the ship's computers.

Willhelmina blinked a few times, then turned to perform her own systems checks. She had never been to Mars before and was looking forward to it, although Riana's sudden mood shift concerned her.

The Kestrel settled lightly onto the landing pad which retracted into an alcove that would be the ship's berth until their business was done. The large air lock trundled closed, sealing the shuttle within the chamber, and a sharp hissing noise filled the room as breathable air was cycled in. Riana and Willhelmina were out of their seats and back into the preparation area, checking their gear even before the pressure door had fully closed.

The reactive armor they wore was matte black. It covered their chest and back, shoulders, and the front and back of both arms and legs. All in all, they looked like a pair of the extreme sports junkies Riana had seen on the video terminals.

Riana buckled a series of straps around her thighs, waist, shoulders and upper arms, securing high strength combat webbing over top of her armor, the webbing's myriad of pouches and holsters filled with various items, extra ammunition for her weapons, electronic counter measures, small explosives, grenades, and much more. Quickly she removed her chosen weapons from their storage bays and checked them over before loading and cocking them, then securing them to her. An auto pistol went in the holster on her right thigh and its mate under her left arm. The bull-pup design snub nosed machine gun was then secured to the webbing on her right shoulder so that it hung easily between her right arm and body. The last touch was a long, fitted coat that shimmered in the light of the ship's cabin, seemingly changing colors as she moved about, fastening its buckles around her waist to cover her armor and artillery followed by a thick, plated head band that supported a comm unit and a personal heads up display reticule.

Riana turned to look at Willhelmina who was just seating her own head set and adjusting her mic. "Are we ready for this?" She asked her sister seriously.

"Whether we are or not, we don't have much choice at this point. All we can do is stay on guard and roll with the punches." Willhelmina was trying to be light hearted, but Riana could see the worry behind her eyes. This was the mission that Kilishandra had warned them about. If anything was going to happen, it would be here, today, now.

With a grunt of understanding, Riana activated the door circuit and there was a rush of air as the hatch cycled open. Their heavy, buckled boots clomped as they stepped out onto the landing pad. Securing the Kestrel's hatch behind them, they headed for the door and into the Achilles space port.

44

Passing on their courier credentials, they made it through customs with ease, especially considering the artillery they were carrying. It took less than fifteen minutes for them to get through the spaceport and into the Achilles arcology where, once again, Riana's breath came up short.

The spaceport was at the very top of the arcology, just beneath the dome that kept the breathable atmosphere in while allowing sunlight to stream in from outside. There was a wide platform between the spaceport and a railing that looked over a deep chasm. Moving to the railing, Riana looked down more than a mile into the bowels of the planet. The arcology was arranged in a series of rings, stacked on top of one another, layer after layer of buildings and structures, many of which were carved directly into the bedrock of the planet.

Between the railing on the inside of the rings and the various structures on the outside, a set of rails accommodated a pair of monorails that spiraled around the central shaft, moving people rapidly from one level of the arcology to another.

"This. Is amazing." She breathed out as she looked down the shaft into the darkness below them where a few lights twinkled dimly.

"Over eight-thousand feet straight down." Willhelmina responded, equally awed by the sight. "It's the deepest hole mankind has ever excavated for the purpose of habitation."

"For never having been here before, you seem to know quite a bit." Riana looked askance at her friend as they continued to hang over the edge of the railing.

"Well, you don't go your entire life without hearing something about an eight-thousand foot deep hole. Besides, I picked up this visitor's guide from the spaceport." She dangled a brightly colored pamphlet absently by its corner as she peered into the depths of the hole.

"Nice." Riana laughed. "Where are we headed? We need to get this over with."

"Right." Katrina agreed. "Our info says the facility we are looking for is on the very bottom level. Somewhere along the opposite edge of the shaft there." She pointed vaguely into the blackness below them.

Riana nodded, then pushed off of the railing, turning around in a fluid spin to face the area behind them. "So, we will need to get a ride then. How about these big train things here?" She pointed at a stopping monorail curiously.

"That should be just fine." Willhelmina responded, snapping up Riana's arm as she sprinted toward the transport.

A moment later they were on board the monorail, seated at the back where they could see everyone else on the transport. All of the other passengers were careful to stay as far from them as possible. The train picked up speed very quickly, rushing in a wide circle around the outside of the vertical city. Riana was about to ask why she wasn't getting dizzy when she noticed the floor seemed to be drifting up the wall of the tubular vehicle, keeping their center of gravity below them through the continuous spiral.

Within thirty minutes, after numerous stops to allow passengers to get on and off, they were on solid ground at the bottom of the city.

Looking up from the bottom was a different experience from looking down from the top. The light was artificial; the sunlight streaming in the transparent dome was only visible as a speck above their heads.

Looking around them, Riana saw a solid wall of blank grey building fronts circling around them in a grand, sweeping arc, punctuated occasionally by an alley that looked just wide enough to accommodate a small vehicle. The alleys were darkened, covered in deep, black shadows. The ground around them was that of the natural Martian bedrock, a powdery orange color, pounded flat and worn smooth over untold years of use it was littered with debris. Riana spotted a stuffed bear not far away from them and wondered if some child had accidentally misplaced it, or simply outgrown it.

"Where does all of this come from?" She wondered aloud.

"Probably from up there." Willhelmina pointed upwards, towards the far off upper levels of the shaft.

"Oh yeah." Riana said, silently chiding herself. Nearly a year and she still sounded like a kid every time she saw something.

"There it is." Willhelmina piped up a moment later, pointing her gloved finger toward a blank section of wall with an unimpressive brown door in its center. "Twenty-one eighty-seven. You ready for this sis?"

Riana looked at the plain door, then to her sister. Steeling herself for a fight, she nodded. "Let's do it."

Quickly and silently, they picked their way through the refuse, moving toward the door that they had been warned would hide an ambush.

Riana's hand slipped comfortably around the grip of her snub-nosed machine gun, lifting its length silently up from under her coat and seating the butt of the weapon snuggly against her shoulder just as they arrived on either side of the door.

With a tap on a wrist control, Riana shifted her HUD into thermal view and scanned the wall for any traces of warm bodies. Silently she nodded at Willhelmina who slowly put pressure on the door's opening panel. Silently the door slid out of the way, revealing an oppressive darkness. Checking their line of sight with thermal sensors, they both nodded the all clear and Riana crept silently through the open door.

Half a dozen steps into the unknown room, she froze. She tried to wave Willhelmina back with her left arm, but it refused to move. Her legs and arms were all immobile. Throwing caution and stealth to the wind she hissed over her shoulder, "Kat, run for it. I can't move."

"Oh I don't think we'll be having any of that my dear." A scratchy voice responded from behind her.

In a flash, the room was full of light. Riana was surrounded by a dozen armored troops, all bearing rifles of various sizes and shapes, all pointed at her. She blinked at them, unable to move anything more than her eyes, and lips. She scanned as much of the room as she could from her frozen position. It was a cavernous space, or would have been had it not been packed floor to ceiling with shipping and storage crates of all shapes and sizes.

The soldiers she could see all wore full helmets with protective masks that hid their faces. Her mind raced. What was this? Who was behind it? What was going on? What could she do about it? She couldn't move her arms or legs; couldn't squeeze the hair trigger of her machine gun, all she could do was look around frantically at the menacing forms of dark, armored figures pointing weapons at her.

"Who are you?" Was all she could think to ask.

"I am your salvation, my child." The raspy voice replied, this time from her left side.

Riana threw her eyes to the left, desperate for a glimpse of her sister, or the source of the voice. Immediately she wished she hadn't looked. Moving slowly into view on her left side she saw Willhelmina, her arms restrained behind her back and a gloved hand covering her mouth. Struggling against her captor, she was having no success at all. The man behind her was barely her height, and unlike the soldiers his head wasn't covered. He had an unkempt mass of curly platinum hair covering his head, with random clumps draped over his face. He was of average build, belying his strength as he seemed to hold Willhelmina with no effort at all. He wore a simple set of blue denim overalls that revealed a hint of a tattered white shirt beneath and heavy work boots.

"Who are you? What do you want?" Riana hissed at him angrily. She pushed with all her might against the invisible bonds that held her fast. If she could just pull the trigger and blast one of the bastards to hell, maybe it would disrupt the strange hold they had on her.

"Who I am, child, is not of consequence. We are here to discuss you and your, ah, potential, shall we say?" He smiled a strange, cruel smile as he continued to drag Willhelmina around, finally stopping in front of Riana's frozen form.

"I don't know what you're talking about." Riana spat at the man. "Let us go now and I'll take it easy on you." She had no idea what she was going to do, but she felt as though she was obliged to say something defiant.

The man simply laughed at her, a toneless, hollow laugh that sent chills running up and down her spine. "By all means child, be as hard on us as you like." Then he gave her that evil grin again. "As hard as you can, at any rate. While totally incapacitated."

Riana glared at him icily, all words gone from her, she had nothing but contempt for this man, whoever he was, and wanted to hurt him with all of her being.

"I think, perhaps, that it would be more amusing to us all if we had some play time with your friend here." He gave Willhelmina a hard shake by way of explanation. She lashed out at his shins and feet with her heavy boots, but even though she landed every blow as intended, he did not so much as flinch.

"What do you want from us?" Riana shouted at him, trying to burn him to dust with her gaze alone.

"I want you to do something for me, child. And when this thing is done, I shall set the both of you free, until such time as I have need of you again." He leveled his gaze on her and she could see that he was deadly serious.

"I am not your slave. I will not do your bidding simply because you say I should." Her voice was laced with venom, she pushed and pushed on her body with her mind, straining to make it move, any piece of it. A finger, a toe, anything.

"Ah, but that is where you are mistaken little one. You ARE my slave. And here in my arms I hold proof." He gave Willhelmina a violent shake again, this time Riana could hear her gasp from the whiplash-inducing movement.

"What do you want?" Riana said almost instantly at the sound of Willhelmina's pain.

"I want the trinket that you retrieved for Xavier Quinn in Rathalon recently. I want the rune." He smiled at her again, his steely grey eyes boring into her soul.

"I don't know where it is. Xavier has it somewhere." She pushed harder, pressing the weight of her soul against her immobile limbs, focusing her energy on her right index finger. Pressing harder and harder with her mind. *'Move! Move damn you!'*

"He keeps it in his apartment. Aboard the Tyconderoga." He said simply.

"I've never seen his apartment. I have no idea where it even is! What makes you think he will let me in there?" Her index finger moved almost imperceptibly, squeezing the trigger slightly as she threw her mind at it again and again with all the force of will she could muster.

"Easy child, you just ask him. Tell him his daughter's life hangs in the balance." He smiled his sinister smile at her again and then twisted Willhelmina's head cruelly upwards, looking into her green eyes with murderous intent. "That will, after all, be the case."

Riana panicked, she didn't even want to consider what she would do without Willhelmina. She was the closest thing to real family Riana had, and she was not about to let some madman hurt her. Overcome with a blinding rage, she pushed again on her immobile body, willing it into motion again. She didn't feel it when her limbs began to obey her commands once more. She didn't even register the sharp inhalations of breath through atmospheric filters all around her as the armored figures realized what was going on. All she saw was the madman holding her sister as she aimed the bull-pup at the elbow of the arm he was using to hold Willhelmina's head.

"I won't do what you ask, and I won't allow you to hurt my sister!" She bellowed as she squeezed the trigger. Her bull-pup pressed into her shoulder as fire erupted from its barrel and a hail of high density, armor piercing projectiles covered the short distance between them in an instant. The man's elbow erupted in a spray of fluid that looked nothing like blood. A few bits of metal showered out from the gaping hole in his arm as it went limp and then the room erupted in a deafening roar of gunfire all around them.

She felt her reactive armor stiffen in response to the torrent of gunfire that rained in on her from all sides. She knew the armor could withstand a lot of punishment, but this situation would soon overcome it and yet, she found that she didn't care. Her own safety was the last thing in her mind. Without thinking any more on it, she stripped two grenades off of her combat webbing and dropped them to the floor at her feet as she dove forward into a roll towards Willhelmina and the man with the hateful laugh.

Bullets ricocheted off of the armor on her back as she tumbled forward, her long color-shifting duster was already torn to shreds and she could feel every single impact, bruising her skin through the armored second skin. She was certain that she felt multiple bullets cutting through the armor's soft spots and tearing into her flesh, but she focused her mind on the task of freeing her sister from the clutches of this unknown madman.

Coming up from her forward roll she set the barrel of her machine-gun against the man's exposed knee, between Willhelmina's legs, and squeezed the trigger. His leg erupted in a spray of machine fluids and parts as he crumbled to the ground, grinning his maniacal grin all the while.

Not stopping for an instant, Riana kept her momentum moving forward carrying her shoulder into Willhelmina's mid-section, lifting her bodily off the ground and slamming her other shoulder into one of the soldiers —

eliciting a sick, breaking sound from somewhere in the man's chest as her body impacted his— as she dashed past and leapt behind a nearby crate.

Slamming to the ground behind the huge shipping crate Riana suddenly began to feel all of the wounds on her body. She knew her armor was destroyed, but between its protection and her cyborg body, she had managed to pull her sister out of the fray, looking down into Willhelmina's green eyes she saw a wan smile from the other woman as she readied her own machine-gun now that her arms were free.

"Hold that thought a moment." Riana whispered.

"The hell with that. I want to hurt those bastards!"

"You'll get your chance, just wait a second."

As if on queue, a pair of explosions sounded from the other side of the crate. Their cover shook with the force of the explosions, and dust and debris rained down from above them. There were bits of armor, chunks of the floor and ceiling, and fifty years of dust that had been suddenly dislodged from the tops of the light fixtures. The lights dimmed as many of the fixtures were destroyed and a few faint voices could be heard from the other side of their cover, shouting, confused voices, some of them wails of pain at some unseen damage.

"Ok. Now we can go." Riana said flatly as she slapped another magazine onto the top of her bull-pup and slid the cocking mechanism home.

Together the pair of them rounded the crate and set their backs against one another. Side stepping towards the door, they scanned the smoke and dust filled area for any signs of aggression. Once or twice someone moved to fire at them and was quickly dispatched with a burst of armor piercing slugs from one of their rifles. In moments they were through the front door, back in the refuse-covered courtyard.

Growling in anger, Willhelmina stripped two of her own grenades from her webbing and tossed them back into the building behind them, her lips twisting into a perversely satisfied smile as she heard the two explosions and a plume of dust and smoke billowed through the doorway, swirling around them like a dust devil.

"Uh, sis?"

"Yeah Ree?" Willhelmina turned around again to look at the taller woman questioningly.

"I think we better find some cover." Riana pointed across the court yard as she spoke. Her eyes narrowed at something in an expression of disgust.

Following her sister's extended index finger across the way, squinting to see through the cloud they were standing in, Willhelmina cursed under her breath, "Dammit."

Emerging from several buildings on the far side of the shaft was a dozen or more of the same unknown soldiers, all clad in the same black, environmental armor and bearing a wide variety of weapons. The soldiers were making their way toward the sisters who were still obscured by the cloud of dust from the grenades.

"C'mon, in here." Riana grabbed Willhelmina's arm and dragged her into the narrow alley next to the building they had just blown up. Rushing through the darkness of the alley they realized that their situation had not improved. The narrow corridor was a dead end. There was nothing else in the shadowed alcove but themselves and a large refuse bin at the very back.

Willhelmina ejected the clip from her rifle and slapped another one home, jerking the cocking mechanism with a grunt, "We're in trouble here."

"You may be right about that."

"Well. We'd better get to it." Willhelmina took a step forward, reaching for another grenade on her webbing. She sounded as though she was walking into a death trap and had resigned herself to her fate.

"Wait a sec." Riana was looking at the back of the alley as she spoke.

"What? Did you find something?"

"I'm not sure. Remember, Kilishandra said we would get ambushed here."

"Yeah, and?"

"What else did she say?"

Willhelmina looked perplexed at the question, as though she thought it was an extremely odd thing to be talking about under the circumstances. "Is this really the time?"

"I think it's the perfect time." Riana said as she put her hands on the refuse bin and gave it a yank. The heavy metal container moved forward with a lurch, its metal feet grinding on the stone of the floor and producing a high pitched screeching noise that resounded off the walls of the alley loudly.

"Um. I think you just let them know where we are."

"Never mind that. C'mere a sec, and tell me if you can operate this thing."

Cautiously, Willhelmina made her way to the dumpster and looked around behind it at what Riana was talking about. There, in a small alcove carved into the rock wall behind the bin was a sleek motorcycle that looked like it was moving over one hundred miles per hour just sitting there.

"Oddly enough. I think I can." Willhelmina whispered under her breath as she tried to get a better look at the vehicle in the shrouded darkness of the dead end alley. "Now, if we could just get it out from behind this dumpster, it's too tight in here to squeeze the bike past it."

"Hey! You! Down there! Come out here with your hands up." An amplified voice shot down the narrow alley and slammed into them like a physical blow.

"Get on the other side of the dumpster, I'll move it."

Willhelmina shrugged at her sister and clambered over the trash bin with her.

"Get it going. I'm going to get this out of our way." Riana grunted as she set her shoulder against the dumpster and began to push it down the alley at a trot. Sparks showered behind the metal bin as it ground its way down the alley.

Quickly, Willhelmina turned and bent down by the motorcycle, fiddling with some adjustments and then straddling the vehicle and kicking it to life with the press of a button.

The dumpster picked up speed as it moved down the alley, propelled by Riana's cybernetic strength. It burst out into the open area, slamming into two of the soldiers and knocking them aside like a pair of bowling pins. Their comrades jumped aside to avoid the blow only to be caught by Riana's flurry of punches and kicks as she leapt from behind the dumpster.

Another hail of gun fire splashed into her back, forcing Riana to her knees. She knew instantly that her armor was done for as she felt the bullets tear into her flesh and a fresh trickle of blood ran down her back. Spinning around in her crouching position, she loosed a spray of bullets in a wide arc, forcing the soldiers to duck, and then flung a flash-bang toward them as Willhelmina screeched to a halt next to her, the bike's engine humming loudly beneath her.

Continuing her spin Riana came around and mounted the bike behind Willhelmina. Wrapping her left arm around the other woman's waist, they started moving rapidly toward the spiraling ramp that would lead them upward to the top of the arcology.

A loud bang and a flash of brilliant white light issued from behind them when the flash-bang went off, knocking most of their assailants to the ground and temporarily blinding them.

Speeding away from the scene of the conflict, the motorcycle's engine hummed away beneath them, carrying them inexorably upwards, round and round the wide spiral of the arcology. After a few minutes Riana began to feel the adrenalin wearing off, her limbs became shaky and the cool chills across her back told her that she was still covered in blood and that her back was at least partially bared through her tattered armor, although she barely felt the wounds.

As they made it up several tiers of the spiraling arcology, a high pitched whining noise began to top the constant thrum of the motorcycle's engine.

"What's that noise?" Riana's ears perked up, trying to get a better idea of what it was or where it was coming from.

"Sounds like a hover system." Willhelmina's voice fell back from the front of the speeding bike. She was concentrating on avoiding pedestrians as she throttled through the busy arcology. It was obviously not designed for motor vehicles as they were forced to dodge and weave through the wide pedestrian walkway.

"It sounds like it's getting louder."

"There shouldn't be any hover vehicles in here. This is a pedestrian only arcology."

"And yet here we are on the back of a dangerously speeding motorcycle." Riana tossed her gaze over her shoulder as she spoke, just in time to see two vehicles that looked very much like their motorcycle drop down from above them and start skimming along just above the ground behind them. The riders of the hover bikes looked just like the soldiers at the bottom of the shaft, and they were all bearing weapons. Riana swallowed hard as her right hand moved to the handle of her machine gun, and her left arm clenched a bit tighter around Willhelmina's waist.

"Ouch! Stop that Ree!"

"Kat. I think you had better get this thing moving."

The bike was already moving well beyond a safe speed as Willhelmina wove it in and out around groups of startled people on the wide walkway. As they moved higher into the arcology, the density of the crowds increased.

"I don't think I can get any more out of it in here. We're barely staying on as it is."

"That's what I thought, but I had to ask." Clicking the safety off, she half-turned and raised the weapon toward the nearest of the two hover bikes.

The pilot reacted instantly, pressing a control on the handle of his vehicle. Two barrels on the front of the hover bike belched flame as the machine guns opened fire. He kept the stream of bullets going for a moment before cutting them off and dodging off to the side.

Riana's aim came up short as the stream of bullets cut into her side and arm, what was left of her armor tried to repel them, but most of them passed straight through and bit into her flesh. Gouts of pain scorched her nerves for an instant before they went mercifully numb.

Leveling her weapon at the vehicle again Riana pulled the trigger and sent a stream of bullets toward the pilot's body, hunched over his controls. He rolled the vehicle to the side, avoiding the spray of projectiles and Riana was suddenly blasted again from the other side, this time the bullets dug into the armor on her exposed front side.

"Dammit!" She shouted as she tried to regain her aim.

"These bastards don't seem to care who they get while trying for us Ree. We need to put a stop to this."

The motorcycle jerked sharply as another volley of bullets slammed into Riana's back causing her to wince in momentary pain.

"Keep going. I'll catch up with you!" She yelled at her friend.

"What the hell are you talking about?" Willhelmina tried to reach back and grab hold of Riana but she instantly had to put it back on the controls again as the bike tried to come out from under them.

Riana dropped her machine gun to her side and slipped her feet up under her. With one clean movement she spun around and leapt off the motorcycle, straight at one of the hover cycles. The pilot seemed so surprised, he sat up nearly straight on his vehicle. Riana hit the front of the machine roughly, rolling into a ball as her momentum carried her over the handlebars and into the soldier. Knocking him bodily off the bike, he made a sick squishing sound as he hit the ground with Riana on top of his chest. The hover cycle careened away and fell down the central shaft of the arcology out of sight.

Slamming into the ground with enough force to crack the super dense pavement, Riana rolled to a crouching position and snapped up her machine gun again, scanning the area for signs of danger. All around her people had stopped what they were doing and were looking at her with wide eyes. Picking through the crowd hurriedly, she caught sight of a throng of people gathered around something. Briefly she caught a glimpse of the crumpled form of the armored soldier laying motionless on the ground, and then returned her scanning eyes back to the air just in time to see the other hover bike barreling toward her.

Throwing herself to the side she opened up on the vehicle with the remains of her ammunition. Her volley caught the front and side of it, tearing up some of the frame and armored plates, but the damage didn't seem to cause it too much distress. The pilot cut loose with a sustained burst from his own guns, strafing the area.

Coming up from a sideways roll, she jerked her gun off of its shoulder strap and threw it at the pilot's head. The man ducked out of the way almost casually as he watched the weapon fly past him in a graceful arc, returning his scrutiny back to his quarry only to realize too late what he had done. Riana had used the soaring weapon as a distraction and pulled her shoulder holstered pistol out.

With a grunt of resignation, the man fell off the hovering bike, an armor piercing bullet imbedded deep within his brain.

Wasting no time, Riana leapt onto the vehicle and scanned the controls. They seemed similar to those of the Kestrel, if somewhat less complicated. Holstering her pistol again she kicked the vehicle into forward and sped up the spiral of the arcology, skimming above the heads of the stunned crowd.

-45-

"What about the bullets?" Riana asked Gayle as she lay face down on the examination table, the other woman wiping clotted and dried blood from her back with a woefully small, alcohol soaked gauze patch.

"Your body's already absorbed them." Gayle responded coolly, sticking her finger tentatively into one of the shallow depressions that had recently been a bullet hole. "Looks like the micro-weave is already reknitting. The skin will be quick after that. There should be no signs whatever within a few days."

"What do you mean absorbed them?" Riana shifted her torso around, raising up to her elbows and twisting her head around to look at the blonde woman.

"The nanites in your body have broken them down into raw materials to use in repairing the damage to your body."

"Nanites." Riana repeated.

"Yes. Nanites."

"Ok. Nanites it is then." She lay back down on the table for a moment, but just as Gayle resumed cleaning Riana's back, the purple haired woman twisted around again to look at her. "What the hell is a nanite?"

"A nanite," Xavier's voice rolled smoothly through the examination room causing Riana to gasp and lay back down on the table, feeling suddenly very self-conscious, "is a microscopic robot. Smaller than a living cell, that is capable of performing certain tasks within a living organism. In your case, they break down any foreign material and use it to affect repairs on your body."

"Um. Ok. Thanks." Any part of her that wasn't covered in clotted blood must have burned scarlet. She buried her face into the depression at the head of the table, trying to disappear into the furniture.

"I've just come from Willhelmina's room. She is doing well." Xavier's baritone continued silkily.

"Good." Riana spoke into the table. "She isn't bullet proof, like I apparently am."

"Not bullet proof per se, just highly resistant. Gayle, how did our friend fare?"

"I haven't had a chance to inspect all of the wounds yet, sir. She sustained a great deal of damage, but all of her internal systems seem to be one hundred percent. Sensors indicate that only a few rounds made it past the skin weave and the nanites got everything back up to speed in short order."

"So the skin weave was an effective deterrent then?"

"It seems to be sir. If we were to increase its density by another three or four percent it would be extremely effective."

"What skin weave?" Riana mumbled loudly into the depression on the table, trying to remind them that she was in the room.

"Your skin, Miss Thorindal, is composed of several layers of the same woven fibers that are used in reactive armors. Then the living tissue and blood vessels are grown on and through that weave. It makes you extremely durable." Xavier explained patiently.

"I noticed. So who were those people?"

"We have yet to discern their origins, or designs."

"Which is Xavier-speak for you have no idea. On both counts?"

"That is correct Miss Thorindal. However we have had some luck tracking down information based upon the surveillance information you were able to provide us. This man…" at that he pressed a control at the room's computer console and the lights dimmed a bit. Riana looked up to see a hologram of the man that had been restraining Willhelmina.

The image stood there motionless, wearing the same denim overalls and a dirty white T-shirt. His curly platinum hair creating a halo around his head. Riana's stomach turned over seeing him again. She was overtaken by a desire to choke the life out of him.

"Who is he?" She hissed at the image.

"He," Xavier replied nonplussed, "Is a mercenary by the name of Gregory Shantal. He has been on military radar for nearly fifty years, and he carries a well-deserved reputation for being brutally efficient at his assigned tasks."

"A mercenary? So he is hired muscle?"

"That would seem a likely prospect Miss Thorindal. What remains to be determined is who has hired him and to what end."

"Ok. So you say he is a well-known mercenary?"

"Indeed." Xavier said simply, without managing to sound bored.

"Well then he probably commands a pretty high salary right?"

"Correct."

"So, all you need to do is figure out who can afford to pay his wages, along with those of his private army, and has interest in SO's business."

There was a long pause that was filled only by the sound of Gayle scrubbing the blood off of Riana's body.

Finally Riana hoisted herself back up to her elbows, tucking her hands under her chest to cover herself as she looked at Xavier who was looking at her with a tinge of amusement.

"What?" She said incredulously.

"Nothing Miss Thorindal."

"So?"

"I have people working on it as we speak. I simply wanted to inform you as to what we had discerned thus far. I would ask that the two of you remain on stand-by in case we learn the whereabouts of the prototype you were sent to retrieve."

Riana slumped back down onto the table, eliciting a disappointed sigh from Gayle. "Yes sir." She spoke into the table again.

There was silence again, but this time Riana was determined not to fill it first. She forced herself to keep her head in the indentation. She would not break the silence.

"What is that?" For the first time she could remember, Xavier sounded upset about something.

Looking up at him, she followed the line of his gaze down to the inside of her left wrist, dangling over the edge of the table. There, standing out starkly against her light skin was the now brightly colored, blue glyph that had appeared there of its own accord.

"Uh. It's elven." She said quickly.

"I realize that Miss Thorindal. Where did you get it?"

"Oh. I had it done in Achilles. A little place just outside the spaceport."

"Why? Does this mark hold some significance to you?"

Riana looked at him. His dark eyes were boring through her. Trying to discover any signs of…falsehood? She wasn't sure. She could tell he was upset about something. "Yes sir, mom and Kat and I used this symbol to mark anything that was of value to the family. I wanted to have a reminder of her."

"I see." He said shortly, staring at her for a moment longer before shutting off the holographic emitter and heading toward the door. "I will have this information sent to your quarters so that you may review it. Gayle, I want a full report in one hour."

He didn't wait for either of them to respond. He simply stepped through the door and was gone.

"So what did you tell him?" Willhelmina asked with a raised eyebrow as she looked at her sister's concerned face.

"I told him you and mom and I used this symbol to mark things that were important to us, and that I had it done at a shop near the spaceport in Achilles." Riana's eyes dropped down and looked for something interesting to stare at on the floor. She was ashamed about having lied to Xavier. Somehow explaining that she had a vision of her long-dead mother in a video game and then the mark had spontaneously appeared on her arm didn't seem appropriate either.

"Ok. I'll make sure to tell him the same thing if he asks me."

Riana looked up at her sister's sparkling green eyes suddenly. She could not even express in words how that simple statement made her feel. "Thanks Kat. I really appreciate it."

Willhelmina smiled fondly, then shifted gears suddenly. "So the intel on this Gregory Shantal fellow is ominous eh?"

"Yeah. It looks like he is over ninety percent artificial. Most of his body has been replaced due to injuries, but some parts were done quite willingly. He has enhanced strength, almost unlimited endurance. Quickened reflexes. Most of the specifics are unknown though. It doesn't seem like anyone who has gotten close enough to find out more has ever returned."

"This doesn't bode well for us if we run into him again."

"Tell me about it." Riana tapped away at the controls on her computer terminal, scanning through pages and pages of information about the mercenary and his past deeds. "Says here he has a class two martial arts rating. This guy is going to be a tough fight if we meet up with him again. I somehow doubt if he will let me blast his arm and leg off again."

"You're probably right about that. This is assuming that he wasn't scragged by those grenades, you know."

"Thus far, my luck has not proven to be that good." Riana quipped, never taking her eyes off of the data floating in front of her.

Willhelmina grimaced at her sister; she didn't like it much when Riana was talking negatively. "So what's our next move?"

"Good question. Xavier wants us on stand-by until they figure out where that processor is. Then he wants us to retrieve it. I say we go to Kalijor and see if we can track down any information about this rune everyone is after."

"Ok. Who should we ask?"

"Well. Gornin for one. Then I was thinking that maybe we should go to the Magic Academy and use the library to look it up. I figure the fewer people we speak to about it the better off we'll be."

"Alright. I'll let Xavier know we are going into Kalijor for a bit. Meet me on the game deck in ten minutes."

"Ok. See you there."

Ten minutes later Willhelmina strolled toward the game pods. Riana had set everything up already. She was talking to one of the technicians about something and turned to face her as soon as she saw her coming.

"Heyas sis. Ready to go?"

Willhelmina smiled. "Of course. Xavier said not to be gone too long though. I guess they are close to something."

"Ok. They are going to log us in at Cohai, then we can portal over to the Magic Academy from there."

"Sounds like a plan. Let's get a move on."

-47-

The cool, fresh air of the Uraval Mountains washed over her like an old friend saying hello. She inhaled deeply, realizing how much she missed it. The sky was a deep sapphire color and as clear of clouds as she had ever seen it before.

Riana stretched languidly as though she were a cat waking up from a long nap in a sun beam, then had a look around her. Katrina stood next to her, already digging through her pack for her spell book. The two of them stood in a small alcove just inside the main gate of the Cohai Observatory. Looking out on the lush, well tended garden and the blue sky beyond, they could see several people wandering here and there taking care of the various trees and flowers. Others sat and meditated or sparred with one another.

"Business as usual here." Riana said with a small smile on her lips.

"Probably always will be." Katrina said absently, flipping pages in her thick spell book, looking intent on finding some elusive spell or cantrip.

"Ladies. It has been a while. How may I be of service?" Gornin's gravelly voice rumbled from behind them, causing them both to jump.

"Master Gornin!" Riana managed to collect herself enough to face him and bow.

Katrina recovered her spell book from the ground and dusted it off with a look of indignation on her face, as though she had just been slapped. "You shouldn't sneak up on people like that!"

"My apologies ladies. I did not mean to startle you." He bowed low to them, his blue eyes almost glowing in the shadowed alcove.

"We were wondering if you would mind talking to us in private for a moment?" Riana rolled her eyes in exasperation towards her sister as she spoke.

"I will always have time for the ladies Thorindal." Gornin nodded for them to continue. "What would you like to talk about?"

Riana knelt down and drew the elven glyph in the dirt on the ground with her index finger, then looked up at Gornin. His seven foot height seemed even more imposing from near ground level. "The last time we were in Rathalon we made a trade with a man named Malice for a large blue stone that had this elven glyph in it. Since then it has come up several times in... various situations. We were wondering if you knew anything about it?"

Gornin looked at the symbol passively for a long moment before sighing heavily. Thoroughly eradicating the image with his foot, the troll looked at them each in turn. When he finally spoke, his voice was low and conspiratorial for the first time either of them could remember. "This item you speak of is one of the five keys. The fact that it is in the open again after so long does not bode well." The girls looked at him curiously, Riana hauling herself back to a standing position, her ears perked up in interest at his reaction.

"Keys to what?" Katrina asked with interest as she closed her book.

"This is a long tale. You of course remember the stories of the Great War?" Gornin asked them.

"Yes." They replied in unison.

"It was a conflict between the dwarves and the elves concerning who had the most powerful magic and should rule the realm." Katrina added.

"That is what everyone has been led to believe." Gornin replied, his voice growing lower and lower by the moment. "The truth is something much different, and possibly the most closely guarded secret in Kalijor. I only tell you this because you now have a much more unique understanding of the world." He closed his eyes as though he were recalling some memory that was long ago tucked away in a chest and locked up forever. "The truth is that there was an unexplained event that occurred just before the war began. No one has yet determined what caused it, but we know well the ramifications. The event, whatever it was, tore open a hole in this reality that allowed some immense evil to begin seeping into our world. It happened on what is now the dark side of the Uraval Mountains, near the north shore of the Dead Sea."

"At the time, that region was a lush forested area that was inhabited by the elves. They had built their capital city there and it was a marvelous sight indeed, built into the tops of the great trees. But it was not meant to be. As the evil seeped into the forest it began corrupting the elves that lived there, twisting their hearts and minds toward darkness and hatred. Over time they formed an army, using their skills in metallurgy and arcane magic to equip themselves with some of the most powerful weapons and armor this realm has ever known." Gornin took a long breath and held it for a moment before slowly letting it go and continuing his story, "once their army was built, they marched against the other nations of the realm and destroyed everything they encountered. No one was safe, and it seemed that no one could mount any kind of resistance that stood a chance against their might."

"Finally, the dwarves began working their forges and foundries, producing most of the powerful magical weapons and armor that are still in use to this day in the services of good. The dwarves worked tirelessly, night and day in order to supply weapons for those that would fight against the corrupted elven empire. When the time came for the armies of darkness and light to clash, the Plain of Serenity was washed red with spilled blood. In the end the corrupted elven army was laid to waste and the elven people were all but eradicated from our world, along with most of the dwarves."

"We thought we had won. We had not known the source of their corruption, and so we had not known to go and seek it out. As time marched on the elves' home became a barren and parched land overrun by monsters and the undead. One of these undead would prove to be the nemesis of all things living. The former king of their once great empire, King Tinaan's body was possessed by the evil that now lived in the Plain of Sorrow. What was left of his mind was slowly twisted and deformed into a parody of its former greatness. Calling back all of his fallen soldiers as undead minions, he christened himself the Lich King."

"Again his army marched across the land, and this time they nearly destroyed the entire world. No one could destroy them. No weapon could halt their advance or send them back to the grave." He paused, his voice grinding to a stop as his eyes drifted over their heads. "A single, solitary warrior appeared. He battled constantly, night and day. When his blades stopped swinging, the entire undead army lay in ruin, utterly destroyed. This hero then pressed on into the Plain of Sorrow and fought against the Lich King himself. Only through both of their destruction was the warrior able to seal the rift that was allowing the evil into our world."

"It was later discovered that some of the remaining, uncorrupted elves had opened themselves up to the shadow realm, increasing their magical powers immeasurably. This bond allowed them to forge the weapons and armor that had carried the solitary warrior on his journey of salvation for our world. However, these elves paid a terrible price for their pact with the shadows. After the rift was sealed they asked two boons of the world they had saved. They asked that they be allowed to disappear forever into the peaks of the Uraval Mountains and never be bothered again."

"The other request brings us back to your key. We agreed to take the items they had given to that nameless warrior and scatter them throughout the realm. Massive ziggurats were erected and sealed with the most powerful magics we could muster. Each was protected by a series of deadly traps and protective enchantments. Each was locked by a key and each key was in turn secreted away and protected by similar means." His eyes focused first on Riana then on Katrina. "We locked away their most powerful artifacts and let them disappear into the mountains, where they have remained to this day. They call themselves the Obscuri now. The shadow elves."

The girls stared at Gornin, engrossed in his story. There was a long silence between them before anyone spoke again.

"What... What price did they pay?" Katrina asked in a barely audible voice, she sounded as though she didn't really want to know the answer, but she was compelled to ask.

"No one knows the extent of the price, Katrina, but we do know that they no longer feel any emotions. At least, not in the same sense that we do. They would not, and still have not, spoken of it. Anyone who climbs the mountains, whether to seek out the Obscuri, or just out of idle curiosity is never seen again."

"So this jewel. Is one of the five keys to the Obscuri artifacts then?" Riana finally spoke.

"That is correct Riana."

"But why would Xavier and this mercenary be after it? Why would they want such items? What good could they possibly do them in the real world?" Riana spoke under her breath.

Gornin sighed heavily again, sounding almost defeated. "You still do not understand Riana. Our worlds are inexorably connected. What affects one, can affect the other, and often in ways you would not expect."

Riana stared at him for a long moment, trying to figure out how he knew of the 'real world'. "Master Gornin, I just don't understand how that is possible."

"It is not my place to reveal such things Riana. You must discover some truths for yourself."

"Dammit Gornin I hate it when you do this! I NEED to know what is going on here!" Riana's face was flushed with rage, her ears cocked back aggressively and her fists clenched tightly, white-knuckled. She didn't even seem to notice the fact that Gornin was speaking to them almost as if he was a player.

"I understand your frustration Riana, but even for me there are rules. There are many things that I can do and many more that I can not. You must discover these things for yourself, as much as I would like to be able to reveal them to you."

"Fine." Riana's anger was a nearly tangible force radiating from her body. Her tattoos were all glowing brightly as she tried, with minimal effect, to control her fury. "Then at least tell us where the key has gone. We had it with us when we logged out that day, and now it's gone. Where do these things go when we log out?"

"They are stored in a secure location that is inaccessible to any but those with power over the world."

"So only a Game Master can get them?" Katrina piped in smartly.

"That is not exactly correct."

"Alright. So if a Game Master can't get at these items, then who can?" Riana hissed.

"Only adventurers may retrieve the keys. Once an adventurer has obtained a key then the gods may intervene."

Riana glared at Gornin, staring up into his calm blue eyes. He was not going to tell her about the connections between the real world and this one. What was at stake? How did she fit in? And why was she being treated like a child? Finally she spoke again, still glaring into his calm visage. "And I suppose I still can't speak to my mom?"

"I am sorry Riana. She is still indisposed. I will pass along any message you wish the next time I meet her."

"Don't bother yourself Gornin. It's obvious you could care less. Let's go Kat. We're supposed to be on stand-by, not mucking about in Kalijor."

Riana vanished without a sound right in front of them. Katrina looked at the empty space that had been her sister only a moment ago then back to Gornin. "I'm sorry Master Gornin. She has been kind of on edge lately. We got shot up pretty badly the other day."

"I am aware of your exploits. You handled yourselves admirably." His low voice was almost soothing despite its rough edge.

"Thank you. Well. I had better go after her. Make sure she doesn't hurt somebody in the sparring ring or something."

"Very well, Katrina. It was good seeing you both again. Please stop in whenever you like and remind your sister that the power is still hers. She need only take it."

"What does that mean Gornin?" It was a simple question, not an accusation or demand.

"One day she will understand. Until then, that is all I am able to say."

"Alright. I'll tell her, but I don't think it will help her mood any."

"I very much doubt it."

Katrina looked at the troll's gnarly face, his piercing blue eyes—as sharp as any she had ever seen—were a stark contrast to his otherwise unappealing body. She knew he was trying to help. Somehow, he was constrained by the system in which he lived and yet had managed to find some ways to get around the barriers. All they had to do was discover how that system worked and she had a feeling that many of their questions would be answered. "Well. Thanks again Master Gornin. I'll see you later."

They bowed to one another before Katrina also disappeared in a soundless blink.

Gornin sighed again before turning toward the gardens of Cohai and heading out to speak with his other pupils.

48

"There you are!" Willhelmina grinned as she approached her sister.

Riana didn't look away from the large view port. She simply stared straight ahead offering no acknowledgement.

"What are you doing up here? I was sure you would be in the gym embarrassing the Class Three folks."

"I can't do that any more."

"Do what? Embarrass the Class Threes?"

"Fight."

"You can't fight anymore?" Willhelmina screwed up her face in confusion.

"I can't fight with people around here anymore." Riana continued staring out the view port at cargo haulers offloading large crates from a transport vessel in the station's local space.

"Ok. Why?"

Finally, Riana turned and looked at her friend, violet eyes wide with fear and a hint of something else. "I'm afraid I might hurt someone. I'm scared to death of what could happen."

"What's gong on Ree?"

"Look."

Willhelmina watched with growing awe as Riana put her right hand on an emergency hand rail near the view port and tore the solid steel bar from its fusion welded anchor points on the wall. She then proceeded to twist the three foot long bar into a malformed ball without the slightest appearance of exertion.

Setting the mangled piece of steel on a near-by table she looked up at Willhelmina and waited.

"That... was pretty cool."

"Kat be serious. I could seriously hurt someone. And that isn't the end of it. My reflexes are super-human now as well. Just about everything about me is… more powerful than before. I'm really scared."

"So let's go talk to Wayne and have him take a look at you."

"No!" She almost shouted the word then turned back toward the carefully orchestrated space ballet that was progressing outside the station in the emptiness of space.

"Why? If anyone could fix it he would be the one."

"I know but… I don't want it fixed. Not like they would fix it."

Willhelmina looked seriously at her sister for a long moment. She had suspected that something deeper was going on here, but now she was sure of it. "What's the matter Ree? I can't help you if you won't talk to me."

Riana took a deep breath and let it go slowly, eyeing Willhelmina's reflection in the wide view port. "I don't want to be their lab rat any more. I don't want to be under their control. They use this to keep me manageable." Gently she fingered the shiny metal encircling her neck in a seamless collar. "Somehow, since the incident on Mars it has stopped working entirely, and I don't want them to know about it, but I am scared to death I may hurt someone if I can't control my strength."

Riana's voice drifted off into silence. The dead air hung between them for a long moment as they stared out the view port into the void. Finally, Willhelmina broke the tension.

398

"I understand Ree. But I honestly don't think they are trying to keep you docile with that collar. Doesn't it seem reasonable that they are using it to help you? For the very same reasons you are scared right now. Scared of hurting people."

"Call it whatever you want Kat. It's a leash." Her voice grew taut. "They can shut me down if they want. From who knows how far away? Maybe the other side of the station. Maybe on another planet. I don't know. But I don't like the thought of it. I don't like being held hostage in my own body, made to do as they please."

"Ree, nobody here is going to make you do anything you don't want to! They built this body for you! Why would they force you to do things you didn't want to?"

"What if I wanted to leave? To go away and live in Tranquility or Achilles? Or get myself a ship and run charter flights around the Sol system? What if I wanted nothing to do with this whole Obscuri ultimate weapon thing and just disappeared? What do you think they would do?"

Willhelmina looked at her friend. Riana's eyes were clear and bright, but her face was contorted into the visage of a person wracked with painful sobs. Her ears drooping down low and flushed red with sadness.

"I can't even cry. They didn't give me my own tears to cry Kat. I don't think they were being as generous as you think when they built this body for me. I think there is something else behind it." Her voice was breaking up and her breath was ragged. Without the tears it all seemed oddly contrived.

"What purpose Ree? What could possibly motivate them beyond what they have already told you?" Willhelmina was crying now, really crying, with real tears and real sobs.

"I don't know Kat. But something feels wrong and I don't want to be their attack dog, or puppet, or whatever they have planned for me. If I tell them that I shut down the inhibitor collar, they will fix it. Maybe fix it so I can't get around it again, assuming I can figure out how I did it the first time."

"You want to leave? You want to move away from me?" Willhelmina's eyes searched Riana's.

"No Kat. I don't want to leave. But I don't want to be forced to stay by some invisible fence either. If we are going to figure out what is going on with mom and all of this other stuff, that no one will tell us about, then we will need to be here to do it."

Riana snatched up the metal from the table and crushed it into a tighter mass, the size of a softball which she gently returned to the center of the small table. "I won't let them keep me on a chain."

Willhelmina looked at the ball of metal on the table. Turning her emerald eyes on Riana she quirked a small smile, "I bet that would surprise that Gregory Shantal fellow."

"I bet it would." Riana sighed heavily, sitting down with a plop in a contoured plastic and steel chair that complained loudly about her deceptive weight. "Look Kat, you are the only person here that I truly trust which is why I am confiding in you. Between what Gornin said, and what we know about the other parties involved in this, I am not inclined to take anyone's word at face value, except yours."

"Ok. So what are you proposing?" Willhelmina sat down in a chair opposite Riana's.

"Just that we stick together at this point. I have a bad feeling about Xavier, I'm not really sure why."

"Ree, I will always stick with you, no matter what. But I really think Xavier is ok. He has been like a father to me ever since my parents…"

"I know Kat. But even the best people have weaknesses. Vices. Dirty little secrets."

"Courier team Alpha to Briefing Room Seven please. Courier team Alpha to Briefing Room Seven." A harsh female voice cut through the room, interrupting their conversation with the cold chill of duty waiting to be done.

"Here we go." Riana sighed, looking into Willhelmina's emerald eyes. "Are you with me?"

"I'll always be with you Ree. I won't say anything about your collar but you're going to have to get your body under control. If you suddenly stop going to see Master Jonin people will get suspicious."

Riana stared long and hard at her sister, plumbing the depths of her emotions and convictions as much as she could as an outsider to her mind. She felt that she knew Willhelmina well enough after essentially growing up together, to know when she was serious. "Alright. I'll keep at it. Maybe It's time to take Master Jonin up on those meditation lessons."

"Definitely." Willhelmina offered a small smile in support. "We should get down to room seven before they send out a search party."

"Let's go." Riana stood up and offered a hand to Willhelmina, hoisting her up out of the form fitting plastic chair. As they turned to leave the room, Riana snatched the mangled metal and slipped it into a waste disposal unit.

49

They had barely found seats in the briefing room when Xavier began speaking. He seemed slightly flustered. His face was stern rather than its usual neutral calm. His eyes showed a hint of anger, or disappointment at something, and his normally controlled baritone voice was slightly rushed as he spoke.

"Mr. Shantal has contacted us with instructions on how to recover the prototype that he stole from Achilles."

"Good." Riana nodded at him vigorously. "Tell us where he is and we'll go smear him all over a wall." She made no attempt at all to hide her anger.

"I'm afraid it is not that easy Miss Thorindal. He has asked for a trade, and on very specific terms."

"What does he want?" Willhelmina piped in, cutting Riana off intentionally before she could say something to give away what knowledge they had acquired.

"Interestingly enough, he wants this." Xavier pressed a button on his usual podium and the holographic display twinkled to life, showing a revolving image of the key.

Willhelmina feigned surprise, again cutting Riana off before she could speak. "That looks familiar. Where have I… OH! Isn't that what we got from that Malice fellow at the Crossed Swords?"

"It is the very same item." Xavier looked at them each in turn.

"So how are we doing this exchange?" Riana finally broke in over Willhelmina. "We drop off the item and he tells us where to get the processor?"

"No. The exchanges are to happen at the same time."

"Ok. So which one are we in charge of and who's doing the other?"

"You will be handling both. As per his instructions."

Riana grimaced, her ears drooping down in frustration at the news. "We can't be in two places at once, sir."

"You can if you split up. Mr. Shantal has demanded that Willhelmina deliver the item to one of his men in the Crossed Swords in Rathalon, while you pick up the prototype from him personally on the Mars space platform."

Riana and Willhelmina looked at one another with wide eyes. "You want us…" Willhelmina said.

"…to split up?" Riana finished with a tone of indignation in her voice that she made no attempt to conceal.

"In point of fact, no. I don't want you to split up. But the fact remains that those were his demands and that prototype must be recovered at all costs. So we are, unfortunately, forced to capitulate."

"I don't like it." Riana was scowling now, half out of her seat but at the same time not sure where she was going.

"Nor do I Miss Thorindal. But as I say, we must recover that prototype, all other concerns are secondary."

"ALL other concerns?" Her violet eyes focused on him like laser beams.

"You were made very aware of the risks when you accepted the job Miss Thorindal. Rest assured that every step will be taken to ensure your safety, but in the end your well-being may rest more on your own abilities than any amount of preparation on our part."

Riana glared at him and he glared back at her. For a moment it looked as though they might actually attack one another, until Willhelmina broke the silence.

"When does all of this happen then?" She asked plainly, directing Riana and Xavier forward into other matters. Both of the others looked at her for a long moment before Xavier spoke again.

"Miss Thorindal will leave for Mars within the hour. Her trip should take less than a day. The exchange is the day after tomorrow. Noon, station time."

"So you are sending us into the enemy's den just like that?" Riana shouted, gesturing at him angrily.

"Miss Thorindal. As I said, you were made aware of the risks of being a courier before you signed on. You are expected to take these duties in stride. If you find them to be too trying, just say the word and I will have the technicians shoehorn your mind back into Kalijor!" Xavier's voice was barely under control as he spoke. Menace dripped from every word as he glared at her, leaving no impression that he might be kidding.

Willhelmina gasped at the threat. Riana met his eyes, tossing daggers with her mind.

"Yes sir. Is that all sir? I would like to prepare for my mission SIR." She finally spat out, never averting her eyes from his.

Willhelmina was looking back and forth between them with a look of sheer terror on her face. She had never seen Xavier lose his control before, let alone threaten someone openly.

"Yes Miss Thorindal. That will be all." His voice still dripped ice as his gaze fought against hers. The tension in the room was nearly a solid wall between them.

"I'll be prepping the Kestrel for departure if you need me, sir!" She spat the last word out like poison from a wound as she stood up and turned her back on them both. In an instant she was through the door and running at a blinding speed toward the shuttle bay where the Kestrel was docked. Her heart sank as she tried to force tears from her eyes, but they would not come.

-50-

"Ree?" Willhelmina's voice lilted over the hum of the ship's engines as they went through their warm-up cycle.

Riana was at the controls, running the vessel through its preflight check list. Ignoring Willhelmina, she continued to fiddle with the controls.

"Ree. C'mon. Talk to me."

"I don't know what to say Kat." Riana kept her back on the other woman.

"Ree. Xavier's mad. Really mad. I've never seen him like that before." Willhelmina hugged herself tightly as she recalled the odd battle that had taken place less than thirty minutes ago.

"I'm sure it won't be the last time." Riana said shortly, jabbing a button with her finger. The small green button shattered under the force of her unintended attack. "Dammit!"

"Ree. You need to calm down. You're going to need the Kestrel to take care of you while we're apart."

Riana choked back a tearless sob as she reached across the console to the copilot's side and pressed the redundant button. She was forcing herself to go through the motions when what she really wanted was to curl up under her bed —like she did when she was younger— and cry herself to sleep.

"Talk to me Ree. Please?" Willhelmina's voice was wavering on the edge of tears as well. She was scared.

Riana stopped what she was doing and spun the chair around so she could see her friend. The closest person she had to family in the entire world. "Kat. I'm scared. We've never really been apart. Now we will be millions of miles away from one another, and in different worlds besides."

"It'll be ok Ree. We'll see each other again soon." Willhelmina slipped into the copilot's seat and turned to face her sister, snatching up her hand and holding it tightly in her own.

"I know we will. I just…" She sighed heavily, staring at the smooth chrome deck plates of the ship's floor. "I don't think Xavier has our best interests at heart Kat. I think there is something else going on here."

"He just hates to lose." Willhelmina looked at Riana imploringly, unsure what to make of Xavier's sudden change in behavior.

"So do I. But you don't see me threatening people's lives. I TOLD you this thing was a leash, and now he is tugging on it."

"Ree. He has a company to run. Tens of thousands of people work for him and he has a responsibility to them." She squeezed Riana's hand tightly and it occurred to her how normal it felt, exactly like a human hand should feel. It was even warm to the touch and she could feel blood coursing through the veins. "Still, he scared the hell out of me in there. I've never seen him make such serious threats before."

Riana snorted. "Seems I am capable of bringing out the best in him. It's great that he is so concerned for everyone else's well-being. My concerns are a little more immediate. Namely our well-being." She paused for emphasis. "I don't like being split up."

"Neither do I. But look…" Willhelmina shifted in her seat and opened a concealed panel in the right arm rest. Inside the tiny compartment was a data jack, identical to the one in Riana's game pod on the game deck of the Tyconderoga. "I asked the tech guys to install this last week when all of this weirdness started. I figured we could use the transit time to get into Kalijor and get some research done. Plus, we can keep in touch through Kalijor while you are en route." She grinned a mischievous grin as she looked back at Riana.

"Wow. They've been busy uh?" Riana felt her seat's armrest, finally finding the release mechanism for a similar panel there; she opened it and found the same connection in her own seat.

"Yeah, and they finally got the traction drive working as well. The Kestrel is now super-luminal!"

"I was wondering what these new navigational systems were about." Riana said, pointing at a bank of shiny new controls on the right side of her console.

"They upgraded the weapons systems as well." Willhelmina's eyes gleamed with excitement. "The Kestrel's packing a bit more punch now. Still not a fighter by any means though." Receptacles for charging energy weapon clips have been installed in the weapon rack in the back as well."

Riana's face brightened a bit at the change of subject so she kept up with her line of conversation. "Maybe I should grab a plasma rifle then." Riana said with a genuine grin on her face.

"Could be fun. I've never used one outside of the firing range before," Willhelmina's own mouth stretched into a wide grin.

Abruptly, Riana's face lost its smile. Her voice turned serious again as she spoke. "Kat. I…" Her voice cracked again as she searched for words, "I don't know…"

"We'll be fine. Both of us. SO will be watching me in Kalijor and without me to watch over, you will be able to do what you have to in order to come out of that station ok."

"I love you sis." Riana stammered, nearly tripping over the words.

"I know Ree. I love you too. You take care of yourself, and I'll see you soon."

Without warning, Willhelmina jumped out of the copilot's seat and embraced Riana in a tight hug. Then she was gone from the small ship leaving Riana alone with her thoughts.

51

The Mars space station hung in geosynchronous orbit over the equator of the red planet. The huge man-made structure was essentially a platform dotted with landing strips for larger craft and recessed docking bays for smaller craft such as the Kestrel. The basic idea was to have a location in space already where the much larger vessels could dock, refuel, and repair. Cargo could be easily transferred from ship to ship in a zero-G environment where smaller vessels could then ferry it down to the planet's surface.

Most inhabited planets and planetoids had a similar setup. Especially when new colonies were forming somewhere. Having a platform in the space above allowed them to have a good set of eyes, so to speak, watching them from above, keeping an eye out for harsh weather or other potential hazards. The Mars station had been in service for so long –being one of humanity's first space outposts away from the Earth— that it had taken on additional duties over the decades. It was now more than an orbiting space port. It had been expanded and refitted numerous times, adding habitation areas, commercial areas and even some light fabrication, especially in fields that required a zero-G environment.

"Mars station this is the Kestrel, registration number Sierra-Omega-two-one-dash-one-one-three-eight on approach from Tyconderoga. Requesting clearance for docking and approach vector." Riana spoke into the mic as though she had been doing it her entire life. Although when she thought about it she realized how true the statement really was. She had only been in THIS life for a few months now, her life in Kalijor was almost a dream. She longed for those simpler days now, when she wanted for nothing but a bit of fun with her sister.

"Roger Kestrel, we have you on approach. You are cleared for docking in bay eleven. Approach on relative point five negative. Welcome to Mars station, Kestrel. We hope you enjoy your stay."

Riana flipped off the mic circuit before saying, "Not likely." Guiding the ship toward the underside of the station, she followed the trajectory the control tower sent her.

Thirty minutes later, she sat on a bench inside the main hatch of the ship. Her new suit of reactive armor was tightly wrapped around her body. The combat webbing was snuggly strapped in place, and all of her weapons and equipment were securely stored and ready for use. Sitting with her bull-pup machine gun laying across her thighs, she stared at the closed hatch with a blank expression on her face. She had been sitting there, ready to head to the meeting for more than ten minutes now, but still she waited.

She wasn't even sure what she was waiting for, except to convince herself to go. Why she was getting ready to risk her life. If everything Gornin said was true, then they would be delivering one of the keys to an unknown party. *'Surely, Xavier knew what he had. Why would he be so willing to give it up, knowing what it was for? More to the point, what does he intend to do with the keys if he manages to acquire them all?'*

It was very clear to her though that he was deadly serious about the acquisition of this prototype processor. *'So serious that he had threatened nothing short of removing my mind from my body and putting it back in Kalijor.'* The fact that everyone told her that was impossible only served to make her fear the threat even more rather than consider it false. Xavier was not the kind of man that fell behind on little details like that, and for him to say such a thing was tantamount to threatening murder.

"There will be a reckoning on that score," she said to herself softly. Amazed she had managed to keep her voice steady, Riana realized she was more nervous than she could ever remember having been before.

"So, I'll get him his processor and then quit. I'll go somewhere and do something else." She spoke again, looking at the bulkhead. The ship's wall stood stoically silent despite her obvious need for a response of some kind.

"Yeah right. He is not going to let me out of his control. Especially with this body he built." The ship's bulkhead was not giving her sufficient response, so she answered herself.

During the flight here she had done some research on cybernetics and the supporting sciences. As it turned out there was nothing like her body on record as having ever even been attempted before. Most other cybernetics

415

technology was still using mini hydraulics and micro servo systems over crude composite frames, covered up with synthetic polymers for skin.

Yet here she was. Carbon fiber honeycomb core titanium alloy bones, advanced artificial musculature and impact absorbent/dampening joints. Her organs were constructed using artificial materials fully integrated with organic tissues that had been cloned and custom tailored for the purpose of ultra high performance under the worst of conditions. Highly tuned and tweaked, her cloned nervous system, and the bullet proof material woven right into her living skin was unheard of in the cybernetics industry. Yes, she was indeed the pinnacle of human achievement in the field. By her estimate her body had probably cost hundreds of billions and the likelihood that Xavier would ever willingly let her go was infinitesimal at best.

"What I need is some leverage. Something I can use to make him let me go." She focused her violet eyes on the dim reflection of herself on the inside of the main hatch. "But what about Kat?"

With no answer forthcoming she sat there in silence for another long moment before standing up. Attaching the machine gun to her webbing, she slipped on her flowing, prismatic coat.

"Well. Time to go to work. I can figure all of this out after I am done with this jerk."

No hesitation showed as she cycled the hatch open and stepped out into the small hangar bay. Cycling the hatch closed again, she activated the Kestrel's security system and swept out of the small docking bay.

416

A wide, high-ceilinged corridor that was lined on either side with merchant's tents and kiosks sold every type of item imaginable. Food, weapons, clothing, household items, animals, cybernetic body parts and modifications, and a plethora of other items she had never even conceived of before. The corridor was packed with people, moving from tent to tent, haggling with one another and making deals in the shadows.

She was struck with how different these people were from those she had seen in Tranquility and Achilles. Those people had been clean and fairly well appointed. They had held themselves with confidence and, for lack of a better term, grace. These people on the other hand wore rags or clothes that looked as though they had gone years without being changed or cleaned. They were filthy for the most part and walked hunched over, looking at other people's feet instead of their eyes. These were people that had likely never known a good meal or a new article of clothing.

'Worlds within worlds within worlds.' She thought to herself as she dodged around a corner into another corridor that looked nearly identical to the one she had just been in. She noticed that as she moved down the crowded market corridor, people moved out of her way. She wasn't sure if it was because they could see or sense the arsenal she was carrying, or if they were just so used to being pushed around by other people that they had long ago learned to avoid them. Either way, it made her mad to think about these people being beaten down by whatever forces oppressed them. She had a sudden, seething desire for vengeance on their behalf. To right the wrongs that had been heaped upon them.

Before she could give it further thought, the small metal door leading to the appointed hangar stood before her. She stared at it for a long moment before mentally running over her equipment again. She reviewed the layout of the hangar, according to the stations blueprints. It occurred to her that even that could have been changed, ether structurally or just by the strategic placement and stacking of shipping crates or machinery. She was truly walking blind into a dragon's lair.

With a heavy breath she cleared her mind and cycled the door open, ready for anything.

52

"Welcome my child." Gregory Shantal's voice came to her as soon as the door had opened fully.

Looking into the hangar, Riana took a quick count of the black armor-clad soldiers forming a wide semicircle around the mercenary. Shantal stood in the very center facing the door.

The familiar halo of hair and dirty overalls looked almost comical as a centerpiece to the armor and artillery on the other occupants. Other than a small pistol that was secured in a low-slung thigh holster on his right leg, he carried no visible weapons. He stood with his arms folded casually across his chest and a wide smile on his face. Next to him on his left side, a small metal case stood on the deck.

Riana took a deep breath, then stepped through the doorway into the small hangar. The door slid home behind her with a final clang locking her in with the group.

"Mr. Shantal. My employer has sent me to collect the prototype processor as per your request. Someone should be delivering your item shortly." She fought to keep her voice under control. The man's grin made her want to remove it for him. She reminded herself to stay in control.

"Your employer. Don't you mean your keeper? Your slaver?" His voice was like dragging alloy fasteners across a bulkhead, raising the hairs on the back of her neck. "I mean, sure he pays you and all. But do you really think that collar is about helping you fit in?"

Riana glared at the man icily. *'Keep control. All I have to do is pick up the prototype and walk away. Stay in control.'* Quietly she moved to the center of the circle and stood face to face with the man taunting her.

"Mr. Shantal, I would appreciate it if you left my personal life out of this exchange. I am only here to pick up Solidarity Online's property." Keep control.

"Of course you are. Merely doing your master's bidding. Of course, of course. Well, here you are then. The object of your master's desire." He kicked the metal case forward with a screeching sound of metal on metal.

Riana knelt down and opened the case, inspecting its contents and comparing them against the images Xavier had sent her. Satisfied that all was well, she snapped the case closed again and stood up, holding it in her left hand. "Thank you."

420

Baring his perfect, brilliantly white teeth the man grinned at her. "My pleasure child."

She fought the desire to jump on him and pound his face. Her body twitched as she restrained herself. By the look of things, Shantal knew what was going on in her mind as his smile to widened even more.

"You want a reason to hit me child. You don't need a reason. Just do it. Indulge yourself. Hit me! You want me to pay for what I did to your sister the last time we met!" His voice was striking her nerves. It felt as though he were in her head, speaking directly into her mind.

"If you are satisfied that our business is finished Mr. Shantal, I would like to get back to my ship." She was unable to keep the menace out of her voice.

Suddenly his face grew very serious and he stood up to his full height, his lanky arms at his sides. "Oh. Everything is quite to my satisfaction. Go child, back to your master's house. Report to him that all is as it should be."

Riana stared at him, a look of pure hatred on her face, that she could not conceal. She could barely contain it. Then in a flash she was standing in the Crossed Swords tavern in Rathalon, surrounded by jeering people. Startled, she looked around and saw that they were all watching the pit in the center of the room.

In the pit her sister was fighting a losing battle against Malice. His giant black sword in his right hand, the blade resting on his shoulder, he laughed at Katrina. She was crouching on one knee —her staff, Chavan, clutched tightly in her right hand— sweat and blood pouring from her head and arms as she panted heavily.

Riana screamed at them, but no one paid her any notice. She rushed to the edge and tried to climb over the railing but an invisible barrier barred her way. She pounded on it with her fists and screamed with all of her strength, but she could not break through.

She watched in horror as Malice kicked Katrina in the side, toppling her over sideways. She coughed up a clump of blood onto the dirt floor of the small pit and rolled over onto her stomach, Chavan still clutched tightly in her right hand. Forcing herself to her knees, she slowly stumbled to a standing position.

Riana looked at her sister in horror. Her robes were sliced to ribbons and she was bleeding profusely from numerous places on her over-exposed body. Her look was one of pure determination, but it was obvious that she had lost already.

"Accept it cow! He killed them! You are working and living with a murderer. Cold and heartless. You always wanted to know why it happened. I have told you and yet you refuse to believe! Accept it!" Malice was yelling at her, pointing accusingly at her with his left hand.

Katrina just kept shaking her head, clutching her staff and leaning heavily on it. "You lie! He didn't do it! He has given me everything!"

"Fine! Then I have no sympathy for you. You deserve this." He sneered at her as he held his giant sword and swung the flat of the blade at her temple. The blow knocked her across the pit and into a wall where she slumped to the ground, unmoving.

Riana couldn't tell if she was dead or just unconscious as Malice walked over to her, raising his arms in triumph to the cheering crowd. Kneeling down he grabbed Katrina by her platinum hair and roughly lifted her off the ground by her scalp. Katrina's right hand still clung to the magical staff as her limp form was dragged back to the center of the arena where Malice turned to face Riana directly. He looked into her eyes with a twinkle in his own and smiled broadly. Then he motioned with his giant, black sword and a series of blue rings appeared in the arena. As he smiled again at Riana he dragged Katrina's body into the center of the hovering rings and vanished in a blue flash, leaving no sign that he had been there.

Riana screamed out as loud as she could, "No! You bastard! Bring her back!"

"Something troubling you my child?"

Gregory Shantal's grating voice brought her back to her senses in a flash. She was back in the hangar, surrounded by armed soldiers and still standing toe to toe with the maddening mercenary. She looked back into his eyes and saw his amusement at her situation there.

"You... you arranged it didn't you?" Riana was panting now, her breath coming in ragged gasps even though she knew her cybernetic body should be keeping it steady.

"Arranged what my child?" He smiled at her condescendingly.

"Kat. What have you done with Kat?"

His smile faltered for a fraction of a second before widening again. "You couldn't possibly... But then again you did override my control signal somehow, maybe it is possible. At any rate, suffice to say that she will be well taken care of. Which is more than Xavier would do had I tried to play him the fool as he has done me!"

"What are you talking about? Where did he take my sister?!" She was screaming at him, fury building up inside her, she knew what it was he was talking about. Xavier had not given Willhelmina the real key to deliver. He had gambled with her life, and he had lost.

"I think you know my child. Now, you go and tell your master..."

He never finished his sentence. Riana spun around and flung the metal case at a pair of soldiers as she drew her bull-pup from under her coat.

It lasted mere moments. She had a vague impression of bullets impacting against her reactive armor, but her mind stayed focused on destroying the soldiers. Her movements became a ballet in fast forward as she moved around the circle, her weapon belching gouts of flame. The soldiers dropped one or two at a time, some to her weapon's fire, others to the blunt force of her punches and kicks.

When it was all over she stood in a circle of bodies, bloody and mangled. Her prismatic coat was in tatters, riddled with bullet holes. Her armor was in better shape than the last encounter, but it had taken its share of hits.

Gregory Shantal still stood calmly in the center of the circle of now-deceased soldiers. His face still bore a wide grin and his eyes were alight with admiration at what had just happened around him.

"Oh ho! Xavier's boys really struck gold with you eh? I've never seen anyone move like that before! Very impressive child! Very impressive indeed!"

"You have two seconds to come clean or I'll do the same to you." She intoned flatly as she dropped her empty machine gun on the floor, kicking it aside.

"Oh I don't think so. Not this time. You only get one chance to take me down, and you already blew it. No. Willhelmina will be staying with me for a while. In the mean time I suggest that you and Xavier have a heart to heart and work things out."

"Bastard!" Riana lashed out with a punch that would have ripped a normal man's head off, but Gregory snatched her fist out of the air midway between them and twisted her arm around, forcing her to spin her back to him in order to keep him from locking her arm up.

Wrenching on her arm he tried to force her to the floor. Instead she sprang into a forward flip, wrenching her arm free of his grasp. She landed solidly and wheeled on him with a reverse side kick.

He ducked under it and lunged toward her with both fists extended. Rolling, she planted her hands on his shoulders and went over his back. Coming to her feet, she pulled hard on him and launched him over her head into the back wall of the small hangar.

He hit the wall with a solid metal on metal clang and then fell to the ground, landing on his feet and grinning ear to ear again.

"Not bad my child. But you don't have what it takes to beat me. Your heart just isn't in it."

"I'll show you how 'in it' my heart is." She growled as she drew her pistols. Unloading them in his direction, she sprinted toward him. In a flash—faster than she could even see—he was on top of her. He grabbed her fists and squeezed, crushing the guns in her hands and breaking her fingers with a series of sickening snapping sounds.

She felt every bone in both of her hands break as he smiled. There was a brief flash of blinding pain before the nanites in her body shut off the signal to her brain and she knew it was over for her, just as it had been for her sister in the arena with Malice.

"I am going to let you go child. Otherwise Xavier would not be able to see what he has done first hand. But, I am not letting you leave here intact. I am taking something of yours with me as a souvenir." Then he twisted her left hand and there was a sickening crunch as the metal bones and reinforced tissues gave way under great duress.

She couldn't feel it because of the nanites, but she knew what he had done almost instantly. Then he backed up a few steps and showed her. In his hand, he cradled her left hand, still mangled and clenched around the crushed pistol. Looking down she saw the blood already clotting around the metallic stump of her wrist.

"Now you go back to your master and you tell him that worse is coming if he doesn't meet my demands. I have your sister's mind in custody and I will not hesitate to kill her if Xavier continues to play games with me." His smile was gone. "Go. Get out of my sight."

Riana stared at him in shock. Her mind reeled as everything hit her all at once. Willhelmina, her hand, Xavier's betrayal. In a haze, she made her way back to the Kestrel where she managed to somehow get the ship out of the hangar and set the auto pilot to take her back to the Tyconderoga.

53

"How DARE you trade her life for a virtual trinket! Who are you?!" Riana was laying on her back on a bed in the infirmary, her right hand and the ugly growth that was becoming her new left hand were both secured in small vats of some kind of sludge that had a ruddy, amber color to it and felt like something that came out the back end of a fire beetle. It had been three days since she had returned to the Tyconderoga and she had been stuck to this bed with her hands in these fluid tanks—which were regularly refilled—ever since.

"Miss Thorindal, your contracts stipulate that you are to undertake any mission that I outline for you no matter the risk or possible outcome. You are of course free to breach that contract at any time, however I will be forced to reacquire any of our technology that you may have on, or in your person when you leave."

"You know what that would mean Xavier. You can't kill me off that easily. ESPECIALLY since I have to clean up your mess still." She glared at him across the infirmary.

"I will assign your next task just as soon as you are returned to active duty by your doctors and technicians, which they tell me will be at least a week at this rate."

"You should be flogged for what you did to Willhelmina! She trusts you. You're the closest thing she has to a father."

"I will continue to be so, do not mistake any of this for ambivalence on my part, I did what had to be done."

"You callous, sanctimonious…"

"Now Miss Thorindal, let's not regress to name calling," he cut her off. "All things considered, we didn't come out that badly. And I have decided not to fine you. That should raise your spirits some."

"FINE ME?! For what? Blithely following your directions when I should have had my brain engaged and thinking for itself?!"

"No Miss Thorindal. Your contract clearly stipulates that if you should loose a package, parcel, or other company property including one of a kind or particularly expensive weapons and/or equipment, that you shall potentially be held liable for the monetary value of said property either immediately or through a period of payroll garnishing."

"Well excuse me for not bringing your damn processor back! Under the circumstances you're lucky I didn't hand it back to the guy with my compliments!"

"While the processor is a significant loss for Solidarity Online, that is not the property to which I was referring." An expression of smugness crept across his face then. He knew she was clueless as to his line of thought.

"What the hell are you getting at Xavier?" She was not in the mood to play games. Her sister was still in Kalijor somewhere, and she could be in there looking for her right now if Xavier wasn't standing across the room wasting her time with his bureaucratic nonsense.

"Your hand Miss Thorindal. You left your hand behind. In the competition's possession. A piece of equipment that I have had the value quoted to me as being nearly twenty million credits by itself. As valuable as that processor prototype is to us, you are much more so. Or at the very least, your body is."

She simply stared at him with her mouth open. She could not believe that he looked at her as a piece of corporate hardware instead of a person. It almost made sense to her, although she despised him for it. The fact that he was able to run Solidarity Online like his own personal kingdom had gone to his head. She was unsure if his 'employees' were allowed to leave if they didn't like it, but the fact that he had gambled so casually with the life of someone that could have—SHOULD have—been his daughter was unthinkable to her. She would stay here until she was able to find and free her sister. Then she would leave this damnable place and find somewhere else to be and something else to do.

Calmly, she looked up at the man on the other side of the room, casually standing there in his expensive suit, holding his wooden cane. Slowly, she formed her face into a grim smile, staring unblinkingly into his eyes. "I want a connection to Kalijor in here, today. I will spend as much time as is necessary in there. I will search high and low, and I will take that damn place apart one stone at a time until I find Kat. And if you try to stop me…"

"What, Miss Thorindal? What will you do?" His smirk told her that he didn't believe she had any bargaining cards. He thought he had all the aces.

"I'll take this damn station apart one bolt at a time. And you won't be able to stop me, because your leash is broken." She then dislodged her right hand from it's fluid bath, breaking the seals around it with ease, and reached up to the shiny chrome collar around her neck. Gently she placed her hand on the collar and gave it a twist. There was a metallic scraping noise as she tore through the metal and then pulled it off of her neck and casually tossed it across the room at Xavier's feet.

For a long moment he looked at the twisted remains of the collar. Finally he raised his gaze to her and offered a weak smile. "Very well Miss Thorindal. I will have a Kalijor feed put in this afternoon. But please understand that the inhibitor collar was not our sole means of controlling you. We have other—more extreme—methods of keeping you under control if circumstances demand."

"Whatever. Just as long as we are clear on where we both stand."

"Indeed we are Miss Thorindal. Indeed we are."

www.ingramcontent.com/pod-product-compliance
Lightning Source LLC
Chambersburg PA
CBHW031142050726
47495CB00018B/365